주석과 함께 읽는

햄릿

HAMLET: PRINCE OF DENMARK

주석과 함께 읽는
햄릿

전상범 지음

한국문화사

주석과 함께 읽는 햄릿

1판1쇄 발행 2018년 11월 10일

지 은 이 전상범
펴 낸 이 김진수
펴 낸 곳 **한국문화사**
등   록 1991년 11월 9일 제2-1276호
주   소 서울특별시 성동구 광나루로 130 서울숲 IT캐슬 1310호
전   화 02-464-7708
팩   스 02-499-0846
이 메 일 hkm7708@hanmail.net
홈페이지 www.hankookmunhwasa.co.kr

ISBN 978-89-6817-686-9   93840

이 도서의 국립중앙도서관 출판예정도서목록(CIP)은 서지정보유통지원시스템 홈페이지(http://seoji.nl.go.kr)와
국가자료공동목록시스템(http://www.nl.go.kr/kolisnet)에서 이용하실 수 있습니다.(CIP제어번호: CIP2018033037)

전공이 영어영문학이라고 하면 으레 Shakespeare 몇 편은 읽었을 것으로 짐작한다. 그런데 영어영문학과가 있는 상위 52개 대학에서 Shakespeare를 필수과목으로 개설하고 있는 대학은 4개 대학에 불과하다는 통계가 있다. 우리나라의 통계가 아니라 미국의 통계이다.[1] 짐작컨대 우리나라 어느 대학에서도 Shakespeare가 필수과목으로 설정된 곳은 없으리라고 생각된다. 다시 말해 Shakespeare 한 편 읽지 않고도 영어영문학과를 졸업할 수 있다는 말이 된다. Milton이나 Chaucer는 더 말할 나위도 없다.

언제부터인가 우리나라 대학가에서 대학원중심대학이라는 말이 유행하기 시작한 적이 있다. 쉽게 말해 본격적인 전공 공부는 대학원에서 하고, 대학에서는 그 준비를 위한 폭넓은 기초 교육을 제공한다는 것이다. 그 결과 눈에 띄게 달라진 점은 첫째, 전체적인 이수 학점 수가 줄었고, 둘째, 전공보다 교양과목이나 부전공을 장려하는 경향이 생겨나게 되었고, 셋째, 필수과목을 줄인 결과 예전보다 전공필수과목의 이수 학점이 현저히 줄게 되었다.

필수과목이 줄어든 결과 학생들이 상대적으로 부담스러운 Shakespeare나 영시 같은 과목들을 기피하는 현상이 생겨났다. 세태가 이렇다 보니 학생들 사이에 인기 있는 과목은 역시 말하고 듣기와 관련된 과목들이다. 예전에 필자가 학과장 일을 맡고 있던 어떤 해에 「영국희곡」 과목에

---

[1] *U. S. News and World Report*, 2015. 홍지수 씨의 TV 대담에서 인용 (2018. 3. 31).

비전공 수강생들이 너무 많이 몰려 그 이유를 알아본 적이 있다. 영어회화에 도움이 될 것 같다는 대답을 듣고 과의 교수 일동이 적이 놀랐던 일이 있다.

그런데 대학원중심대학의 문제점은 우리나라에서 아직은 선택된 일부 학생들만이 대학원에 간다는 사실이다. 학부가 최종 학벌인 대부분의 학생들은 본격적인 전공 공부를 위한 기초 교양만 쌓다가 학교를 떠나게 된다.

Shakespeare라고 하면 영국 사람들이 인도하고도 바꾸지 않을 작가라든가, 또는 언어 구사의 마술사라는 말을 듣는다. 그러나 이런 사실들은 번역본이나 하물며 연극이나 영화를 통해서는 알 수 없다. 그가 수없이 사용하는 pun만 해도 그렇다. Hamlet이 Polonius를 죽이고 그 시체를 끌고 가면서 죽고 나니 이제 Polonius가 grave해졌다고 말할 때 그것은 죽어서 말 수가 적어졌다(somber)는 뜻인 동시에 시체가 무겁다(weighty)는 뜻도 되고, 동시에 이제 갈 곳은 무덤(grave)이라는 뜻도 깔려 있다. 수도 없이 사용되는 이와 같은 pun의 재미를 번역본이나 영화, 연극에서 맛볼 수 없는 것은 자명하다.

본서와 같은 저술이 독창적일 수는 없다. 선행 연구들의 성과를 필자 나름대로 취사선택하였으며, 주로 Deighton (1959), Ichikawa & Mine (2000), Main (1963), Miola (2011), Mowat & Werstine (2012), Rowse (1978), Thompson & Taylor (2016), Verity (1953) 등의 주석본들에서 많은 도움을 받았다.

그 밖에 金在枏, 李京植 두 분의 번역을 비롯한 국내 학자들의 번역, 그리고 일본의 野島秀勝(노지마 히데가츠), 福田恒存(후쿠다 쯔네아리) 교수를 비롯한 몇몇 분들의 번역에서도 많은 도움을 받았다.

단어의 뜻풀이는 C.T. Onions의 *A Shakespeare Glossary*의 풀이를 우

선적으로 사용하였으며, 여기에 게재되지 않은 경우에는 *COD (Concise Oxford Dictionary)*나 *SOD (Shorter Oxford Dictionary)*를 사용하였다.

오래 전 필자는 여름 한 학기를 Oxford 대학에서 보낸 적이 있다. 학교 기숙사에 도착해서 방 열쇠를 받는데, 수위 아저씨가 "당신 방은 전에 Richard Burton이 쓰던 방이다"라고 해서 약간 놀란 적이 있다. 그가 Elizabeth Taylor와 결혼했다 이혼한 사실이 얼마간 신문을 떠들썩하게 했던 일이 있었기 때문이다. 그러나 그 뒤 곧 그가 영국민의 존경을 받는 Shakespeare 배우이며, 최고의 Hamlet 배우 가운데 한 사람이라는 사실을 알게 되어, 그와 같은 침대를 사용한다는 사실에 기분이 야릇해졌던 기억이 있다.

여름의 Oxford 대학은 문자 그대로 문학 장마당이다. 매일과 같이 문학 강연이나 시 낭송회가 있고, 또 거의 매일과 같이 Shakespeare의 연극 공연이 있다. 대개 대학생들의 아마추어 공연이다. 입장료 같은 것은 없고, 대신 비번의 배우들이 분장한 채 공연 도중에 관중석을 돌며 초콜릿을 팔았다. 예쁘게 분장한 Ophelia가 와서 웃으며 초콜릿 상자를 내밀면 누구나 한두 개는 팔아주게 된다. 그러던 Ophelia가 자기 차례가 되면 초콜릿 상자를 다른 배우에게 맡기고 급하게 무대에 뛰어 올라 연기를 계속하던 모습이 지금도 눈에 선하다.

무릇 영어에 종사하는 사람들은 Shakespeare 한 편쯤은 꼼꼼하게 읽을 필요가 있다는 필자의 평소 신념이 이런 모양의 책이 된 것으로 생각한다. 우리나라 영문학의 품격을 높이는 일에 작으나마 도움이 되기를 바라는 바이다.

차례

W. Shakespeare (1564-1616)

Wikipedia에서 Chaucer의 항목을 찾아보면 생년월일이 (c. 1343-25 October 1400)로 나와 있다. 출생연도 앞의 c.는 라틴어 circa(= about)의 약자로서, 다시 말해 출생 연도를 정확히 알지 못한다는 뜻이다. Shakespeare의 경우에는 (26 April 1564 (baptised)-23 April 1616)로 나와 있거나 사전에 따라서는 (c. 1564-1616)로 나와 있기도 하다. 유아세례는 보통 태어난 지 사나흘 만에 받음으로 Shakespeare는 생일과 기일이 같은 것으로 알려져 있다. 유명인들의 기일은 정확히 기록되면서 출생 연도가 불분명한 것은 어쩌면 당연하다고 할 수 있다.

Shakespeare는 London 서북부 100마일쯤 떨어진 곳에 있는 Stratford-upon-Avon이라는 작은 마을에서 태어났다. London에서 기차나 버스로 한 시간 반쯤 걸리는 작은 마을이며, Avon이라는 작은 강이 가까이에 있다. Stratford 뒤의 upon-Avon은 또 다른 곳의 Stratford와 구별하기 위한 것이다. 독일의 Frankfurt am Main의 경우와 같다.

예수의 소년 시절과 청년 시절에 대해서 알려진 바가 거의 없듯이 Shakespeare의 소년 시절과 청년 시절에 대해서도 알려진 바가 거의 없다. Shakespeare는 비교적 부유한 집안에 태어났으므로 당시 청소년들이 밟은 교육과정을 밟았으리라고 짐작할 뿐이다. Stratford-upon-Avon에 있던 King's New School은 어린이들에게 라틴어 문법 교육을 목적으로 세워진 이른바 grammar school로서 매우 뛰어난 학교였다. 당시 어린이들은 네다섯 살에 학교에 들어가 우선 영어의 읽기 쓰기를 배우고, 2년 뒤엔 grammar school의 저학년 반(lower form)에 들어가 라틴어 문법을 배우기 시작하고, 상급반(upper form)이 되는 열 살, 내지 열한 살이 되면 라틴어로 연설문을 쓰고, 이어서 그리스어로 신약성경 공부를 한 것으로 알려져 있다. Shakespeare가 마을의 grammar school을 다녔다는 기록은 없으나, 여러 사실들이 그가 상기와 같은 교육을 받았을 것이라는 점을 말해주고 있다.

그는 1582년(18세)에 Anne Hathaway와 결혼하고, 1583년에 딸 Susanna를, 그리고 1585년에 Judith와 Hamnet 쌍둥이 남매를 얻는다. 그의 작품에 가끔 쌍둥이가 등장하는 것은 이와 무관하지 않을 것이다 (*Twelfth Night, The Comedy of Errors*). 당시 그가 어떻게 생계를 꾸렸는지, 또 언제 어떻게 그가 London에 가서 1590년 초에 유명 인사가 되었는지 우리는 알지 못한다. 그는 배우 겸 극작가, 시인으로 이름을 날리게 된다. *Hamlet*의 유령 역은 그가 맡아 한 것으로 알려져 있다.

1593년에 최초로 *Venus and Adonis*라는 서사시를 발표했고, 이어 1594년에는 *The Rape of Lucrece*를 발표한다. 이때는 London에 전염병이 돌아 극장들이 휴관하고 있던 때인데, 1594년 극장 문이 다시 열리자 그는 배우와 극작가라는 이중생활을 하는 한편 극장의 주를 가지게 되어 안정된 수입을 올리게 된다. 이와 같은 생활은 약 20년간 계속되었다.

1599년 Shakespeare 일당은 London 시의 강남에 Globe라는 극장을 짓는다. 그의 작품은 주로 이 극장에서 상연되었으나, 지방에서도 많이 상연되었다.

1613년에 Globe Theatre가 불에 탄 뒤 그는 고향인 Stratford-upon-Avon으로 돌아와 두 딸과 그 남편들과 함께 살았다. 그의 아들 Hamnet은 1596년에 죽었다. 그는 배우와 극작가로서 얻은 수입, 극장의 주에서 얻은 수입, 그리고 그 수입을 현명하게 투자해서 얻은 수입으로 유복한 생활을 즐길 수 있었다. 한편 1596년에는 그가 그처럼 오랫동안 원했던 문장(coat of arms)을 그의 아버지 John Shakespeare가 받았다. 그는 1616년 4월 23일(52세)에 죽어 마을의 Holy Trinity Church에 묻혔다.

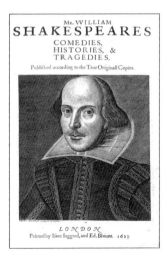

Mr. William Shakespeares Comedies, Histories, & Tragedies (First Folio, 1623)

그가 사망한 7년 뒤에 그의 작품 전집 *Mr. William Shakespeares Comedies, Histories, & Tragedies* (First Folio)가 출간되었다.

19세기 중반 이후 가짜 Shakespeare 설이 나돌았다. Shakespeare는 가공의 인물이고, 그의 작품을 쓴 것은 사실은 Francis Bacon, Christopher Marlowe, 심지어는 Elizabeth 여왕이라는 주장이다. 증명된 바 없으며, 이것은 거꾸로 말해 Shakespeare가 그만큼 위대한 작가라는 주장이 될 수 있다.

셰익스피어의 영어

통상적으로 영어의 역사는 대개 다음 세 단계로 나누어진다.[2]

　　고대영어: 450　－　1100
　　중세영어: 1100　－　1500
　　근대영어: 1500　－

초기의 근대영어는 지금으로부터 500년도 더 지난 시대의 영어로서 현대영어와는 많은 차이가 난다. 그리하여 근대영어를 초기근대영어와 후기근대영어(현대영어)로 구분하기도 한다.

아래에 「주기도문」(The Lord's Prayer (*Matthew* 4:9-13))의 처음 두 문장을 위 세 단계의 영어로 제시해 두었다.

Old English

Fæder ure þu þe eart on heofonum, sie þin nama gehalgod.
Tobecume þin rice.

Middle English

Oure fadir that art in heuenes, halewid be thi name;
thi kyngdoom come to;

---

[2]　이 부분의 보다 자세한 설명을 위해서는 전상범, 『영어학개론』(서울: 한국문화사)의 3장을 참고할 것.

Modern English

Our father which art in heaven, hallowed be thy name.
Thy kingdom come.

Shakespeare(1564-1616)의 영어는 그의 활동연대로 보아 초기근대영어에 속한다. 따라서 근본적으로 그의 영어는 현재의 영어와 크게 다르지 않다. 그러나 16세기의 영어가 현대영어와 동일할 수는 없다. 주의해 읽지 않으면 오해할 표현이 적지 않다. 예를 들어 notorious는 단순히 well-known의 뜻만을 가지며, success는 good success나 bad success 등의 표현에서 알 수 있듯이 중립적인 단어이다. 현대영어의 success는 Shakespeare의 good success에 해당한다. notorious와 success는 지금과 달리 뜻이 중립적인 경우이지만 반대로 지금의 중립적인 뜻이 Shakespeare 시대에는 그렇지 않았던 경우도 있다. 예를 들어 companion은 '패거리'라는 나쁜 뜻으로 사용되었다.

당시는 Elizabeth(1558-1603) 여왕의 치세에 속하며, 문화사적으로 영국은 문예부흥의 전성기였다. 문예부흥 시대의 가장 대표적인 작가로 Shakespeare를 천거하는 데에는 이의가 없을 것이다. 그는 영어에서 굴절이 소실되고 난 다음의 최초의 작가로서, 과도기의 언어가 갖는 유연성을 최대한도로 이용한 언어의 마술사였다. Caxton이 1478년에 인쇄를 시작한 이래 철자법은 급속히 자리를 잡아가고 있었으나 아직도 통일되기까지는 거리가 멀었으며, 문법도 과도기의 언어답게 확실하게 정해진 것이 없던 때였다. 그의 타고난 천재성에도 불구하고 그가 만약 200년 뒤의 후기근대영어 시대에 태어났다면 그는 우리가 알고 있는 주옥같은 작품들을 남기지 못했을 것이다. 그의 문학적 업적은 문예부흥이라는 시대정신과 아직 고정되지 않은 언어라는 토양에서 자라날 수 있었던 그의 문학정신의 소산이라고 할 수 있다. 어떤 이의 비유처럼 그에게 있어 당시의 '영어는 천재의 손에 쥐어진 점토'(It was a plastic medium ready for the modeling hand of genius.)와 같은 것이었다.

Shakespeare의 영어를 말할 때 흔히 사람들은 그의 풍부한 어휘에 대해 말한다. 대개 2만개 이상의 어휘를 그가 사용한 것으로 알려져 있다. 알고 있는 단어와 실제로 사용하는 단어의 수는 같지 않으므로 그가 알고 있던 어휘의 수는 이보다 훨씬 더 많았을 것이다. 참고로 동시대의 Milton의 시에서는 7,800개의 어휘가 발견되며, 구약성서와 신약성서에는 각기 5,643개와 4,800개의 단어가 들어있다.

주의할 것은 어휘 수만을 가지고 문학의 우열을 논할 수는 없다는 점이다. Milton의 산문에는 시에는 나타나지 않는 어휘가 들어있다. 그러고 보면 시에 농기구 이름이나 주방기구 이름이 들어갈 가능성은 희박해 보인다. 이것은 바꿔 말해 Shakespeare의 어휘가 풍부하다는 것은 그가 그만큼 다양한 주제를 다루었다는 방증이 된다. 다음과 같은 Jespersen의 말은 귀담아 들을 필요가 있다.

> 따라서 Shakespeare 정신의 위대성은 그가 2만 개의 단어를 알고 있었다는 사실에서가 아니라 그가 그처럼 다양한 주제에 관해 글을 썼으며, 그처럼 많은 인간사와 인간관계를 다루었기 때문에 그가 자기 작품에 그처럼 많은 수의 단어를 필요로 했다는 사실에서 나타난다.

Shakespeare의 영어를 대할 때 우리는 그가 대단한 언어의 자유주의자이며 실험가라는 것을 알게 된다. 그가 영문학 사상 드물게 많은 어휘를 사용한 것이 Jespersen의 말처럼 그의 다양한 주제와 밀접한 관계가 있기는 하나, 전적으로 주제의 탓이라고만 생각한다면 그것은 잘못이다. Shakespeare는 관습에 구애됨이 없이 대담하게 언어에 대한 실험을 해나갔다. *OED (Oxford English Dictionary)*를 보면 그가 처음으로 쓴 단어가 무수히 발견된다. 그중 몇 개만 예를 들면 다음과 같다.

accommodation, apostrophe, assassination, indistinguishable, frugal, misanthrope, obscene, pedant, premeditated, reliance

그의 언어적 대담성과 실험정신은 수없이 많은 경우에 목격된다. 예를 들어 그는 You can *happy* your friend에서처럼 형용사를 동사로 사용한다든지, 혹은 You can speak *free*에서처럼 형용사를 부사로 사용하는 등의 대담성을 보인다. 이것은 지금이라도 되살리고 싶은 표현 방식들이다.

Shakespeare의 언어적 대담성과 실험성은 합성어에서 돋보인다. 언어의 실험가답게 많은 새로운 합성어를 만들어 사용하였다. 또한 그는 필요하다면 방언의 사용도 서슴치 않았다. 그러나 관객이 주로 런던사람들이었으므로 그가 사용하는 방언은 청중이 이해할 수 있는 범위의 것이었으며, 또 그것은 등장인물의 성격상 꼭 필요한 경우에 한했다. 그는 외래어에 대해서도 편협하지 않았으나 절대로 필요 이상으로 사용하는 일은 없었다.

앞서 지적한 것처럼 Shakespeare의 영어는 현대영어와는 거리가 있다. 그 가운데서도 눈에 띄는 몇 가지 중요한 차이는 첫째, 대명사의 2인칭에서 thou와 you를 구별했다는 점, 둘째, 이른바 문법에서 말하는 *do*-support가 아직 발달하기 전의 모양을 사용하고 있다는 점이다. 아래에 현대영어와의 차이를 대비시켜 놓았다.

Shakespeare	현대영어
I heard it not.	I didn't hear it.
Go not there!	Don't go there!
Stay'd it long?	Did it stay long?
Sit we down.	Let us sit down.
What says Polonius?	What does Polonius say?
Saw you not his face?	Didn't you see his face?
Looks it not like the king?	Doesn't it look like the king?

그 밖에 단어의 모양은 같으나 뜻이나 뜻의 뉘앙스가 현대영어와 같지 않은 경우가 허다하다. 그러나 그와 같은 미세한 차이를 무시한다면 그의 영어는 역시 우리와 동시대의 영어임에 틀림없다.

Shakespeare의 작품을 읽기 전에 알아두어야 할 중요한 사실은 그의 작품이 시라는 점이다. 모든 행이 대문자로 시작되는 것은 그 까닭이다. 흔히 그의 작품을 시극詩劇이라고 한다. 쉽게 말해 오페라라고 생각하면 된다.

나라마다 시에는 정해진 패턴이 있다. 이를테면 일본의 시는 5,7조, 한국은 3,4조, 영어는 약강5음보(iambic pentameter)가 대표적인 기본형이다. 약강의 강세를 갖는 2음절을 하나의 음보(meter)라고 할 때, 약강5음보는 다음과 같은 모양을 갖는다.

$$\times \; \acute{-} \; / \; \times \; \acute{-} \; / \; \times \; \acute{-} \; / \; \times \; \acute{-} \; / \; \times \; \acute{-}$$
Toge / ther with / that fair / and war / like form

(Together with that fair and warlike form)

그러나 가끔 시가 산문으로 바뀌는 경우가 있다. 예를 들면 II. ii. 168-221이 그렇다. 이것은 오페라에서도 가끔 노래가 아닌 보통 대사가 나오는 경우와 같다. 이야기의 속도를 높이고자 할 때 흔히 볼 수 있다.

HAMLET
PRINCE OF DENMARK

DRAMATIS PERSONÆ

CLAUDIUS [klɔ́:diəs], King of Denmark.

HAMLET [hǽmlit], son to the late, and nephew to the present king.

POLONIUS [polóuniəs], lord chamberlain.

HORATIO [horéiʃiou], friend to Hamlet.

LAERTES [leiə́:tiz], son to Polonius.

VOLTIMAND [vɔ́ltimənd],

CORNELIUS [kɔ:ní:liəs],

ROSENCRANTZ [róuzənkrænts],　　　　　　courtiers.

GUILDENSTERN [gíldənstə:n],

OSRIC [ɔ́zrik],

A Gentleman,

A Priest.

MARCELLUS [mɑ:séləs],　　　　　　officers.

BERNARDO [bənɑ́:dou],

FRANCISCO [frænsískou],　a soldier.

REYNALDO [renǽldou], servant to Polonius.

Players.

Two Clowns, grave-diggers.

FORTINBRAS [fɔ́:tinbræs], prince of Norway.

A Captain.

English Ambassadors.

GERTRUDE, queen of Denmark, and mother to Hamlet.

OPHELIA [ofi:liə], daughter to Polonius.

Lords, Ladies, Officers, Soldiers, Sailors, Messengers, and other Attendants.

Ghost of Hamlet's Father.

SCENE: *Denmark.*

Act I

SCENE I

Elsinore. A platform before the castle.

FRANCISCO *at his post. Enter to him* BERNARDO.

Ber.   Who's there?

Fran.   Nay, answer me.   Stand, and unfold yourself.

Ber.   Long live the king!

Fran.   Bernardo?

Ber.   He.   5

Fran.   You come most carefully upon your hour.

Ber.   'Tis now struck twelve.   Get thee to bed,
   Francisco.

Fran.   For this relief much thanks.   'Tis bitter cold,
   And I am sick at heart.

Ber.   Have you had quiet guard?

Fran.   Not a mouse stirring.   10

Ber.   Well, good-night.

If you do meet Horatio and Marcellus,

The rivals of my watch, bid them make haste.

Enter HORATIO *and* MARCELLUS.

Fran.   I think I hear them.   Stand, ho! Who's there?

Hor.   Friends to this ground.

Mar.   And liegemen to the Dane.   15

Fran.   Give you good-night.

Mar.   O, farewell, honest soldier.

Who hath reliev'd you?

Fran.   Bernardo has my place.

Give you good-night.   [*Exit.*

Mar.   Holla! Bernardo!

Ber.   Say,

What, is Horatio there?

Hor.   A piece of him.

Ber.   Welcome, Horatio;   welcome, good Marcellus.   20

Hor.   What, has this thing appear'd again to-night?

Ber.   I have seen nothing.

Mar.   Horatio says 'tis but our fantasy,

And will not let belief take hold of him

Touching this dreaded sight, twice seen of us;   25

Therefore I have entreated him along

With us to watch the minutes of this night,

That if again this apparition come,

He may approve our eyes and speak to it.

Hor.   Tush, tush, 'twill not appear.

Ber.   Sit down awhile,   30

And let us once again assail your ears,

That are so fortified against our story,

What we have two nights seen.

Hor.   Well, sit we down,

And let us hear Bernardo speak of this.

Ber.   Last night of all,   35

When yond same star that's westward from the pole

Had made his course to illume that part of heaven

Where now it burns, Marcellus and myself,

The bell then beating one,—

Enter Ghost.

Mar.   Peace, break thee off! Look, where it comes

again!   40

Ber.   In the same figure, like the king that's dead.

Mar.   Thou art a scholar; speak to it, Horatio.

Ber.   Looks it not like the King? Mark it, Horatio.

Hor.   Most like; it harrows me with fear and wonder.

Ber.   It would be spoke to.

Mar.   Question it, Horatio.   45

Hor.   What art thou that usurp'st this time of night,

Together with that fair and warlike form

I. i]

In which the majesty of buried Denmark

Did sometimes march? By heaven I charge thee, speak!

Mar. It is offended.

Ber.   See, it stalks away!   50

Hor. Stay! speak, speak! I charge thee, speak!

[Exit Ghost.

Mar. 'Tis gone, and will not answer.

Ber. How now, Horatio! you tremble and look pale.

Is not this something more than fantasy?

What think you on't?   55

Hor. Before my God, I might not this believe

Without the sensible and true avouch

Of mine own eyes.

Mar.   Is it not like the King?

Hor. As thou art to thyself.

Such was the very armour he had on   60

When he the ambitious Norway combated.

So frown'd he once, when, in an angry parle,

He smote the sledded Polacks on the ice.

'Tis strange.

Mar. Thus twice before, and jump at this dead hour,   65

With martial stalk hath he gone by our watch.

Hor. In what particular thought to work I know not;

But, in the gross and scope of my opinion,

This bodes some strange eruption to our state.

Mar. Good now, sit down, and tell me, he

that knows,   70

Why this same strict and most observant watch

So nightly toils the subject of the land,

And why such daily cast of brazen cannon,

And foreign mart for implements of war;

Why such impress of shipwrights, whose sore task   75

Does not divide the Sunday from the week.

What might be toward, that this sweaty haste

Doth make the night joint-labourer with the day,

Who is't that can inform me?

Hor.   That can I;

At least, the whisper goes so. Our last king   80

Whose image even but now appear'd to us,

Was, as you know, by Fortinbras of Norway,

Thereto prick'd on by a most emulate pride,

Dared to the combat; in which our valiant Hamlet⌐

For so this side of our known world esteem'd him⌐   85

Did slay this Fortinbras; who, by a seal'd compact,

Well ratified by law and heraldry,

Did forfeit, with his life, all those his lands

Which he stood seiz'd of, to the conqueror;

Against the which, a moiety competent   90

Was gaged by our king; which had return'd

To the inheritance of Fortinbras,

Had he been vanquisher; as, by the same covenant,

And carriage of the article design'd,

His fell to Hamlet. Now, sir, young Fortinbras,   95
Of unimproved mettle hot and full,
Hath in the skirts of Norway here and there
Shark'd up a list of landless resolutes,
For food and diet, to some enterprise
That hath a stomach in't; which is no other⁻   100
As it doth well appear unto our state⁻
But to recover of us, by strong hand
And terms compulsatory, those foresaid lands
So by his father lost; and this, I take it,
Is the main motive of our preparations,   105
The source of this our watch, and the chief head
Of this post-haste and romage in the land.

Ber.   I think it be no other but e'en so.
Well may it sort that this portentous figure
Comes armed through our watch; so like the king   110
That was and is the question of these wars.

Hor.   A mote it is to trouble the mind's eye.
In the most high and palmy state of Rome,
A little ere the mightiest Julius fell,
The graves stood tenantless and the sheeted dead   115
Did squeak and gibber in the Roman streets;
As stars with trains of fire and dews of blood,
Disasters in the sun; and the moist star
Upon whose influence Neptune's empire stands
Was sick almost to doomsday with eclipse;   120

And even the like precurse of fierce events,

As harbingers preceding still the fates

And prologue to the omen coming on,

Have heaven and earth together demonstrated

Unto our climatures and countrymen. —   125

Re-enter Ghost.

But soft, behold!   Lo, where it comes again!

I'll cross it, though it blast me.   Stay, illusion!

If thou hast any sound, or use of voice,

Speak to me:

If there be any good thing to be done,   130

That may to thee do ease and grace to me,

Speak to me: [*Cock crows.*

If thou art privy to thy country's fate,

Which, happily, foreknowing may avoid,

O speak!   135

Or if thou hast uphoarded in thy life

Extorted treasure in the womb of earth,

For which, they say, you spirits oft walk in death,

Speak of it: stay, and speak!   Stop it, Marcellus.

Mar.   Shall I strike at it with my partisan?   140

Hor.   Do, if it will not stand.

Ber.   'Tis here!

Hor.   'Tis here!

I. i]

Mar.　'Tis gone!　　　　　　　　　　　*[Exit Ghost.*

　　We do it wrong, being so majestical,

　　To offer it the show of violence;

　　For it is, as the air, invulnerable,　　　　　　　145

　　And our vain blows malicious mockery.

Ber.　It was about to speak, when the cock crew.

Hor.　And then it started like a guilty thing

　　Upon a fearful summons. I have heard,

　　The cock, that is the trumpet to the morn,　　150

　　Doth with his lofty and shrill-sounding throat

　　Awake the god of day; and, at his warning,

　　Whether in sea or fire, in earth or air,

　　The extravagant and erring spirit hies

　　To his confine; and of the truth herein　　155

　　This present object made probation.

Mar.　It faded on the crowing of the cock.

　　Some say that ever 'gainst that season comes

　　Wherein our Saviour's birth is celebrated,

　　The bird of dawning singeth all night long;　160

　　And then, they say, no spirit dare stir abroad;

　　The nights are wholesome; then no planets strike,

　　No fairy takes, nor witch hath power to charm,

　　So hallow'd and so gracious is the time.

Hor.　So have I heard and do in part believe it.　165

　　But, look, the morn, in russet mantle clad,

　　Walks o'er the dew of yon high eastward hill.

Break we our watch up;   and, by my advice,

Let us impart what we have seen to-night

Unto young Hamlet;   for, upon my life,   170

This spirit, dumb to us, will speak to him.

Do you consent we shall acquaint him with it,

As needful in our loves, fitting our duty?

Mar.   Let's do 't, I pray;   and I this morning know

Where we shall find him most convenient.   175

[Exeunt.

SCENE II

A room of state in the castle.

Enter the KING, QUEEN, HAMLET, POLONIUS,
LAERTERS, VOLTMAND, CORNELIUS, Lords, *and* Attendants.

King.   Though yet of Hamlet our dear brother's death

The memory be green, and that it us befitted

To bear our hearts in grief, and our whole kingdom

To be contracted in one brow of woe,

Yet so far hath discretion fought with nature   5

That we with wisest sorrow think on him,

Together with remembrance of ourselves.

Therefore our sometime sister, now our queen,

The imperial jointress of this warlike state,

Have we, as 'twere with a defeated joy,— 10

With one auspicious and one dropping eye,

With mirth in funeral and with dirge in marriage,

In equal scale weighing delight and dole,—

Taken to wife; nor have we herein barr'd

Your better wisdoms, which have freely gone 15

With this affair along. For all, our thanks.

Now follows, that you know, young Fortinbras,

Holding a weak supposal of our worth,

Or thinking by our late dear brother's death

Our state to be disjoint and out of frame, 20

Colleagued with the dream of his advantage,

He hath not fail'd to pester us with message

Importing the surrender of those lands

Lost by his father, with all bonds of law,

To our most valiant brother. So much for him. 25

Now for ourself and for this time of meeting,

Thus much the business is: we have here writ

To Norway, uncle of young Fortinbras,—

Who, impotent and bed-rid, scarcely hears

Of this his nephew's purpose,—to suppress 30

His further gait herein; in that the levies,

The lists and full proportions, are all made

Out of his subject; and we here dispatch

You, good Cornelius, and you, Voltimand,

For bearers of this greeting to old Norway; 35

Giving to you no further personal power

To business with the king, more than the scope

Of these delated articles allow.

Farewell, and let your haste commend your duty.

Cor. & Vol.   In that and all things will we show

our duty.   40

King.   We doubt it nothing;   heartily farewell.

[*Exeunt Voltimand and Cornelius.*

And now, Laertes, what's the news with you?

You told us of some suit;   what is 't, Laertes?

You cannot speak of reason to the Dane,

And lose your voice: what wouldst thou beg, Laertes,   45

That shall not be my offer, not thy asking?

The head is not more native to the heart,

The hand more instrumental to the mouth,

Than is the throne of Denmark to thy father.

What wouldst thou have, Laertes?

Laer.   My dread lord,   50

Your leave and favour to return to France;

From whence though willingly I came to Denmark

To show my duty in your coronation,

Yet now, I must confess, that duty done,

My thoughts and wishes bend again toward France   55

And bow them to your gracious leave and pardon.

King.   Have you your father's leave? What says

Polonius?

Pol.   He hath, my lord, wrung from me my
  slow leave

  By laboursome petition, and at last

  Upon his will I seal'd my hard consent: 60

  I do beseech you, give him leave to go.

King.   Take thy fair hour, Laertes;   time be thine,

  And thy best graces spend it at thy will!

  But now, my cousin Hamlet, and my son,—

Ham.   [*Aside*]   A little more than kin, and less than
  kind.   65

King.   How is it that the clouds still hang on you?

Ham.   Not so, my lord;   I am too much in the sun.

Queen.   Good Hamlet, cast thy nighted colour off,

  And let thine eye look like a friend on Denmark.

  Do not for ever with thy vailed lids   70

  Seek for thy noble father in the dust.

  Thou know'st 'tis common;   all that lives must die,

  Passing through nature to eternity.

Ham.   Ay, madam, it is common.

Queen.   If it be,

  Why seems it so particular with thee?   75

Ham.   Seems, madam! Nay, it is;   I know not
  'seems.'

  'Tis not alone my inky cloak, good mother,

  Nor customary suits of solemn black,

  Nor windy suspiration of forced breath,

No, nor the fruitful river in the eye,   80

Nor the dejected 'haviour of the visage,

Together with all forms, moods, shapes of grief,

That can denote me truly. These indeed seem,

For they are actions that a man might play;

But I have that within which passeth show;   85

These but the trappings and the suits of woe.

King.   'Tis sweet and commendable in your nature, Hamlet,

To give these mourning duties to your father;

But, you must know, your father lost a father;

That father lost, lost his; and the survivor bound   90

In filial obligation for some term

To do obsequious sorrow. But to persever

In obstinate condolement is a course

Of impious stubbornness; 'tis unmanly grief;

It shows a will most incorrect to heaven,   95

A heart unfortified, a mind impatient,

An understanding simple and unschool'd;

For what we know must be, and is as common

As any the most vulgar thing to sense,

Why should we in our peevish opposition   100

Take it to heart? Fie! 'tis a fault to heaven,

A fault against the dead, a fault to nature,

To reason most absurd; whose common theme

Is death of fathers, and who still hath cried,

From the first corse till he that died to-day,   105
'This must be so.' We pray you, throw to earth
This unprevailing woe, and think of us
As of a father; for, let the world take note,
You are the most immediate to our throne;
And with no less nobility of love   110
Than that which dearest father bears his son,
Do I impart towards you. For your intent
In going back to school in Wittenberg,
It is most retrograde to our desire;
And we beseech you, bend you to remain   115
Here, in the cheer and comfort of our eye,
Our chiefest courtier, cousin, and our son.

Queen.   Let not thy mother lose her prayers, Hamlet,
    I pray, thee, stay with us; go not to Wittenberg.

Ham. I shall in all my best obey you, madam.   120

King.   Why, 'tis a loving and a fair reply.
    Be as ourself in Denmark. Madam, come;
    This gentle and unforc'd accord of Hamlet
    Sits smiling to my heart; in grace whereof,
    No jocund health that Denmark drinks to-day,   125
    But the great cannon to the clouds shall tell,
    And the King's rouse the heavens shall bruit again,
    Re-speaking earthly thunder. Come away.

                    [Exeunt all but Hamlet.

Ham.   O, that this too too solid flesh would melt,

Thaw, and resolve itself into a dew! 130

Or that the Everlasting had not fix'd

His canon 'gainst self-slaughter! O God! God!

How weary, stale, flat, and unprofitable,

Seems to me all the uses of this world!

Fie on't! ah fie! 'tis an unweeded garden, 135

That grows to seed; things rank and gross in nature

Possess it merely. That it should come to this!

But two months dead! Nay, not so much, not two.

So excellent a king; that was, to this,

Hyperion to a satyr; so loving to my mother 140

That he might not beteem the winds of heaven

Visit her face too roughly. Heaven and earth!

Must I remember? Why, she would hang on him,

As if increase of appetite had grown

By what it fed on; and yet, within a month,— 145

Let me not think on't!—Frailty, thy name is woman!—

A little month, or ere those shoes were old

With which she followed my poor father's body,

Like Niobe, all tears,—why she, even she—

O God! a beast, that wants discourse of reason, 150

Would have mourn'd longer—married with mine uncle,

My father's brother, but no more like my father

Than I to Hercules; within a month,

Ere yet the salt of most unrighteous tears

Had left the flushing of her galled eyes, 155

She married. O, most wicked speed, to post

With such dexterity to incestuous sheets!

It is not, nor it cannot come to good.

But break my heart, for I must hold my tongue.

Enter HORATIO, MARCELLUS, *and* BERNARDO.

Hor.   Hail to your lordship!

Ham.   I am glad to see you well: 160

Horatio,—or I do forget myself.

Hor.   The same, my lord, and your poor servant ever.

Ham.   Sir, my good friend; I'll change that name

with you.

And what make you from Wittenberg, Horatio?

Marcellus?   165

Mar.   My good lord!

Ham.   I am very glad to see you. [*To Ber.*] Good

even, sir.—

But what, in faith, make you from Wittenberg?

Hor.   A truant disposition, good my lord.

Ham.   I would not hear your enemy say so,   170

Nor shall you do mine ear that violence,

To make it truster of your own report

Against yourself. I know you are no truant.

But what is your affair in Elsinore?

We'll teach you to drink deep ere you depart.   175

Hor. My lord, I came to see your father's funeral.

Ham. I pray thee, do not mock me, fellow-student;

I think it was to see my mother's wedding.

Hor. Indeed, my lord, it followed hard upon.

Ham. Thrift, thrift, Horatio! The funeral baked meats 180

Did coldly furnish forth the marriage tables.

Would I had met my dearest foe in heaven

Or ever I had seen that day, Horatio!

My father!—methinks I see my father.

Hor. Where, my lord?

Ham. In my mind's eye, Horatio. 185

Hor. I saw him once; he was a goodly king.

Ham. He was a man, take him for all in all,

I shall not look upon his like again.

Hor. My lord, I think I saw him yesternight.

Ham. Saw? Who? 190

Hor. My lord, the King your father.

Ham. The King my father!

Hor. Season your admiration for a while

With an attent ear, till I may deliver,

Upon the witness of these gentlemen,

This marvel to you.

Ham. For God's love, let me hear. 195

Hor. Two nights together had these gentlemen,

Marcellus and Bernardo, on their watch,

In the dead vast and middle of the night,

Been thus encount'red. A figure like your father,

Armed at point exactly, cap-a-pe, 200

Appears before them, and with solemn march

Goes slow and stately by them; thrice he walk'd

By their oppress'd and fear-surprised eyes,

Within his truncheon's length; whilst they, distill'd

Almost to jelly with the act of fear, 205

Stand dumb and speak not to him. This to me

In dreadful secrecy impart they did,

And I with them the third night kept the watch;

Where, as they had deliver'd, both in time,

Form of the thing, each word made true and good, 210

The apparition comes. I knew your father;

These hands are not more like.

Ham.   But where was this!

Mar.   My lord, upon the platform where we watch'd.

Ham.   Did you not speak to it?

Hor.   My lord, I did;

But answer made it none. Yet once methought 215

It lifted up it head and did address

Itself to motion, like as it would speak;

But even then the morning cock crew loud,

And at the sound it shrunk in haste away,

And vanish'd from our sight.

Ham.   'Tis very strange. 220

Hor. As I do live, my honour'd lord, 'tis true,

And we did think it writ down in our duty

To let you know of it.

Ham. Indeed, indeed, sirs. But this troubles me.

Hold you the watch to-night?

Mar. & Ber. We do, my lord. 225

Ham. Arm'd, say you?

Mar. & Ber. Arm'd, my lord.

Ham. From top to toe?

Mar. & Ber. My lord, from head to foot.

Ham. Then saw you not his face?

Hor. O, yes, my lord; he wore his beaver up. 230

Ham. What, look'd he frowningly?

Hor. A countenance more in sorrow than in anger.

Ham. Pale, or red?

Hor. Nay, very pale.

Ham. And fix'd his eyes upon you?

Hor. Most constantly.

Ham. I would I had been there. 235

Hor. It would have much amazed you.

Ham. Very like, very like. Stay'd it long?

Hor. While one with moderate haste might tell a

hundred.

Mar. & Ber. Longer, longer.

Hor. Not when I saw 't.

Ham. His beard was grizzled,—no? 240

Hor.   It was, as I have seen it in his life,

    A sable silver'd.

Ham.   I will watch to-night;

    Perchance 'twill walk again.

Hor.   I warrant you it will.

Ham.   If it assume my noble father's person,

    I'll speak to it, though hell itself should gape   245

    And bid me hold my peace. I pray you all,

    If you have hitherto conceal'd this sight,

    Let it be tenable in your silence still;

    And whatsoever else shall hap to-night,

    Give it an understanding, but no tongue.   250

    I will requite your loves. So, fare you well.

    Upon the platform 'twixt eleven and twelve,

    I'll visit you.

All.   Our duty to your honour.

Ham.   Your loves, as mine to you;   farewell.

                   [*Exeunt all but Hamlet.*

    My father's spirit in arms! All is not well;   255

    I doubt some foul play. Would the night were come!

    Till then sit still, my soul. Foul deeds will rise,

    Though all the earth o'erwhelm them, to men's eyes.

                         [*Exit.*

SCENE III

A room in Polonius' house.

Enter LAERTES *and* OPHELIA *his sister.*

Laer.   My necessaries are embark'd: farewell:
    And, sister, as the winds give benefit
    And convoy is assistant, do not sleep,
    But let me hear from you.

Oph.   Do you doubt that?

Laer.   For Hamlet and the trifling of his favour,   5
    Hold it a fashion and a toy in blood,
    A violet in the youth of primy nature,
    Forward, not permanent, sweet, not lasting,
    The perfume and suppliance of a minute;
    No more.

Oph.   No more but so?

Laer.   Think it no more: 10
    For nature, crescent, does not grow alone
    In thews and bulk, but, as this temple waxes,
    The inward service of the mind and soul
    Grows wide withal.   Perhaps he loves you now,
    And now no soil nor cautel doth besmirch   15
    The virtue of his will;   but you must fear,
    His greatness weigh'd, his will is not his own;
    For he himself is subject to his birth:

He may not, as unvalued persons do,

Carve for himself, for on his choice depends   20

The sanity and health of the whole state;

And therefore must his choice be circumscrib'd

Unto the voice and yielding of that body

Whereof he is the head.   Then, if he says he loves you,

It fits your wisdom so far to believe it   25

As he in his particular act and place

May give his saying deed;   which is no further

Than the main voice of Denmark goes withal.

Then weigh what loss your honour may sustain,

If with too credent ear you list his songs,   30

Or lose your heart, or your chaste treasure open

To his unmast'red importunity.

Fear it, Ophelia, fear it, my dear sister,

And keep you in the rear of your affection,

Out of the shot and danger of desire.   35

The chariest maid is prodigal enough,

If she unmask her beauty to the moon.

Virtue itself 'scapes not calumnious strokes.

The canker galls the infants of the spring

Too oft before the buttons be disclosed,   40

And in the morn and liquid dew of youth

Contagious blastments are most imminent.

Be wary then;   best safety lies in fear;

Youth to itself rebels, though none else near.

Oph. I shall the effect of this good lesson keep,   **45**

    As watchman to my heart. But, good my brother,

    Do not, as some ungracious pastors do,

    Show me the steep and thorny way to heaven,

    Whiles, like a puff'd and reckless libertine,

    Himself the primrose path of dalliance treads,   **50**

    And recks not his own rede.

Laer.   O, fear me not.

    I stay too long: but here my father comes.

Enter POLONIUS.

    A double blessing is a double grace;

    Occasion smiles upon a second leave.

Pol.   Yet here, Laertes! Aboard, aboard, for shame!   **55**

    The wind sits in the shoulder of your sail,

    And you are stay'd for. There; my blessing with thee!

    And these few precepts in thy memory

    See thou character. Give thy thoughts no tongue,

    Nor any unproportion'd thought his act.   **60**

    Be thou familiar, but by no means vulgar.

    The friends thou hast, and their adoption tried,

    Grapple them to thy soul with hoops of steel;

    But do not dull thy palm with entertainment

    Of each new-hatch'd, unfledg'd comrade. Beware   **65**

    Of entrance to a quarrel; but being in,

Bear't that the opposed may beware of thee.

Give every man thine ear, but few thy voice;

Take each man's censure, but reserve thy judgement.

Costly thy habit as thy purse can buy,   70

But not express'd in fancy;   rich, not gaudy;

For the apparel oft proclaims the man,

And they in France of the best rank and station

Are of a most select and generous chief in that.

Neither a borrower nor a lender be;   75

For loan oft loses both itself and friend,

And borrowing dulls the edge of husbandry.

This above all: to thine own self be true,

And it must follow, as the night the day,

Thou canst not then be false to any man.   80

Farewell;   my blessing season this in thee!

Laer.   Most humbly do I take my leave, my lord.

Pol.   The time invites you;   go, your servants tend.

Laer.   Farewell, Ophelia;   and remember well

What I have said to you.

Oph.   'Tis in my memory lock'd,   85

And you yourself shall keep the key of it.

Laer.   Farewell.   [*Exit.*

Pol.   What is 't, Ophelia, he hath said to you?

Oph.   So please you, something touching the Lord

Hamlet.

Pol.   Marry, well bethought.   90

'Tis told me, he hath very oft of late

Given private time to you, and you yourself

Have of your audience been most free and bounteous.

If it be so—as so 'tis put on me,

And that in way of caution—I must tell you,   95

You do not understand yourself so clearly

As it behoves my daughter and your honour.

What is between you? Give me up the truth.

Oph.   He hath, my lord, of late made many tenders

Of his affection to me.   100

Pol.   Affection! pooh! You speak like a green girl,

Unsifted in such perilous circumstance.

Do you believe his tenders, as you call them?

Oph.   I do not know, my lord, what I should think.

Pol.   Marry, I'll teach you: think yourself a baby   105

That you have ta'en these tenders for true pay,

Which are not sterling. Tender yourself more dearly;

Or—not to crack the wind of the poor phrase,

Running it thus—you'll tender me a fool.

Oph.   My lord, he hath importun'd me with love   110

In honourable fashion.

Pol.   Ay, fashion you may call it; go to, go to.

Oph.   And hath given countenance to his speech,

my lord,

With almost all the holy vows of heaven.

Pol.   Ay, springes to catch woodcocks. I do know,   115

When the blood burns, how prodigal the soul
Lends the tongue vows. These blazes, daughter,
Giving more light than heat, extinct in both,
Even in their promise, as it is a-making,
You must not take for fire. From this time   120
Be somewhat scanter of your maiden presence;
Set your entreatments at a higher rate
Than a command to parley. For Lord Hamlet,
Believe so much in him, that he is young,
And with a larger tether may he walk   125
Than may be given you; In few, Ophelia,
Do not believe his vows; for they are brokers,
Not of that dye which their investments show,
But mere implorators of unholy suits,
Breathing like sanctified and pious bawds,   130
The better to beguile. This is for all:
I would not, in plain terms, from this time forth,
Have you so slander any moment leisure
As to give words or talk with the Lord Hamlet.
Look to 't, I charge you. Come your ways.   135
Oph.   I shall obey, my lord.   [*Exeunt.*

SCENE IV

The platform.

HAMLET, HORATIO, *and* MARCELLUS.

Ham.   The air bites shrewdly;   it is very cold.

Hor.   It is a nipping and an eager air.

Ham.   What hour now?

Hor.   I think it lacks of twelve.

Mar.   No, it is struck.

Hor.   Indeed? I heard it not.   Then it draws near
the season   5
Wherein the spirit held his wont to walk.
>   [*A flourish of trumpets, and two
>   pieces go off within.*

What does this mean, my lord?

Ham.   The King doth wake to-night and takes
his rouse,
Keeps wassail, and the swaggering up-spring reels;
And, as he drains his draughts of Rhenish down,   10
The kettle-drum and trumpet thus bray out
The triumph of his pledge.

Hor.   Is it a custom?

Ham.   Ay, marry, is 't;
But to my mind, though I am native here
And to the manner born, it is a custom   15

More honour'd in the breach than the observance.

This heavy-headed revel east and west

Makes us traduc'd and tax'd of other nations:

They clepe us drunkards, and with swinish phrase

Soil our addition;   and indeed it takes   20

From our achievements, though perform'd at height,

The pith and marrow of our attribute.

So, oft it chances in particular men,

That for some vicious mole of nature in them,

As, in their birth—wherein they are not guilty,   25

Since nature cannot choose his origin—

By their o'ergrowth of some complexion,

Oft breaking down the pales and forts of reason,

Or by some habit that too much o'er-leavens

The form of plausive manners, that these men,   30

Carrying, I say, the stamp of one defect,

Being nature's livery, or fortune's star,

Their virtues else—be they as pure as grace,

As infinite as man may undergo—

Shall in the general censure take corruption   35

From that particular fault.   The dram of eale

Doth all the noble substance of a doubt

To his own scandal.

Enter Ghost.

Hor.   Look, my lord, it comes!

Ham.   Angels and ministers of grace defend us!

Be thou a spirit of health or goblin damn'd,   40

Bring with thee airs from heaven or blasts from hell,

Be thy intents wicked or charitable,

Thou comest in such a questionable shape

That I will speak to thee. I'll call thee Hamlet,

King, father, royal Dane. O, answer me!   45

Let me not burst in ignorance, but tell

Why thy canonized bones, hearsed in death,

Have burst their cerements; why the sepulchre,

Wherein we saw thee quietly inurn'd,

Hath oped his ponderous and marble jaws,   50

To cast thee up again. What may this mean,

That thou, dead corse, again in complete steel

Revisits thus the glimpses of the moon,

Making night hideous, and we fools of nature

So horridly to shake our disposition   55

With thoughts beyond the reaches of our souls?

Say, why is this? wherefore? What should we do?

                    [*Ghost beckons Hamlet.*

Hor.   It beckons you to go away with it,

As if it some impartment did desire

To you alone.

Mar.   Look, with what courteous action   60

It waves you to a more removed ground.

But do not go with it.

Hor.　　　　No, by no means.

Ham.　It will not speak;　then will I follow it.

Hor.　Do not, my lord.

Ham.　　　　　Why, what should be the fear?

I do not set my life at a pin's fee;　　　　　　　65

And for my soul, what can it do to that,

Being a thing immortal as itself?

It waves me forth again;　I'll follow it.

Hor.　What if it tempt you toward the flood,

my lord,

Or to the dreadful summit of the cliff　　　　　70

That beetles o'er his base into the sea,

And there assume some other horrible form,

Which might deprive your sovereignty of reason

And draw you into madness? Think of it.

The very place puts toys of desperation,　　　　75

Without more motive, into every brain

That looks so many fathoms to the sea

And hears it roar beneath.

Ham.　　　　　It waves me still.

Go on, I'll follow thee.

Mar.　You shall not go, my lord.

Ham.　　　　　　　Hold off your hands.　　　80

Hor.　Be rul'd;　you shall not go.

Ham.   My fate cries out,
  And makes each petty artery in this body
  As hardy as the Nemean lion's nerve.
  Still am I call'd. Unhand me, gentlemen.
  By heaven, I'll make a ghost of him that lets me!   85
  I say, away! Go on, I'll follow thee.
                      [Exeunt Ghost and Hamlet.

Hor.   He waxes desperate with imagination.
Mar.   Let's follow; 'tis not fit thus to obey him.
Hor.   Have after. To what issue will this come?
Mar.   Something is rotten in the state of Denmark.   90
Hor.   Heaven will direct it.
Mar.   Nay, let's follow him. *[Exeunt.*

Scene V

Another part of the platform.

Enter Ghost *and* HAMLET.

Ham.   Where wilt thou lead me? Speak, I'll
  go no further.
Ghost.   Mark me.
Ham.   I will.
Ghost.   My hour is almost come,
  When I to sulphurous and tormenting flames

Must render up myself.

Ham.　　　　Alas, poor ghost!

Ghost.　Pity me not, but lend thy serious hearing　　　　　　5

To what I shall unfold.

Ham.　　　　　Speak; I am bound to hear.

Ghost.　So art thou to revenge, when thou shalt hear.

Ham.　What?

Ghost.　I am thy father's spirit,

Doom'd for a certain term to walk the night,　　　　　　10

And for the day confin'd to fast in fires,

Till the foul crimes done in my days of nature

Are burnt and purg'd away.　But that I am forbid

To tell the secrets of my prison-house,

I could a tale unfold whose lightest word　　　　　　15

Would harrow up thy soul, freeze thy young blood,

Make thy two eyes, like stars, start from their spheres,

Thy knotted and combined locks to part

And each particular hair to stand an end,

Like quills upon the fretful porpentine.　　　　　　20

But this eternal blazon must not be

To ears of flesh and blood.　List, Hamlet, O, list!

If thou didst ever thy dear father love—

Ham.　O God!

Ghost.　Revenge his foul and most unnatural murder.　　　　　　25

Ham.　Murder!

Ghost.　Murder most foul, as in the best it is;

But this most foul, strange, and unnatural.

Ham.   Haste me to know 't, that I, with wings as
swift
As meditation or the thoughts of love,   30
May sweep to my revenge.

Ghost.   I find thee apt;
And duller shouldst thou be than the fat weed
That roots itself in ease on Lethe wharf,
Wouldst thou not stir in this. Now, Hamlet, hear.
'Tis given out that, sleeping in mine orchard,   35
A serpent stung me; so the whole ear of Denmark
Is by a forged process of my death
Rankly abus'd; but know, thou noble youth,
The serpent that did sting thy father's life
Now wears his crown.

Ham.   O my prophetic soul!   40
Mine uncle!

Ghost.   Ay, that incestuous, that adulterate beast,
With witchcraft of his wit, with traitorous gifts,—
O wicked wit and gifts, that have the power
So to seduce!—won to his shameful lust   45
The will of my most seeming-virtuous queen.
O Hamlet, what a falling-off was there!
From me, whose love was of that dignity
That it went hand in hand even with the vow
I made to her in marriage, and to decline   50

Upon a wretch whose natural gifts were poor

To those of mine!

But virtue, as it never will be moved,

Though lewdness court it in a shape of heaven,

So lust, though to a radiant angel link'd,   55

Will sate itself in a celestial bed

And prey on garbage.

But, soft! methinks I scent the morning air.

Brief let me be. Sleeping within mine orchard,

My custom always of the afternoon,   60

Upon my secure hour thy uncle stole,

With juice of cursed hebenon in a vial,

And in the porches of mine ears did pour

The leperous distilment;   whose effect

Holds such an enmity with blood of man   65

That swift as quicksilver it courses through

The natural gates and alleys of the body,

And with a sudden vigour it doth posset

And curd, like eager droppings into milk,

The thin and wholesome blood. So did it mine,   70

And a most instant tetter bark'd about,

Most lazar-like, with vile and loathsome crust,

All my smooth body.

Thus was I, sleeping, by a brother's hand

Of life, of crown, of queen, at once dispatch'd;   75

Cut off even in the blossoms of my sin,

Unhousel'd, disappointed, unanel'd;

No reckoning made, but sent to my account

With all my imperfections on my head.

O, horrible! O, horrible! most horrible! 80

If thou hast nature in thee, bear it not;

Let not the royal bed of Denmark be

A couch for luxury and damned incest.

But, howsoever thou pursuest this act,

Taint not thy mind, nor let thy soul contrive 85

Against thy mother aught;   leave her to heaven

And to those thorns that in her bosom lodge,

To prick and sting her.   Fare thee well at once!

The glow-worm shows the matin to be near,

And 'gins to pale his uneffectual fire. 90

Adieu, adieu! Hamlet, remember me.   [*Exit.*

Ham.   O all you host of heaven!   O earth!

What else?

And shall I couple hell? O, fie!   Hold, hold my heart;

And you, my sinews, grow not instant old,

But bear me stiffly up.   Remember thee! 95

Ay, thou poor ghost, while memory holds a seat

In this distracted globe.   Remember thee!

Yea, from the table of my memory

I'll wipe away all trivial fond records,

All saws of books, all forms, all pressures past, 100

That youth and observation copied there,

And thy commandment all alone shall live

Within the book and volume of my brain,

Unmix'd with baser matter. Yes, by heaven!

O most pernicious woman!   105

O villain, villain, smiling, damned villain!

My tables,—meet it is I set it down

That one may smile, and smile, and be a villain;

At least I'm sure it may be so in Denmark.

[Writing.

So, uncle, there you are. Now to my word;   110

It is 'Adieu, adieu! remember me.'

I have sworn 't.

Mar. & Hor.   [*Within*]   My lord, my lord!

Mar.   [*Within*]   Lord Hamlet!

Hor.   [*Within*]   Heaven secure him!

Ham.   So be it!

Mar.   [*Within*]   Illo, ho, ho, my lord!   115

Ham.   Hillo, ho, ho, boy! Come, bird, come.

Enter HORATIO *and* MARCELLUS.

Mar.   How is 't, my noble lord?

Hor.   What news, my lord?

Ham.   O, wonderful!

Hor.   Good my lord, tell it.

Ham.   No;   you'll reveal it.

Hor.   Not I, my lord, by heaven.

Mar.   Nor I, my lord.   120

Ham.   How say you, then;   would heart of man
    once think it?

    But you'll be secret?

Hor. & Mar.   Ay, by heaven, my lord.

Ham.   There's ne'er a villain dwelling in all
    Denmark

    But he's an arrant knave.

Hor.   There needs no ghost, my lord, come from
    the grave   125

    To tell us this.

Ham.   Why, right;   you are i' the right;
    And so, without more circumstance at all,
    I hold it fit that we shake hands and part;
    You, as your business and desires shall point you;
    For every man has business and desire,   130
    Such as it is;   and for mine own poor part,
    Look you, I'll go pray.

Hor.   These are but wild and whirling words,
    my lord.

Ham.   I'm sorry they offend you, heartily;
    Yes, faith, heartily.

Hor.   There's no offence, my lord.   135

Ham.   Yes, by Saint Patrick, but there is, Horatio,
    And much offence too.   Touching this vision here,

It is an honest ghost, that let me tell you.

For your desire to know what is between us,

O'ermaster 't as you may. And now, good friends,   **140**

As you are friends, scholars, and soldiers,

Give me one poor request.

Hor.　What is 't, my lord? We will.

Ham.　Never make known what you have seen
to-night.

Hor. & Mar.　My lord, we will not.

Ham.　　　　　　　　Nay, but swear 't.

Hor.

　　　　In faith,   **145**

My lord, not I.

Mar.　Nor I, my lord, in faith.

Ham.　Upon my sword.

Mar.　　　　　We have sworn, my lord, already.

Ham.　Indeed, upon my sword, indeed.

Ghost.　[*Beneath*] Swear!

Ham.　Ah, ha, boy! say'st thou so? Art thou there,
truepenny?   **150**

Come on;　you hear this fellow in the cellarage.

Consent to swear.

Hor.　Propose the oath, my lord.

Ham.　Never to speak of this that you have seen.

Swear by my sword.

Ghost.　[*Beneath*]　Swear.   **155**

Ham. Hic et ubique? Then we'll shift our ground.

Come thither, gentlemen,

And lay your hands again upon my sword;

Never to speak of this that you have heard,

Swear by my sword.   160

Ghost. [*Beneath*] Swear.

Ham. Well said, old mole! Canst work i' the earth

so fast?

A worthy pioner! Once more remove, good friends.

Hor. O day and night, but this is wondrous strange!

Ham. And therefore as a stranger give it

welcome.   165

There are more things in heaven and earth, Horatio,

Than are dreamt of in your philosophy.

But come;

Here, as before, never, so help you mercy,

How strange or odd soe'er I bear myself,   170

As I perchance hereafter shall think meet

To put an antic disposition on —

That you, at such times seeing me, never shall,

With arms encumber'd thus, or this headshake,

Or by pronouncing of some doubtful phrase,   175

As 'Well, well, we know,' or 'We could, an if we

would,'

Or "If we list to speak," or "There be, an if they

might,"

Or such ambiguous giving out, to note

That you know aught of me,—this not to do,

So grace and mercy at your most need help you,   180

Swear.

Ghost.   [*Beneath*]   Swear.

Ham.   Rest, rest, perturbed spirit! [*They swear.*]

So, gentlemen,

With all my love I do commend me to you.

And what so poor a man as Hamlet is   185

May do, to express his love and friending to you,

God willing, shall not lack.   Let us go in together;

And still your fingers on your lips, I pray.

The time is out of joint: O cursed spite,

That ever I was born to set it right!   190

Nay, come, let's go together.   [*Exeunt.*

Act II

SCENE I

A room in Polonius' house.

Enter POLONIUS *and* REYNALDO.

Pol. Give him this money and these notes, Reynaldo.

Rey. I will, my lord.

Pol. You shall do marvellous wisely, good Reynaldo,
    Before you visit him, to make inquire
    Of his behaviour.

Rey.   My lord, I did intend it.   5

Pol. Marry, well said; very well said. Look
    you, sir,
    Inquire me first what Danskers are in Paris;
    And how, and who, what means, and where they
    keep,
    What company, at what expense; and finding
    By this encompassment and drift of question   10

That they do know my son, come you more nearer
Than your particular demands will touch it:
Take you, as 'twere, some distant knowledge of him;
As thus, 'I know his father and his friends,
And in part him.' Do you mark this, Reynaldo?　　　　15

Rey.　Ay, very well, my lord.

Pol.　'And in part him;　but,' you may say,
　'not well.
　But, if 't be he I mean, he's very wild;
　Addicted so and so;'　and there put on him
　What forgeries you please;　marry, none so rank　　20
　As may dishonour him;　take heed of that;
　But, sir, such wanton, wild, and usual slips
　As are companions noted and most known
　To youth and liberty.

Rey.　　　As gaming, my lord.

Pol.　Ay, or drinking, fencing, swearing, quarrelling,　25
　Drabbing;　you may go so far.

Rey.　My lord, that would dishonour him.

Pol.　'Faith, no;　as you may season it in the charge.
　You must not put another scandal on him,
　That he is open to incontinency;　　　　30
　That's not my meaning.　But breathe his faults so quaintly
　That they may seem the taints of liberty,
　The flash and outbreak of a fiery mind,
　A savageness in unreclaimed blood,

Of general assault.

Rey.   But, my good lord,— 35

Pol.   Wherefore should you do this?

Rey.   Ay, my lord,
I would know that.

Pol.   Marry, sir, here's my drift,
And, I believe, it is a fetch of wit:
You laying these slight sullies on my son,
As 'twere a thing a little soil'd i' the working, 40
Mark you,
Your party in converse, him you would sound,
Having ever seen in the prenominate crimes
The youth you breathe of guilty, be assur'd
He closes with you in this consequence; 45
'Good sir,' or so, or 'friend,' or 'gentleman,'
According to the phrase and the addition
Of man and country.

Rey.   Very good, my lord.

Pol.   And then, sir, does he this—he does—
What was I about to say? By the mass, I was 50
about to say something. Where did I leave?

Rey.   At 'closes in the consequence,' at 'friend
or so,' and 'gentleman.'

Pol.   At 'closes in the consequence,' ay, marry.
He closes thus: 'I know the gentleman. 55
I saw him yesterday, or t' other day,

Or then, or then; with such, or such; and, as you say,

There was 'a gaming; there o'ertook in 's rouse;

There falling out at tennis;' or, perchance,

'I saw him enter such a house of sale,'   60

    Videlicet, a brothel, or so forth.

See you now;

Your bait of falsehood takes this carp of truth;

And thus do we of wisdom and of reach,

With windlasses and with assays of bias,   65

By indirections find directions out:

So by my former lecture and advice,

Shall you my son. You have me, have you not?

Rey.   My lord, I have.

Pol.   God be wi' you; fare you well.

Rey.   Good my lord!   70

Pol.   Observe his inclination in yourself.

Rey.   I shall, my lord.

Pol.   And let him ply his music.

Rey.   Well, my lord.

Pol.   Farewell!   [*Exit Reynaldo.*

Enter OPHELIA.

    How now, Ophelia! what's the matter?

Oph.   O, my lord, I have been so affrighted!   75

Pol.   With what, i' the name of God?

Oph. My lord, as I was sewing in my closet,
    Lord Hamlet, with his doublet all unbrac'd,
    No hat upon his head, his stockings foul'd,
    Ungarter'd, and down-gyved to his ankle;   **80**
    Pale as his shirt, his knees knocking each other,
    And with a look so piteous in purport
    As if he had been loosed out of hell
    To speak of horrors,—he comes before me.

Pol. Mad for thy love?

Oph.   My lord, I do not know,   **85**
    But truly, I do fear it.

Pol.   What said he?

Oph. He took me by the wrist and held me hard;
    Then goes he to the length of all his arm,
    And, with his other hand thus o'er his brow,
    He falls to such perusal of my face   **90**
    As he would draw it. Long stay'd he so.
    At last, a little shaking of mine arm,
    And thrice his head thus waving up and down,
    He rais'd a sigh so piteous and profound
    As it did seem to shatter all his bulk   **95**
    And end his being. That done, he lets me go;
    And, with his head over his shoulder turn'd,
    He seem'd to find his way without his eyes,
    For out o' doors he went without their helps,
    And, to the last, bended their light on me.   **100**

Pol.   Come, go with me. I will go seek the King.

This is the very ecstasy of love,

Whose violent property fordoes itself

And leads the will to desperate undertakings

As oft as any passion under heaven   105

That does afflict our natures. I am sorry,—

What, have you given him any hard words of late?

Oph.   No, my good lord, but, as you did command,

I did repel his letters and denied

His access to me.

Pol.   That hath made him mad.   110

I am sorry that with better heed and judgement

I had not quoted him. I fear'd he did but trifle,

And meant to wreck thee; but beshrew my jealousy!

By heaven, it is as proper to our age

To cast beyond ourselves in our opinions   115

As it is common for the younger sort

To lack discretion. Come, go we to the King.

This must be known, which, being kept close, might
move

More grief to hide than hate to utter love.   [*Exeunt.*

SCENE **II**

A room in the castle.

Enter KING, QUEEN, ROSENCRANTZ, GUILDENSTERN,
and Attendants.

King.   Welcome, dear Rosencrantz and Guildenstern!
    Moreover that we much did long to see you,
    The need we have to use you did provoke
    Our hasty sending. Something have you heard
    Of Hamlet's transformation; so I call it,   5
    Sith nor the exterior nor the inward man
    Resembles that it was. What it should be,
    More than his father's death, that thus hath put him
    So much from the understanding of himself,
    I cannot dream of. I entreat you both,   10
    That, being of so young days brought up with him,
    And sith so neighbour'd to his youth and haviour,
    That you vouchsafe your rest here in our court
    Some little time; so by your companies
    To draw him on to pleasures, and to gather,   15
    So much as from occasions you may glean,
    Whether aught, to us unknown, afflicts him thus,
    That, open'd, lies within our remedy.
Queen.   Good gentlemen, he hath much talk'd of
    you;

And sure I am two men there is not living   20

To whom he more adheres. If it will please you

To show us so much gentry and good will

As to expend your time with us a while

For the supply and profit of our hope,

Your visitation shall receive such thanks   25

As fits a king's remembrance.

Ros.   Both your Majesties

Might, by the sovereign power you have of us,

Put your dread pleasures more into command

Than to entreaty.

Guil.   But we both obey.

And here give up ourselves, in the full bent   30

To lay our services freely at your feet,

To be commanded.

King.   Thanks, Rosencrantz and gentle Guildenstern.

Queen.   Thanks, Guildenstern and gentle Rosencrantz,

And I beseech you instantly to visit   35

My too much changed son. Go, some of you,

And bring the gentlemen where Hamlet is.

Guil.   Heavens make our presence and our practices

Pleasant and helpful to him!

Queen.   Ay, Amen!

[*Exeunt Rosencrantzs, Guildenstern, and*
and some Attendants].

Enter POLONIUS.

Pol.   The ambassadors from Norway, my good lord,   40

   Are joyfully return'd.

King.   Thou still hast been the father of good news.

Pol.   Have I, my lord? Assure you, my good liege,

   I hold my duty as I hold my soul,

   Both to my God and to my gracious King.   45

   And I do think, or else this brain of mine

   Hunts not the trail of policy so sure

   As it hath us'd to do, that I have found

   The very cause of Hamlet's lunacy.

King.   O, speak of that; that do I long to hear.   50

Pol.   Give first admittance to the ambassadors;

   My news shall be the fruit to that great feast.

King.   Thyself do grace to them, and bring them in.

                           [*Exit Polonius.*

   He tells me, my dear Gertrude, he hath found

   The head and source of all your son's distemper.   55

Queen.   I doubt it is no other but the main;

   His father's death and our o'erhasty marriage.

King.   Well, we shall sift him.

Re-enter POLONIUS, *with* VOLTIMAND *and* CORNELIUS.

Welcome, my good friends!

Say, Voltimand, what from our brother Norway?

Volt.   Most fair return of greetings and desires.   60

Upon our first, he sent out to suppress

His nephew's levies;   which to him appear'd

To be a preparation 'gainst the Polack;

But, better look'd into, he truly found

It was against your Highness.   Whereat grieved,   65

That so his sickness, age, and impotence

Was falsely borne in hand, sends out arrests

On Fortinbras;   which he, in brief, obeys;

Receives rebuke from Norway, and in fine

Makes vow before his uncle never more   70

To give the assay of arms against your Majesty.

Whereon old Norway, overcome with joy,

Gives him three thousand crowns in annual fee,

And his commission to employ those soldiers,

So levied as before, against the Polack;   75

With an entreaty, herein further shown,

                    [Giving a paper.

That it might please you to give quiet pass

Through your dominions for this enterprise,

On such regards of safety and allowance

As therein are set down.

King.   It likes us well;   80

And at our more consider'd time we'll read,

Answer, and think upon this business.

Meantime we thank you for your well-took labour.

Go to your rest;   at night we'll feast together.

Most welcome home!

　　　　　　[*Exeunt Voltimand and Cornelius.*

Pol.　　　　　This business is well ended.　　　　　　　　85

My liege, and madam, to expostulate

What majesty should be, what duty is,

Why day is day, night night, and time is time,

Were nothing but to waste night, day, and time.

Therefore, since brevity is the soul of wit　　　　　　90

And tediousness the limbs and outward flourishes,

I will be brief.   Your noble son is mad.

Mad call I it;   for, to define true madness,

What is 't but to be nothing else but mad?

But let that go.

Queen.　　More matter, with less art.　　　　　　　95

Pol.　　Madam, I swear I use no art at all.

That he is mad, 'tis true;   'tis true 'tis pity,

And pity 'tis 'tis true.   A foolish figure!

But farewell it, for I will use no art.

Mad let us grant him, then;   and now remains　　　100

That we find out the cause of this effect,

Or rather say, the cause of this defect,

For this effect defective comes by cause.

Thus it remains, and the remainder thus.

Perpend.　　　　　　　　　　　　　　　　105

I have a daughter⁻have whilst she is mine⁻

Who, in her duty and obedience, mark,

Hath given me this.　Now gather, and surmise.

　　　　　　　　　　　　　　　　　[Reads.

'To the celestial and my soul's idol, the most

beautified Ophelia,'⁻　　　　　　　　　　　　110

That's an ill phrase, a vile phrase;　'beautified' is

a vile phrase.　But you shall hear.　Thus: *[Reads.*

'In her excellent white bosom, these, &c.'

Queen.　Came this from Hamlet to her?

Pol.　Good madam, stay a while;　I will be

faithful.　　　　　　　　　　　*[Reads.*　　115

　　'Doubt thou the stars are fire;

　　　Doubt that the sun doth move;

　　Doubt truth to be a liar,

　　　But never doubt I love.

'O dear Ophelia, I am ill at these numbers.　I have　　120

not art to reckon my groans;　but that I love thee best,

O most best, believe it.　Adieu.

　Thine evermore, most dear lady, whilst

　　this machine is to him, HAMLET.'

This, in obedience, hath my daughter shown me,　　125

And more above, hath his solicitings,

As they fell out by time, by means, and place,

All given to mine ear.

King.　　　　　But how hath she

Receiv'd his love?

Pol.   What do you think of me?

King.   As of a man faithful and honourable.   130

Pol.   I would fain prove so. But what might
you think,
When I had seen this hot love on the wing, ⎯
As I perceiv'd it, I must tell you that,
Before my daughter told me, ⎯what might you,
Or my dear Majesty your queen here, think,   135
If I had play'd the desk or table-book,
Or given my heart a winking, mute and dumb,
Or look'd upon this love with idle sight;
What might you think? No, I went round to work,
And my young mistress thus I did bespeak;   140
'Lord Hamlet is a prince, out of thy star;
This must not be:' and then I prescripts gave her,
That she should lock herself from his resort,
Admit no messengers, receive no tokens.
Which done, she took the fruits of my advice;   145
And he, repulsed ⎯a short tale to make ⎯
Fell into a sadness, then into a fast,
Thence to a watch, thence into a weakness,
Thence to a lightness, and, by this declension,
Into the madness wherein now he raves,   150
And all we wail for.

King.   Do you think 'tis this?

Queen.   It may be, very likely.

Pol.   Hath there been such a time—I'd fain
know that—
That I have positively said, ''Tis so,'
When it prov'd otherwise?

King.   Not that I know.   155

Pol.   [*Pointing to his head and shoulder*] Take
this from this, if this be otherwise.
If circumstances lead me, I will find
Where truth is hid, though it were hid indeed
Within the centre.

King.   How may we try it further?

Pol.   You know, sometimes he walks four hours
together   160
Here in the lobby.

Queen.   So he does, indeed.

Pol.   At such a time I'll loose my daughter to him.
Be you and I behind an arras then;
Mark the encounter. If he love her not
And be not from his reason fall'n thereon,   165
Let me be no assistant for a state,
But keep a farm and carters.

King.   We will try it.

Enter HAMLET, *reading on a book.*

Queen. But look where sadly the poor wretch
  comes reading.

Pol. Away, I do beseech you, both away:
  I'll board him presently.

        [*Exeunt KING, QUEEN and Attendants.*

        O, give me leave;   170
  How does my good Lord Hamlet?

Ham. Well, God-a-mercy.

Pol. Do you know me, my lord?

Ham. Excellent well; you are a fishmonger.

Pol. Not I, my lord.   175

Ham. Then I would you were so honest a man.

Pol. Honest, my lord!

Ham. Ay, sir; to be honest, as this world goes,
  is to be one man pick'd out of ten thousand.

Pol. That's very true, my lord.   180

Ham. For if the sun breed maggots in a dead
  dog, being a good kissing carrion,—Have you a
  daughter?

Pol. I have, my lord.

  Ham. Let her not walk i' the sun. Conception   185
  is a blessing, butnot as your daughter may
  conceive. Friend, look to 't.

Pol. [*Aside*] How say you by that? Still
  harping on my daughter. Yet he knew me not at
  first; he said I was a fishmonger. He is far gone,   190

far gone.   And truly in my youth I suff'red much
extremity for love;   very near this.   I'll speak to
him again.—What do you read, my lord?

Ham.   Words, words, words.

Pol.   What is the matter, my lord?   195

Ham.   Between who?

Pol.   I mean, the matter you read, my lord.

Ham.   Slanders, sir;   for the satirical rogue
says here that old men have grey beards, that
their faces are wrinkled, their eyes purging thick   200
amber or plum-tree gum, and that they have a
plentiful lack of wit, together with weak
hams;   all which, sir, though I most powerfully
and potently believe, yet I hold it not honesty to
have it thus set down;   for you yourself, sir, should be   205
old as I am, if like a crab you could go backward.

Pol.   [*Aside*]   Though this be madness, yet
there is method in 't.   —Will you walk out of the
air, my lord?

Ham.   Into my grave?   210

Pol.   Indeed, that is out o' the air.   [*Aside*]
How pregnant sometimes his replies are! a
happiness that often madness hits on, which
reason and sanity could not so prosperously be
deliver'd of.   I will leave him, and suddenly   215
contrive the means of meeting between him and

my daughter. ‒My honourable lord, I will most
humbly take my leave of you.

Ham. You cannot, sir, take from me anything
that I will more willingly part withal,‒   220
[*Aside*] except my life, except my life, except my life.

Pol. Fare you well, my lord.

Ham. These tedious old fools!

Enter ROSENCRANTZ *and* GUILDENSTERN.

Pol. You go to seek the Lord Hamlet;   there he is.

Ros. [*To Polonius*]   God save you, sir!   225

[*Exit Polonius.*

Guil. Mine honour'd lord!

Ros. My most dear lord!

Ham. My excellent good friends!   How dost
thou, Guildenstern?   Ah, Rosencrantz!   Good
lads, how do ye both?   230

Ros. As the indifferent children of the earth.

Guil. Happy, in that we are not the over-happy;
On fortune's cap we are not the very button.

Ham. Nor the soles of her shoe?

Ros. Neither, my lord.   235

Ham. Then you live about her waist, or in the
middle of her favour?

Guil. Faith, her privates we.

Ham.   In the secret parts of fortune?   O, most
        true;   she is a strumpet.   What's the news?   240
Ros.   None, my lord, but that the world's grown
        honest.
Ham.   Then is doomsday near.   But your news
        is not true. Let me question more in particular.
        What have you, my good friends, deserved at the   245
        hands of Fortune, that she sends you to prison
        hither?
Guil.   Prison, my lord!
Ham.   Denmark's a prison.
Ros.   Then is the world one.   250
Ham.   A goodly one, in which there are many
        confines, wards, and dungeons, Denmark being
        one o' the worst.
Ros.   We think not so, my lord.
Ham.   Why, then 'tis none to you;   for there   255
        is nothing either good or bad, but thinking makes
        it so.   To me it is a prison.
Ros.   Why, then your ambition makes it one;
        'tis too narrow for your mind.
Ham.   O God, I could be bounded in a   260
        nutshell and count myself a king of infinite space,
        were it not that I have bad dreams.
Guil.   Which dreams indeed are ambition, for
        the very substance of the ambitious is merely the

shadow of a dream.   265

Ham.   A dream itself is but a shadow.

Ros.   Truly, and I hold ambition of so airy

and light a quality that it is but a shadow's shadow.

Ham.   Then are our beggars bodies, and our

monarchs and outstretch'd heroes the beggar's   270

shadows. Shall we to the court? for, by my fay,

I cannot reason.

Ros. & Guil.   We'll wait upon you.

Ham.   No such matter. I will not sort you

with the rest of my servants, for, to speak to you   275

like an honest man, I am most dreadfully attended.

But in the beaten way of friendship, what make

you at Elsinore?

Ros.   To visit you, my lord; no other occasion.

Ham.   Beggar that I am, I am even poor in   280

thanks;   but I thank you;   and sure, dear friends,

my thanks are too dear a halfpenny. Were you

not sent for? Is it your own inclining? Is it a

free visitation? Come, deal justly with me.

Come, come; nay, speak.   285

Guil.   What should we say, my lord?

Ham.   Why, any thing, but to the purpose.

You were sent for; and there is a kind of

confession in your looks which your modesties have

not craft enough to colour. I know the good   290 king and queen have sent for you.

Ros. To what end, my lord?

Ham. That you must teach me. But let me
conjure you, by the rights of our fellowship, by
the consonancy of our youth, by the obligation of   295
our ever-preserved love, and by what more dear
a better proposer could charge you withal, be
even and direct with me, whether you were sent
for or no!

Ros. [*Aside to Guil.*] What say you?   300

Ham. [*Aside*] Nay, then, I have an eye of
you.─If you love me, hold not off.

Guil. My lord, we were sent for.

Ham. I will tell you why; so shall my
anticipation prevent your discovery, and your secrecy   305
to the King and Queen moult no feather. I have of
late─but wherefore I know not─lost all my mirth,
foregone all custom of exercises; and indeed it
goes so heavily with my disposition that this
goodly frame, the earth, seems to me a sterile   310
promontory, this most excellent canopy, the air,
look you, this brave o'erhanging firmament, this
majestical roof fretted with golden fire, why, it
appears no other thing to me than a foul and
pestilent congregation of vapours. What a piece   315
of work is a man! How noble in reason! How

infinite in faculty! In form and moving how express
and admirable! in action how like an angel!
in apprehension how like a god! the beauty of
the world! the paragon of animals! And yet, to   320
me, what is this quintessence of dust? Man delights
not me, ⁻no, nor woman neither, though by your
smiling you seem to say so.

Ros. My lord, there was no such stuff in my
thoughts.   325

Ham. Why did you laugh then, when I said,
'Man delights not me'?

Ros. To think, my lord, if you delight not in
man, what lenten entertainment the players shall
receive from you. We coted them on the way;   330
and hither are they coming to offer you service.

Ham. He that plays the king shall be welcome;
his majesty shall have tribute of me; the adventurous
knight shall use his foil and target; the
lover shall not sigh gratis; the humorous man   335
shall end his part in peace; the clown shall make
those laugh whose lungs are tickle o' the sere;
and the lady shall say her mind freely, or the
blank verse shall halt for 't. What players are
they?   340

Ros. Even those you were wont to take delight
in, the tragedians of the city.

Ham.　How chances it they travel?　Their
residence, both in reputation and profit, was better
both ways.　　　　　　　　　　　　　　　　345

Ros.　I think their inhibition comes by the
means of the late innovation.

Ham.　Do they hold the same estimation they
did when I was in the city?　Are they so
followed?　　　　　　　　　　　　　　　　350

Ros.　No, indeed, they are not.

Ham.　How comes it?　Do they grow rusty?

Ros.　Nay, their endeavour keeps in the wonted
pace;　but there is, sir, an aery of children, little
eyases, that cry out on the top of question, and　　355
are most tyrannically clapp'd for 't.　These
are now the fashion, and so berattle the common
stages—so they call them—that many wearing
rapiers are afraid of goose-quills and dare scarce
come thither.　　　　　　　　　　　　　　360

Ham.　What, are they children?　Who
maintains 'em?　How are they escoted?　Will they
pursue the quality no longer than they can sing?
Will they not say afterwards, if they should grow
themselves to common players,—as it is most like,　365
if their means are no better—their writers do them
wrong, to make them exclaim against their own
succession?

Ros.   Faith, there has been much to do on
both sides;   and the nation holds it no sin to tarre   370
them to controversy.   There was for a while no
money bid for argument, unless the poet and the
player went to cuffs in the question.

Ham.   Is 't possible?

Guil.   O, there has been much throwing about   375
of brains.

Ham.   Do the boys carry it away?

Ros.   Ay, that they do, my lord;   Hercules and
his load too.

Ham.   It is not strange;   for mine uncle is   380
King of Denmark, and those that would make mows
at him while my father lived, give twenty, forty,
fifty, an hundred ducats apiece for his picture in
little.   'Sblood, there is something in this more
than natural, if philosophy could find it out.   385

                    [*Flourish of trumpets within.*

Guil.   There are the players.

Ham.   Gentlemen, you are welcome to Elsinore.
Your hands, come then;   the appurtenance
of welcome is fashion and ceremony.   Let me
comply with you in this garb, lest my extent to   390
the players, which, I tell you, must show fairly
outward, should more appear like entertainment
than yours.   You are welcome;   but my

uncle-father and aunt-mother are deceiv'd.

Guil.   In what, my dear lord?   395

Ham.   I am but mad north-north-west.   When the
wind is southerly I know a hawk from a handsaw.

Enter POLONIUS.

Pol.   Well be with you, gentlemen!

Ham.   Hark you, Guildenstern, and you too,
at each ear a hearer: that great baby you   400
see there is not yet out of his swaddling-clouts.

Ros.   Happily he is the second time come to
them;   for they say an old man is twice a
child.

Ham.   I will prophesy he comes to tell me of   405
the players;   mark it.   [*Aloud*] You say right, sir;
o'Monday morning;   'twas so indeed.

Pol.   My lord, I have news to tell you.

Ham.   My lord, I have news to tell you.
When Roscius was an actor in Rome, —   410

Pol.   The actors are come hither, my lord.

Ham.   Buzz, buzz!

Pol.   Upon mine honour, —

Ham.   Then came each actor on his ass, —

Pol.   The best actors in the world, either for   415
tragedy, comedy, history, pastoral, pastoral —

comical, historical-pastoral, tragical-historical,
tragical-comical-historical-pastoral, scene individable,
or poem unlimited; Seneca cannot be too
heavy, nor Plautus too light. For the law of   420
writ and the liberty, these are the only men.

Ham. O Jephthah, judge of Israel, what a treasure
hadst thou!

Pol. What a treasure had he, my lord?

Ham. Why,   425

    'One fair daughter, and no more,
    The which he loved passing well.'

Pol. [*Aside*] Still on my daughter.

Ham. Am I not i' the right, old Jephthah?

Pol. If you call me Jephthah, my lord, I   430
have a daughter that I love passing well.

Ham. Nay, that follows not.

Pol. What follows, then, my lord?

Ham. Why,

    'As by lot, God wot,'   435
and then, you know,

    'It came to pass, as most like it was,' —
The first row of the pious chanson will show you
more; for look where my abridgement comes.

Enter four or five Players.

You're welcome, masters; welcome all. ─I am   **440**
glad to see thee well. ─Welcome, good friends.
─O, my old friend! Thy face is valanc'd since I
saw thee last; com'st thou to beard me in
Denmark? ─What, my young lady and mistress!
By'r lady, your ladyship is nearer to heaven   **445**
than when I saw-you last, by the altitude of a
chopine. Pray God, your voice, like a piece of
uncurrent gold, be not crack'd within the ring.
Masters, you are all welcome. We'll e'en to 't
like French falconers, fly at any thing we see.   **450**
We'll have a speech straight. Come, give us a
taste of your quality; come, a passionate speech.

1. Play.   What speech, my lord?

Ham.   I heard thee speak me a speech once,
but it was never acted; or, if it was, not above   **455**
once. For the play, I remember, pleas'd not the
million; 'twas caviare to the general; but it was
─as I receiv'd it, and others, whose judgements
in such matters cried in the top of mine─an
excellent play, well digested in the scenes, set down   **460**
with as much modesty as cunning. I remember,
one said there were no sallets in the lines to make
the matter savoury, nor no matter in the phrase
that might indict the author of affectation; but
call'd it an honest method, as wholesome as   **465**

sweet, and by very much more handsome than
fine. One speech in it I chiefly lov'd; 'twas
Æneas' tale to Dido, and thereabout of it especially
where he speaks of Priam's slaughter. If it
live in your memory, begin at this line: let me   470
see, let me see—

  'The rugged Pyrrhus, like the Hyrcanian beast,'—
It is not so; it begins with Pyrrhus:—
  'The rugged Pyrrhus, he whose sable arms,
Black as his purpose, did the night resemble   475
When he lay couched in the ominous horse,
Hath now this dread and black complexion smear'd
With heraldry more dismal; head to foot
Now is he total gules, horribly trick'd
With blood of fathers, mothers, daughters, sons,   480
Bak'd and impasted with the parching streets,
That lend a tyrannous and damned light
To their lord's murders. Roasted in wrath and fire,
And thus o'er-sized with coagulate gore,
With eyes like carbuncles, the hellish Pyrrhus   485
Old grandsire Priam seeks.'

  So, proceed you.

Pol. 'Fore God, my lord, well spoken, with good
accent and good discretion.

1. Play. 'Anon he finds him   490
  Striking too short at Greeks; his antique sword,

Rebellious to his arm, lies where it falls,

Repugnant to command. Unequal match'd,

Pyrrhus at Priam drives, in rage strikes wide;

But with the whiff and wind of his fell sword   495

The unnerved father falls. Then senseless Ilium,

Seeming to feel this blow, with flaming top

Stoops to his base, and with a hideous crash

Takes prisoner Pyrrhus' ear;   for, lo! his sword,

Which was declining on the milky head   500

Of reverend Priam, seem'd i' the air to stick.

So, as a painted tyrant, Pyrrhus stood

And like a neutral to his will and matter,

Did nothing.

But, as we often see, against some storm,   505

A silence in the heavens, the rack stand still,

The bold winds speechless and the orb below

As hush as death, anon the dreadful thunder

Doth rend the region;   so, after Pyrrhus' pause,

Aroused vengeance sets him new a-work;   510

And never did the Cyclops' hammers fall

On Mars's armour forg'd for proof eterne

With less remorse than Pyrrhus' bleeding sword

Now falls on Priam.

Out, out, thou strumpet, Fortune! All you gods,   515

In general synod, take away her power;

Break all the spokes and fellies from her wheel,

And bowl the round nave down the hill of heaven,

As low as to the fiends!'

Pol. This is too long. 520

Ham. It shall to the barber's, with your beard.

Prithee, say on; he's for a jig or a tale of bawdry,

or he sleeps. Say on; come to Hecuba.

1. Play. 'But who, O, who had seen the mobled

queen'— 525

Ham. 'The mobled queen?'

Pol. That's good; 'mobled queen' is good.

1. Play.

'Run barefoot up and down, threat'ning the flames

With bisson rheum, a clout about that head

Where late the diadem stood, and for a robe, 530

About her lank and all o'er-teemed loins,

A blanket, in the alarm of fear caught up;

Who this had seen, with tongue in venom steep'd,

'Gainst Fortune's state would treason have

pronounc'd.

But if the gods themselves did see her then, 535

When she saw Pyrrhus make malicious sport

In mincing with his sword her husband's limbs,

The instant burst of clamour that she made,

Unless things mortal move them not at all,

Would have made milch the burning eyes of

heaven, 540

And passion in the gods.'

Pol.   Look, whe'er he has not turn'd his
colour and has tears in's eyes.   Pray you, no
more.

Ham.   'Tis well;   I'll have thee speak out the   545
rest soon.   Good my lord, will you see the
players well bestow'd?   Do you hear, let them
be well us'd;   for they are the abstracts and brief
chronicles of the time;   after your death you were
better have a bad epitaph than their ill report   550
while you live.

Pol.   My lord, I will use them according to
their desert.

Ham.   God's bodykins, man, much better.
Use every man after his desert, and who should   555
'scape whipping?   Use them after your own honour
and dignity.   The less they deserve, the more
merit is in your bounty.   Take them in.

Pol.   Come, sirs.   [*Exit.*

Ham.   Follow him, friends;   we'll hear a play   560
to-morrow.   [*Exeunt all the Players but the First.*]
Dost thou hear me, old friend;   Can you play 'The
Murder of Gonzago'?

1. Play.   Ay, my lord.

Ham.   We'll ha't to-morrow night.   You   565
could, for a need, study a speech of some dozen

or sixteen lines, which I would set down and
insert in't, could you not?

1. Play.   Ay, my lord.

Ham.   Very well. Follow that lord; and look   570
you mock him not.   [*Exit First Player.*]   My
good friends, I'll leave you till night. You are
welcome to Elsinore.

Ros.   Good my lord!

        [*Exeunt Rosencrantz and Guildenstern.*]

Ham.   Ay, so, God be wi' ye; Now I am alone.   575
O, what a rogue and peasant slave am I!
Is it not monstrous that this player here,
But in a fiction, in a dream of passion,
Could force his soul so to his own conceit
That from her working all his visage wann'd,   580
Tears in his eyes, distraction in's aspect,
A broken voice, and his whole function suiting
With forms to his conceit? And all for nothing!
For Hecuba!
What's Hecuba to him, or he to Hecuba,   585
That he should weep for her? What would he do,
Had he the motive and the cue for passion
That I have? He would drown the stage with tears
And cleave the general ear with horrid speech,
Make mad the guilty and appal the free,   590
Confound the ignorant, and amaze indeed

The very faculties of eyes and ears.

Yet I,

A dull and muddy-mettled rascal, peak,

Like John-a-dreams, unpregnant of my cause, 595

And can say nothing; no, not for a king,

Upon whose property and most dear life

A damn'd defeat was made. Am I a coward?

Who calls me villain, breaks my pate across,

Plucks off my beard and blows it in my face, 600

Tweaks me by the nose, gives me the lie i' the throat

As deep as to the lungs, who does me this?

Ha!

'Swounds, I should take it; for it cannot be

But I am pigeon-liver'd and lack gall 605

To make oppression bitter, or ere this

I should have fatted all the region kites

With this slave's offal. Bloody, bawdy villain!

Remorseless, treacherous, lecherous, kindless villain!

O, vengeance! 610

Why, what an ass am I! This is most brave,

That I, the son of a dear father murdered,

Prompted to my revenge by heaven and hell,

Must, like a whore, unpack my heart with words,

And fall a-cursing, like a very drab, 615

A scullion!

Fie upon 't! Foh! About, my brain! I have heard

That guilty creatures sitting at a play

Have by the very cunning of the scene

Been struck so to the soul that presently   620

They have proclaim'd their malefactions;

For murder, though it have no tongue, will speak

With most miraculous organ.   I'll have these players

Play something like the murder of my father

Before mine uncle.   I'll observe his looks;   625

I'll tent him to the quick.   If he but blench,

I know my course.   The spirit that I have seen

May be the devil;   and the devil hath power

To assume a pleasing shape;   yea, and perhaps

Out of my weakness and my melancholy,   630

As he is very potent with such spirits,

Abuses me to damn me.   I'll have grounds

More relative than this.   The play's the thing

Wherein I'll catch the conscience of the King.

[Exit.

Act III

Scene I

A room in the castle.

Enter King, Queen, Polonius, Ophelia,
Rosencrantz, *and* Guildenstren.

King. And can you, by no drift of circumstance,
Get from him why he puts on this confusion,
Grating so harshly all his days of quiet
With turbulent and dangerous lunacy?
Ros. He does confess he feels himself distracted; 5
But from what cause he will by no means speak.
Guil. Nor do we find him forward to be sounded,
But, with a crafty madness, keeps aloof
When we would bring him on to some confession
Of his true state.
Queen. Did he receive you well? 10
Ros. Most like a gentleman.

Guil. But with much forcing of his disposition.

Ros. Niggard of question; but, of our demands,

Most free in his reply.

Queen.   Did you assay him

To any pastime?   15

Ros. Madam, it so fell out, that certain players

We o'er-raught on the way; of these we told him;

And there did seem in him a kind of joy

To hear of it. They are about the court,

And, as I think, they have already order   20

This night to play before him.

Pol.   'Tis most true;

And he beseech'd me to entreat your Majesties

To hear and see the matter.

King. With all my heart; and it doth much

content me

To hear him so inclin'd.   25

Good gentlemen, give him a further edge,

And drive his purpose on to these delights.

Ros. We shall, my lord.

          [*Exeunt Rosencrantz and Guildenstern.*]

King.   Sweet Gertrude, leave us too;

For we have closely sent for Hamlet hither,

That he, as 'twere by accident, may here   30

Affront Ophelia.

Her father and myself, lawful espials,

Will so bestow ourselves that, seeing unseen,

We may of their encounter frankly judge,

And gather by him, as he is behaved,   35

If 't be the affliction of his love or no

That thus he suffers for.

Queen.   I shall obey you.

And for your part, Ophelia, I do wish

That your good beauties be the happy cause

Of Hamlet's wildness;   so shall I hope your virtues   40

Will bring him to his wonted way again,

To both your honours.

Oph.   Madam, I wish it may.   [*Exit Queen.*]

Pol.   Ophelia, walk you here.   Gracious, so please

      you,

We will bestow ourselves.   [*To Ophelia*]   Read on this

book,

That show of such an exercise may colour   45

Your loneliness.   We are oft to blame in this,⎯

'Tis too much prov'd⎯that with devotion's visage

And pious action we do sugar o'er

The devil himself.

King. [*Aside*]   O, 'tis too true!

      How smart a lash that speech doth give

      my conscience!   50

The harlot's cheek, beautied with plast'ring art,

Is not more ugly to the thing that helps it

Than is my deed to my most painted word.

O heavy burden!

Pol. I hear him coming. Let's withdraw, my lord. 55

[*Exeunt King and Polonius.*

Enter HAMLET.

Ham. To be, or not to be: that is the question;

Whether 'tis nobler in the mind to suffer

The slings and arrows of outrageous fortune,

Or to take arms against a sea of troubles,

And by opposing end them? To die; to sleep; 60

No more; and by a sleep to say we end

The heart-ache and the thousand natural shocks

That flesh is heir to. 'Tis a consummation

Devoutly to be wish'd. To die; to sleep;

To sleep; perchance to dream. Ay, there 's the rub; 65

For in that sleep of death what dreams may come,

When we have shuffl'd off this mortal coil,

Must give us pause. There's the respect

That makes calamity of so long life;

For who would bear the whips and scorns of time, 70

The oppressor's wrong, the proud man's contumely,

The pangs of despis'd love, the law's delay,

The insolence of office and the spurns

That patient merit of the unworthy takes,

When he himself might his quietus make   75
With a bare bodkin?   Who would fardels bear,
To grunt and sweat under a weary life,
But that the dread of something after death,
The undiscover'd country from whose bourn
No traveller returns, puzzles the will   80
And makes us rather bear those ills we have
Than fly to others that we know not of?
Thus conscience does make cowards of us all;
And thus the native hue of resolution
Is sicklied o'er with the pale cast of thought,   85
And enterprises of great pitch and moment
With this regard their currents turn awry,
And lose the name of action. ―Soft you now!
The fair Ophelia!   Nymph, in thy orisons
Be all my sins remember'd.

Oph.   Good my Lord,   90
How does your honour for this many a day?

Ham.   I humbly thank you, well, well, well.

Oph.   My lord, I have remembrances of yours
That I have longed long to re-deliver.
I pray you, now receive them.

Ham.   No, not I;   95
I never gave you aught.

Oph.   My honour'd lord, you know right well
you did,

And, with them, words of so sweet breath compos'd

As made the things more rich; their perfume lost,

Take these again; for to the noble mind   100

Rich gifts wax poor when givers prove unkind.

There, my lord.

Ham. Ha ha! are you honest?

Oph. My lord?

Ham. Are you fair?   105

Oph. What means your lordship?

Ham. That if you be honest and fair, your

honesty should admit no discourse to your beauty.

Oph. Could beauty, my lord, have better

commerce than with honesty?   110

Ham. Ay, truly; for the power of beauty

will sooner transform honesty from what it is to a

bawd than the force of honesty can translate

beauty into his likeness. This was sometime a

paradox, but now the time gives it proof. I did   115

love you once.

Oph. Indeed, my lord, you made me believe so.

Ham. You should not have believ'd me; for

virtue cannot so inoculate our old stock but we

shall relish of it. I loved you not.   120

Oph. I was the more deceived.

Ham. Get thee to a nunnery; why wouldst

thou be a breeder of sinners? I am myself

indifferent honest, but yet I could accuse me of
such things that it were better my mother had   125
not borne me: I am very proud, revengeful,
ambitious, with more offences at my beck than I
have thoughts to put them in, imagination to give
them shape, or time to act them in. What should
such fellows as I do crawling between earth and   130
heaven? We are arrant knaves, all; believe
none of us. Go thy ways to a nunnery. Where's
your father?

Oph.   At home, my lord.

Ham.   Let the doors be shut upon him, that   135
he may play the fool nowhere but in 's own
house. Farewell!

Oph.   O, help him, you sweet heavens!

Ham.   If thou dost marry, I'll give thee this
plague for thy dowry: be though as chaste as ice,   140
as pure as snow, thou shalt not escape calumny.
Get thee to a nunnery, go, farewell! Or, if thou
wilt needs marry, marry a fool; for wise men
know well enough what monsters you make of
them. To a nunnery, go, and quickly too.   145
Farewell!

Oph.   O heavenly powers, restore him!

Ham.   I have heard of your paintings too,
well enough. God has given you one face and

you make yourselves another. You jig, you   150
amble, and you lisp and nick-name God's
creatures, and make your wantonness your ignorance.
Go to, I'll no more on 't;   it hath made me mad.
I say, we will have no more marriages. Those
that are married already, all but one, shall live;   155
the rest shall keep as they are. To a nunnery,
go.   [*Exit.*

Oph.   O, what a noble mind is here o'erthrown!
    The courtier's, soldier's, scholar's, eye, tongue, sword;
    The expectancy and rose of the fair state,   160
    The glass of fashion and the mould of form,
    The observ'd of all observers, quite, quite down!
    And I, of ladies most deject and wretched,
    That suck'd the honey of his music vows,
    Now see that noble and most sovereign reason,   165
    Like sweet bells jangled, out of tune and harsh;
    That unmatch'd form and feature of blown youth
    Blasted with ecstasy. O, woe is me,
    To have seen what I have seen, see what I see!

                Re-enter KING *and* POLONIUS.

King.   Love! his affections do not that way tend;   170
    Nor what he spake, though it lack'd form a little,
    Was not like madness. There's something in his soul

O'er which his melancholy sits on brood;

And I do doubt the hatch and the disclose

Will be some danger;   which for to prevent,   175

I have in quick determination

Thus set it down: he shall with speed to England

For the demand of our neglected tribute.

Haply the seas and countries different

With variable objects shall expel   180

This something-settled matter in his heart,

Whereon his brains still beating puts him thus

From fashion of himself.   What think you on't?

Pol.   It shall do well;   but yet do I believe

The origin and commencement of this grief   185

Sprung from neglected love.   How now, Ophelia!

You need not tell us what Lord Hamlet said;

We heard it all.   My lord, do as you please;

But, if you hold it fit, after the play

Let his queen mother all alone entreat him   190

To show his griefs.   Let her be round with him,

And I'll be plac'd, so please you, in the ear

Of all their conference.   If she find him not,

To England send him, or confine him where

Your wisdom best shall think.

King.   It shall be so: 195

Madness in great ones must not unwatch'd go.

[Exeunt.

SCENE **II**

A hall in the castle.

Enter HAMLET *and* Players.

Ham. Speak the speech, I pray you, as I
   pronounc'd it to you, trippingly on the tongue;
   but if you mouth it, as many of your players do,
   I had as lief the town-crier spoke my lines. Nor
   do not saw the air too much with your hand,   5
   thus, but use all gently; for in the very torrent,
   tempest, and, as I may say, the whirlwind of
   passion, you must acquire and beget a temperance
   that may give it smoothness. O, it offends
   me to the soul to hear a robustious periwig-pated   10
   fellow tear a passion to tatters, to very rags, to
   split the ears of the groundlings, who for the most
   part are capable of nothing but inexplicable
   dumb-shows and noise. I would have such a
   fellow whipp'd for o'erdoing Termagant. It   15
   out-herods Herod. Pray you, avoid it.
1. Play. I warrant your honour.
Ham. Be not too tame neither, but let your
   own discretion be your tutor. Suit the action to
   the word, the word to the action; with this   20
   special observance, that you o'erstep not the modesty

of nature;   for anything so overdone is from the
purpose of playing, whose end, both at the first
and now, was and is, to hold, as 'twere, the mirror
up to nature;   to show virtue her own feature,   25
scorn her own image, and the very age and body
of the time his form and pressure.   Now this
overdone, or come tardy off, though it makes the
unskilful laugh, cannot but make the judicious
grieve;   the censure of the which one must, in   30
your allowance, o'erweigh a whole theatre of
others.   O, there be players that I have seen
play, and heard others praise, and that highly,
not to speak it profanely, that, neither having the
accent of Christians nor the gait of Christian,   35
pagan, nor man, have so strutted and bellowed
that I have thought some of Nature's journeymen
had made men and not made them well, they
imitated humanity so abominably.

1. Play.   I hope we have reform'd that   40
indifferently with us, sir.

Ham.   O, reform it altogether.   And let those
that play your clowns speak no more than is set
down for them;   for there be of them that will
themselves laugh to set on some quantity of   45
barren spectators to laugh too, though in the
meantime some necessary question of the play

be then to be considered. That's villanous, and
shows a most pitiful ambition in the fool that
uses it. Go, make you ready.   50

                    [Exeunt Players.

      Enter POLONIUS, ROSENCRANTZ, *and* GUILDENSTERN.

How now, my lord! Will the King hear this piece
of work?
Pol.   And the Queen too, and that presently.
Ham.   Bid the players make haste. *[Exit Polonius.*
Will you two help to hasten them?   55
Ros. & Guil.   We will, my lord.
           [Exeunt ROSENCRANTZ and GUILDENSTERN.
Ham.   What ho! Horatio.

           Enter HORATIO.

Hor.   Here, sweet lord, at your service.
Ham.   Horatio, thou art e'en as just a man
As e'er my conversation coped withal.   60
Hor.   O, my dear lord,—
Ham.   Nay, do not think I flatter;
For what advancement may I hope from thee
That no revenue hast but thy good spirits
To feed and clothe thee? Why should the poor

be flatter'd?

No, let the candied tongue lick absurd pomp,   65

And crook the pregnant hinges of the knee

Where thrift may follow fawning.   Dost thou hear?

Since my dear soul was mistress of her choice

And could of men distinguish, her election

Hath seal'd thee for herself;   for thou hast been   70

As one, in suffering all, that suffers nothing,

A man that Fortune's buffets and rewards

Hath ta'en with equal thanks;   and blest are those

Whose blood and judgement are so well commingled,

That they are not a pipe for Fortune's finger   75

To sound what stop she please.   Give me that man

That is not passion's slave, and I will wear him

In my heart's core, ay, in my heart of heart,

As I do thee. ⌐Something too much of this.⌐

There is a play to-night before the King;   80

One scene of it comes near the circumstance

Which I have told thee of my father's death.

I prithee, when thou seest that act afoot,

Even with the very comment of thy soul

Observe mine uncle.   If his occulted guilt   85

Do not itself unkennel in one speech,

It is a damned ghost that we have seen,

And my imaginations are as foul

As Vulcan's stithy.   Give him heedful note;

For I mine eyes will rivet to his face,   90

And after we will both our judgements join

To censure of his seeming.

Hor.   Well, my lord.

If he steal aught the whilst this play is playing,

And 'scape detecting, I will pay the theft.

Danish march. A flourish. Enter KING, QUEEN,

POLONIUS, OPHELIA, ROSENCRANTZ, GUILDENSTERN,

and other Lords *attendant, with the* Guard *carrying torches.*

Ham.   They are coming to the play; I must be idle.   95

Get you a place.

King.   How fares our cousin Hamlet?

Ham.   Excellent, i' faith; of the chameleon's

dish. I eat the air, promise-cramm'd. You cannot

feed capons so.   100

King.   I have nothing with this answer, Hamlet;

these words are not mine.

Ham.   No, nor mine now. [*To Polonius*] My

lord, you play'd once i' the university, you say?

Pol.   That did I, my lord, and was accounted   105

a good actor.

Ham.   What did you enact?

Pol.   I did enact Julius Cæsar. I was kill'd

i' the Capitol; Brutus kill'd me.

Ham. It was a brute part of him to kill so 110
capital a calf there. —Be the players ready?

Ros. Ay, my lord; they stay upon your
patience.

Queen. Come hither, my good Hamlet, sit by
me. 115

Ham. No, good mother, here's metal more
attractive.

Pol. [*To the King*] O, ho! do you mark that?

Ham. Lady, shall I lie in your lap?

[*Lying down at Ophelia's feet.*]

Oph. No, my lord. 120

Ham. I mean, my head upon your lap?

Oph. Ay, my lord.

Ham. Do you think I meant country matters?

Oph. I think nothing, my lord.

Ham. That's a fair thought to lie between 125
maids' legs.

Oph. What is, my lord?

Ham. Nothing.

Oph. You are merry, my lord.

Ham. Who, I? 130

Oph. Ay, my lord.

Ham. O God, your only jig-maker. What
should a man do but be merry? For, look you,
how cheerfully my mother looks, and my father

died within's two hours.   135

Oph.   Nay, 'tis twice two months, my lord.

Ham.   So long? Nay then, let the devil wear
black, for I'll have a suit of sables.   O heavens!
die two months ago, and not forgotten yet?
Then there's hope a great man's memory may   140
outlive his life half a year;   but, by'r lady, he
must build churches, then;   or else shall he suffer
not thinking on, with the hobby-horse, whose
epitaph is, 'For, O, for, O, the hobby-horse is
forgot.'   145

Hautboys play.   The dumb-show enters.

Enter a King *and* Queen *very lovingly, the*
Queen *embracing him, and he her.   She*
kneels and makes show of protestation unto
him.   He takes her up, and declines his head
upon her neck: lays him down upon a bank of
flowers;   she, seeing him asleep, leaves him.
Anon comes in a fellow, takes off his crown,
kisses it, and pours poison in the King's *ears,*
and exit.   *The* Queen *returns, finds the*
King *dead, and makes passionate action.   The*
Poisoner, *with some two or three* Mutes,
comes in again, seeming to lament with her.

The dead body is carried away. *The* Poisoner *woos the* Queen *with gifts; she seems loath and unwilling awhile, but in the end accepts his* love. [*Exeunt.*

Oph. What means this, my lord?

Ham. Marry, this is miching mallecho; that means mischief.

Oph. Belike this show imports the argument of the play. **150**

Enter Prologue.

Ham. We shall know by this fellow: the players cannot keep counsel; they'll tell all.

Oph. Will they tell us what this show meant?

Ham. Ay, or any show that you'll show him. Be not you asham'd to show, he'll not shame to **155** tell you what it means.

Oph. You are naught, you are naught. I'll mark the play.

Pro. For us, and for our tragedy, Here stooping to your clemency, **160** We beg your hearing patiently. [*Exit.*

Ham. Is this a prologue, or the posy of a ring?

Oph. 'Tis brief, my lord.

Ham. As woman's love.

Enter two Players, KING *and* QUEEN.

P. King.　　Full thirty times hath Phœbus'　　　　　165

cart gone round

Neptune's salt wash and Tellus' orbed ground,

And thirty dozen moons with borrowed sheen

About the world have times twelve thirties been,

Since love our hearts and Hymen did our hands

Unite commutual in most sacred bands.　　　　　170

P. Queen.　　So many journeys may the sun

and moon

Make us again count o'er ere love be done!

But, woe is me, you are so sick of late,

So far from cheer and from your former state,

That I distrust you.　Yet, though I distrust,　　　175

Discomfort you, my lord, it nothing must;

For women's fear and love holds quantity,

In neither aught, or in extremity.

Now, what my love is, proof hath made you know;

And as my love is siz'd, my fear is so.　　　　　180

Where love is great, the littlest doubts are fear;

Where little fears grow great, great love grows there.

P. King.　　Faith, I must leave thee, love,

and shortly too:

My operant powers their functions leave to do;

And thou shalt live in this fair world behind,　　185

Honour'd, belov'd;   and haply one as kind.

For husband shalt thou⸺

P. Queen.   O, confound the rest!

Such love must needs be treason in my breast.

In second husband let me be accurst!

None wed the second but who kill'd the first.   190

Ham.   [*Aside*] Wormwood, wormwood.

P. Queen.   The instances that second marriage

move

Are base respects of thrift, but none of love.

A second time I kill my husband dead,

When second husband kisses me in bed.   195

P. King.   I do believe you think what now

you speak;

But what we do determine oft we break.

Purpose is but the slave to memory,

Of violent birth, but poor validity;

Which now, like fruit unripe, sticks on the tree;   200

But fall unshaken when they mellow be.

Most necessary 'tis that we forget

To pay ourselves what to ourselves is debt.

What to ourselves in passion we propose,

The passion ending, doth the purpose lose.   205

The violence of either grief or joy

Their own enactures with themselves destroy.

Where joy most revels, grief doth most lament;

Grief joys, joy grieves, on slender accident.

This world is not for aye, nor 'tis not strange   **210**

That even our loves should with our fortunes change,

For 'tis a question left us yet to prove,

Whether love lead fortune, or else fortune love.

The great man down, you mark his favourite flies;

The poor advanc'd makes friends of enemies.   **215**

And hitherto doth love on fortune tend;

For who not needs shall never lack a friend;

And who in want a hollow friend doth try,

Directly seasons him his enemy.

But, orderly to end where I begun,   **220**

Our wills and fates do so contrary run

That our devices still are overthrown;

Our thoughts are ours, their ends none of our own.

So think thou wilt no second husband wed;

But die thy thoughts when thy first lord is dead.   **225**

P. Queen.   Nor earth to me give food, nor
heaven light!

Sport and repose lock from me day and night!

To desperation turn my trust and hope!

An anchor's cheer in prison be my scope!

Each opposite that blanks the face of joy   **230**

Meet what I would have well and it destroy!

Both here and hence pursue me lasting strife,

If, once a widow, ever I be wife!

Ham. If she should break it now!

P. King. 'Tis deeply sworn. Sweet, leave
me here awhile; 235
My spirits grow dull, and fain I would beguile
The tedious day with sleep. [*Sleeps.*

P. Queen. Sleep rock thy brain,
And never come mischance between us twain! [*Exit.*

Ham. Madam, how like you this play?

Queen. The lady doth protest too much, methinks. 240

Ham. O, but she'll keep her word.

King. Have you heard the argument? Is
there no offence in 't?

Ham. No, no, they do but jest, poison in jest;
no offence i' the world. 245

King. What do you call the play?

Ham. The Mouse-trap. Marry, how?
Tropically. This play is the image of a murder done
in Vienna: Gonzago is the duke's name; his
wife, Baptista. You shall see anon. 'Tis a knavish 250
piece of work; but what o' that? Your Majesty
and we that have free souls, it touches us not. Let
the gall'd jade wince, our withers are unwrung.

Enter LUCIANUS.

This is one Lucianus, nephew to the king.

Oph.　You are as good as a chorus, my lord.　　255

Ham.　I could interpret between you and your
　　love, if I could see the puppets dallying.

Oph.　You are keen, my lord, you are keen.

Ham.　It would cost you a groaning to take
　　off my edge.　　260

Oph.　Still better, and worse.

Ham.　So you mistake your husbands.　Begin,
　　murderer;　pox, leave thy damnable faces
　　and begin.　Come;　'the croaking raven doth
　　bellow for revenge.'　　265

Luc.　Thoughts black, hands apt, drugs fit,
　　and time agreeing;
　　Confederate season, else no creature seeing;
　　Thou mixture rank, of midnight weeds collected,
　　With Hecate's ban thrice blasted, thrice infected,
　　Thy natural magic and dire property　　270
　　On wholesome life usurp immediately.

　　　　　[*Pours the poison into the sleeper's* ears.

Ham.　He poisons him i' the garden for 's
　　estate.　His name's Gonzago;　the story is extant,
　　and writ in choice Italian.　You shall see anon
　　how the murderer gets the love of Gonzago's wife.　　275

Oph.　The King rises.

Ham.　What, frighted with false fire!

Queen.　How fares my lord?

Pol. Give o'er the play.

King. Give me some light. Away! 280

All. Lights, lights, lights!

           [Exeunt all but Hamlet and Horatio.

Ham. Why, let the strucken deer go weep,

       The hart ungalled play;

    For some must watch, while some must sleep;

       So runs the world away. 285

Would not this, sir, and a forest of feathers ⁻if
the rest of my fortunes turn Turk with me⁻with
two Provincial roses on my raz'd shoes, get me a
fellowship in a cry of players, sir?

Hor. Half a share. 290

Ham. A whole one, I.

    For thou dost know, O Damon dear,

       This realm dismantled was

    Of Jove himself; and now reigns here

       A very, very⁻pajock. 295

Hor. You might have rhym'd.

Ham. O good Horatio, I'll take the ghost's
word for a thousand pound. Didst perceive?

Hor. Very well, my lord.

Ham. Upon the talk of the poisoning? 300

Hor. I did very well note him.

Ham. Ah, ha! Come, some music! Come,
the recorders!

For if the king like not the comedy,

Why, then, belike, he likes it not, perdy.   305

Come, some music!

Re-enter Rosencrantz *and* Guildenstern.

Guil.   Good my lord, vouchsafe me a word
with you.

Ham.   Sir, a whole history.

Guil.   The King, sir,—   310

Ham.   Ay, sir, what of him?

Guil.   Is in his retirement marvellous
distemper'd.

Ham.   With drink, sir?

Guil.   No, my lord, rather with choler.   315

Ham.   Your wisdom should show itself more
richer to signify this to his doctor;   for, for me to
put him to his purgation would perhaps plunge
him into far more choler.

Guil.   Good my lord, put your discourse into   320
some frame, and start not so wildly from my affair.

Ham.   I am tame, sir. Pronounce.

Guil.   The Queen, your mother, in most great
affliction of spirit, hath sent me to you.

Ham.   You are welcome.   325

Guil.   Nay, good my lord, this courtesy is not

of the right breed. If it shall please you to make
me a wholesome answer, I will do your mother's
commandment; if not, your pardon and my return
shall be the end of my business. 330

Ham. Sir, I cannot.

Guil. What, my lord?

Ham. Make you a wholesome answer; my
wit's diseas'd. But, sir, such answers as I can
make, you shall command; or, rather, as you say, 335
my mother. Therefore no more, but to the matter:
my mother, you say,⁻

Ros. Then thus she says: your behaviour hath
struck her into amazement and admiration.

Ham. O wonderful son, that can so astonish 340
a mother! But is there no sequel at the heels of
this mother's admiration? Impart.

Ros. She desires to speak with you in her
closet ere you go to bed.

Ham. We shall obey, were she ten times our 345
mother. Have you any further trade with us?

Ros. My lord, you once did love me.

Ham. So I do still, by these pickers and
stealers.

Ros. Good my lord, what is your cause of 350
distemper? You do surely bar the door upon
your own liberty, if you deny your griefs to your

friend.

Ham.   Sir, I lack advancement.

Ros.   How can that be, when you have the   355
voice of the King himself for your succession in
Denmark?

Ham.   Ay, sir, but 'While the grass grows,'—
the proverb is something musty.

Re-enter Players *with recorders.*

O, the recorders! Let me see. —To withdraw   360
with you: —why do you go about to recover the
wind of me, as if you would drive me into a toil?

Guil.   O, my lord, if my duty be too bold, my
love is too unmannerly.

Ham.   I do not well understand that.   Will   365
you play upon this pipe?

Guil.   My lord, I cannot.

Ham.   I pray you.

Guil.   Believe me, I cannot.

Ham.   I do beseech you.   370

Guil.   I know no touch of it, my lord.

Ham.   'Tis as easy as lying: govern these
ventages with your fingers and thumb, give it
breath with your mouth, and it will discourse
most eloquent music. Look you, these are the   375

stops.

Guil.   But these cannot I command to any
utterance of harmony;   I have not the skill.

Ham.   Why, look you now, how unworthy a
thing you make of me! You would play upon   380
me;   you would seem to know my stops;   you
would pluck out the heart of my mystery;   you
would sound me from my lowest note to the top
of my compass;   and there is much music, excellent
voice, in this little organ, yet cannot you   385
make it speak.   'Sblood, do you think that I am easier
to be play'd on than a pipe? Call me what
instrument you will, though you can fret me, yet you
cannot play upon me.

Enter POLONIUS.

God bless you, sir.   390

Pol.   My lord, the Queen would speak with
you, and presently.

Ham.   Do you see that cloud that's almost
in shape of a camel?

Pol.   By the mass, and it's like a camel, indeed.   395

Ham.   Methinks it is like a weasel.

Pol.   It is back'd like a weasel.

Ham.   Or like a whale?

Pol.   Very like a whale.

Ham.   Then will I come to my mother by and   **400**

    by. [*Aside*] They fool me to the top of my bent.

    —I will come by and by.

Pol.   I will say so.

Ham.   'By and by' is easily said. [*Exit Polonius.*

    Leave me, friends.   **405**

                          [*Exeunt all but Hamlet.*

'Tis now the very witching time of night,

When churchyards yawn and hell itself breathes out

Contagion to this world.   Now could I drink hot blood,

And do such bitter business as the day

Would quake to look on.   Soft! now to my mother.   **410**

O heart, lose not thy nature;   let not ever

The soul of Nero enter this firm bosom:

Let me be cruel, not unnatural:

I will speak daggers to her, but use none.

My tongue and soul in this be hypocrites;   **415**

How in my words soever she be shent

To give them seals never, my soul, consent!   [*Exit.*

SCENE **III**

A room in the castle.

Enter KING, ROSENCRANTZ, *and* GUILDENSTERN.

King. I like him not, nor stands it safe with us
　　To let his madness range. Therefore prepare you;
　　I your commission will forthwith dispatch,
　　And he to England shall along with you.
　　The terms of our estate may not endure　　　　　5
　　Hazard so near us as doth hourly grow
　　Out of his lunacies.
Guil.　　　　We will ourselves provide.
　　Most holy and religious fear it is
　　To keep those many many bodies safe
　　That live and feed upon your Majesty.　　　　　10
Ros. The single and peculiar life is bound
　　With all the strength and armour of the mind
　　To keep itself from noyance; but much more
　　That spirit upon whose weal depends and rests
　　The lives of many. The cease of majesty　　　　15
　　Dies not alone, but, like a gulf, doth draw
　　What's near it with it. It is a massy wheel,
　　Fixed on the summit of the highest mount,
　　To whose huge spokes ten thousand lesser things
　　Are mortis'd and adjoin'd; which, when it falls,　　20

Each small annexment, petty consequence,

Attends the boisterous ruin.   Never alone

Did the King sigh, but with a general groan.

King.   Arm you, I pray you, to this speedy voyage;

For we will fetters put upon this fear,   25

Which now goes too free-footed.

Ros. & Guil.   We will haste us.

[*Exeunt* Rosencrantz *and* Guildenstern.

Enter POLONIUS.

Pol.   My lord, he's going to his mother's closet.

Behind the arras I'll convey myself,

To hear the process.   I'll warrant she'll tax him home;

And, as you said, and wisely was it said,   30

'Tis meet that some more audience than a mother,

Since nature makes them partial, should o'erhear

The speech, of vantage.   Fare you well, my liege.

I'll call upon you ere you go to bed,

And tell you what I know.

King.   Thanks, dear my lord.   35

[*Exit Polonius.*

O, my offence is rank, it smells to heaven;

It hath the primal eldest curse upon 't,

A brother's murder.   Pray can I not,

Though inclination be as sharp as will.

My stronger guilt defeats my strong intent,   40
And, like a man to double business bound,
I stand in pause where I shall first begin,
And both neglect.   What if this cursed hand
Were thicker than itself with brother's blood,
Is there not rain enough in the sweet heavens   45
To wash it white as snow?   Whereto serves mercy
But to confront the visage of offence?
And what's in prayer but this twofold force,
To be forestalled ere we come to fall,
Or pardon'd being down? Then I'll look up;   50
My fault is past.   But, O, what form of prayer
Can serve my turn?   'Forgive me my foul murder'?
That cannot be;   since I am still possess'd
Of those effects for which I did the murder,
My crown, mine own ambition, and my queen.   55
May one be pardon'd and retain the offence?
In the corrupted currents of this world
Offence's gilded hand may shove by justice,
And oft 'tis seen the wicked prize itself
Buys out the law.   But 'tis not so above.   60
There is no shuffling, there the action lies
In his true nature;   and we ourselves compell'd,
Even to the teeth and forehead of our faults,
To give in evidence.   What then? What rests?
Try what repentance can.   What can it not?   65

Yet what can it when one cannot repent?

O wretched state!   O bosom black as death!

O limed soul, that, struggling to be free,

Art more engag'd!   Help, angles! Make assay!

Bow, stubborn knees;   and heart with strings of steel,   70

Be soft as sinews of the new-born babe!

All may be well.   [*Retires and kneels.*

Enter HAMLET.

Ham.   Now might I do it pat, now he is praying.

And now I'll do 't.   And so he goes to heaven,

And so am I reveng'd.   That would be scann'd: 75

A villain kills my father;   and for that,

I, his sole son, do this same villain send

To heaven.

Oh, this is hire and salary, not revenge.

He took my father grossly, full of bread,   80

With all his crimes broad blown, as flush as May;

And how his audit stands who knows save heaven?

But in our circumstance and course of thought

'Tis heavy with him;   and am I then reveng'd

To take him in the purging of his soul,   85

When he is fit and season'd for his passage?

No!

Up, sword, and know thou a more horrid hent.

When he is drunk asleep, or in his rage,

Or in the incestuous pleasure of his bed;   90

At gaming, swearing, or about some act

That has no relish of salvation in 't;

Then trip him, that his heels may kick at heaven,

And that his soul may be as damn'd and black

As hell, whereto it goes.   My mother stays.   95

This physic but prolongs thy sickly days.   [*Exit.*

King.   [*Rising*]   My words fly up, my thoughts

remain below.

Words without thoughts never to heaven go.   [*Exit.*

SCENE IV

The Queen's closet.

Enter QUEEN *and* POLONIUS.

Pol.   He will come straight.   Look you lay home to him.

Tell him his pranks have been too broad to bear with,

And that your Grace hath screen'd and stood between

Much heat and him.   I'll silence me e'en here.

Pray you, be round with him.   5

Ham.   [*Within*]   Mother, mother, mother!

Queen.   I'll warrant you,

Fear me not.   Withdraw, I hear him coming.

[*Polonius hides behind the arras.*

Enter HAMLET.

Ham. Now, mother, what's the matter?

Queen. Hamlet, thou hast thy father much offended.

Ham. Mother, you have my father much offended.   10

Queen. Come, come, you answer with an idle tongue.

Ham. Go, go, you question with a wicked tongue.

Queen. Why, how now, Hamlet!

Ham.   What's the matter now?

Queen. Have you forgot me?

Ham.   No, by the rood, not so:

 You are the Queen, your husband's brother's wife; 15

 And—would it were not so!—you are my mother.

Queen. Nay, then, I'll set those to you that

 can speak.

Ham. Come, come, and sit you down; you

 shall not budge.

 You go not till I set you up a glass

 Where you may see the inmost part of you.   20

Queen. What wilt thou do? Thou wilt not

 murder me?

 Help, help, ho!

Pol. [*Behind*] What, ho! help, help, help!

Ham. [*Drawing*] How now! A rat? Dead,

for a ducat, dead!

> [*Kills Polonius with a pass through the arras.*]

Pol.   [*Behind*]   O, I am slain!   [*Falls and dies.*

Queen.   O me, what hast thou done?

Ham.   Nay, I know not;   25
   Is it the King?

Queen.   O, what a rash and bloody deed is this!

Ham.   A bloody deed! ⁻almost as bad, good mother,
   As kill a king, and marry with his brother.

Queen.   As kill a king!

Ham.   Ay, lady, 'twas my word.   30

> [*Lifts up the arras and discovers Polonius.*

   Thou wretched, rash, intruding fool, farewell!
   I took thee for thy better.   Take thy fortune;
   Thou find'st to be too busy is some danger.
   ⁻Leave wringing of your hands.   Peace! Sit you down,
   And let me wring your heart;   for so I shall,   35
   If it be made of penetrable stuff,
   If damned custom have not braz'd it so
   That it be proof and bulwark against sense.

Queen.   What have I done, that thou dar'st wag
   thy tongue
   In noise so rude against me?

Ham.   Such an act   40
   That blurs the grace and blush of modesty,
   Calls virtue hypocrite, takes off the rose

From the fair forehead of an innocent love
And sets a blister there, makes marriage-vows
As false as dicers' oaths. O, such a deed   45
As from the body of contraction plucks
The very soul, and sweet religion makes
A rhapsody of words. Heaven's face doth glow
Yea, this solidity and compound mass,
With tristful visage, as against the doom,   50
Is thought-sick at the act.
Queen.   Ay me, what act,
That roars so loud and thunders in the index?
Ham.   Look here, upon this picture, and on this,
The counterfeit presentment of two brothers.
See, what a grace was seated on this brow;   55
Hyperion's curls;   the front of Jove himself;
An eye like Mars, to threaten or command;
A station like the herald Mercury
New-lighted on a heaven-kissing hill;
A combination and a form indeed,   60
Where every god did seem to set his seal,
To give the world assurance of a man.
This was your husband. Look you now what follows:
Here is your husband, like a mildew'd ear,
Blasting his wholesome brother. Have you eyes?   65
Could you on this fair mountain leave to feed,
And batten on this moor? Ha! have you eyes?

You cannot call it love;   for at your age
The hey-day in the blood is tame, it's humble,
And waits upon the judgement;   and what judgement   70
Would step from this to this?   Sense, sure you have,
Else could you not have motion;   but sure, that sense
Is apoplex'd;   for madness would not err,
Nor sense to ecstasy was ne'er so thrall'd
But it reserv'd some quantity of choice,   75
To serve in such a difference.   What devil was't
That thus hath cozen'd you at hoodman-blind?
Eyes without feeling, feeling without sight,
Ears without hands or eyes, smelling sans all,
Or but a sickly part of one true sense   80
Could not so mope.
O shame!   where is thy blush?   Rebellious hell,
If thou canst mutine in a matron's bones,
To flaming youth let virtue be as wax,
And melt in her own fire;   proclaim no shame   85
When the compulsive ardour gives the charge,
Since frost itself as actively doth burn
And reason panders will.

Queen.   O Hamlet, speak no more!
Thou turn'st mine eyes into my very soul;
And there I see such black and grained spots   90
As will not leave their tinct.

Ham.   Nay, but to live

In the rank sweat of an enseamed bed,
Stew'd in corruption, honeying and making love
Over the nasty sty,—

Queen.   O, speak to me no more!
These words, like daggers, enter in mine ears;   95
No more, sweet Hamlet!

Ham.   A murderer and a villain!
A slave that is not twentieth part the tithe
Of your precedent lord;   a vice of kings;
A cutpurse of the empire and the rule,
That from a shelf the precious diadem stole,   100
And put it in his pocket!

Queen.   No more!

Enter Ghost.

Ham.   A king of shreds and patches,—
Save me, and hover o'er me with your wings,
You heavenly guards! What would your gracious
figure?

Queen.   Alas, he's mad!   105

Ham.   Do you not come your tardy son to chide,
That, laps'd in time and passion, lets go by
The important acting of your dread command?
O, say!

Ghost.   Do not forget!   This visitation   110

Is but to whet thy almost blunted purpose.

But, look, amazement on thy mother sits.

O, step between her and her fighting soul.

Conceit in weakest bodies strongest works.

Speak to her, Hamlet.

Ham.   How is it with you, lady?   115

Queen.   Alas, how is 't with you,

That you do bend your eye on vacancy

And with the incorporal air do hold discourse?

Forth at your eyes your spirits wildly peep,

And, as the sleeping soldiers in the alarm,   120

Your bedded hair, like life in excrements,

Start up and stand an end. O gentle son,

Upon the heat and flame of thy distemper

Sprinkle cool patience. Whereon do you look?

Ham. On him, on him! Look you, how pale

he glares!   125

His form and cause conjoin'd, preaching to stones,

Would make them capable. Do not look upon me,

Lest with this piteous action you convert

My stern effects: then what I have to do

Will want true colour; tears perchance for blood.   130

Queen. To whom do you speak this?

Ham.   Do you see nothing there?

Queen. Nothing at all; yet all that is I see.

Ham. Nor did you nothing hear?

III. iv]

Queen.   No, nothing but ourselves.

Ham.   Why, look you there! Look, how it
   steals away!
   My father, in his habit as he lived!   135
   Look, where he goes, even now, out at the portal!

                                          [*Exit Ghost.*

Queen.   This is the very coinage of your brain.
   This bodiless creation ecstasy
   Is very cunning in.

Ham.   Ecstasy!
   My pulse, as yours, doth temperately keep time,   140
   And makes as healthful music. It is not madness
   That I have uttered. Bring me to the test,
   And I the matter will re-word, which madness
   Would gambol from. Mother, for love of grace,
   Lay not that flattering unction to your soul,   145
   That not your trespass, but my madness speaks:
   It will but skin and film the ulcerous place,
   Whilst rank corruption, mining all within,
   Infects unseen. Confess yourself to heaven;
   Repent what's past; avoid what is to come;   150
   And do not spread the compost on the weeds,
   To make them ranker. Forgive me this my virtue,
   For in the fatness of these pursy times
   Virtue itself of vice must pardon beg,
   Yea, curb and woo for leave to do him good.   155

Queen.　O Hamlet, thou hast cleft my heart
　　in twain.

Ham.　O, throw away the worser part of it,
　　And live the purer with the other half.
　　Good-night: but go not to mine uncle's bed;
　　Assume a virtue, if you have it not.　　　　　　160
　　That monster, custom, who all sense doth eat,
　　Of habits devil, is angel yet in this,
　　That to the use of actions fair and good
　　He likewise gives a frock or livery,
　　That aptly is put on.　Refrain to-night,　　　　165
　　And that shall lend a kind of easiness
　　To the next abstinence;　the next more easy;
　　For use almost can change the stamp of nature,
　　And either master the devil or throw him out,
　　With wondrous potency.　Once more, good-night;　　170
　　And when you are desirous to be blest,
　　I'll blessing beg of you.　For this same lord,
　　　　　　　　　　　[Pointing to Polonius.
　　I do repent;　but Heaven hath pleas'd it so,
　　To punish me with this and this with me,
　　That I must be their scourge and minister.　　175
　　I will bestow him, and will answer well
　　The death I gave him.　So, again, good-night.
　　I must be cruel, only to be kind;
　　Thus bad begins and worse remains behind.

One word more, good lady.

Queen.   What shall I do?   **180**

Ham. Not this, by no means, that I bid you do:

Let the bloat king tempt you again to bed;

Pinch wanton on your cheek;   call you his mouse;

And let him, for a pair of reechy kisses,

Or paddling in your neck with his damn'd fingers,   **185**

Make you to ravel all this matter out,

That I essentially am not in madness,

But mad in craft.   'Twere good you let him know;

For who, that's but a queen, fair, sober, wise,

Would from a paddock, from a bat, a gib,   **190**

Such dear concernings hide?   Who would do so?

No, in despite of sense and secrecy,

Unpeg the basket on the house's top,

Let the birds fly, and like the famous ape,

To try conclusions, in the basket creep,   **195**

And break your own neck down.

Queen. Be thou assur'd, if words be made of
breath,

And breath of life, I have no life to breathe

What thou hast said to me.

Ham. I must to England;   you know that?

Queen.   Alack,   **200**

I had forgot. 'Tis so concluded on.

Ham. There's letters sealed;   and my two

school-fellows,

Whom I will trust as I will adders fang'd,

They bear the mandate; they must sweep my way,

And marshal me to knavery. Let it work;   205

For 'tis the sport to have the enginer

Hoist with his own petar; and 't shall go hard

But I will delve one yard below their mines,

And blow them at the moon. O, 'tis most sweet,

When in one line two crafts directly meet.   210

This man shall set me packing.

I'll lug the guts into the neighbour room.

Mother, good-night. Indeed this counsellor

Is now most still, most secret, and most grave,

Who was in life a foolish prating knave.   215

Come, sir, to draw toward an end with you.

Good-night, mother.

    [*Exeunt severally; Hamlet tugging in Poonius.*

Act IV

SCENE I

A room in the castle.

Enter KING, QUEEN, ROSENCRANTZ, *and* GUILDENSTERN.

King. There's matter in these sighs; these profound heaves
You must translate; 'tis fit we understand them.
Where is your son?
Queen. Bestow this place on us a little while.
　　　　　[*Exeunt* ROSENCRANTZ *and* GUILDENSTERN.
Ah, mine own lord, what have I seen to-night!　　　　5
King. What, Gertrude? How does Hamlet?
Queen. Mad as the seas and wind, when both contend
Which is the mightier. In his lawless fit,
Behind the arras hearing something stir,
Whips out his rapier out, cries, 'A rat, a rat!'　　　　10

And, in his brainish apprehension, kills

The unseen good old man.

King.   O heavy deed!

It had been so with us, had we been there.

His liberty is full of threats to all;

To you yourself, to us, to every one.   15

Alas, how shall this bloody deed be answer'd?

It will be laid to us, whose providence

Should have kept short, restrain'd, and out of haunt,

This mad young man.   But so much was our love,

We would not understand what was most fit;   20

But, like the owner of a foul disease,

To keep it from divulging, let it feed

Even on the pith of life.   Where is he gone?

Queen.   To draw apart the body he hath kill'd;

O'er whom his very madness, like some ore   25

Among the mineral of metals base,

Shows itself pure;   he weeps for what is done.

King.   O Gertrude, come away!

The sun no sooner shall the mountains touch,

But we will ship him hence;   and this vile deed   30

We must, with all our majesty and skill,

Both countenance and excuse.   Ho, Guildenstern!

Re-enter ROSENCRANTZ *and* GUILDENSTERN.

Friends both, go join you with some further aid:
Hamlet in madness hath Polonius slain,
And from his mother's closet hath he dragg'd him;   35
Go seek him out;   speak fair, and bring the body
Into the chapel.   I pray you, haste in this.
　　　　[*Exeunt* ROSENCRANTZ *and* GUILDENSTERN.
Come, Gertrude, we'll call up our wisest friends
And let them know both what we mean to do
And what's untimely done;   [so, haply, slander,]   40
Whose whisper o'er the world's diameter,
As level as the cannon to his blank,
Transports his poison'd shot, may miss our name,
And hit the woundless air.   O, come away!
My soul is full of discord and dismay.   [*Exeunt.*   45

SCENE II

Another room in the castle.

Enter HAMLET.

Ham.　Safely stowed.
Ros. & Guil.　[*Within*]　Hamlet!　Lord Hamlet!
Ham.　But soft, what noise?　Who calls on Hamlet?
　O, here they come!

Enter ROSENCRANTZ *and* GUILDENSTERN.

Ros.　What have you done, my lord, with the

dun dead body?　　　　　　　　　　　　　　　　5

Ham.　Compounded it with dust, whereto 'tis kin.

Ros.　Tell us where 'tis, that we may take it thence

And bear it to the chapel.

Ham.　Do not believe it.

Ros.　Believe what?　　　　　　　　　　　　10

Ham.　That I can keep your counsel and not mine

own.　Besides, to be demanded of a sponge, what

replication should be made by the son of a king?

Ros.　Take you me for a sponge, my lord?　　　15

Ham.　Ay, sir, that soaks up the King's

countenance, his rewards, his authorities.　But such

officers do the King best service in the end.　He

keeps them, like an ape, in the corner of his

jaw;　first mouth'd, to be last swallowed;　when　　20

he needs what you have glean'd, it is but

squeezing you, and, sponge, you shall be dry

again.

Ros.　I understand you not, my lord.

Ham.　I am glad of it;　a knavish speech sleeps　　25

in a foolish ear.

Ros.　My lord, you must tell us where the

body is, and go with us to the King.

Ham.   The body is with the King, but the

    King is not with the body. The King is a thing⁻   30

Guil.   A thing, my lord!

Ham.   Of nothing. Bring me to him. Hide

    fox, and all after.   [*Exeunt.*

SCENE III

Another room in the castle.

Enter KING, *attended.*

King.   I have sent to seek him, and to find the body.

    How dangerous is it that this man goes loose!

    Yet must not we put the strong law on him:

    He's lov'd of the distracted multitude,

    Who like not in their judgement, but their eyes;   5

    And where 'tis so, the offender's scourge is weigh'd,

    But never the offence. To bear all smooth and even,

    This sudden sending him away must seem

    Deliberate pause. Diseases desperate grown

    By desperate appliance are relieved,   10

    Or not at all.

Enter ROSENCRANTZ.

How now! What hath befall'n?

Ros.   Where the dead body is bestow'd, my lord,

We cannot get from him.

King.   But where is he?

Ros.   Without, my lord;   guarded, to know

your pleasure.

King.   Bring him before us.   15

Ros.   Ho, Guildenstern!   bring in my lord.

Enter HAMLET *and* GUILDENSTERN.

King.   Now, Hamlet, where's Polonius?

Ham.   At supper.

King.   At supper!   Where?

Ham.   Not where he eats, but where he is   20

eaten;   a certain convocation of politic worms

are e'en at him.   Your worm is your only

emperor for diet: we fat all creatures else to fat

us, and we fat ourselves for maggots;   your fat

king and your lean beggar is but variable service,   25

two dishes, but to one table.   That's the end.

Alas, alas!

Ham.   A man may fish with the worm that

hath eat of a king, and eat of the fish that hath

fed of that worm.   30

King.   What dost thou mean by this?

Ham. Nothing but to show you how a king
may go a progress through the guts of a beggar.

King. Where is Polonius?

Ham. In heaven; send thither to see. If your   35
messenger find him not there, seek him i' the
other place yourself. But indeed, if you find him
not within this month, you shall nose him as you
go up the stairs into the lobby.

King. Go seek him there.   40

[To some Attendants.

Ham. He will stay till ye come.

[Exeunt Attendants.

King. Hamlet, this deed of thine, for thine especial
safety,—
Which we do tender, as we dearly grieve
For that which thou hast done,—must send thee hence
With fiery quickness. Therefore prepare thyself;   45
The bark is ready, and the wind at help,
The associates tend, and everything is bent
For England.

Ham.   For England!

King.   Ay, Hamlet.

Ham.   Good.

King. So is it, if thou knew'st our purposes.

Ham. I see a cherub that sees them. But   50
come; for England! Farewell, dear mother.

King. Thy loving father, Hamlet.

Ham. My mother: father and mother is man
and wife; man and wife is one flesh; and so, my
mother. Come, for England!

     [*Exit.*   **55**

King. Follow him at foot; tempt him with
speed aboard;
Delay it not; I'll have him hence to-night.
Away! for everything is seal'd and done
That else leans on the affair. Pray you, make haste.

   [*Exeunt* ROSENCRANTZ *and* GUILDENSTERN.

And, England, if my love thou hold'st at aught,— **60**
As my great power thereof may give thee sense,
Since yet thy cicatrice looks raw and red
After the Danish sword, and thy free awe
Pays homage to us—thou mayst not coldly set
Our sovereign process; which imports at full, **65**
By letters congruing to that effect,
The present death of Hamlet. Do it, England;
For like the hectic in my blood he rages,
And thou must cure me. Till I know 'tis done,
Howe'er my haps, my joys were ne'er begun. **70**

         [*Exit.*

Scene IV

A plain in Denmark.

Enter FORTINBRAS, a Captain, *and* Soldiers *marching.*

For.   Go, captain, from me greet the Danish king.
　　Tell him that, by his license, Fortinbras
　　Craves the conveyance of a promis'd march
　　Over his kingdom.   You know the rendezvous.
　　If that his Majesty would aught with us,　　　　　5
　　We shall express our duty in his eye;
　　And let him know so.
Cap.　　　　I will do't, my lord.
For.   Go softly on.

　　　　　　　　　[*Exeunt* FORTINBRAS *and Soldiers.*

Enter HAMLET, ROSENCRANTZ, GUILDENSTERN,
and others

Ham.   Good sir, whose powers are these?
Cap.   They are of Norway, sir.　　　　　　　　10
Ham.   How purpos'd, sir, I pray you?
Cap.   Against some part of Poland.
Ham.   Who commands them, sir?
Cap.   The nephew to old Norway, Fortinbras.
Ham.   Goes it against the main of Poland, sir,　　15

Or for some frontier?

Cap.　Truly to speak, and with no addition,

We go to gain a little patch of ground

That hath in it no profit but the name.

To pay five ducats, five, I would not farm it;　　20

Nor will it yield to Norway or the Pole

A ranker rate, should it be sold in fee.

Ham.　Why, then the Polack never will defend it.

Cap.　Yes, it is already garrison'd.

Ham.　Two thousand souls and twenty thousand

ducats　　25

Will not debate the question of this straw.

This is the imposthume of much wealth and peace,

That inward breaks, and shows no cause without

Why the man dies.　I humbly thank you, sir.

Cap.　God buy you, sir.　　　　　　　[*Exit.*

Ros.　　　　　Will't please you go, my lord?　　30

Ham.　I'll be with you straight.　Go a little before.

　　　　　　　　　[*Exeunt all except HAMLET.*

How all occasions do inform against me,

And spur my dull revenge!　What is a man,

If his chief good and market of his time

Be but to sleep and feed?　A beast, no more.　　35

Sure, he that made us with such large discourse,

Looking before and after, gave us not

That capability and god-like reason

To fust in us unus'd. Now, whether it be

Bestial oblivion, or some craven scruple   40

Of thinking too precisely on the event,—

A thought which, quarter'd, hath but one part wisdom

And ever three parts coward,—I do not know

Why yet I live to say 'This thing's to do',

Sith I have cause and will and strength and means   45

To do't. Examples gross as earth exhort me;

Witness this army of such mass and charge

Led by a delicate and tender prince,

Whose spirit with divine ambition puff'd

Makes mouths at the invisible event,   50

Exposing what is mortal and unsure

To all that fortune, death and danger dare,

Even for an egg-shell. Rightly to be great

Is not to stir without great argument,

But greatly to find quarrel in a straw   55

When honour's at the stake. How stand I then,

That have a father kill'd, a mother stain'd,

Excitements of my reason and my blood,

And let all sleep, while to my shame I see

The imminent death of twenty thousand men,   60

That, for a fantasy and trick of fame,

Go to their graves like beds, fight for a plot

Whereon the numbers cannot try the cause,

Which is not tomb enough and continent

To hide the slain?   O, from this time forth,   65
My thoughts be bloody, or be nothing worth!

[Exit.

SCENE V

Elsinore. A room in the castle.

Enter QUEEN, HORATIO *and a* Gentleman.

Queen.   I will not speak with her.
Gent. She is importunate, indeed distract.
   Her mood will needs be pitied.
Queen.   What would she have?
Gent. She speaks much of her father;   says
   she hears
   There's tricks i' the world, and hems, and beats
   her heart;   5
   Spurns enviously at straws;   speaks things in doubt,
   That carry but half sense. Her speech is nothing,
   Yet the unshaped use of it doth move
   The hearers to collection;   they aim at it,
   And botch the words up fit to their own thoughts;   10
   Which, as her winks and nods and gestures yield them,
   Indeed would make one think there might be thought,
   Though nothing sure, yet much unhappily.

Hor. 'Twere good she were spoken with; for she
    may strew

    Dangerous conjectures in ill-breeding minds.   15

Queen. Let her come in.   *[Exit Gentleman.*

[*Aside*] To my sick soul, as sin's true nature is,

    Each toy seems prologue to some great amiss.

    So full of artless jealousy is guilt,

    It spills itself in fearing to be spilt.   20

        Enter OPHELIA, *distracted.*

Oph.   Where is the beauteous majesty of Denmark?

Queen.   How now, Ophelia!

Oph. [*Sings*]

      How should I your true love know

        From another one?

      By his cockle hat and staff,   25

        And his sandal shoon.

Queen.   Alas, sweet lady, what imports this song?

Oph.   Say you? Nay, pray you, mark.

[*Sings*] He is dead and gone, lady,

      He is dead and gone;   30

      At his head a grass-green turf

      At his heels a stone.

Queen.   Nay, but, Ophelia,—

Oph.   Pray you, mark.

[*Sings*]   White his shroud as the mountain snow,' —   **35**

Enter KING.

Queen.   Alas, look here, my lord.
Oph. [*Sings*]
    Larded with sweet flowers;
        Which bewept to the grave did not go
    With true-love showers.
King.   How do you, pretty lady?   **40**
Oph.   Well, God 'ild you! They say the owl
was a baker's daughter.   Lord, we know what we
are, but know not what we may be.   God be at
your table!
King.   Conceit upon her father.   **45**
Oph.   Pray you, let's have no words of this;
but when they ask you what it means, say you this:
[*Sings*] To-morrow is Saint Valentine's day,
    All in the morning betime,
    And I a maid at your window,   **50**
        To be your Valentine.
    Then up he rose and donn'd his clothes,
        And dupp'd the chamber door;
    Let in the maid, that out a maid
        Never departed more.'   **55**
King.   Pretty Ophelia!

Oph. Indeed, la, without an oath I'll make
an end on't.

[*Sings*] By Gis, and by Saint Charity,
Alack! and, fie for shame! 60
Young men will do't, if they come to 't;
By Cock, they are to blame.
Quoth she, 'Before you tumbled me,
You promis'd me to wed'.
So would I ha' done, by yonder sun, 65
An thou hadst not come to my bed.

King. How long hath she been thus?

Oph. I hope all will be well. We must be
patient; but I cannot choose but weep, to think
they should lay him i' the cold ground. My 70
brother shall know of it; and so I thank you for
your good counsel. Come, my coach! Good
night, ladies; good-night, sweet ladies; good
night, good-night. [*Exit.*

King. Follow her close; give her good watch,
I pray you.

[*Exit Horatio.* 75

O, this is the poison of deep grief; it springs
All from her father's death. O Gertrude, Gertrude,
When sorrows come, they come not single spies,
But in battalions. First, her father slain;
Next, your son gone; and he most violent author 80

Of his own just remove; the people muddied,

Thick and unwholesome in their thoughts and whispers,

For good Polonius' death; and we have done but
greenly,

In hugger-mugger to inter him; poor Ophelia

Divided from herself and her fair judgement,   **85**

Without the which we are pictures, or mere beasts;

Last, and as much containing as all these,

Her brother is in secret come from France;

Feeds on his wonder, keeps himself in clouds,

And wants not buzzers to infect his ear   **90**

With pestilent speeches of his father's death;

Wherein necessity, of matter beggar'd,

Will nothing stick our person to arraign

In ear and ear. O my dear Gertrude, this,

Like to a murdering-piece, in many places   **95**

Gives me superfluous death.   *[A noise within.*

Queen.   Alack, what noise is this?

King. Where are my Switzers? Let them guard
the door.

Enter a Gentleman.

What is the matter?

Gent.   Save yourself, my lord:

The ocean, overpeering of his list,

Eats not the flats with more impetuous haste   100

Than young Laertes, in a riotous head,

O'erbears your officers.   The rabble call him lord;

And, as the world were now but to begin,

Antiquity forgot, custom not known,

The ratifiers and props of every word,   105

They cry, 'Choose we! Laertes shall be king!'

Caps, hands, and tongues applaud it to the clouds,

'Laertes shall be king, Laertes king!'

Queen.   How cheerfully on the false trail they
cry!

O, this is counter, you false Danish dogs!   110

King.   The doors are broke.   [*Noise within.*

Enter LAERTES, *armed;* Danes *following.*

Laer.   Where is this king? Sirs, stand you all
without.

Danes.   No, let's come in.

Laer.   I pray you, give me leave.

Danes.   We will, we will.

                    [*They retire without the door.*

Laer.   I thank you;   keep the door.   O thou
vile king,   115

Give me my father!

Queen.   Calmly, good Laertes.

Laer.　That drop of blood that's calm proclaims
　　me bastard,
　　Cries cuckold to my father, brands the harlot
　　Even here, between the chaste unsmirched brow
　　Of my true mother.

King.　　　What is the cause, Laertes,　　　　　　　120
　　That thy rebellion looks so giant-like?
　　Let him go, Gertrude;　do not fear our person:
　　There's such divinity doth hedge a king,
　　That treason can but peep to what it would,
　　Acts little of his will.　Tell me, Laertes,　　　　125
　　Why thou art thus incens'd.　Let him go, Gertrude.
　　Speak, man.

Laer.　Where's my father?

King.　　　　　　　　　　Dead.

Queen.　　　　　　　　　　　　But not by him.

King.　Let him demand his fill.

Laer.　How came he dead?　I'll not be
　　juggl'd with.　　　　　　　　　　　　　　130
　　To hell, allegiance! vows, to the blackest devil!
　　Conscience and grace, to the profoundest pit!
　　I dare damnation.　To this point I stand,
　　That both the worlds I give to negligence,
　　Let come what comes;　only I'll be reveng'd　　　135
　　Most throughly for my father.

King.　　　　　　　　Who shall stay you?

Laer. My will, not all the world.

And for my means, I'll husband them so well,

They shall go far with little.

King. Good Laertes,

If you desire to know the certainty 140

Of your dear father's death, is't writ in your revenge

That, swoopstake, you will draw both friend and foe,

Winner and loser?

Laer. None but his enemies.

King. Will you know them then?

Laer. To his good friends thus wide I'll ope

my arms, 145

And like the kind life-rend'ring pelican,

Repast them with my blood.

King. Why, now you speak

Like a good child and a true gentleman.

That I am guiltless of your father's death,

And am most sensibly in grief for it, 150

It shall as level to your judgement pierce

As day does to your eye.

[*A noise within*: 'Let her come in!'

Laer. How now! what noise is that?

Re-enter OPHELIA.

O heat, dry up my brains! tears seven times salt

Burn out the sense and virtue of mine eye!   155

By heaven, thy madness shall be paid with weight

Till our scale turns the beam. O rose of May!

Dear maid, kind sister, sweet Ophelia!

O heavens! is't possible, a young maid's wits

Should be as mortal as an old man's life?   160

Nature is fine in love, and where 'tis fine,

It sends some precious instance of itself

After the thing it loves.

Oph.   [*Sings.*]

They bore him barefac'd on the bier;

Hey non nonny, nonny, hey nonny;   165

And in his grave rains many a tear, —

Fare you well, my dove!

Laer.   Hadst thou thy wits, and didst persuade

revenge,

It could not move thus.

Oph.   You must sing, 'Down a-down, and you   170

call him a-down-a.' O, how the wheel becomes it!

It is the false steward, that stole his master's

daughter.

Laer.   This nothing's more than matter.

Oph.   There's rosemary, that's for remembrance;   175

pray, love, remember; and there is pansies,

that's for thoughts.

Laer.   A document in madness, thoughts and

remembrance fitted.

Oph. There's fennel for you, and columbines.   **180**

There's rue for you, and here's some for me.

We may call it herb of grace o' Sundays. O, you

must wear your rue with a difference. There's

a daisy. I would give you some violets, but they

wither'd all when my father died. They say he   **185**

made a good end, —

    [*Sings.*]

      For bonny sweet Robin is all my joy.

Laer. Thought and affliction, passion, hell

itself,

She turns to favour and to prettiness.

Oph. [*Sings.*]

      And will he not come again?   **190**

      And will he not come again?

        No, no, he is dead;

        Go to thy death-bed;

      He never will come again.

      His beard as white as snow,   **195**

      All flaxen was his poll.

        He is gone, he is gone,

        And we cast away moan:

      God ha' mercy on his soul!

And of all Christian souls, I pray God. God buy

you. [*Exit.* **200**

Laer. Do you see this, O God?

King. Laertes, I must commune with your grief,

Or you deny me right. Go but apart,

Make choice of whom your wisest friends you will,

And they shall hear and judge 'twixt you and me. **205**

If by direct or by collateral hand

They find us touch'd, we will our kingdom give,

Our crown, our life, and all that we call ours,

To you in satisfaction; but if not,

Be you content to lend your patience to us, **210**

And we shall jointly labour with your soul

To give it due content.

Laer. Let this be so.

His means of death, his obscure funeral—

No trophy, sword, nor hatchment o'er his bones,

No noble rite nor formal ostentation— **215**

Cry to be heard, as 'twere from heaven to earth,

That I must call't in question.

King. So you shall;

And where the offence is let the great axe fall.

I pray you, go with me. [*Exeunt.*

SCENE VI

Another room in the castle.

Enter HORATIO *and a* Servant.

Hor. What are they that would speak with me?

Att. Sailors, sir. They say they have letters
for you.

Hor. Let them come in.   [*Exit Attendant.*
I do not know from what part of the world
I should be greeted, if not from Lord Hamlet.   5

Enter Sailors.

Sail. God bless you, sir.

Hor. Let Him bless thee too.

Sail. He shall, sir, an 't please Him.
There's a letter for you, sir—it comes from the
ambassador that was bound for England—if your   10
name be Horatio, as I am let to know it is.

Hor. [*Reads*] 'Horatio, when thou shalt have
overlook'd this, give these fellows some means to
the King; they have letters for him. Ere we were
two days old at sea, a pirate of very warlike   15
appointment gave us chase. Finding ourselves
too slow of sail, we put on a compelled valour,

and in the grapple I boarded them. On the instant
they got clear of our ship; so I alone became
their prisoner. They have dealt with me like   20
thieves of mercy; but they knew what they did:
I am to do a good turn for them. Let the King
have the letters I have sent; and repair thou to
me with as much speed as thou wouldest fly death.
I have words to speak in thine ear will make thee   25
dumb; yet are they much too light for the bore
of the matter. These good fellows will bring
thee where I am. Rosencrantz and Guildenstern
hold their course for England; of them I have
much to tell thee. Farewell.   30

   'He that thou knowest thine, HAMLET.'
Come, I will give you way for these your letters;
And do't the speedier, that you may direct me
To him from whom you brought them. [*Exeunt.*

SCENE VII

Another room in the castle.

Enter KING *and* LAERTES.

King. Now must your conscience my acquittance
seal;

And you must put me in your heart for friend,
Sith you have heard, and with a knowing ear,
That he which hath your noble father slain
Pursued my life.

Laer.   It well appears. But tell me   5
Why you proceeded not against these feats,
So crimeful and so capital in nature,
As by your safety, wisdom, all things else,
You mainly were stirr'd up.

King.   O, for two special reasons,
Which may to you, perhaps, seem much unsinew'd,   10
But yet to me they are strong. The Queen his mother
Lives almost by his looks; and for myself—
My virtue or my plague, be it either which—
She's so conjunctive to my life and soul,
That, as the star moves not but in his sphere,   15
I could not but by her. The other motive ,
Why to a public count I might not go,
Is the great love the general gender bear him;
Who, dipping all his faults in their affection,
Would, like the spring that turneth wood to stone,   20
Convert his gyves to graces; so that my arrows,
Too slightly timber'd for so loud a wind,
Would have reverted to my bow again,
And not where I had aim'd them.

Laer.   And so have I a noble father lost,   25

A sister driven into desperate terms,

Whose worth, if praises may go back again,

Stood challenger on mount of all the age

For her perfections.　But my revenge will come.

King.　Break not your sleeps for that.　You

must not think　　　　　　　　　　　　　30

That we are made of stuff so flat and dull

That we can let our beard be shook with danger

And think it pastime.　You shortly shall hear more.

I lov'd your father, and we love our self;

And that, I hope, will teach you to imagine—　35

Enter a Messenger with letters.

How now! What news?

Mess.　　　Letters, my lord, from Hamlet:

This to your Majesty;　this to the Queen.

King.　From Hamlet! Who brought them?

Mess.　　Sailors, my lord, they say;　I saw them not.

They were given me by Claudio.　He receiv'd them　40

Of him that brought them.

King.　　　　Laertes, you shall hear them.

Leave us.　　　　　　　　　　[*Exit Messenger.*

[*Reads*] 'High and mighty, You shall know I

am set naked on your kingdom.　To-morrow

shall I beg leave to see your kingly eyes;　when　45

I shall, first asking your pardon thereunto,

recount the occasion of my sudden and more

strange return.

                        HAMLET.'

What should this mean? Are all the rest come back?   50

Or is it some abuse, or no such thing?

Laer.   Know you the hand?

King.   'Tis Hamlet's character. 'Naked!'

And in a postscript here, he says, 'alone.'

Can you advise me?

Laer.   I'm lost in it, my lord. But let him come;   55

It warms the very sickness in my heart

That I shall live and tell him to his teeth,

'Thus didest thou.'

King.   If it be so, Laertes, —

As how should it be so? how otherwise? —

Will you be rul'd by me?

Laer.   Ay, my lord;   60

So you'll not o'errule me to a peace.

King.   To thine own peace. If he be now return'd,

As checking at his voyage, and that he means

No more to undertake it, I will work him

To an exploit, now ripe in my device,   65

Under the which he shall not choose but fall;

And for his death no wind of blame shall breathe,

But even his mother shall uncharge the practice

And call it accident.

Laer.   My lord, I will be rul'd;

The rather, if you could devise it so   70

That I might be the organ.

King.   It falls right.

You have been talk'd of since your travel much,

And that in Hamlet's hearing, for a quality

Wherein, they say, you shine. Your sum of parts

Did not together pluck such envy from him   75

As did that one, and that, in my regard,

Of the unworthiest siege.

Laer.   What part is that, my lord?

King.   A very riband in the cap of youth,

Yet needful too; for youth no less becomes

The light and careless livery that it wears   80

Than settled age his sables and his weeds,

Importing health and graveness. Two months since,

Here was a gentleman of Normandy; —

I've seen myself, and serv'd against, the French,

And they can well on horseback; but this gallant   85

Had witchcraft in 't. He grew unto his seat,

And to such wondrous doing brought his horse,

As had he been incorps'd and demi-natur'd

With the brave beast. So far he topp'd my thought,

That I, in forgery of shapes and tricks,   90

Come short of what he did.

Laer. A Norman, was't?

King. A Norman.

Laer. Upon my life, Lamord.

King. The very same.

Laer. I know him well. He is the brooch indeed

And gem of all the nation. 95

King. He made confession of you,

And gave you such a masterly report

For art and exercise in your defence,

And for your rapier most especial,

That he cried out, 'twould be a sight indeed 100

If one could match you. The scrimers of their nation,

He swore, had neither motion, guard, nor eye,

If you oppos'd them. Sir, this report of his

Did Hamlet so envenom with his envy

That he could nothing do but wish and beg 105

Your sudden coming o'er to play with him.

Now, out of this —

Laer. What out of this, my lord?

King. Laertes, was your father dear to you?

Or are you like the painting of a sorrow,

A face without a heart?

Laer. Why ask you this? 110

King. Not that I think you did not love your father,

But that I know love is begun by time,

And that I see, in passages of proof,

Time qualifies the spark and fire of it.

There lives within the very flame of love   115

A kind of wick or snuff that will abate it;

And nothing is at a like goodness still;

For goodness, growing to a plurisy,

Dies in his own too much. That we would do,

We should do when we would; for this 'would'

changes,   120

And hath abatements and delays as many

As there are tongues, are hands, are accidents;

And then this 'should' is like a spendthrift sigh,

That hurts by easing. But, to the quick o' the ulcer:—

Hamlet comes back. What would you undertake,   125

To show yourself your father's son in deed

More than in words?

Laer.   To cut his throat i' the church.

King.   No place, indeed, should murder sanctuarize;

Revenge should have no bounds. But, good Laertes,

Will you do this, keep close within your chamber?   130

Hamlet return'd shall know you are come home.

We'll put on those shall praise your excellence

And set a double varnish on the fame

The Frenchman gave you, bring you, in fine, together

And wager on your heads. He, being remiss,   135

Most generous and free from all contriving,

Will not peruse the foils; so that, with ease,

Or with a little shuffling, you may choose

A sword unbated, and in a pass of practice

Requite him for your father.

Laer.   I will do 't;   140

And, for that purpose, I'll anoint my sword.

I bought an unction of a mountebank,

So mortal that, but dip a knife in it,

Where it draws blood no cataplasm so rare,

Collected from all simples that have virtue   145

Under the moon, can save the thing from death

That is but scratch'd withal.   I'll touch my point

With this contagion, that, if I gall him slightly,

It may be death.

King.   Let's further think of this;

Weigh what convenience both of time and means   150

May fit us to our shape.   If this should fail,

And that our drift look through our bad performance,

'Twere better not assay'd;   therefore this project

Should have a back or second, that might hold

If this should blast in proof.   Soft! let me see.   155

We'll make a solemn wager on your cunnings,—

I ha't!

When in your motion you are hot and dry—

As make your bouts more violent to that end—

And that he calls for drink, I'll have prepar'd him   160

A chalice for the nonce, whereon but sipping,

If he by chance escape your venom'd stuck,

Our purpose may hold there. But stay; what noise?

Enter QUEEN.

                    How now, sweet queen!

Queen.   One woe doth tread upon another's heel,

So fast they follow. Your sister's drown'd, Laertes.   **165**

Laer.   Drown'd! O, where?

Queen.   There is a willow grows aslant a brook,

That shows his hoar leaves in the glassy stream;

There with fantastic garlands did she come

Of crow-flowers, nettles, daisies, and long purples   **170**

That liberal shepherds give a grosser name,

But our cold maids do dead men's fingers call them.

There, on the pendent boughs her coronet weeds

Clamb'ring to hang, an envious silver broke;

When down her weedy trophies and herself   **175**

Fell in the weeping brook. Her clothes spread wide

And, mermaid-like, awhile they bore her up;

Which time she chanted snatches of old tunes,

As one incapable of her own distress,

Or like a creature native and indued   **180**

Unto that element; but long it could not be

Till that her garments, heavy with their drink,

Pull'd the poor wretch from her melodious lay

To muddy death.

Laer.   Alas, then, is she drown'd?

Queen.   Drown'd, drown'd.   185

Laer.   Too much of water hast thou, poor Ophelia,

And therefore I forbid my tears;   but yet

It is our trick;   nature her custom holds,

Let shame say what it will.   When these are gone,

The woman will be out.   Adieu, my lord.   190

I have a speech of fire that fain would blaze,

But that this folly douts it.   [*Exit.*

King.   Let's follow, Gertrude.

How much I had to do to calm his rage!

Now fear I this will give it start again;

Therefore let's follow.   [*Exeunt.*   195

Act V

Scene I

A churchyard.

Enter two Clowns, *with spades and pickaxes.*

1. Clo.   Is she to be buried in Christian
burial that wilfully seeks her own salvation?

2. Clo.   I tell thee she is;   and therefore
make her grave straight.   The crowner hath sat on
her, and finds it Christian burial.   5

1. Clo.   How can that be, unless she drown'd
herself in her own defence?

2. Clo.   Why, 'tis found so.

1. Clo.   It must be 'se offendendo';   it
cannot be else.   For here lies the point: if I   10
drown myself wittingly, it argues an act;   and
an act hath three branches;   it is, to act, to do, and
to perform;   argal, she drown'd herself wittingly.

2. Clo.   Nay, but hear you, Goodman
Delver, ─   15

1. Clo.   Give me leave. Here lies the
water; good. Here stands the man; good. If the
man go to this water and drown himself, it is,
will he, nill he, he goes, ─mark you that; but if
the water come to him and drown him, he drowns   20
not himself; argal, he that is not guilty of his
own death shortens not his own life.

2. Clo.   But is this law?

1. Clo.   Ay, marry, is 't; crowner's quest
law.   25

2. Clo.   Will you ha' the truth on 't? If this
had not been a gentlewoman, she should have
been buried out o' Christian burial.

1. Clo.   Why, there thou say'st; and the
more pity that great folk should have countenance   30
in this world to drown or hang themselves,
more than their even Christian. Come,
my spade. There is no ancient gentlemen but
gardeners, ditchers, and grave-makers; they hold
up Adam's profession.   35

2. Clo.   Was he a gentleman?

1. Clo.   A' was the first that ever bore
arms.

2. Clo.   Why, he had none.

1. Clo.   What, art a heathen? How dost   40
thou understand the Scripture? The Scripture
says 'Adam digg'd'; could he dig without arms?
I'll put another question to thee. If thou
answerest me not to the purpose, confess thyself—

2. Clo.   Go to.   45

1. Clo.   What is he that builds stronger
than either the mason, the shipwright, or the
carpenter?

2. Clo.   The gallows-maker; for that frame
outlives a thousand tenants.   50

1. Clo.   I like thy wit well; in good faith
The gallows does well; but how does it well? It
does well to those that do ill. Now, thou dost ill
to say the gallows is built stronger than the
church; argal, the gallows may do well to thee. 55
To't again, come.

2. Clo.   'Who builds stronger than a mason,
a shipwright, or a carpenter?'

1. Clo.   Ay, tell me that, and unyoke.

2. Clo.   Marry, now I can tell.   60

1. Clo.   To't.

2. Clo.   Mass, I cannot tell.

Enter HAMLET *and* HORATIO, *afar off.*

1. Clo.   Cudgel thy brains no more about
   it, for your dull ass will not mend his pace with
   beating;   and, when you are ask'd this question   65
   next, say 'a grave-maker';   the houses that he
   makes lasts till doomsday.   Go, get thee to
   Yaughan;   fetch me a stoup of liquor.

                    [*Exit Second Clown.*

                    [*He digs, and sings.*

       In youth, when I did love, did love,
              Methought it was very sweet,   70
       To contract, O, the time for-a my behove,
              O, methought, there-a was nothing-a meet.

Ham.   Has this fellow no feeling of his
   business, that he sings at grave-making?

Hor.   Custom hath made it in him a property   75
   of easiness.

Ham.   'Tis e'en so;   the hand of little
   employment hath the daintier sense.

1. Clo.   [*Sings.*]

       But age, with his stealing steps,
              Hath claw'd me in his clutch,   80
       And hath shipped me intil the land,
              As if I had never been such.

                    [*Throws up a skull.*

Ham.   That skull had a tongue in it, and could
   sing once.   How the knave jowls it to the ground,

as if it were Cain's jaw-bone, that did the first 85

murder! It might be the pate of a politician,

which this ass now o'er-reaches; one that would

circumvent God, might it not?

Hor. It might, my lord.

Ham. Or of a courtier, which could say, 90

'Good morrow, sweet lord! How dost thou,

good lord?' This might be my lord such-a-one,

that prais'd my lord such-a-one's horse, when he

meant to beg it; might it not?

Hor. Ay, my lord. 95

Ham. Why, e'en so; and now my Lady

Worm's; chapless, and knock'd about the

mazzard with a sexton's spade. Here's fine revolution,

if we had the trick to see't. Did these bones

cost no more the breeding, but to play at loggats 100

with'em? Mine ache to think on 't.

1. Clo. [*Sings*]

A pick-axe, and a spade, a spade,

For and a shrouding sheet:

O, a pit of clay for to be made

For such a guest is meet.' 105

[*Throws up another skull.*

Ham. There's another. Why may not that

be the skull of a lawyer? Where be his quiddities

now, his quillets, his cases, his tenures, and his

tricks? Why does he suffer this rude knave now
to knock him about the sconce with a dirty shovel,   110
and will not tell him of his action of battery?
Hum! This fellow might be in 's time a great
buyer of land, with his statutes, his recognizances,
his fines, his double vouchers, his recoveries. Is
this the fine of his fines, and the recovery of his   115
recoveries, to have his fine pate full of fine dirt?
Will his vouchers vouch him no more of his
purchases, and double ones too, than the length and
breadth of a pair of indentures? The very
conveyances of his lands will hardly lie in this box,   120
and must the inheritor himself have no more, ha?

Hor.   Not a jot more, my lord.

Ham.   Is not parchment made of sheep-skins?

Hor.   Ay, my lord, and of calf-skins too.

Ham.   They are sheep and calves which seek   125
out assurance in that. I will speak to this fellow.
Whose grave 's this, sirrah?

1. Clo.   Mine, sir.   [*Sings*]
    O, a pit of clay for to be made
        For such a guest is meet.   130

Ham.   I think it be thine indeed, for thou
liest in't.

1. Clo.   You lie out on't, sir, and therefore
it is not yours. For my part, I do not lie in 't,

and yet it is mine. 135

Ham. Thou dost lie in't, to be in't and say

it is thine; 'tis for the dead, not for the quick;

therefore thou liest.

1. Clo. 'Tis a quick lie, sir; 'twill away

again, from me to you. 140

Ham. What man dost thou dig it for?

1. Clo. For no man, sir.

Ham. What woman, then?

1. Clo. For none, neither.

Ham. Who is to be buried in't? 145

1. Clo. One that was a woman, sir; but,

rest her soul, she's dead.

Ham. How absolute the knave is! We must

speak by the card, or equivocation will undo us.

By the Lord, Horatio, these three years I have 150

taken note of it; the age is grown so picked

that the toe of the peasant comes so near the heel

of our courtier, he galls his kibe. How long hast

thou been a grave-maker?

1. Clo. Of all the days i' the year, I came 155

to 't that day that our last king Hamlet overcame

Fortinbras.

Ham. How long is that since?

1. Clo. Cannot you tell that? Every fool

can tell that: it was the very day that young 160

Hamlet was born; he that was mad, and sent into
England.

Ham. Ay, marry, why was he sent into
England?

1. Clo. Why, because 'a was mad: he 165
shall recover his wits there; or, if he do not, it's
no great matter there.

Ham. Why?

1. Clo. 'Twill not be seen in him there;
there the men are as mad as he. 170

Ham. How came he mad?

1. Clo. Very strangely, they say.

Ham. How 'strangely?

1. Clo. Faith, e'en with losing his wits.

Ham. Upon what ground? 175

1. Clo. Why, here in Denmark. I have
been sexton here, man and boy, thirty years.

Ham. How long will a man lie i' the earth
ere he rot?

1. Clo. I' faith, if he be not rotten before 180
he die—as we have many pocky corses now-a-days,
that will scarce hold the laying in—he will
last you some eight year or nine year. A tanner
will last you nine year.

Ham. Why he more than another? 185

1. Clo. Why, sir, his hide is so tann'd

with his trade that he will keep out water a great
while, and your water is a sore decayer of your
whoreson dead body. Here's a skull now; this
skull has lain in the earth three and twenty   190
years.

Ham. Whose was it?

1. Clo. A whoreson mad fellow's it was.
Whose do you think it was?

Ham. Nay, I know not.   195

1. Clo. A pestilence on him for a mad
rogue! 'A pour'd a flagon of Rhenish on my head
once. This same skull, sir, was Yorick's skull,
the King's jester.

Ham. This?   200

1. Clo. E'en that.

Ham. Let me see. [*Takes the skull.*]
Alas, poor Yorick! I knew him, Horatio; a
fellow of infinite jest, of most excellent fancy; he
hath borne me on his back a thousand times. And   205
now how abhorred in my imagination it is! My
gorge rises at it. Here hung those lips that I
have kiss'd I know not how oft. Where be your
gibes now, your gambols, your songs, your
flashes of merriment, that were wont to set the   210
table on a roar? Not one now, to mock your
own grinning? Quite chap-fallen? Now get you

to my lady's chamber, and tell her, let her paint
an inch thick, to this favour she must come;
make her laugh at that. Prithee, Horatio, tell   215
me one thing.

Hor.   What 's that, my lord?

Ham.   Dost thou think Alexander look'd o'
this fashion i' the earth?

Hor.   E'en so.   220

Ham.   And smelt so? Pah!

> [*Puts down the skull.*

Hor.   E'en so, my lord.

Ham.   To what base uses we may return,
Horatio! Why may not imagination trace the
noble dust of Alexander, till he find it stopping a   225
bung-hole?

Hor.   'Twere to consider too curiously, to
consider so.

Ham.   No, faith, not a jot; but to follow him
thither with modesty enough, and likelihood to   230
lead it, as thus: Alexander died, Alexander was
buried, Alexander returneth to dust; the dust
is earth; of earth we make loam; and why of
that loam whereto he was converted might they
not stop a beer-barrel?   235

   Imperious Cæsar, dead and turn'd to clay,
   Might stop a hole to keep the wind away.

O, that that earth, which kept the world in awe,

Should patch a wall to expel the winter's flaw!

But soft! but soft! Aside! Here comes the King,   240

Enter KING, QUEEN, LAERTES, *and a coffin, with* Lords

attendant.

The Queen, the courtiers. Who is this they follow?

And with such maimed rites? This doth betoken

The corse they follow did with desperate hand

Fordo it own life. 'Twas of some estate.

Couch we awhile, and mark.   245

          [*Retiring with* HORATIO.

Laer.   What ceremony else?

Ham.   That is Laertes,

    a very noble youth. Mark.

Laer.   What ceremony else?

Priest.   Her obsequies have been as far enlarg'd

As we have warrantise. Her death was doubtful;   250

And, but that great command o'ersways the order,

She should in ground unsanctified have lodg'd

Till the last trumpet; for charitable prayers,

Shards, flints, and pebbles should be thrown on her;

Yet here she is allowed her virgin crants,   255

Her maiden strewments, and the bringing home

Of bell and burial.

Laer.   Must there no more be done?

Priest.   No more be done.

We should profane the service of the dead

To sing such requiem and such rest to her   260

As to peace-parted souls.

Laer.   Lay her i' the earth;

And from her fair and unpolluted flesh

May violets spring! I tell thee, churlish priest,

A minist'ring angel shall my sister be,

When thou liest howling.

Ham.   What, the fair Ophelia!   265

Queen.   Sweets to the sweet;   farewell!

                              [*Scattering flowers.*

I hop'd thou shouldst have been my Hamlet's wife;

I thought thy bride-bed to have deck'd, sweet maid,

And not have strew'd thy grave.

Laer.   O, treble woe

Fall ten times treble on that cursed head   270

Whose wicked deed thy most ingenious sense

Depriv'd thee of! Hold off the earth awhile,

Till I have caught her once more in mine arms.

                              [*Leaps into the grave.*

Now pile your dust upon the quick and dead,

Till of this flat a mountain you have made   275

To o'ertop old Pelion, or the skyish head

Of blue Olympus.

Ham.   [*Advancing.*]   What is he whose grief

    Bears such an emphasis, whose phrase of sorrow

    Conjures the wand'ring stars, and makes them stand

    Like wonder-wounded hearers? This is I,   280

    Hamlet, the Dane!   [*Leaps into the grave.*

Laer.   The devil take thy soul!

                       [*Grappling with him.*

Ham.   Thou pray'st not well.

    I prithee, take thy fingers from my throat;

    For, though I am not splenitive and rash,

    Yet have I something in me dangerous,   285

    Which let thy wiseness fear.   Hold off thy hand.

King.   Pluck them asunder.

Queen.   Hamlet, Hamlet!

All.   Gentlemen,—

Hor.   Good my lord, be quiet.

         [*The Attendants part them, and they

               come out of the grave.*

Ham.   Why, I will fight with him upon this theme

    Until my eyelids will no longer wag.   290

Queen.   O my son, what theme?

Ham.   I lov'd Ophelia: forty thousand brothers

    Could not, with all their quantity of love,

    Make up my sum.   What wilt thou do for her?

King.   O, he is mad, Laertes.   295

Queen.   For love of God, forbear him.

Ham. 'Swounds, show me what thou 'lt do:

Woo 't weep? woo 't fight? Woo 't fast? woo't
tear thyself?

Woo't drink up eisel? eat a crocodile?

I'll do 't. Dost thou come here to whine? 300

To outface me with leaping in her grave?

Be buried quick with her, and so will I;

And, if thou prate of mountains, let them throw

Millions of acres on us, till our ground,

Singeing his pate against the burning zone, 305

Make Ossa like a wart! Nay, an thou 'lt mouth,

I'll rant as well as thou.

Queen.   This is mere madness;

And thus awhile the fit will work on him;

Anon, as patient as the female dove,

When that her golden couplets are disclos'd, 310

His silence will sit drooping.

Ham.   Hear you, sir:

What is the reason that you use me thus?

I lov'd you ever. But it is no matter.

Let Hercules himself do what he may,

The cat will mew and dog will have his day. 315

       [*Exit.*

King. I pray thee, good Horatio, wait upon him.

      [*Exit HORATIO.*

[*To LAERTES*] Strengthen your patience in our

last night's speech;

We'll put the matter to the present push.

Good Gertrude, set some watch over your son.

This grave shall have a living monument.　　　　**320**

An hour of quiet shortly shall we see;

Till then, in patience our proceeding be.　　[*Exeunt.*

SCENE **II**

A hall in the castle.

Enter HAMLET *and* HORATIO.

Ham. 　So much for this, sir;　shall you

　see the other.

　You do remember all the circumstance?

Hor. 　Remember it, my lord!

Ham. 　Sir, in my heart there was a kind of

　fighting,

　That would not let me sleep. Methought I lay　　**5**

　Worse than the mutines in the bilboes. Rashly,

　And prais'd be rashness for it;　let us know

　Our indiscretion sometimes serves us well,

　When our deep plots do pall;　and that should teach us

　There 's a divinity that shapes our ends,　　**10**

　Rough-hew them how we will,—

Hor.   That is most certain.

Ham.   Up from my cabin,

My sea-gown scarf'd about me, in the dark

Grop'd I to find out them;   had my desire;

Finger'd their packet, and, in fine withdrew   15

To mine own room again, making so bold,

My fears forgetting manners, to unseal

Their grand commission;   where I found, Horatio,—

O royal knavery!—an exact command,

Larded with many several sorts of reason   20

Importing Denmark's health and England's too,

With, ho! such bugs and goblins in my life,

That, on the supervise, no leisure bated,

No, not to stay the grinding of the axe,

My head should be struck off.

Hor.   Is 't possible?   25

Ham.   Here's the commission;   read it at more

leisure.

But wilt thou hear me how I did proceed?

Hor.   I beseech you.

Ham.   Being thus be-netted round with villainies,—

Ere I could make a prologue to my brains,   30

They had begun the play,—I sat me down,

Devis'd a new commission, wrote it fair.

I once did hold it, as our statists do,

A baseness to write fair, and labour'd much

How to forget that learning;   but, sir, now   35

It did me yeoman's service.   Wilt thou know

The effect of what I wrote?

Hor.   Ay, good my lord.

Ham.   An earnest conjuration from the King,

As England was his faithful tributary,

As love between them like the palm should flourish,   40

As peace should still her wheaten garland wear

And stand a comma 'tween their amities,

And many such-like as-es of great charge,

That, on the view and knowing of these contents,

Without debatement further, more or less,   45

He should the bearers put to sudden death,

Not shriving time allow'd.

Hor.   How was this seal'd?

Ham.   Why, even in that was Heaven ordinant.

I had my father's signet in my purse,

Which was the model of that Danish seal;   50

Folded the writ up in form of the other,

Subscrib'd it, gave 't the impression, plac'd it safely,

The changeling never known.   Now, the next day

Was our sea-fight;   and what to this was sequent

Thou know'st already.   55

Hor.   So Guildenstern and Rosencrantz go to 't.

Ham.   Why, man, they did make love to this

employment;

They are not near my conscience; their defeat

Does by their own insinuation grow:

'Tis dangerous when the baser nature comes   60

Between the pass and fell incensed points

Of mighty opposites.

Hor.   Why, what a king is this!

Ham.   Does it not, thinks't thee, stand me now

upon⎺

He that hath kill'd my king and whor'd my mother;

Popp'd in between the election and my hopes,   65

Thrown out his angle for my proper life,

And with such cozenage⎺is 't not perfect conscience,

To quit him with this arm? And is 't not to be damn'd,

To let this canker of our nature come

In further evil?   70

Hor.   It must be shortly known to him from England

What is the issue of the business there.

Ham.   It will be short; the interim is mine,

And a man's life's no more than to say 'One'.

But I am very sorry, good Horatio,   75

That to Laertes I forgot myself;

For, by the image of my cause, I see

The portraiture of his. I'll court his favours.

But, sure, the bravery of his grief did put me

Into a tow'ring passion.

Hor.   Peace! who comes here?   80

Enter young OSRIC.

Osr. Your lordship is right welcome back to
Denmark.

Ham. I humbly thank you, sir. [*Aside to Horatio*]
Dost know this water-fly?

Hor. [*Aside to Hamlet*] No, my good lord.   85

Ham. [*Aside to Horatio*] Thy state is the more
gracious; for 'tis a vice to know him. He hath much
land, and fertile; let a beast be lord of beasts, and
his crib shall stand at the King's mess. 'Tis a chough;
but, as I say, spacious in the possession of dirt.   90

Osr. Sweet lord, if your lordship were at
leisure, I should impart a thing to you from his
Majesty.

Ham. I will receive it, sir, with all diligence
of spirit. Put your bonnet to his right use; 'tis   95
for the head.

Osr. I thank your lordship, 'tis very hot.

Ham. No, believe me, 'tis very cold; the wind
is northerly.

Osr. It is indifferent cold, my lord, indeed.   100

Ham. But yet methinks it is very sultry and
hot for my complexion.

Osr. Exceedingly, my lord; it is very sultry,—
as 'twere,—I cannot tell how. But, my lord, his

Majesty bade me signify to you that he has laid   105
a great wager on your head. Sir, this is the
matter, ─

Ham.   I beseech you, remember ─

       [*HAMLET moves him to put on his hat.*]

Osr.   Nay, good my lord;   for mine ease, in
good faith. Sir, here is newly come to court   110
Laertes;   believe me, an absolute gentleman, full
of most excellent differences, of very soft society
and great showing.   Indeed, to speak feelingly of
him, he is the card or calendar of gentry, for you
shall find in him the continent of what part a   115
gentleman would see.

Ham.   Sir, his definement suffers no perdition
in you;   though, I know, to divide him inventorially
would dizzy the arithmetic of memory, and
yet but yaw neither, in respect of his quick sail.   120
But, in the verity of extolment, I take him to be
a soul of great article;   and his infusion of such
dearth and rareness, as, to make true diction of
him, his semblable is his mirror;   and who else
would trace him, his umbrage, nothing more.   125

Osr.   Your lordship speaks most infallibly of
him.

Ham.   The concernancy, sir? Why do we wrap
the gentleman in our more rawer breath?

Osr. Sir? 130

Hor. [*Aside to Hamlet*] Is 't not possible to understand in another tongue? You will do 't, sir, really.

Ham. What imports the nomination of this
gentleman?

Osr. Of Laertes? 135

Hor. [*Aside*] His purse is empty already. All 's
golden words are spent.

Ham. Of him, sir.

Osr. I know you are not ignorant⌐

Ham. I would you did, sir; yet, in faith, if 140
you did, it would not much approve me. Well,
sir?

Osr. You are not ignorant of what excellence
Laertes is⌐

Ham. I dare not confess that, lest I should 145
compare with him in excellence; but to know a
man well were to know himself.

Osr. I mean, sir, for his weapon; but in the
imputation laid on him by them, in his meed he's
unfellowed. 150

Ham. What's his weapon?

Osr. Rapier and dagger.

Ham. That's two of his weapons; but well.

Osr. The King, sir, has wag'd with him
six Barbary horses, against the which he has 155

impon'd, as I take it, six French rapiers and
poniards, with their assigns, as girdle, hangers,
and so.　Three of the carriages, in faith, are very
dear to fancy, very responsive to the hilts, most
delicate carriages, and of very liberal conceit.　　　　160

Ham.　What call you the carriages?

Hor.　[*Aside to Hamlet*] I knew you must be
edified by the margent ere you had done.

Osr.　The carriages, sir, are the hangers.

Ham.　The phrase would be more germane to　　　　165
the matter, if we could carry cannon by our sides;
I would it might be hangers till then.　But, on:
six Barbary horses against six French swords,
their assigns, and three liberal-conceited carriages;
that 's the French bet against the Danish.　Why　　　　170
is this 'impon'd,' as you call it?

Osr.　The King, sir, hath laid, sir, that in a dozen
passes between you and him, he shall not exceed
you three hits;　he hath laid on twelve for
nine;　and that would come to immediate trial, if　　　　175
your lordship would vouchsafe the answer.

Ham.　How if I answer 'no'?

Osr.　I mean, my lord, the opposition of your
person in trial.

Ham.　Sir, I will walk here in the hall;　if it　　　　180
please his Majesty, 'tis the breathing time of day

with me: let the foils be brought, the gentleman
willing, and the King hold his purpose, I will win
for him an I can; if not, I'll gain nothing but
my shame and the odd hits.   185

Osr.   Shall I re-deliver you e'en so?

Ham.   To this effect, sir; after what flourish
your nature will.

Osr.   I commend my duty to your lordship.

Ham.   Yours, yours. [*Exit OSRIC.*] He does   190
well to commend it himself; there are no tongues
else for 's turn.

Hor.   This lapwing runs away with the shell
on his head.

Ham.   He did comply with his dug before he   195
suck'd it. Thus has he, and many more of the
same bevy that I know the drossy age dotes on,
only got the tune of the time and outward habit
of encounter; a kind of yesty collection, which
carries them through and through the most fond   200
and winnowed opinions; and do but blow them
to their trial, the bubbles are out.

Enter a Lord.

Lord.   My lord, his Majesty commended him
to you by young Osric, who brings back to him,

  that you attend him in the hall. He sends to know   205

  if your pleasure hold to play with Laertes, or that

  you will take longer time.

Ham. I am constant to my purposes; they

  follow the King's pleasure. If his fitness speaks,

  mine is ready, now or whensoever, provided I be   210

  so able as now.

Lord. The King and Queen and all are coming

  down.

Ham. In happy time.

Lord. The Queen desires you to use some   215

  gentle entertainment to Laertes before you fall

  to play.

Ham. She well instructs me. [*Exit Lord.*

Hor. You will lose this wager, my lord.

Ham. I do not think so; since he went into   220

  France, I have been in continual practice. I shall

  win at the odds. But thou wouldst not think how

  ill all's here about my heart. But it is no matter.

Hor. Nay, good my lord,—

Ham. It is but foolery; but it is such a kind of   225

  gain-giving, as would perhaps trouble a woman.

Hor. If your mind dislike anything, obey it.

  I will forestall their repair hither, and say you are

  not fit.

Ham. Not a whit, we defy augury: there's a   230

special providence in the fall of a sparrow. If it
be now, 'tis not to come; if it be not to come, it
will be now; if it be not now, yet it will come;
the readiness is all. Since no man has aught of
what he leaves, what is 't to leave betimes? Let be.   235

Enter KING, QUEEN, LAERTES, OSRIC, Lords,
and other Attendants *with foils and gauntlets;*
a table and flagons of wine on it

King.   Come, Hamlet, come, and take this
hand from me.
    [*The* KING *puts* LAERTES*'s hand into* HAMLET*'s.*
Ham.   Give me your pardon, sir. I've done
you wrong;
But pardon 't, as you are a gentleman.
This presence knows,
And you must needs have heard, how I am punish'd   240
With sore distraction. What I have done
That might your nature, honour, and exception
Roughly awake, I here proclaim was madness.
Was 't Hamlet wrong'd Laertes? Never Hamlet.
If Hamlet from himself be ta'en away,   245
And when he's not himself does wrong Laertes,
Then Hamlet does it not, Hamlet denies it.
Who does it, then? His madness. If 't be so,

Hamlet is of the faction that is wrong'd;

His madness is poor Hamlet's enemy.   250

Sir, in this audience,

Let my disclaiming from a purpos'd evil

Free me so far in your most generous thoughts,

That I have shot mine arrow o'er the house

And hurt my brother.

Laer.   I am satisfied in nature,   255

Whose motive, in this case, should stir me most

To my revenge;   but in my terms of honour

I stand aloof, and will no reconcilement,

Till by some elder masters of known honour

I have a voice and precedent of peace,   260

To keep my name ungor'd.   But till that time,

I do receive your offer'd love like love,

And will not wrong it.

Ham.   I embrace it freely;

And will this brother's wager frankly play.

Give us the foils.   Come on.

Laer.   Come, one for me.   265

Ham.   I'll be your foil, Laertes;   in mine

ignorance

Your skill shall, like a star i' the darkest night,

Stick fiery off indeed.

Laer.   You mock me, sir.

Ham.   No, by this hand.

King.   Give them the foils, young Osric.   Cousin
 Hamlet,   **270**

 You know the wager?

Ham. Very well, my lord;

 Your Grace hath laid the odds o' the weaker side.

King.   I do not fear it;   I have seen you both;

 But since he is better'd, we have therefore odds.

Laer.   This is too heavy, let me see another.   **275**

Ham.   This likes me well.   These foils have

 all a length?   *[They prepare to play.*

Osr.   Ay, my good lord.

King.   Set me the stoups of wine upon that table.

 If Hamlet give the first or second hit,

 Or quit in answer of the third exchange,   **280**

 Let all the battlements their ordnance fire;

 The King shall drink to Hamlet's better breath,

 And in the cup an union shall he throw,

 Richer than that which four successive kings

 In Denmark's crown have worn.   Give me the cups; **285**

 And let the kettle to the trumpets speak,

 The trumpet to the cannoneer without,

 The cannons to the heavens, the heaven to earth,

 'Now the King drinks to Hamlet.' Come, begin —

 And you, the judges, bear a wary eye.   **290**

Ham.   Come on, sir.

Laer.   Come, my lord. *[They play.*

Ham. One.

Laer. No.

Ham. Judgement.

Osr. A hit, a very palpable hit.

Laer. Well; again.

King. Stay, give me drink. Hamlet, this

    pearl is thine;

    Here's to thy health!

        [*Trumpets sound, and shot goes off within.*

        Give him the cup.

Ham. I'll play this bout first; set it by a while.   295

    Come. [*They play.*] Another hit; what say you?

Laer. A touch, a touch, I do confess.

King. Our son shall win.

Queen. He's fat, and scant of breath.

    Here, Hamlet, take my napkin, rub thy brows.

    The Queen carouses to thy fortune, Hamlet.   300

Ham. Good madam!

King. Gertrude, do not drink.

Queen. I will, my lord; I pray you, pardon me.

King. [*Aside*] It is the poison'd cup; it is too

    late.

Ham. I dare not drink yet, madam; by and by.

Queen. Come, let me wipe thy face.   305

Laer. My lord, I'll hit him now.

King. I do not think 't.

Laer.   [*Aside*] And yet 'tis almost 'gainst my
    conscience.

Ham.   Come, for the third, Laertes; you but dally;
    I pray you, pass with your best violence;
    I am afeard you make a wanton of me.   310

Laer.   Say you so? Come on.   [*They play.*

Osr.   Nothing, neither way.

Laer.   Have at you now!
        [*LAERTES wounds HAMLET; then, in scuffling,*
            they change rapiers, and Hamlet wounds
    Laertes.

King.   Part them; they are incens'd.

Ham.   Nay, come, again.   [*The Queen falls.*

Osr.   Look to the Queen there! Ho!

Hor.   They bleed on both sides. How is it,
    my lord!   315

Osr.   How is 't, Laertes?

Laer.   Why, as a woodcock to mine own springe,
    Osric;
    I am justly kill'd with mine own treachery.

Ham.   How does the Queen?

King.   She swounds to see them bleed.

Queen.   No, no, the drink, the drink,—O my
    dear Hamlet,—   320
    The drink, the drink! I am poison'd.   [*Dies.*

Ham.   O villainy! Ho! let the door be lock'd:

Treachery!   Seek it out.

Laer.   It is here, Hamlet.   Hamlet, thou art slain.

No medicine in the world can do thee good;   325

In thee there is not half an hour of life;

The treacherous instrument is in thy hand,

Unbated and envenom'd.   The foul practice

Hath turn'd itself on me;   lo, here I lie,

Never to rise again.   Thy mother's poison'd.   330

I can no more: The King, the King's to blame.

Ham.   The point envenom'd too!

Then, venom, to thy work.   [*Stabs the King.*

All.   Treason! treason!

King.   O, yet defend me, friends;   I am but hurt.   335

Ham.   Here, thou incestuous, murderous, damned
Dane,

Drink off this potion.   Is thy union here?

Follow my mother!   [*King dies.*

Laer.   He is justly serv'd;

It is a poison temp'red by himself.

Exchange forgiveness with me, noble Hamlet,   340

Mine and my father's death come not upon thee,

Nor thine on me!   [*Dies.*

Ham.   Heaven make thee free of it!   I follow
thee.

I am dead, Horatio.   Wretched queen, adieu!

You that look pale and tremble at this chance,   345

That are but mutes or audience to this act,

Had I but time—as this fell sergeant, Death,

Is strict in his arrest—O, I could tell you—

But let it be. Horatio, I am dead;

Thou liv'st. Report me and my cause aright   350

To the unsatisfied.

Hor.   Never believe it.

I am more an antique Roman than a Dane;

Here's yet some liquor left.

Ham.   As thou 'rt a man,

Give me the cup. Let go! By heaven, I'll have't.

O good Horatio, what a wounded name,   355

Things standing thus unknown, shall live behind me!

If thou didst ever hold me in thy heart,

Absent thee from felicity awhile

And in this harsh world draw thy breath in pain,

To tell my story.

         [*March afar off, and shot within.*

       What warlike noise is this?   360

Osr.   Young Fortinbras, with conquest come

from Poland,

To the ambassadors of England gives

This warlike volley.

Ham.   O, I die, Horatio;

The potent poison quite o'er-crows my spirit.

I cannot live to hear the news from England,   365

But I do prophesy the election lights

On Fortinbras; he has my dying voice.

So tell him, with the occurrents, more and less,

Which have solicited —The rest is silence.   [*Dies.*

Hor.   Now cracks a noble heart. Good-night,

sweet prince,   370

And flights of angels sing thee to thy rest!

Why does the drum come hither?

[*March within.*

Enter FORTINBRAS *and* English Ambassadors,

with drum, colours, and Attendants.

Fort.   Where is this sight?

Hor.   What is it ye would see?

If aught of woe or wonder, cease your search.

Fort.   This quarry cries on havoc. O proud death,   375

What feast is toward in thine eternal cell,

That thou so many princes at a shot

So bloodily hast struck?

Amb.   The sight is dismal;

And our affairs from England come too late:

The ears are senseless that should give us hearing,   380

To tell him his commandment is fulfill'd,

That Rosencrantz and Guildenstern are dead.

Where should we have our thanks?

Hor.   Not from his mouth,

Had it the ability of life to thank you:

He never gave commandment for their death.   385

But since, so jump upon this bloody question,

You from the Polack wars, and you from England,

Are here arrived, give order that these bodies

High on a stage be placed to the view;

And let me speak to the yet unknowing world   390

How these things came about. So shall you hear

Of carnal, bloody, and unnatural acts,

Of accidental judgements, casual slaughters,

Of deaths put on by cunning and forc'd cause,

And, in this upshot, purposes mistook   395

Fall'n on the inventors' heads: all this can I

Truly deliver.

Fort.   Let us haste to hear it,

And call the noblest to the audience.

For me, with sorrow I embrace my fortune;

I have some rights of memory in this kingdom,   400

Which now to claim my vantage doth invite me.

Hor.   Of that I shall have also cause to speak,

And from his mouth whose voice will draw on more.

But let this same be presently perform'd

Even while men's minds are wild, lest more mischance,   405

On plots and errors, happen.

Fort.   Let four captains

Bear Hamlet, like a soldier, to the stage,
For he was likely, had he been put on,
To have prov'd most royally;   and, for his passage,
The soldiers' music and the rites of war   410
Speak loudly for him.
Take up the bodies.   Such a sight as this
Becomes the field, but here shows much amiss.
Go, bid the soldiers shoot.

> [*Exeunt marching, bearing off the
> dead bodies; after which a peal of
> ordnance are shot* off.

NOTES·

Act I

· 약어 목록 · ───────────────

cf. = compare
esp. = especially
fig. = figuratively
i.e. = that is to say
SC. = that is to say
SD. = stage direction
viz. = namely

Scene I

SD   **Elsinore** [elsinɔ́:] 덴마크의 셸란 섬의 동북부에 위치한 항구
도시로서 현재의 Helsingør(헬싱외르)이다. Copenhagen에서
북쪽으로 백리쯤 떨어진 곳에 있다.

    platform = terrace「성벽 위의 길」.

    post = place of duty「근무지」.

1.   **Nay** = no. 일종의 감탄사.

    Nay, answer me =「아니, 네가 대답해라」.

    me = 강조형.

    unfold yourself = declare who you are, tell me who you are
「신분을 밝히라」. 원래는 근무 중인 Francisco가 새로 등장하는
Bernardo에게 수하 誰何하는 것이 정상이다. 교대하러 온
Bernardo가 보초의 모습을 보고 누구냐고 먼저 수하하는 것은
그가 이틀 밤이나 연달아 유령을 보아 겁에 질려 있기 때문이
다. Shakespeare의 기교가 빛나는 부분이다.

3.   **Long live the king!**「국왕 만세!」. 보초들 사이에 주고받는 이날
밤의 암호(watchword)로 보인다. 그러나 13행에서 Francisco의
동일한 수하에 대해 Horatio와 Bernado가 각기 다른 대답

(Friends, liegemen)을 하고 있는 것을 보면 아는 사람들 사이에 목소리로 자기를 알리기 위한 편한 암호로 보인다.

6. **upon your hour** = just at your hour 「정각에」. 이 대목은 「왜 좀 미리 오지 않고 겨우 시간에 맞춰 오느냐」는 원망의 뜻으로 읽힐 수도 있다. 그런데 Francisco는 사병이고 Bernard는 장교이다. 장교가 사병과 근무 교대한다는 것은 부자연스럽다.

7. **'Tis** = It is.
   now = just this moment.
   get thee to bed = go to bed. 명령문에서 thou 대신 대격의 thee가 사용되는 경우가 흔히 있다.

8. **relief** = 「교대」.
   bitter cold = bitterly cold. 여기서 bitter는 부사이다. cf. piping hot 「팔팔 끓는」.

9. **sick at heart** = heartily weary, thoroughly exhausted, with watching in such weather 「심신이 지쳤다」.

10. **Have you had quiet guard?** = has your watch been undisturbed by any alarm? 「별일 없었는가?」.

12. **do meet** = meet. 여기서 do는 강조의 뜻은 없이 운을 맞추기 위해 사용되고 있다.

13. **rivals** = partners, companions, associates 「짝」.
    watch = guard.
    bid them make haste = 「서두르라고 일러주게」. 혼자 있기 두려워하는 Bernardo의 심정을 나타내고 있다.

14. **ho!** = 감탄사. 여기서는 stop! 정도의 뜻.

15. **ground** = land 「나라」.
    liegemen [líːdʒmən] = subjects 「신하」.
    the Dane = the Danish king.
    liegemen to Dane = men who have sworn allegiance to the King of Denmark 「덴마크 왕에게 충성을 맹서한 사람들」. Friends

to this ground과 Liegemen to the Dane은 모두 암호.

16.   **Give you good night** = May God give you good night, I wish you a good night.

        honest soldier = honest는 good이나 worthy처럼 칭찬을 위한 막연한 뜻으로 사용되었다.

18.   **Give you good-night** = 이처럼 Francisco가 작별 인사를 두 번씩이나 하는 것은 근무를 마치고 난 그의 안도감을 나타낸다.
        Holla [hólə] = 주의를 끌거나 가벼운 놀라움을 나타내기 위한 감탄사. 여기서는 Hello 정도의 뜻.

19.   **What** = 상대방의 주의를 끌기 위한 가벼운 뜻의 감탄사.「그런데」정도의 뜻.

        A piece of him = Horatio가 손을 내밀면서「이것이 Horatio의 한 부분일세」라고 농담을 하거나, 아니면「날이 추워 내가 이렇게 졸아들었네」라고 장난하고 있는 것으로 해석할 수 있다. 아무튼 유령 때문에 겁에 질린 Bernardo를 Horatio가 놀리고 있다.

        a piece = a fragment「조각」.

21.   **What, has this thing appear'd again tonight?** = 여기서 this thing은「그 유령인가 뭔가 하는 것」정도의 뜻. 유령의 존재를 믿지 않는 Horatio의 태도를 나타낸다. 판본에 따라서는 이 부분이 Marcellus가 한 말로 된 곳이 있으나 곧 이어 유령을 this dreaded sight라고 말하는 그가 유령을 this thing이라고 부르는 것은 어울리지 않는다.

        What = 가벼운 뜻의 감탄사.「그런데」정도의 뜻.

23.   **'tis but our fantasy** = it is only our fancy「그것은 우리의 환상에 지나지 않는다」.

        fantasy = imagination「허깨비, 환상」.

        but = only.

24.   **will not let belief take hold of him** = refuses to believe, will

not allow himself to believe 「믿으려 하지 않는다」.

25. **Touching~** = as regards, concerning 「~에 관하여」.

dreaded = dreadful 「무서운」.

twice seen of us = which has been seen by us twice.

26. **entreated him along** = entreated him to come along.

entreated = asked earnestly 「간청하다」.

27. **watch the minutes of this night** = stay awake or keep watch through this night 「밤새 망을 보다」.

28. **apparition** = ghost 「유령」.

29. **approve our eyes** = confirm our observation 「우리 눈을 믿어준다」.

speak to it = speak to the apparition 「유령한테 말을 부친다」. 유령을 쫓기 위해서는 라틴어를 사용해야 한다고 믿고 있었다. Horatio는 Hamlet과 마찬가지로 Wittenberg 대학의 학생이다.

30. **Tush** = 강한 불신이나 경멸, 짜증을 나타내는 감탄사. 「흥, 쳇」.

Sit down awhile = 세 사람이 서 있으면 곧 나타날 유령의 모습에 관객의 주목을 끌기가 힘들다.

awhile = for a time.

31. **assail your ears** = attack your ears.

31-2. **your ears…story** = 「우리말을 듣지 않으려고 단단히 무장한 당신의 귀」.

32. **fortified** = strengthened, equipped. assail이나 fortify 모두 군인들이 쓸 만한 표현이다.

33. **What** = with what.

sit we down = let us sit down. 이른바 1칭 명령문인데, 이것은 다음 줄의 And let us hear에서 보듯 let과 함께 쓰이기도 했다.

35. **Last night of all** [nights] = this very last night.

36-8. **When…burns** = 「저기 북극성 서쪽에 있는 바로 저 별이 지금 밝히고 있는 하늘 저 근처까지 왔을 때」. 다시 말해 바로 어제

와 같은 시간이라는 뜻.

36. **yond** = yonder, there 「저편에서」. yond는 부사이며, 같은 뜻의 형용사는 yon(저편의)이다.

    same = that very. **yond same**에서 same은 this same이나 that same의 경우와 마찬가지로 앞의 지시사의 뜻을 강화한다.

    pole = polar star. 「북극성」.

37. **his course** = its course.

    illumine = illuminate 「비추다」.

36. **pole** = Polaris, the North Star.

37. **his** = its.

39. **beating** = striking, tolling. beat가 toll보다 한밤중에 시끄러운 소리를 내는 느낌이 더 든다.

40. **Peace** = Be silent.

    break thee off = cease speaking. 여기서도 7행의 get thee to bed 에서처럼 thou 대신 대격의 thee가 사용되고 있다.

    Look, where it comes again! = where는 there로 바꿔도 무방하다.

41. **in the same figure** = in the same shape and dress. 여기서 same은 보통 「어제 밤과 마찬가지」(as last night)의 뜻으로 해석되나, 「돌아가신 임금님과 마찬가지」의 뜻으로 해석될 수도 있다.

42. **scholar** = exorcism(푸닥거리나 살풀이)에서는 통상적으로 라틴어가 사용되었다. Marcellus는 Horatio에게 당신은 배운 게 많고 따라서 라틴어를 할 수 있으니까 유령에게 말을 해보라는 뜻.

43. **Looks it not like the king?** = Doesn't it look like the king?

    the King = the dead king, Hamlet's father.

    Mark it = look at it, observe it closely.

44. **harrows** = vexes, confounds, lacerate, torments 「괴롭히다」.

    harrow = 「써레」.

45. **It would be spoke to** = It(= the ghost) desires to be spoken

to 「말을 건네주기를 원한다」. 유령은 누가 말을 먼저 건네기 전에는 말을 하지 못한다.

Question = Speak to.

46. **What are thou that usurp'st this time of night** = 「이 시간을 아랑곳하지 않고 나타나는 너는 누구냐」.

    usurp'st = intrudes upon 「밀고 들어가다」. usurp의 2인칭 단수형.

47. **Together with** = and also (usurp'st).

    fair and warlike form = beautiful and soldierly form.

48. **the majesty of buried Denmark** = His Majesty the buried King of Denmark = Hamlet's father. 나라 이름으로 그 나라 왕을 나타내는 Shakespeare에서 흔히 발견되는 제유(synecdoche)이다.

49. **sometimes** = formerly. 즉 임금님이 아직 살아 계실 때.

    charge = call upon to give answer 「대답할 것을 요구한다」.

50. **offended** = got angry 「화가 났다」. Horatio에게 선왕의 모습을 가장한 악마 취급을 당했기 때문에 화가 났다.

    stalks = stride with a slow and stately step 「젠체하며 걷다」.

52. **will not** = is determined not to. 강한 의지의 표현.

53. **How now?** = How is it now? 「어떻게 된 거요?」.

55. **on't** = of it.

56. **Before my God** = I swear before my God 「맹세컨대」.

    might not = could not, would not be able to.

57-8. **Without…eyes** = had it not been vouched for by the certain warrant of my visual sense 「내 자신의 눈으로 확실히 보지 않았더라면」.

57. **sensible** = able to be sensed or felt 「(오감으로) 느낄 수 있는」.

    true = trustworthy 「믿을 수 있는」.

    avouch = witness, guarantee, warrant, testimony.

59. **As thou art to thyself** = 「네가 너이듯이 그는 틀림없이 선왕이

었다」.

61.   **Norway** = the king of Norway. 아버지 Fortinbras. 48행의
Denmark(= the king of Denmark)와 동일한 제유의 경우이다.
combated = met in personal combat 「결투했다」. 나중에 알게
되지만 이 결투가 벌어진 것은 지금부터 30년 전이다. 바로
이날 Hamlet이 태어났고 따라서 그의 친구인 Horatio가 당시의
왕의 모습을 기억할 리가 없다. 그러나 이와 같은 콘티
(continuity)의 모순이나 논리의 모순은 당시로서는 하나의 애
교에 불과했다.

62.   **when, in an angry parle** = when, on the occasion of a conference
which ended in angry words.

parle [pɑ:l] = parley, meeting, conference 「교섭, 담판」.

63.   **smote** = attacked, or perhaps, defeated.

the sledded Polacks = Polis soldiers on sleds.

65.   **jump at this dead hour** = just at this very hour of dead stillness.

jump = just, exactly, precisely 「바로, 정확히」.

dead hour = 「온 세상이 잠든 시간」.

dead = still, midnight.

66.   **stalk** = walk.

gone by our watch = gone past us as we stood on watch 「망보고
있는 우리들 옆을 지나갔다」.

67.   **In what particular thought to work I know not** = I know not
what special line of thought to follow 「어떻게 갈피를 잡아야
할지 모르겠다」.

68.   **gross and scope** = overall view.

gross and scope는 nice and warm(쾌적하게 따뜻한)처럼 두 단
어로 하나의 뜻을 나타내는 경우이다. gross는 scope를 수식하
는 형용사.

69.   **bodes** = foreshows, foretells.

strange eruption = (전쟁이나 돌림병 등의) 발생.

70.   **Good now** = very well, then. 「자, 그럼」 정도의 뜻.

    tell me, he that knows = let him who knows tell me 「누군가 아는 사람이 있으면 말해주시오」.

71.   **this same** = 여기서 same은 36행의 yond same과 마찬가지로 선 행하는 this의 뜻을 강조한다.

71-2.   **Why this⋯land** = why, night after night, the king's subjects are worn out by their vigilance so strictly observed.

    observant = attentive 「주의 깊은, 엄중한」.

72.   **toils** = cause to labour 「힘들게 하다」.

    subject of the land = subject of the realm.

    subject = subjects 「신하들」.

73.   **why such daily cast of brazen cannon** = why, day after day, the casting of cannon proceeds without interruption 「왜 밤낮을 가리지 않고 놋쇠를 부어 대포를 만드는가」.

    cast = 「주조하다」.

    brazen cannon = 「놋쇠로 만든 대포」.

74.   **And foreign mart for implements of war** = and why there is this constant trade with foreign countries for the purchase of implements of war 「왜 끊임없이 외국에서 무기를 사 들이는 가」.

    foreign mart = purchasing in foreign countries, international trade.

    implements of war = 「무기」.

75-6.   **Why such⋯week** = why shipwrights are compelled to work in the docks week-days and Sundays.

75.   **impress** = forced labour, enforced service 「강제 동원」.

    shipwright = 「배 대목, 조선공」.

76.   **Does not divide the Sunday from the week** = 「휴일도 없이」.

the week = week-days.

77-8.　　**What might…day** = what can possibly be in preparation that all this heavy labour goes on day and night.

　　　　　toward = imminent, coming 「임박한, 다가올」.

78.　　　**make the night joint-labourer with the day** = 「밤낮의 구별을 없애다」.

　　　　　joint-labourer = fellow-labourer.

80.　　　**whisper** = rumour.

81.　　　**image** = semblance of a person 「닮은 모양새」.

　　　　　even but now = only just now.

83.　　　**Thereto prick'd on by a most emulate pride** = stirred to do this (i.e. to dare King Hamlet to combat) by a proud desire to rival the Danish king.

　　　　　prick'd on = incited.

　　　　　emulate = rivalling, ambitious.

84.　　　**Dared** = challenged 「도전했다」. 82행의 Was에 연결된다.

　　　　　the combat = that (famous) single combat 「결투」. 정관사 the 가 이 결투가 이미 잘 알려진 것임을 말해준다.

　　　　　valiant = courageous.

85.　　　**this side of our known world** = the inhabitants of this portion of the world that is known to us 「이쪽 세상 사람들」, 즉 Europe.

86.　　　**seal'd compact** = binding agreement, contract bearing a seal guaranteeing its authenticity 「옥쇄가 찍힌 계약」.

　　　　　compáct = contract 「계약」.

87.　　　**ratified** = confirmed or accepted (an agreement) by formal consent, signature.

　　　　　law and heraldry = heraldic law 「가문의 명예를 건 의전상의 법」. 이것도 hendiadys의 예.

88.　　　**forfeit** = 「몰수당하다」.

| | with his life = when forfeiting, losing, his life 「목숨과 더불어 (재산도 잃고)」. |

with his life = when forfeiting, losing, his life 「목숨과 더불어 (재산도 잃고)」.

all those his lands = those lands of his.

89. **stood seized of** = legally possessed. Shakespeare는 자주 stood를 강조를 위한 조동사로 사용하였다.

90. **Against the which** = against which. which 앞에 전치사가 오는 경우 흔히 그 사이에 the가 와서 관계대명사의 뜻을 강화한다.

a moiety competent = a sufficient share, an equivalent amount of lands 「버금가는 크기의 땅」.

moiety [mɔ́iəti] = share, portion.

competent = adequate, sufficient.

91. **gaged** [-id] = engaged, pledged, staked, wagered 「담보하다, (내기에) 걸다」.

91-2. **which had ⋯ Fortinbras** = and this would have gone as an inheritance to Fortinbras; would have passed into his possession.

91. **which had** = which would have.

92. **inheritance** = possession. Elizabeth 왕조 시대에 inherit는 자주 「상속」의 뜻은 없이 단순히 「소유」를 나타내는 동사로 사용되었다.

93. **covenant** = an agreement, a contract 「계약, 약속」.

93-5. **as, by the same ⋯ Hamlet** = in the same way that, by the agreement of which I have spoken, and the tenor of the stipulation formally drawn up between them, his possessions passed to Hamlet.

94 **carriage** = terms, import, bearing 「의미, 취지」.

article = a clause or provision in a law or treaty or agreement 「(법이나 계약, 조약 등의) 항목」.

design'd = drawn up 「(문서를) 작성하다」.

95. **His fell to Hamlet** = his (land) was forfeit to Hamlet. 「그의 땅은

Hamlet에게 몰수당했다」.

His = his lands.

sir = Horatio는 지금 Marcellus의 질문에 답하고 있으므로 sir는 Marcellus를 가리킨다.

young Fortinbras = Fortinbras's son.

96. **Of unimproved mettle hot and full** = of fiery and full-blooded courage that has not yet been disciplined in action.

unimproved [-id] = undisciplined, untested 「규율이 없는, 막돼 먹은」.

mettle = a person's make-up, character, disposition, temperament 「사람의 됨됨이, 품성」.

mettle hot and full = 「성격이 불같은 이 녀석」.

hot and full = fully hot. hendiadys이 예.

97. **skirts** = borders, outskirts 「변방」. 당시 변방에는 할 일없는 젊은이들이 많았다.

98. **Shark'd up** = greedily swept up, as the shark voraciously sweeps up all prey that come in its way; picked up without distinction, as a shark picks up its prey 「상어가 먹이를 쓸어 담듯이 모아들 였다」.

a list = a gang, a number 「다수의」.

lawless resolutes = wild-blooded young fellows ready for any enterprise however desperate and unjustifiable 「무뢰한들」.

resolutes = resolved desperate men, desperadoes 「무법자」.

99. **For food and diet** = merely for their keep, caring nothing about being paid 「(급여는 없이) 먹이기만 하면 되는」. 또 다른 해석은 「그들을 먹어버릴 위험한 사업에 먹잇감으로」 제공한다는 뜻.

99-100. **some···in't** = an action that requires courage.

100. **stomach** = courage, spirit of adventure. 옛날 용기는 위 속에 들

어 있다고 생각되었다. 우리말의 「뱃심」.

which is no other = and this enterprise is nothing else than 「바로
그것이다」. 102행의 But으로 연결된다.

101. **doth well appear** = is evident enough.

    our state = the Danish authorities, government 「덴마크 정부 당
국」.

102. **But** = 위의 no other에 연결됨으로 지금 같아서는 than이 사용
되었을 것이다.

    recover of us = recover from us.

    of = from.

102-3. **by strong…compulsatory** = by force of arms, and on compulsory
conditions 「강제적인 방법으로」.

103. **terms** = condition, circumstances.

    compulsatory = involving compulsion violent.

    foresaid = 「앞서 말한」.

104. **I take it** = I understand.

106. **head** = fountainhead, source, reason.

107. **post-haste** = extreme haste, rapid activity, urgency, great
expedition. 이 단어는 옛날 전령에게 맡기는 편지에 'Haste,
post, haste'(지급)라고 쓰던 관습에서 유래한 말.

    romage = bustle, commotion, turmoil.

108. **I think it be no other but e'en so** = I think that this and no other
must be the cause of all this bustle.

    I think it be = 「…이 아닌가 하고 생각하다」. be는 가정법으로
사용되고 있으며, 직설법보다 의문의 강도가 더 높다.

    but = except.

    e'en = even.

109. **Well may it sort** = may it turn out well; may it have a good
issue 「잘됐으면 좋겠다」.

sort = happen, turn out이라는 뜻 외에 suit, agree (with the present state of things)라는 뜻도 있다. 그때는 「선왕이 그런 복장으로 우리 옆을 지나간 것은 당연하다」는 뜻이 된다. 여기서는 이 두 가지 뜻으로 사용되었다.

portentous = heralding or foreboding some calamity, ominous 「불길한」.

110. **armed** [-id]

111. **That was and is the question of these wars** = whose action was, and still is, the subject of these wars.

question = subject, cause, focus of the dispute 「논쟁의 주제」.

112. **A mote it is to trouble the mind's eye** = the apparition is a thing as troubling to the mental vision as a particle of dust is to the natural eye.

mote = a particle of dust.

113. **In the most high and palmy state of Rome** = when Rome was at its height of power and glory.

palmy = triumphant, flourishing.

palm = 종려(야자) 잎은 승리의 징표였다.

state = community. 「상태」라는 뜻이 아니다.

114. **ere** = before.

mightiest = supremely mighty. 비교최상급이 아닌 절대최상급.

Julius = Julius Caesar.

115. **stood tenantless** = opened and gave up their dead.

sheeted dead = corpses clad in the shroud.

sheeted = wrapped in shrouds 「수의로 몸을 감싼」.

116. **squeak** = squeal, cry out in a shrill tone as if in anguish 「비명을 지르다」.

gibber = gabble, talk in unintelligible language 「영문 모를 말을 하다」.

117-8. **As stars … in the sun** = 문법적으로 완전하지 못한 이 부분은 한두 줄 탈락한 결과로 여겨진다.

117. **stars with trains of fire** = comets 「혜성」. 옛날에 혜성은 흉조로 알려져 있었다.

118. **Disasters in the sun** = dark spots on the sun. 혹은 「일식」으로 해석되기도 한다.

　Disasters = unfavourable aspects (of a heavenly body), threatening signs. 천문학 술어.

　moist star = moon. 달은 차고 습한 곳으로 알려져 있었다.

119. **Upon whose influence Neptune's empire stands** = by whose influence the sea is controlled. 달이 바다의 조류(ebb and flow of the tides)에 영향을 미친다는 뜻.

　influence = 천문학의 용어로서, 별의 인력이 흘러든다 (in+fluere(= to flow))는 것이 본래의 뜻.

　Neptune = Roman god of the sea.

　stands = depend upon.

120. **Was sick almost to doomsday** = was sick almost to death with the long and entire eclipse it suffered; was so long in a state of complete eclipse as to seem almost doomed to perish.

　sick = of a sickly hue, pale.

　almost to doomsday = almost as if it were the end of the world.

　doomsday = the day of doom or judgement, especially the day of the last judgement, on which the general doom will be pronounced 「최후심판의 날」.

121. **And even the like precurse of fierce events** = the precisely similar signs foreshadowing terrible events.

　precurse = a forerunner, heralding warning sign 「전조」. 124행 demonstrated(= shown)의 목적어.

　fierce = violent. feared로 읽히기도 한다.

122. **harbingers** = forerunners.

still = always, constantly.

the fates = what was fated, that which is destined to happen 「운명적으로 일어날 일들」.

123. **prologue** = prologue to the disastrous events to be enacted here.

omen = ominous event, calamity 「재앙」.

124. **together** = 하늘은 '혜성'과 '일식'으로, 그리고 땅은 '유령'으로 함께.

125. **climatures** = clime, geographic regions 「지역, 고장」.

126. **soft** = be quiet, hold, stop.

lo = look.

127. **I'll cross it, though it blast me** = I will walk across its path, intercept it, even though the result should be that it blast me. 「설사 저주받는 일이 있더라도 내가 앞을 가로 지르겠다」. 귀신을 가로지르면 저주를 받는다는 것은 당시의 미신이었다.

cross it = cross its path, impede its progress, block its path 「앞을 가로 막다」.

blast = strike with pernicious influence, to cause to sicken or wither, destroy 「저주하다」.

illusion = phantom. illusion의 본래의 뜻은 「허깨비」이다. Horatio는 아직도 「유령」의 존재를 의심하고 있다.

131. **That may to thee do ease and grace to me** = that may bring rest to thee and reflect credit on me 「너에게는 안식이 되고, 나에게는 업적이 될 것」.

133. **art privy to** = have private knowledge of, privately aware of.

fate = destiny.

134. **Which, happily, foreknowing may avoid** = foreknowledge of which may perhaps enable us to avoid.

happily = haply, by chance. fortunately라는 해석도 있다. 그러

나 현재의 회의적인 Horatio의 정신 상태를 생각하면 전자의 해석이 타당할 듯.

foreknowing = advance knowledge 「예비지식」. 주어로 사용되었음.

136. **uphoarded** = hoarded up, accumulate 「축적하다」.

137. **womb of earth** = 「땅 속 깊은 곳」.

　　　Extorted = ill-gotten, wrongfully obtained 「부당하게 얻은」.

138. **in death** = 「죽어서」.

140. **partisan** [pátizæn] = a kind of halberd(도끼 창) or long-handled pike(창).

143-4. **We do … of violence** = it is an insult on our part to make an attempt to offer violence to one so majestical in form 「저처럼 장엄한 모습의 유령을 해치려고 했던 것은 잘못이었다」.

143. **majestical** = 「장엄한」.

145. **as the air, invulnerable** = 「공기처럼 공격할 수 없는」.

146. **vain blows** = 「헛된 공격」. 상대가 공기와 같으므로 공격이 헛수고이다.

　　　malicious mockery = a derisory show, mere imitation of hostility, hollow mockery of doing harm derisory 「거짓 해치려는 동작」.

148-9. **started … summons** = 「무서운 호출을 받은 죄인처럼 움찔했다」.

148. **started** = startled 「깜짝 놀랐다」.

149. **fearful summons** = (죄인들이) 무서워하는 출두명령.

　　　I have heard = I have heard that.

150. **The cock, that is the trumpet to the morn** = 「(군대의 나팔수가 아침에 병사들을 깨우듯) 아침을 깨우는 나팔수인 수탉」.

　　　trumpet = trumpeter 「나팔수」, herald.

151. **lofty** = high-sounding.

　　　throat = voice.

152.	**god of day** = the sun-god, Apollo.
	warning = summons.
153.	**sea or fire, in earth or air** = 「(옛사람들이 만물을 이루는 근원이라고 믿은) 4대 원소」.
154.	**extravagant and erring** = vagrant and wandering.
	hies = hurries, hastens.
155.	**confine** = proper home, place of confinement.
155-6.	**of the truth…probation** = this recent sight proves the truth of that supposition.
156.	**This present object** = what we have just seen.
	probation = proof.
157.	**on the crowing of the cock** = when the cock crowed.
158.	**'gainst** = just before, in anticipation of, in expectation of the time when.
	that season = late December.
160.	**bird of dawning** = the cock.
161.	**spirit** [sprit] = 한 음절로 발음할 것. And thén, they sáy, no sp'rít dare stír.
	dare stir = dare move beyond its confine.
162.	**wholesome** = sound, healthy. 밤은 대개 불건강한 것으로 여겨졌다.
	strike = exert evil or destructive influence, blast, destroy by malign influence. 주로 천체에 대해 사용되었다. moonstruck(미친)의 strike와 같은 뜻. 사람이 미치는 것은 달의 인력에 영향을 받은 탓으로 여겨졌다.
163.	**takes** = puts under a magic spell, bewitches, affects with malignant influence.
	charm = enchant 「홀리다」.
164.	**hallow'd** = made holy, sanctified.

gracious = filled with divine grace, blessed.

165.   **in part** = partly.

166.   **in russet mantle clad** = dressed in ruddy hues 「적갈색의 옷을 입고」.

     russet = coarse homespun fabric in reddish brown.

167.   **eastward** = eastern.

168.   **Break we our watch up** = let us bring our guard duty to an end.

     Break we = let us break.

     by my advice = I suggest, if I may advise you, if you take my advice.

169.   **impart** = tell.

170.   **young Hamlet** = 아버지와 아들의 이름이 같으므로 선왕과 구별하기 위해 young이 사용되었다.

     upon my life = I am ready to stake my life 「단언컨대」.

171.   **dumb to us** = though dumb to us.

172.   **acquaint him with it** = let him know it.

173.   **As needful in our loves, fitting our duty?** = as being a thing which the love we all bear to him renders necessary, and one to which our loyal duty makes becoming in us. 「우리의 우정을 생각해서라도 그래야 하고, 또 의무이기도 하다」.

     our loves = Shakespeare 시대에는 앞의 대명사(our)가 복수인 경우 복수형의 추상명사(loves)를 사용하는 것이 관행이었다.

174.   **I pray** = I strongly urge you 「부디, 제발」.

175.   **Where we shall find him most convenient** = 「그를 아주 손쉽게 찾을 수 있는 곳」.

     convenient = conveniently.

Scene II

SD   **room of state** = 「회의실」.

1.   **our dear brother's death** = 여기서 사용되는 **our**나 **we, us**는 군주가 공식적인 자리에서 자신을 지칭하는 이른바 Royal 'we'이다.

2.   **memory be green** = memory is fresh.

        and that = that가 though로 해석되기도 하나, Shakespeare는 since *that*, thought *that*, when *that*처럼 접속사 뒤에 무의미한 that를 첨가하는 경우가 종종 있다.

        us befitted = would have been appropriate for us.

3.   **bear our hearts in grief** = 「슬픔에 잠기다」.

        our whole kingdom = befitted의 목적어. 즉 it is befitted our whole kingdom to be…

4.   **contracted in one brow of woe** = contorted into one expression of grief, drawn together in a frown. kingdom을 의인화하고 있다.

        brow of woe = mourning brow.

5.   **discretion fought with nature** = reason overmastered natural affection 「사리분별이 타고 난 우리의 감정을 이겼다」.

        discretion = polite consideration, prudence 「사리분별」.

        nature = natural emotion, natural inclination 「타고난 감정」.

7.   **Together with remembrance of ourselves** = 「동시에 우리 자신도 잊지 말고」.

8.   **our sometime sister** = 「이전의 나의 형수님」.

        sometime(= formerly)이 여기서는 형용사로 사용되었다. **sister** = sister-in law. 중세 이후의 사회적, 종교적 통념으로는 형수와의 결혼은 근친상간이다.

9.　　**imperial** = royal.

jointress = a widow who inherits her husband's entire estate for her life-time, a holder of a jointure(과부급여).

warlike = martial 「무예를 숭상하는, 상무의」.

10.　　**Have we… ** = 14행의 Taken to wife와 연결된다.

defeated joy = a joy robbed of its completeness 「마냥 기쁘기만 하지 않은 즐거움」.

defeated = marred, spoilt, destroyed.

11.　　**With an auspicious and one dropping eye** = with one eye glad and the other weeping 「한쪽 눈은 기쁨에 반짝이고 다른 한쪽에서는 눈물이 흐르는」.

auspicious = cheerful.

dropping = tearful.

12.　　**mirth** = merriment, laughter.

dirge = a lament for the dead 「만가」.

13.　　**In equal scale weighing delight and dole** = equally balancing joy and grief 「기쁨과 슬픔을 꼭 같은 비중으로」.

equal scale = a perfectly balanced scale 「좌우 무게가 꼭 같은」.

dole = grief, sorrow, lamentation.

14.　　**Taken to wife** = 10행의 Have we에 걸린다. Have we…Taken to wife = we(= I) have taken (our(= my) sometime sister) as wife.

barr'd = excluded 「멀리하다, 막다」.

15-6.　　**freely…along** = willingly approved of this affair.

go along with = agree with, approve of.

16.　　**this affair** = 우선은 형수 Gertrude와의 결혼이고, 다음으로 왕위계승자로 선출되는 일도 포함하고 있다. 당시 Denmark는 궁정의 선거에 의한 군주국이었다. 선거에서 가장 공이 큰 사람이 Polonius였던 것은 의심할 바가 없다.

16.	**For all, our thanks** = For everything you have done, you have my gratitude.

17.	**Now follows** = next I must mention.

	that you know = that which you already know. 삽입절.

	Young Fortinbras = 22행에서 He로 다시 받고 있다.

18.	**Holding a weak supposal of our worth** = supposing that our [military] position is weak「내 실력을 우습게 알고」.

	supposal = estimate, opinion「평가」.

19.	**by** = because of, in consequence of.

20.	**state** = kingdom.

	disjoint = out of joint, distracted, shaken out of its proper form「지리멸렬의」.

	out of frame = out of order, in disorder.

21.	**Colleagued [-id] with the dream of his advantage** = Fortinbras's erroneous view of Denmark's weakness is accompanied by(*colleagued with*) a fantasy of his own advancement.「자기가 유리하다는 (헛된) 꿈에」.

	Colleagued with··· = allied with「···과 겹쳐」.

	advantage = superiority.

22.	**He** = Fortinbras. 17행의 Fortinbras와 너무 거리가 떨어져있어 다시 한 번 주어를 반복하고 있다.

	pester = annoy, trouble, infest「귀찮게 하다」.

22-3.	**message···lands** =「그 땅을 넘기라는 취지의 전갈」.

	Importing··· =「···라는 취지의」.

23.	**import** = bear as its purport, express, state. import를 importune (끈덕지게 조르다)의 같은 뜻으로 해석하는 경우도 있다. 즉「끈질기게 땅의 반환을 요구하는」.

	surrender =「(토지의) 반환」.

24.	**with all bonds of law** = in full accordance with the legal agreement entered into by the two parties「모두 법적인 약조에 의해」.

bonds = binding agreements.

25.   **To our most valiant brother** = To는 앞줄의 Lost에 걸린다.

      So much for him = of him and his acts I need say no more 「그 사람 이야기는 그만 하자」.

26.   **for ourself** = for me. royal "we"의 예. 왕은 한 사람이므로 통상적인 ourselves라고 하지 않는다.

      this time of meeting = this occasion for which we have called you together.

27.   **here writ** = written in this letter.

28.   **Norway** = King of Norway.

      uncle of young Fortinbras = Norway에서도 Denmark와 마찬가지로 아들이 아니라 삼촌이 왕위를 계승한 것으로 보인다.

29.   **impotent** = incapable, helpless.

      bed-rid = bed-ridden 「침대에 누운, 병환중의」.

      scarcely hears = has hardly any knowledge of.

30-1.   **to suppress…herein** = calling upon him to put a stop to his nephew's further proceeding in this matter.

31.   **gait** = going forward, proceeding.

      in that = inasmuch as 「…인 점을 고려하면」.

      the levies = the body of men enrolled 「소집된 군인들」.

32.   **lists** = soldiers.

      proportions = quotas of troops furnished. 「배당된 군인의 수」라는 본래의 뜻에서 여기서는 단순히 「군인들」의 뜻으로 사용되었다.

32-3.   **made Out of** = conscripted or requisitioned for the campaign from among 「징집한」.

33.   **Out of his subject** = from his people.

subject = subjects 「신하들」.

35. **For bearers** = as bearers.

  bearers = carriers or messengers.

36-8. **Giving to···allow** = allowing you no further authority to treat with the king than the limits of these conditions, herein expressly stated.

36-7. **power To business** = power to do business, i.e. negotiate 「(왕과) 협상할 권한」.

38. **delated** = expressly stated, articulated.

  allow = allow의 주어는 앞줄의 scope이므로 단수형의 allows로 해야 되지만 바로 앞의 articles에 속아 복수형이 쓰였다. 문법에서 말하는 이른바 false attraction 현상이다.

39. **let your haste commend your duty** = prove your duty by the speed with which you accomplish your mission 「곧 임무에 착수해서 네 임무를 빛내라, 공을 세워라」.

  commend = recommend, praise.

41. **nothing** = in no way, not at all.

42. **and now, Laertes** = 이하 Laertes의 이름을 말끝마다 네 번씩이나 부르는 것은 그렇게 함으로써 왕이 왕위에 오르도록 도와준 Polonius의 아들 Laertes에 대한 친근감을 나타내기 위함이다.

  what's the news with you? = what have you to tell us about yourself?

43. **You told us of some suit** = you lately spoke to us about some request you had to prefer.

  suit = 「소송, 송사」.

44. **speak of reason** = make any reasonable request.

  the Dane = the King of Denmark

45. **lose your voice** = waste your words, speak in vain, not have your request granted.

45-6. **what wouldst…asking?** = you cannot possibly make any request of us which we would not grant of our own free will, if we only knew what its nature was 「자네가 무슨 부탁을 하던 그것은 자네 부탁이 아니라 내가 즐겨 해주는 것이 아닌 것이 있겠는가?」. 즉 I would give you, even without your asking(자네가 부탁하지 않아도 내가 해주겠다)는 뜻. 여기서 대명사를 you에서 thou(thy)로 바꾼 것은 친밀감을 더하기 위해서임.

47-9. **The head…father** = the head and heart, the hand and mouth, do not work together in more complete sympathy than do your father and myself.

47. **native** = allied by nature, cognate.

48. **instrumental** = serviceable.

50. **dread** = held in awe, revered 「경외하는」.

51. **leave and favour** = permission to depart. hendiadys의 예.

52. **From whence** = whence가 from there의 뜻이므로 엄밀히 말해 from은 필요 없다. 한국어의 「역전 앞」과 같은 경우.

53. **To show my duty in your coronation** = to show myself a loyal subject by attending your coronation 「대관식에 참석해서 (신하의) 의무를 다하다」.

56. **And bow them to your gracious leave and pardon** = and I submit them(= wishes) to your permission 「허락을 간청합니다」.

58. **wrung from me my slow leave** = extorted from me a permission reluctantly granted.
      slow leave = reluctant permission.

59. **By laboursome petition** = by strenuous and persistent begging 「끈질기게 졸라서」.

60. **Upon his will I seal'd my hard consent** = I reluctantly agreed to his wishes 「그의 고집에 마지못해 허가해주었다」.
      seal = 봉인하다. 보통 편지를 봉한 뒤 밀랍을 바르고 그 위에다

반지에 새긴 글자를 눌러 봉인하는 데, 대개 공문서나 유서 등에 사용된다. 여기서 will은 wish의 뜻이지만 동시에 「유서」라는 뜻도 있다. 이처럼 동음이의어(homophone)를 이용한 말장난을 pun이라고 하며 Shakespeare가 흔하게 사용하는 기교 가운데 하나이다.

hard = hard-earned.

62. **Take thy fair hour** = go when you please.

    time be thine = consider yourself at liberty to remain away as long as you may think fit 「있고 싶은 대로 있어라」.

63. **And thy best graces spend it at thy will** = may your virtuous qualities guide you in spending time 「네 장점을 이용해 실컷 즐겨라」.

64. **cousin** = kinsman, nephew. 당시 cousin은 직계 가족 이외의 친족을 나타내는 넓은 뜻의 단어로 사용되었다.

65. [*Aside*] = words spoken in a play for the audience to hear, but supposed not to be heard by the other characters 「방백(傍白)」. 방백을 말하는 배우는 대개 무대 전면에 나와 관객을 향해 방백을 말한다.

    A little more than kin, and less than kind = 여러 가지 해석이 제안된 난해한 구이다. 그중 대표적인 것은 In marrying my mother, you have made yourself something more than my kinsman, and, at the same time, have shown yourself unworthy of our race, our kind이다. 또 다른 해석은 I am indeed something more than merely your kinsman('cousin'), but very far from a 'son' in kind feelings towards to you이다. 결국 kind가 갖는 두 가지 뜻(「종류」와 「친절한」)에 의한 pun인 셈이다. kind는 당시는 [ki:nd]로 발음되어 앞의 kin과 대조를 이루는 jingle(같은 음의 운율적 반복)을 이루고 있다.

67. **too much in the sun** = 「햇볕을 너무 많이 쪼이고 있다」. sun은

son과 발음이 같음으로 이 부분은 「너무 많이 아들 대접을 받고 있다」라는 비꼬는 말로도 해석된다. pun의 예이다. 영어에는 Out of God's blessing into a warm sun(= quitting a better for a worse situation)이라는 속담이 있다. 따라서 Hamlet이 in the sun이라고 한 것은 정당한 왕권의 상속자였던 자기가 삼촌한테 모든 것을 빼앗긴 신세를 한탄하고 있는 것으로도 보인다.

68. **nighted colour** = dark frame of mind 「우울한 기분」. 한편 nighted colour는 black (mourning) clothes(상복)의 뜻도 있다.

69. **like a friend** = in a friendly way, as the eye of a friend would look 「다정하게」.

Denmark = the king of Denmark.

70-1. **Do not ⋯ dust** = do not for all time go about with your eyes cast upon the ground as if you were looking for your father laid in the earth.

vailed [-id] = downcast.

72. **'tis common** = death is common to all.

73. **nature** = the temporary existence in the natural world.

74. **common** = common은 natural이라는 뜻과 함께 base, vulgar(천한)나 심지어 promiscuous(문란한)의 뜻도 있다. 따라서 common 안에는 남편이 죽은 뒤 시동생과 너무나 쉽게 결혼해버린 어머니에 대한 원망과 비꼬임의 뜻도 포함돼 있다. 이것도 pun의 예. cf. common woman = 「창녀」.

75. **Why seems it so particular with thee?** = why do you behave as though it were something special to you?

particular = special, personal.

77-83. **'Tis not ⋯ truly** = it is not only my black clothes, my sighs and ears, my downcast face, and other outward signs of grief that indicate my real feelings.

77. **not alone** = not only.

inky = black. The color symbolized mourning and melancholy.

78. **Nor customary suits of solemn black** = nor the usual sombre dress of mourners.

   customary suits = conventional garments.

   solemn = sad, gloomy.

79. **Nor windy suspiration of forced breath** = nor the forced sighs of insincere grief.

   windy = noisy. 「소리만 요란한」 정도의 뜻.

   suspiration = sighing, deep breathing.

   forced = heavy, panting. 이것은 동시에 한숨이 진지하지 않은 「억지스럽다」는 뜻도 내포하고 있다.

80. **the fruitful river in the eye** = the tears always ready to fall so copiously.

   fruitful = abundant, copious.

81. **dejected 'haviour of the visage** = downcast expression.

   dejected = downcast, depressed.

   'haviour = behaviour.

   visage = face.

82. **moods** = modes, forms; methods of displaying grief externally.

   shapes = external semblances 「겉모양」.

83. **denote** = indicate.

84. **might play** = would be able to act.

   play = perform as on a stage.

85. **passeth show** = goes beyond, is incapable of being represented by, any outward demonstration.

   passeth = surpasses.

   show는 passeth의 목적어.

86. **trappings** = ornamental accessories. 본래는 말의 장식을 일컫는 말. 여기서는 superficial appearances(겉치레)의 뜻.

87. **commendable** [kɔ́məndəbl] = praiseworthy.

88. **to give** = 지금 같아서는 to pay라고 해야 옳다.

90. **That father lost** = that father who was lost.

    survivor = 뒤에 is를 보완할 것.

    bound = was obliged, committed.

91. **In filial obligation** = by the duty he owed as a son 「자식으로서의 도리」.

92. **obsequious sorrow** = sorrow usual to show at the funeral of some one dear.

    obsequious = appropriate to a funeral rite (obsequy).

    persever [pə:sévə] = persevere, persist, continue.

93. **obstinate condolement** = sorrow that refuses comfort.

    condolement = sorrow for the dead, mourning, grieving.

94. **impious** = in not showing resignation to the divine will, irreligious, profane. *impious*에 이어서 부정의 접두사로 시작되는 *unmanly, incorrect, unfortified, impatient, unschool'd*와 같은 단어를 잇달아 사용함으로써 작자는 왕의 불쾌감을 나타내고 있다.

95. **incorrect to heaven** = 「하늘의 섭리를 거역하는」.

    incorrect = disobedient.

96. **unfortified** = not fortified by the consolations of religion.

    impatient = incapable of suffering.

97. **simple** = foolish, dull, ignorant.

    unschool'd = uneducated, untaught.

98. **what** = that which.

    must be = must happen.

99. **any the most vulgar thing to sense** = as anything that is the most familiar object of perception 「가장 흔하게 보고 느낄 수 있는」.

    vulgar = commonly known.

100.	**peevish** = childishly querulous, fretful 「심술궂은」.
101.	**Take it to heart** = cherish it as a wrong done to us.
	Fie! = 놀라움이나 불쾌감, 비난을 나타내는 감탄사.
	fault to heaven = offence against the heaven.
102.	**fault to nature** = refusal to accept a natural law.
103.	**To reason most absurd** = showing an utter deafness to the voice of reason.
	absurd = 라틴어의 ab(from)+surdus(deaf)에서 온 말로서, 여기서는 어원적인 뜻으로 사용되고 있다.
	whose = reason's.
	theme = topic.
104.	**still** = always, habitually.
105.	**corse** = corpse 「시체」.
	first corse = 기독교에서의 인류 최초의 살인은 Cain에 의한 Abel의 살해. cf. *Genesis* 4:8.
	till he = up to the time of him.
	he = him.
106.	**We pray you, throw to earth···** = 기원문과 명령문 어느 쪽으로도 해석이 가능하다. 전자의 경우는 We pray that you may throw to earth···가 될 것이고, 후자의 경우에는 We require that you throw to earth···가 될 것이다.
	throw to earth = completely cast from you 「완전히 땅에 버리다」.
107.	**unprevailing** = unavailing, futile, useless.
	us = me. royal 'we'.
108-9.	**let the world···throne** = I call all men to witness my declaration that I regard you as next in succession to the throne = you are my heir. 그러나 Hamlet은 뒤에서 지금처럼 crown prince가 아니라 왕이었어야 한다고 생각한다.

109. **most immediate** = next in line of succession.

110. **with no less nobility of love** = with a love as full of generous feeling. 이 부분은 문법적으로 어색하다. no less nobility of love 가 112행 impart의 목적어라면 with는 없어야 한다. with를 살리려면 Do I impart towards you를 Do I love you로 했어야 한다.

112. **Do I impart towards you** = 지금까지의 Royal 'we' 대신 보다 친근한 'I'를 사용하고 있다. 이것이 그의 마음이 약해졌음을 나타내는 것인지 아니면 계산된 교활함을 나타내는 것인지는 불분명하다.

 impart = 뒤에 it(= love)를 보충해서 읽을 것.

 For your intent = as regards.

113. **school** = university.

 Wittenberg = 독일의 유명한 대학 소재지. Berlin 남쪽 50마일 지점에 있다. 1502년에 설립되었으며, 이 학교 졸업생인 Luther 는 이 학교 교수로 재직 중에 종교개혁을 일으킨다.

114. **retrograde** = opposite, contrary, opposed to, repugnant. 본래는 천문학의 용어로서 천체가 역행하는 것을 뜻한다.

115. **bend you to remain** = subordinate your wishes to ours by staying 「네 고집을 꺾고 우리와 같이 있자」.

 bend = turn, incline, acquiesce.

 you = yourself.

116. **in the cheer and comfort of our eye** = cheered and encouraged by our presence.

 cheer = face, the look.

117. **Our chiefest courtier…** = 앞에 as를 보충할 것.

 chiefest = highest in rank and importance.

 cousin = Hamlet를 부르는 호격.

118. **lose her prayers** = fail to achieve what she requests.

 lose = waste.

120. **I shall in all my best** = I promise that I will to the best of my ability.

I shall… obey you = 손윗사람의 명령에 대한 대답에 사용된다. 「반드시…하겠습니다」. 여기서 Hamlet은 어머니를 you로 부르고 있다. Shakespeare는 많은 경우에 you와 thou를 구별해 사용함으로써 화자와 청자 사이의 심리적 거리를 나타낸다. you는 thou보다 심리적 거리가 더 크다.

in all my best = to the best of my power.

122. **as ourself** = 「우리처럼」. 즉 enjoying the same privileges and honours의 뜻.

123. **accord** = promise in harmony with our wishes.

124. **Sits smiling** = is pleasant and acceptable, pleases.

in grace whereof = and in order to mark my gratitude by doing honour to your concession 「네가 양보해준 것에 감사하기 위해」.

grace = thanks, gratitude.

125. **No jocund health** = no joyous toast. 앞에 Let there be를 보충해서 읽을 것.

jocund health = joyous toasts to the health of some person.

Denmark = the king of Denmark.

126. **But the great cannon to the clouds shall tell** = without the great cannon telling it to the clouds.

tell = announce.

127. **rouse** = drinking-bout, toast. carouse [kəráuz](폭음)의 축약형인 듯. 뒤에 오는 bruit again의 목적어.

bruit again = echo back.

bruit = make a noise, echo.

128. **Re-speaking earthly thunder** = the skies echoing the report(포성) of the cannon as with heavenly thunder.

129.   이하 159행까지가 이른바 Hamet의 제1독백.

too too = extremely.

solid = sullied(더럽혀진)로 읽히기도 한다. 어머니의 추한 행동에 의해 자기 몸이 더럽혀졌다는 뜻. 그러나 solid가 melt라는 동사와 맞물려 더 강렬한 느낌을 준다.

130.   **resolve** = dissolve.

a dew = a drop of dew.

131.   **the Everlasting** = God.

132.   **canon** = 본래는 a church decree or law(교회법)의 뜻이나, 여기서는 a general law, principle(법도, 규정)의 뜻.

self-slaughter = suicide. 자살은 기독교에서는 금기시되어 있으나 성경에는 일반적인 살인을 금하는 십계명 외에 명확히 자살을 금한 곳은 없다.

133.   **weary** = tiring, tedious 「따분한」.

stale = vapid 「김빠진」.

flat = tasteless, as liquor becomes after standing uncovered for some time.

134.   **all the uses of this world** = the whole routine.

uses = ways, doings.

135.   **'tis** = it is = this world is.

136.   **grows to seed** = 「자라서 열매를 맺다」.

things rank and gross in nature = things which for want of proper attention have become rank and gross in nature.

rank = 「썩은」.

gross = coarse 「추잡한」.

in nature = in their own beings 「천성이, 본성이」.

137.   **Possesses** = seize.

merely = completely, entirely, absolutely.

That it should come to this! = that it works out this way 「일이

이렇게 되다니!」

138. **But two months** = only two months. 3막2장에서 Ophelia는 선왕이 돌아가신 지 넉 달(twice two months)이 되었다고 주장한다. 여기서는 Hamlet이 아버지가 돌아가신 지 얼마 되지도 않아 삼촌과 결혼한 어머니를 비난하기 위해 일부러 과장하고 있다.

139. **to this** = when compared with his uncle, the new king.

140. **Hyperion to a satyr** = like the sun god as compared to a goatlike satyr 「태양신을 반인반수와 비교하는 격이다」.

　　Hyperion = Greek god of the sun, Apollo.

　　satyr [sǽtə] = 그리스나 로마 신화에 나오는 반인반수의 숲의 괴물.

141. **beteem** = allow, permit.

142. **Heaven and earth!** = 「맙소사!」 호격의 간투사.

143. **Must I remember?** = can I not put such thoughts out of my head? must ever be present there? 「이런 생각까지 해야 하나?」

　　hang on him = cling to him in fond embrace 「다정하게 안겼다」.

144-5. **As if…fed on** = as if her loving desire had been made more eager by its mere satisfaction 「아버지가 사랑할수록 어머니의 식욕(= 성욕)은 증가했다」.

145. **within a month** = 바로 앞에서 두 달이라고 해놓고 지금은 한 달이라고 말하고 있다. 과장의 증거.

146. **Let me not think 't!** = oh, that I could forget it!

　　Frailty, thy name is woman! = 「약한 자여, 그대 이름은 여자여라」. 직역하면 「'약한 것'에 이름을 붙이자면 그것은 '여자'이다」. 여기서 frailty는 도덕적으로, 윤리적으로 약하다는 뜻.

147. **A little month** = a short month, scarcely a month.

147. **or ere** = before.

　　or = ere, before. 같은 말의 중첩.

148. **follow** = follow to the grave.

149. **Niobe** [náiobi] = 애 많은 것을 자랑하다가 모두 살해된 뒤 돌이
되었다는 희랍신화에 나오는 여자.

    even she = 「바로 그 여자가」.

150. **wants** = lacks.

    discourse of reason = reasoning faculty.

152-3. **no more like my father Than I to Hercules** = 「내가 Hercules를
닮지 않았듯이 아버지를 닮지 않았다」.

153. **Hercules** [hɔ́:kjuli:z] = 엄청난 힘을 가진 장사.

154. **unrighteous** = false, wicked, insincere.

155. **Had left the flushing of her eyes** = had left before her tears had
had time to redden her eyes.

    flushing = reddening.

    galled [gɔ́:lid] = injured (by tears), sore, irritated.

    gall = wear away.

156. **to post** = to hurry at full speed. post-horse(역마)를 달리듯이.

157. **dexterity** = nimbleness 「민첩함」.

    incestuous = 「근친상간의」. 당시 덴마크 궁정은 인정한 듯하나
유대교에서는 근친상간으로 여겼다.

158. **It is not** = 뒤의 good에 연결된다.

    not, …cannot = 강조를 위한 이중부정이다. 부정하는 말이 둘
(not와 ~not) 있다고 해서 긍정이 되지 않는다. 당시로서는 흔
한 용법이다.

159. **But break my heart** = let my heart break. 이 부분을 break 뒤에
쉼표를 두어(But break, my heart,…) my heart를 호격으로 해석
하기도 한다.

160. **Hail** = 본래는 '건강'을 뜻하는 단어이지만 당시엔 흔하게 사용
되는 인사말.

    I am glad to see you well = 새로 등장한 세 사람 모두에게 하는
인사로서 Hamlet은 아직 독백의 흥분에서 깨어나지 못해 처음

엔 Horatio를 알아보지 못한다.

161.   **or I do forget myself** = or I know not what I am 「내 정신 좀
봐」.

162.   **poor** = humble.

163-4.   **Sir, my good friend** = No, not my poor servant; you are my good
friend.

163.   **I'll change that name with you** = you are my friend, not my
servant. 문자 그대로의 뜻은 servant와 friend라는 말을 맞바꿔
I'll be your servant, and you shall be my friend가 되겠으나
여기서는 I'll exchange that name with you, calling you friend
and expecting you to call me so in return, 즉 servant라는 이름을
friend라는 이름으로 바꾸겠다는 정도의 뜻으로 해석하는 것이
좋을 듯. cf. *John* 15:15. Henceforth I call you not servants:
…but I have called you friends;
change = exchange.
that name = 'friend'.

164.   **what make you from Wittenberg?** = what are you doing here
away from Wittenberg? 「Wittenberg에서 떠나 와 (여기서) 무엇
을 하고 있는가?」.
make = do. 따라서 주어는 뒤의 you. 만약 앞의 what이 주어라
면 makes로 해야 옳다.
from = away from.

167.   **Good even** = Good evening/afternoon. 정오 이후에는 어느 때든
지 사용할 수 있는 인사.

168.   **But what, in faith, make you from Wittenberg?** = but tell me
truly what has brought you all the way from Wittenberg.
in faith = in truth, really.

169.   **A truant disposition** = an idle, wandering nature 「게으른 천성」.
뒤에 has brought me from Wittenberg here를 보충해서 읽을 것.

170. **I would not hear your enemy say so** = I would not let even your enemy say such a thing without objecting「자네 적들이 그런 말을 한데도 내가 곧이듣지 않겠다」.

171. **that** = such.

171-2. **that violence, To···** = such violence as to···.

172-3. **To make···yourself** = as to make it believe your own report when it is one defaming yourself.

report =「(불리한) 증언」.

your own report Against yourself =「자신에게 불리한 증언」.

174. **Elsinore** = 현재의 Helsingør.

175. **We'll teach you···** = if we cannot do anything else, we will at all events teach you···

179. **hard upon** = soon after.

180. **Thrift, thrift** =「돈을 아끼려는 거다」. 예부터 장례식이나 결혼식에 온 손님들에게 음식 대접을 하는데, 장례식과 결혼식이 잇달아 있으면 그만큼 절약하게 된다는 뜻.

the funeral baked meats = the dishes cooked for the funeral ceremony「제삿밥」.

meat = food.

181. **Did coldly furnish forth the marriage tables** = served, when cold, for the wedding feast. 장례식에 차렸던 음식이므로 식기도 하였거니와 옛날엔 관례적으로 문상객에게 차가운 음식을 대접했다. 또한 여기서 coldly는「냉정하게」라는 뜻도 내포한다.

182. **Would I had met my dearest foe in heaven** = I would rather have met my worst enemy in heaven (instead of his being in hell where I should wish him to be)「(그런 날을 당하기보다는) 차라리 천당에서 원수를 만나는 편이 낫겠다」.

dearest foe = deadliest foe「철천지원수」. dear는 애증 간에 단순히 뒤에 오는 말을 강조한다. 따라서 dearest friend나 dearest foe 모두 가능했다.

183. **Or ever** = before.

ㅤ**ever** = 소망을 강조한다.

186. **goodly** = admirable, excellent.

187-8. **He was⋯again** = he was a man whose equal, looking at him in all his characteristics, I shall never see again「어느 모로 보나 그와 같은 사람은 다시 만날 수 없다」.

187. **a man** = 한사람의 훌륭한「남자」라는 뜻.

ㅤ**take him for all in all** =「어느 모로 보나」.

ㅤ**take him** = if one regards him.

ㅤ**for all in all** = for all things in all respects.

189. **yesternight** = last night. 다음도 비슷한 경우이다. yestereve, yestermorn, yesteryear. yesterday를 제외하고는 이들은 시나 고풍스러운 표현에서만 사용된다.

190. **Saw? Who?** =「보았다니 누구를?」Saw와 Who(= whom) 모두 강조형이다. Saw? Who?가 Saw who로 된 판본도 있다. 지금 같아서는 whom이라고 해야 할 곳에 who를 사용하는 경우는 Shakespeare에서 흔히 발견된다.

192-3. **Season your⋯ear** = control your astonishment.

192. **season** = temper, qualify, mature「누그러뜨리다」.

ㅤ**admiration** = wonder, astonishment.

193. **attent** = attentive.

193. **deliver** = relate, narrate「이야기하다」.

194. **Upon the witness of these gentlemen** = resting upon the evidence of these gentlemen which will bear out what I have to say「이분들을 증인으로 하여」.

195. **This marvel** = 193행 deliver의 목적어.

ㅤ**For God's love** = for God's sake.

196-9. **had these⋯encounter'd** = 수동태의 쓰임이 바르지 않다. 바르

게 하려면 these gentlemen had encountered something이라고
하던지, something had appeared to these gentlemen으로 해야
옳다.

197.   **on their watch** = while keeping their watch.

198.   **In the dead vast and middle of the night** = in the silent vacancy
of midnight.

the dead vast = the void still as death itself 「주검처럼 고요한
공허함」.

vast = void, emptiness.

200.   **Armed at point exactly** = in armour complete to the smallest
particular.

at point = at all points 「세세한 부분까지」. at point가 at all
points(모든 면에서)로 된 판본도 있다.

exactly = completely.

cap-a-pe = from head to foot. cap-a-pe는 프랑스어의 cap(=
head)+à(= to)+pied(= foot)에서 온 말.

201-11. **Appears, Goes, Stand, speak, comes** = 이들 동사들은 모두 현재
형으로서 과거에 일어난 일을 지금 눈앞에서 보듯 생생하게
묘사하기 위한 historical present(역사적 현재) 용법이다.

202.   **Goes slow and stately** = passes in front of them in slow and
stately manner.

slow = slowly.

stately = 「위엄 있게」. slow와 stately 모두 부사이다.

203.   **oppress'd** = troubled.

fear-surprised [-id] = 「겁에 질린」.

204.   **Within his truncheon's length** = within the reach of his
truncheon, less than the length of his truncheon away from them.

truncheon = short staff, a symbol of kingly (or other) office 「지
휘봉」.

whilst = while의 소유격으로서 부사로 쓰였다. amongst나 amidst도 마찬가지 경우이다.

204.   **distill'd** = melted.

205.   **act of fear** = action of terror (upon them).

206-7.   **This … did** = they did impart this to me in dreadful secrecy.

207.   **dreadful** = filled with dread.
      impart = make know, tell.

209-11. **as … comes** = the Ghost appeared exactly at the time and in the shape that they had described.

209-10. **both in time, Form of the thing** = both in time and form of the thing.

210.   **each word made true and good** = each word being substantiated 「말 한마디 틀림없이」.

212.   **These hands are not more like** = these two hands of mine (holding them up) are not more like each other than the apparition was like your father.

213.   **platform** = level place constructed for mounting guns in a fort 「총안이 있는 흉벽」.

215.   **answer made it none** = It made no answer의 강조형.
      methought = it seemed to me. methinks의 과거형.

216.   **it head** = its/his head. 당시는 it의 소유격으로 its가 사용되기 시작하던 때로서 Shakespeare는 종종 예전의 it를 사용했다.

216-7.   **did … speak** = began to move as if it would speak.
      address Itself to motion = prepare to move (its lips). **address** = get oneself ready, begin.

217.   **like as it would speak** = just as it would do if it were about to speak.
      like as = like as if = as if.

218.   **even then** = just then, at that very moment.

219.　　**shrunk…away** = shrunk into thin air.

221.　　**As I do live** = as sure as I live.

222.　　**writ down in our duty** = laid down among the items of our duty; required by the loyalty we owe you.
　　　　writ = written.

224.　　**Indeed,…me** = assuredly this troubles me.

226.　　**Arm'd, say you?** = 유령에 관해 하는 말.
　　　　Arm'd = 「갑옷을 입은」.

230.　　**wore his beaver up** = 「턱받이를 위로 올리고 계셨다」.
　　　　beaver = face-guard of a helmet 「(투구의) 얼굴가리개」.

231.　　**What** = how.
　　　　look'd he frowningly? = did he look frowning?

232.　　**A countenance more in sorrow than in anger** = the expression of his features was that of sorrow rather than anger.
　　　　countenance = face, expression.

233.　　**red** = a natural healthy color.

234.　　**Nay** = 강조형. Horatio는 red의 가능성을 강하게 부정하고 있다.

234.　　**constantly** = fixedly, persistently 「뚫어지게」.

235.　　**would** = wish.

236.　　**amazed** = bewildered. 지금보다는 강한 뜻으로 사용되었다.

237.　　**Very like** = perhaps, possibly.
　　　　like = likely.

238.　　**might tell** = could count.

240.　　**grizzled** = of greyish colour, mixed with grey.
　　　　no? = wasn't it?

241.　　**A sable silver'd** = black mixed with gray.
　　　　sable = 「검은 담비(털)」.
　　　　silver'd = streaked with grey.

243. **warrant** = guarantee.

244. **assume my noble father's person** = take on or enact my father's role, present itself in the form of my father 「아버지의 모습으로 나타난다」. 사람들은 유령이 천사나 미녀, 또는 가까운 사람의 모습을 하고 나타난다고 믿었다.

중세 이후 구라파에서는 유령이 연옥에서 빠져나와 현세로 와서 생전에 깊은 관계에 있던 사람에게 나타나는 것으로 믿어왔다. 그러나 신교에서는 연옥의 존재를 믿지 않으며, 프로테스탄트인 Horatio도 유령의 존재를 믿지 않는다.

245. **though hell…peace** = though hell, by opening at my feet, should endeavour to deter me from speaking.

   gape = open one's mouth wide.

246. **hold my peace** = be silent.

248. **tenable in your silence** = kept in your secrecy.

   tenable = withheld, kept secret.

249. **hap** = happen.

250. **Give it an understanding, but no tongue** = take it well into your minds, let it impress itself firmly upon your minds, but do not utter a word about it.

251. **requite** = repay, reward.

   your loves = your friendship.

253. **Our duty to your honour** = we assure you of our loyal obedience.

   your honour = you의 경칭.

254. **Your loves, as mine to you** = it is your affection, not your duty, that I desire, just as it is affection that I feel towards you. 앞에 Promise rather와 같은 말을 보충하면 이해하기 쉬워진다.

255. **My father's spirit in arms!** = 「돌아가신 아버님 혼령이 갑옷을 입다니!」.

   All is not well = something is wrong.

256. **doubt some foul play** = suspect some unfair or treacherous
    dealing.
    foul play = unfair dealing.
257. **sit still** = strive to be composed.
257-8. **Foul deeds ··· eyes** = foul deeds will reveal themselves to men's
    eyes, however thoroughly they may appear to be hidden.
257. **Foul deeds** = unfair dealing.
    rise = reveal themselves.
258. **o'erwhelm** = cover, bury.
    to men's eyes = 앞줄의 rise에 걸린다. 그러나 바로 앞의
    o'erwhelm에 걸린다고 해도 무리는 아니다. 즉. them 뒤의 쉼표
    를 없이 읽는 것이다.

Scene III

3장에서는 Ophelia의 오빠 Laertes와 Laertes의 아버지 Polonius의 입을
통해 숙녀의 몸가짐과 남자의 친구 사귐이나 그 밖의 행실에 대한 충언을
들을 수 있다. 이처럼 극의 전체 내용과 동떨어진 부분을 dramatic relief
라고 부른다. 여기서 우리는 작자의 인생관이나 철학을 엿보게 된다.

1. **necessaries is embarked** = luggage is on board ship.
    embark'd = put on board the vessel.
2. **as the winds give benefit** = when the winds are favourable 「순풍
    일 때」.
    as = at such times as, whenever.
3. **convoy is assistant** = the means of conveyance are ready 「배편이
    있을 때」.

convoy = means of conveyance or transport 「수송, 전달 수단」.

assistant = present to help.

do not sleep = do not be too lazy to write (to me).

4.　　**But let** = without letting.

　　you = Laertes와 Ophelia는 남매 사이이므로 서로를 정중한 대명사 you 대신 thou로 호칭하는 것이 정상이겠으나 당시는 you가 thou의 영역을 침범해 그 기능을 대체해나가던 시대였으므로 양자의 구별이 느슨했다.

5.　　**For Hamlet** = as for Hamlet.

　　the trifling of his favour = his flirting or dallying with you 「그가 너와 노닥거리거나 희롱하는 것」.

　　trifling = frivolous conduct.

6.　　**Hold it a fashion** = regard it as nothing more than a passing fancy, a thing sure to change as quickly as fashion in dress.

　　fashion = passing fancy, temporary enthusiasm 「잠시 스치고 지나가는 감정」.

　　a toy in blood = a mere caprice of impulse, flirtation 「단순한 충동적 변덕」.

　　toy = idle fancy, whim 「변덕」.

　　blood = passion.

7.　　**in the youth of primy nature** = in the early days of its prime 「이른 봄 한창 때에」.

　　primy = in its prime, in its springtime, flourishing.

8.　　**Forward** = premature, precocious, early blooming 「조숙한」.

9.　　**perfume and suppliance of a minute** = the perfume which a minute affords and which with the minute passes away.

　　perfume = Shakespeare는 Sonnet 104에서 perfume을 fleeting pleasures of spring(잠시 스치고 지나가는 봄의 즐거움)의 뜻으로 사용하고 있다.

suppliance = pastime, diversion 「소일거리, 기분전환」.

of a minute = to fill up a minute.

10. **No more but so?** = No more than that?

but = than.

11. **For nature, crescent, does not grow alone** = for a growing human does not increase only in strength and size alone 「사람은 자랄 때 몸만 자라는 것이 아니다」.

crescent = growing.

12. **thews** = sinews, muscular strength 「근육」.

bulk = trunk 「동체」, body (of a person).

temple waxes = body grows.

temple = body (wherein the soul is enshrined). cf. *1. Corinthians* 3:16. Don't you know that you yourselves are God's temple and that God's Spirit lives in you? *2 Corinthians* 6:16. For we are the temple of the living God. 신체는 영혼의 신전으로 여겨진다.

waxes = grows larger, increases.

13. **inward service** = inner life (the activity within the temple) 「내부의 움직임」.

service = 「예배」라는 또 다른 뜻이 있다. 앞줄의 temple과 짝으로 사용되고 있다.

14. **Grows wide withal** = become enlarged with it (the body) at the same time.

withal = with it, at the same time, as well.

15-6. **And now···will** = and at present no evil thought or crafty design stains the essential goodness of his intents towards you.

15. **soil** = moral stain 「도덕적 허물」.

cautel = crafty device, deceit, trickery 「속임수」.

besmirch = soil, contaminate, sully 「더럽히다」.

16. **The virtue of his will** = the sincerity or purity of his intentions.

16-7. **but you⋯own** = but what you have to fear is that, his position in the state being taken into consideration, he is not at liberty to follow his own inclinations.

17. **His greatness weigh'd** = when his greatness is weighed, when you consider his high position (as a crown prince).

greatness = high rank.

weigh'd = properly considered, estimated.

18. **For he himself is subject to his birth** = for he must submit himself to the conditions of his birth.

birth = noble lineage 「지체 높은 가문」.

19-20. **He may not⋯himself** = it is not possible for him, like persons of no consequence, to cut out a path for himself in whatever direction it pleases him.

19. **unvalued** = unimportant or ordinary.

20. **Carve for himself** = help himself to a dish라는 본래의 뜻에서 do as he likes, make his own choice, indulge himself(하고 싶은 대로 하다) 등의 뜻으로 사용되고 있다.

Carve = choose. 식탁에서 고기를 자르는 행위에서 온 은유.

20. **on his choice** = on the choice he makes of a wife.

21. **health** = welfare, well-being.

22-4. **And therefore⋯head** = and therefore must that choice be restricted in accordance with the approval and consent of the body politic, whose head he is.

22-3. **circumscribe'd Unto** = restricted by.

23. **Unto** = according to.

voice and yielding = approval and consent.

that body = the Danish state.

24. **head** = 「(나라의) 수반」. Laertes는 Hamlet이 국왕의 자리를 이

을 것으로 가정하고 있다.

25. **It fits your wisdom so far to believe it** = you would be wise to believe it only so far 「그 정도로만 믿어두는 것이 현명하다」.

26. **in his particular act and place** = in his specific role and situation 「장차 국왕이 된다는 그의 특별한 역할과 형편에 맞게」.

27. **give his saying deed** = put his words into action, fulfil his promise 「언행을 일치시키다」.

27-8. **which is···withal** = and this freedom of action extends no further than it is in accordance with the general wish of the people.

28. **main voice** = general agreement 「(국민) 전반의 찬동」.
    goes withal = consents in addition, approves of.
    withal = along with, in addition.

29. **sustain** = suffer.

30. **credent** = readily believing, gullible, credulous 「쉽사리 믿는」.
    list his songs = listen to his songs, listen to what he says.

31-2. **your chaste treasure open To···** = (if) you open your chaste treasure to his··· = surrender your chastity to··· 「정조를 바치면」.

31. **lose your heart** = yield up your love.
    your chaste treasure = the treasure of your chastity 「순결, 정조」.

32. **unmaster'd importunity** = uncontrolled solicitation.
    unmaster'd = unrestrained 「억제되지 않은」.
    importunity = persistence 「끈질기게 조르는 것」.

33. **it** = the danger of accepting and returning his love.

34-5. **keep···desire** = 여기 사용된 은유는 Hamlet이 Ophelia를 포위하고 공격하고 있는 형상이다.

34. **keep you in the rear of your affection** = hold yourself back from actions your feelings would lead you into 「감정을 적극적으로 나타내지 마라라」.

35. **Out of the shot and danger of desire** = out of the dangerous aim of passion.

shot and danger = dangerous shot.

shot = range of a bow or gun 「사정거리」.

36. **chariest** [tʃéəriist] = most cautious, shy, scrupulous 「신중한」.

maid = maiden, virgin.

prodigal = extravagant and reckless 「방탕한」.

37. **unmask** = show.

moon = symbol of chastity. 달은 순결의 상징.

38. **Virtue itself 'scapes not calumnious strokes** = not even the incarnation of chastity is free from the shafts of calumny.

'scapes = escapes = avoids.

culumnious = slanderous, defamatory 「중상모략적인」.

strokes = blows.

39. **the canker galls the infants of the spring** = the cankerworm destroys the early spring blossoms.

canker = a small worm that eats into and destroys the flower 「자벌레」.

galls = damages, hurts, wounds.

infants = young plants.

40. **buttons** = buds.

disclosed = unclosed, opened.

41. **in the morn and liquid dew of youth** = in their earliest state, which is like a dew-sprinkled morning.

liquid dew = time when dew is fresh and bright.

42. **Contagious** = noxious, pernicious 「고약한」.

blastments = withering blights 「(식물의) 마름병」.

imminent = immediately threatening.

43. **wary** = cautious.

44.   **rebels, though none else near** = loses self-control even when alone 「청춘이란 곁에 상대가 없어도 생겨나는 욕정을 억제할 수 없다」.

45.   **I shall** = 「반드시…하겠습니다」. shall은 손윗사람의 명령에 대한 대답에 사용된다.

       effect = meaning, purport 「취지」.

46.   **watchman to my heart** = guardian to my affection.

       good my brother = my good brother. 이처럼 형용사(good)를 소유대명사(my) 앞에 놓은 것은 호격의 경우에 흔히 있는 어순이다.

47.   **ungracious pastor** = graceless clergymen 「엉터리 성직자」.

       ungracious = devoid of spiritual grace, ungodly, impious 「신앙심이 없는」. 지금은 이런 뜻으로 사용되지 않는다.

       pastor = priest.

48-50. **Show…treads** = show me how to live a strict and virtuous life while he himself follows a life or self-indulgence. cf. *Matthew* 7:13-4.

49.   **puff'd** = swollen with pride 「우쭐한」.

       libertine = one who follows his own inclinations, licentious man 「방탕자」.

50.   **Himself** = 이 부분은 47행의 Do not으로 시작되는 명령문의 일부분이므로 문법적으로는 Yourself라고 하거나, 아니면 ungracious pastors를 빗대서 Themselves라고 해야 옳다.

       primrose path of dalliance = flower-strewn road of pleasure, often seen as the way to hell 「금달맞이꽃이 핀 환락의 길」. primrose path만으로도 path of pleasure의 뜻이 있다.

51.   **recks not his own rede** = pays no attention to his own teaching.

       recks = cares for, heeds.

       rede = advice.

fear me not = do not fear for me, do not be anxious on my account.

me = for me.

53. **A double blessing is a double grace** = to receive one's father's blessing twice is a double favor from heaven. Polonius는 이미 전에 한번 작별을 했다.

   grace = fortune, luck.

54. **Occasion smiles upon a second leave** = Opportunity kindly grants me a second leave; I am fortunate in having a second opportunity of saying goodbye to my father. Occasion을 의인화 했다.

   leave = leave-taking 「작별」.

55. **Aboard, aboard** = get into a ship! 「배에 오르거라」.

   for shame = you ought to be ashamed of yourself for having delayed so long.

56. **sits in the shoulder of your sail** = The sail when blown out looks like a stooping shoulder. 순풍일 때 이런 모양이 된다.

57. **And you are stay'd for** = and your companions are waiting for you.

   stay'd for = awaited.

   There; my blessing = 「자, 내 축복을 받아라」.

   with thee! = go with you!

   thee = 대명사가 you에서 thee로 바뀌면서 친밀감이 더해진다.

58. **precepts** = instruction, direction.

59. **character** [× ⌣ ×] = engrave, write, inscribe. 앞줄의 precepts가 목적어. 시간이 없다고 아들의 출발을 재촉해 놓고 장광설을 늘어놓는 Polonius나 누이동생에게 여인의 몸가짐에 대해 긴 설교를 늘어놓는 부자는 닮은 데가 있다.

60. **Nor any unproportion'd thought his act** = do not act on any

thought that is not properly developed or controlled 「엉뚱한 생각은 그것이 무엇이든 실행에 옮겨서는 안 된다」.

unproportion'd = inordinate, reckless, headlong, intemperate.

his act = its performance, the act which would be the consequence of the thought 「(생각을) 실행하는 것」.

his = its.

61. **Be thou familiar, but by no means vulgar** = be easy in your manners but do not make yourself cheap.

familiar = friendly.

vulgar = common to all, promiscuous 「아무하고나 사귀는」.

62-3. **The friends···steel** = bind to your very soul those friends you have, and whose adoption by you has been put to the proof.

62. **hast** = have, possess 「소유하다」.

their adoption tried = when their suitability for adoption as friends proven 「진짜 친구라는 것이 알려지면」. tried 앞에 being을 첨가해서 읽을 것.

tried = tested.

63. **hoops of steel** = 「(술통의) 쇠테」.

hoops = that which binds together into unity.

64-5. **But do not··· comrade** = but do not make yourself incapable of judging between the value of one man and another by accepting the offer of friendship made by anyone with whom you are thrown, however raw and inexperienced in the world he may be.

64. **dull thy palm** = 「(악수를 많이 해서) 손바닥 감각이 무디어지다」. 손의 감각이 마비되면 선악의 구별이 불가능해진다.

entertainment = reception (as a friend).

65. **new-hatch'd** = newly born (as a bird just hatched from an egg).

unfledg'd = inexperienced, immature 「아직 깃털이 다 나지 않

은」.

comrade [×∠] = 판본에 따라서는 courage로 된 곳도 있다.

65-7. **Beware⋯quarrel** = be cautious about engaging in a quarrel.

66-7. **but being⋯thee** = but once engaged in it, carry matters in such a way that your enemy may in future hesitate about provoking you.

Bear't = carry it on. it는 앞줄의 quarrel.

the opposed [-id] = your opponent.

68. **Give every man thine ear, but few thy voice** = be ready to listen to what each man has to say, but be chary of giving your own views.

69. **Take each man's censure, but reserve thy judgement** = hear each man's opinion but forbear to deliver your own decision as to its merits.

censure = opinion, judgment. 이 단어 본래의 보다 넓은 뜻이다. 지금처럼 unfavourable opinion(비난)의 뜻을 갖게 된 것은 사람들이 칭찬보다 비난을 더 많이 하기 때문일 듯.

70. **Costly thy habit as thy purse can buy** = let your dress be as costly as your means will allow.

habit = dress, clothing. 지금과 같은 「습관」이라는 뜻으로는 Shakespeare 작품에서 단 세 번 사용되었을 뿐이다.

71. **But not express'd in fancy** = but do not let its costliness be shown by its being fanciful, extravagant.

fancy = frivolous fashion, excessive ornament.

rich, not gaudy = expensive but not ostentatious.

72. **For the apparel oft proclaims the man** = for his dress is often an indication of the wearer's character 「옷이 사람을 말해준다」.

73. **And they⋯that** = the men of highest birth and rank in France.

74. **select and generous chief** = excellent and noble preeminence.

generous = noble lineage, high-born.

chief = excellence, eminence, superiority. 판본에 따라서는 generous 뒤에 콤마를 두는 경우도 있다. 그때는 chief를 chiefly 로 읽어 뜻은 the French show their refinement chiefly in the way they choose their apparel이 된다.

in that = in the matter of dress.

76. **For loan oft loses both itself and friend** = for by lending to a friend you often lose both the money itself and the friendship of him to whom you lent.

77. **dulls the edge of husbandry** = takes the fine edge off economy; makes a man less thrifty than he would be if he knew that nobody would lend him money「검약하는 마음이 해이해진다」.

　　edge = blade (as of a knife).

　　husbandry = thrift.

78. **This above all** =「무엇보다 중요한 것은」.

79. **And it must follow…** =「그 결과 틀림없이 …과 같이 된다」.

　　as the night the day = as surely as the night follows the day.

81. **my blessing season this in thee!** = may my blessing make this advice bear fruit in you in due season.

　　season = ripen, mature.

　　this = my advice.

83. **The time invites you** = it is high time that you should.

　　tend = waite for, are expecting you.

86. **And you yourself shall keep the key of it** = and unless you say that it is no longer necessary for me to keep it safely, it shall ever remain there.

89. **So please you** = if it so please you.

　　touching = concerning.

90. **Marry** = indeed, to be sure. by the Virgin Mary(성모 마리아)에

서 온 말로서 가벼운 놀라움을 나타내는 어구.

bethought = thought of.

91.　　**of late** = recently.

92.　　**Given private time to you** = spent upon you in private some of the leisure at his disposal.

private = 방문하는 시간의 성격과 함께 방문 방식에 대해서도 암시하고 있다.

93.　　**Have of your audience been most free and bounteous** = have been more ready to listen to him than you should have been.

audience = hearing, attention to what is said. Hamlet이 하는 말을 Ophelia가 듣는 것.

free and bounteous = 둘 다 「너그럽고 헤프다」는 뜻.

94.　　**as so 'tis put on me** = for so I have been told.

put on = told to.

95.　　**And that in way of caution** = and informed with the object of putting me upon my guard.

that = 그처럼 나에게 알려주는 것.

in way of caution = by way of warning.

96-7.　　**You do not⋯honour** = you have not such a clear conception as you ought to have of what becomes you as my daughter and as a modest maiden.

96.　　**understand yourself** = appreciate your position.

97.　　**behoves** = is appropriate for, suits.

honour = reputation.

98.　　**What is between you?** = What understanding or agreement exists between you?

Give me up the truth = tell me without keeping anything back.

99.　　**tenders** = offers. 이 밖에 tender에는 money or other things that may be legally tendered or offered in payment; currency prescribed by law as that in which payment may be made; token money(어음)(*SOD*)의 뜻도 있어 106행의 true pay와 대비를 이룬다.

100. **affection** = passion 「격정」. 현대의 affection(애정)보다는 강한 뜻.

green = raw, gullible, inexperienced, foolish 「설익은」.

102. **Unsifted in such perilous circumstance** = one that has not been sifted, tried, by experience of such dangerous matters.
Unsifted = untried, untested, inexperienced, naive.
circumstance = matters, circumstances.

106-7. **That you⋯sterling** = for having taken as current coin these offers which are of no sterling value.

106. **That** = in that, for the reason that, because 「~하다니」.
ta'en = taken.
tenders = 「위폐」.
true pay = real money.
sterling = real, lawful (English) money.

107. **Tender yourself more dearly** = (1) regard yourself more lovingly; (2) offer yourself at a higher rate.
tender는 「소중히 하다」(take better care of yourself)라는 뜻 외에 「비싸게 굴다」(offer yourself at a higher rate)라는 뜻도 있다. 마찬가지로 dearly는 「소중하게」라는 뜻 외에 「비싸게」라는 뜻도 있다. Polonius는 99행에서 Ophelia가 한 tenders(제안)라는 말에 빗대 이런 말을 하고 있다. 그리하여 Hamlet의 순수한 연애 감정이 Polonius의 말장난에 의해 흥정의 차원으로 타락하고 있다.

108. **crack the wind of the poor phrase** = exhaust by overuse; ride the phrase to death. 즉 「tender라는 말을 너무 혹사해 숨이 차 죽게 만들다」.

poor phrase = 말(phrase)을 숨이 가쁜 말(horse)에 빗댄 은유 (metaphor).

crack the wind = 「숨차게 만들다」.

phrase = word.

109. **Running it thus** = carrying on the figure of a horse being ridden till, broken-winded, it comes to a stand-still.

tender me a fool = show yourself a fool in my eyes라는 해석과 make me a fool of me라는 두 가지 해석이 모두 가능하다. 한편 귀여운 애기를 fool이라고 부르는 경우를 생각해 present me with a grandchild라는 해석을 시도한 사람도 있다.

tender = exhibit.

110-1. **he hath···fashion** = he has made me urgent proposals of honourable love.

110. **importuned** = persistently solicited 「끈덕지게 조르다」.

111. **fashion** = manner.

112. **Ay, fashion you may call it** = you are quite right to use the word 'fashion', for his proffers of love are but a mere fashion, something that will change quickly enough.

fashion = passing fancy. Ophelia가 fashion을 manner의 뜻으로 사용하고 있는 것에 대해 Polonius는 passing fancy(한 때의 기분)의 뜻으로 사용하고 있다.

go to, go to = nonsense, nonsense; don't be silly 「됐다, 됐어」.

113-4. **And hath···heaven** = and has confirmed his vows by almost every possible appeal to heaven.

113. **given countenance to** = given confirmation to, supported.

countenance = support, credit, authority.

115. **Ay, springes to catch woodcocks** = yes, snares to catch fools.

springes [spríndʒiz] = snares for birds, traps.

woodcock = 「도요새」. 쉽게 잡히기 때문에 흔히 「바보」(fool,

simpleton)와 동의어로 쓰인다.

116.   **When the blood burns** = when passion is strong, when the heart is inflamed with passion, when sexual desire is aroused.

116-7. **how···vows** = how generous the soul is in lending the tongue promises.

116.   **prodigal** = prodigally, liberally, lavishly 「헤프게」.

117-20. **These blazes···fire** = these flashes of passion, which give forth more light than warmth, and of which both the light and the warmth die out even at the moment of their promise, which it is yet in the course of being made, you must not mistake for the fire which burns with steady and comforting warmth.

118-9. **extinct···a-making** = both the light and the heat of such blazes dying out almost as soon as they appear.

118.   **extinct** = extinguished, quenched.

119.   **Even in their promise** = 「타오를 것 같은 낌새가 보일 때에도」.
       as it is a-making = (even) when the blaze is being made.

120.   **take** = mistake.

121.   **Be somewhat scanter of your maiden presence** = show the reserve which becomes a maiden by allowing him fewer opportunities of meeting you.
       scanter = more sparing (less generous), more chary.

122-3. **Set your···parley** = Value yourself and your conversation more highly than to speak with Hamlet simply because he wishes to speak to you. 쉽게 말해 Don't let him see you whenever he wants to.

122.   **entreatments** = conversation. Shakespeare가 만든 단어로서 entreaties(탄원)라는 뜻도 밑에 깔고 있다.

123.   **command to parley** = Hamlet's wish to speak with you.
       parley = 「협상, 담판」.

124-6. **Believe so much in him, that⋯** = so far, and so far only, let your belief go as to bear in mind that⋯「그 정도로만 믿어라」.

124. **in** = of.

125. **larger** = longer, wider.

tether = scope, limit. 본래의 뜻은 a rope etc. by which an animal is tied to confine it to the spot 「가축을 말뚝에 묶어두는 끈」. 따라서 larger tether는 말이 먹을 수 있는 풀밭의 면적, 보다 넓은 활동 범위를 가리킨다.

125-6. **with a⋯you** = to him, as a man, a larger license in making love is allowable than to you in accepting love.

126. **In few** = in short, to sum up shortly.

127-8. **for they⋯show** = for they are go-betweens that do not show themselves in their true colours.

127. **brokers** = go-betweens, esp. in love-affairs. dealers in old clothes 의 뜻도 있다.

128. **that dye** = that colour.

investments = dress, clothes.

129. **mere implorators of unholy suits** = thorough-going solicitors of wicked suits.

implorators = solicitors 「중개자」.

unholy suits = immoral or wicked requests.

suit = 「구혼」과 「의복」의 두 뜻.

130-1. **Breathing⋯beguile** = talking in the language of sanctimonious and hypocritical bawds so as the more effectually to deceive.

130. **Breathing** = speaking.

sanctified = sanctimonious 「신앙심이 깊은 척하는」.

bawds = a woman who runs a brothel, pimps 「뚜쟁이, 포주」.

131. **The better to beguile** = 「더 잘 속이기 위한」.

beguile = cheat.

for all = once for all. i.e. this is the first and last time I am going to tell you this.

132. **in plain terms** = 「알기 쉽게 말해」.

133. **Have you so slander any moment leisure** = have you so misused any moment of your leisure.

slander = abuse, misuse.

moment leisure = moment's leisure.

134. **give words or talk with** = hold conversation with. words와 talk는 동의어라고 할 수 있으나 구태여 구별하자면 전자는 '편지'를 뜻하며 후자는 '대화'로 구분해 볼 수도 있다.

135. **Look to 't** = pay attention to this.

Come your ways = come along, let us go.

ways = way의 복수형이 아니고 way의 소유격이다. 이른바 adverbial genitive(부사적 속격)로서 on your way의 뜻이다.

Scene IV

1. **shrewdly** = keenly, bitterly, severely, sharply.

2. **nipping** = biting.

eager = pungent, acrid, sharp, keen, piercing. 프랑스어의 aigre (날카로운, 찌르는 듯한)에서.

4. **lacks of twelve** = is somewhat short of midnight, i.e. is just before midnight.

5. **season** = time.

6. **held his wont** = has been accustomed.

SD **flourish** = a fanfare played by brass instruments.

pieces = pieces of artillery 「포성」.

8. **wake** = stay up late, keep late revel

takes his rouse = stays awake tonight drinking, drinks deeply, carouses 「진탕 마시다」.

rouse = full draught of liquor, bumper, toast 「가득 채운 축배」. cf. I. ii. 127.

9. **wassail** [wɔ́sl] = revelry, carousing, drinking.

swaggering = walking arrogantly or importantly.

up-spring = wild German dance. 뒤에 오는 reel의 목적어.

reel = stagger along, swing violently. 9행의 the swaggering up-spring reels를 The King reels the swaggering up-spring으로 해석하는 것이 보통이나 주석자에 따라서는 up-spring을 뒤의 reels(= revels)를 수식하는 형용사로 보고 전체를 The King keeps(= holds) blustering new- fangled revels로 해석하는 경우도 있다.

10. **Rhenish** [réniʃ] = Rhine wine. Rhine 지방에서 나는 백포도주.

11. **kettle-drum** = a drum resembling a kettle in shape.

bray out = make a loud, harsh noise. bray는 원래 당나귀 따위 짐승의 울음소리를 나타내는 동사.

12. **The triumph of his pledge** = his feat of emptying the cup in one draft, pledging some one in a toast.

pledge = drinking to a person's health, toast 「축배」.

13. **marry** = by (the Virgin) Mary. 가벼운 뜻의 감탄사. 「아, 글쎄」 정도의 뜻.

14. **to my mind** = to my thinking, in my opinion.

15. **to the manner born** = accustomed to this tradition from birth.

it is a custom = 이하 덴마크인들의 술버릇을 흠잡는 Hamlet의 장광설은 후대의 Folio 판에서는 삭제되었다. 덴마크 출신의 Anne이 James 1세의 왕비가 된 1603년 이후 이와 같은 장광설은 정치적으로 위험할 수 있었을 것이다.

16. **More honour'd in the breach than the observance** = which it is

more honourable to neglect than to observe.

17. **heavy-headed revel** = revelry that ends in a heavy head, a headache.

east and west = everywhere, universally.

18. **Makes us traduc'd and tax'd of other nations** = causes us to be vilified and reproached by other nations.

traduc'd = spoken ill of, defamed.

tax'd = blamed, censured.

of = by.

19. **clepe** = call. yclept(= called (by the name of))가 그 과거분사.

19-20. **with⋯addition** = tarnish our reputation by calling us pigs.

19. **swinish phrase** = as drunk as a pig라는 표현을 참조할 것.

20. **addition** = titles of honor, reputation; something added to a man's name to denote his rank.

it = this drunkenness.

takes = detracts 「손상시키다」.

21. **though perform'd at height** = though performed with the loftiest chivalry and courage; although these may be outstanding.

at height = at the highest point, excellently.

22. **The pith and marrow of our attribute** = the most essential and most valuable part of our reputation.

pith and marrow = essence.

pith = strength, vigour.

marrow = 「골수」.

attribute = credit, reputation.

23-4. **So oft⋯them** = in a similar manner it often happens in the case of particular men.

23. **So** = in the same way.

oft it chances = it often happens with.

particular men = 「개인」.

24. **some vicious mole of nature** = some natural blemish.

mole = a disfiguring spot on the body.

vicious = faulty, wrong, defective. 현재보다는 뜻이 약하다.

mole of nature = natural fault.

mole = blemish 「사마귀, 점」. 한편 mole에는 「두더지」나 hidden undermining presence(잠재적 위험)의 뜻도 있다.

25. **As** = namely, to wit, for example.

wherein they are not guilty = for which defect they cannot be held answerable.

wherein = wherein의 in은 guilty에 걸린다. 현재는 of가 사용된다.

26. **Since nature cannot choose his origin** = since the nature of a man cannot choose from what source it will be derived 「우리는 자신의 출생을 선택할 수 없으므로」.

his = its.

27-8. **By their···reason** = owing to the fact of some particular temperament developing itself to excess, and so breaking down the stronghold of reason.

27. **o'vergrowth** = excess.

complexion = 중세 생물학에서는 인간의 기질(temperament)을 혈액(blood), 점액(phlegm), 황담즙(bile), 흑담즙(black bile)의 네 체액(humours)의 결합(complexion) 상태에 의해 sanguine, phlegmatic, choleric, melancholic의 네 가지로 분류하였다. 이들의 균형이 유지되는 한 인간은 정상적인지만 그 균형이 깨지면 미치게 된다.

28. **breaking down the pales and forts of reason** = which breaks down the guards and strongholds of reason 「이성을 잃게 하다」.

pales = fences, palings 「울타리」.

forts = ramparts 「누벽」.

29-30.　**o'er-leavens … manners** = causes an excess in what would otherwise be acceptable behaviour.

29.　**o'er-leavens** = radically changes (as yeast in dough). 본래의 뜻은 「효모를 과도하게 넣다」. 효모를 과도하게 넣으면 빵이 과도하게 부푼다.

　　leaven = ferment (dough) with leaven

30.　**form** = good order.

　　plausive manners = pleasing morals, pleasant conduct.

　　plausive = worthy of applause, applauded, attractive.

　　that these men = it chances, I say, that these men. 23행의 it chances에 연결된다.

31.　**Carrying, I say, the stamp of one defect** = bearing about upon them the brand of some one defect.

32.　**Being nature's livery, or fortune's star** = which they owe either to nature or to fortune; a blemish they were born with, or one wrought by mischance.

　　nature's livery = something by which one is marked by nature (as in their birth), or the o'ergrowth of some complexion.

　　livery = legal delivery of property into one's possession 「인도, 양여」.

　　fortune's star = something determined by luck.

33.　**Their virtues else** = the other virtues of these men.

　　else = in other respects.

　　be they as pure as grace = even though they are as pure as grace itself.

　　grace = holiness.

34.　**As infinite as man may undergo** = as infinite as it is possible for the nature of man to support 「인간의 천성이 감당할 만큼

무한하다 해도」.

undergo = bear the weight of, sustain.

35-6. **Shall … fault** = are certain in the general estimation of mankind to be looked upon as tainted with evil contracted from that particular fault.

35. **general censure** = the whole estimate formed of a man 「전체 평가」.

35-6. **take corruption From** = be spoilt by, become corrupt.

35. **take** = contract disease 「감염하다」.

36-8. **The dram … scandal** = 해석이 안 되는 것으로 유명한 문장이다. 그리하여 eale을 ease나 base의 잘못으로 보기도 하고, of a doubt를 often dout(= obliterate, extinguish)의 잘못으로 보기도 한다. 대강의 뜻은 a very small amount (dram) of evil makes even something admirable seem disreputable 「아주 작은 결점이 개인을 망가뜨려 세인의 비난을 받게 한다」.

36. **dram** = 무게의 단위 (1.772그램); (hence) very small quantity.
     eale = 뜻이 분명치 않다. 대개 evil의 오식으로 해석한다.

39. **ministers** = angels, agents, messengers.

40. **Be thou a spirit of health of goblin damn'd** = whether you be a good spirit or an evil one condemned to hell.
     thou = 상대가 아버지의 유령이므로 보통 같았으면 you(당신) 라고 해야 할 곳에서 thou(그대, 너)라는 대명사를 사용함으로써 상대에 대한 심리적 거리감이나 강한 회의를 나타내게 된다.
     spirit of health = a healed or saved spirit. of health를 뒤의 damn'd와 대조되는 말로 saved 정도의 뜻으로 보아 이처럼 해석하는 것이 보통이나 spirit of health를 beneficient spirit로 해석하기도 한다.
     goblin = demon 「악마」.

41. **Bring with thee** = whether you bring with you.

airs from heaven or blasts from hell = 미풍과 돌풍을 대비시키고 있다.

43. **Thou comest in such a questionable shape** = you appear in a form which so provokes interrogations.

questionable = inviting question or conversation. 당시에는 현재의 uncertain이나 baffling의 뜻은 없었다.

45. **King, father, royal Dane** = Hamlet이 흥분한 나머지 대답을 얻어내기 위해 아무 이름이나 정신없이 주서대고 있다.

46. **burst in ignorance** = 「알고 싶은 것을 알지 못한 채 폭발하다」.

47. **canonized** [× ◡ ×] = buried according to the canons of the church.

hearsed [-id] = coffined, buried.

hearse [həːrs] = an elaborate framework covering the coffin of a distinguished person during the funeral.

48. **cerements** [síəmənts] = waxed wrappings for the dead, grave-clothes 「수의」.

49. **inurn'd** = interred, entombed 「매장하다」.

50. **ponderous and marble** = ponderous because made of marble. hendiadys의 예.

jaw = 여기서는 무덤의 「뚜껑」.

51. **cast…up** = 「토해내다」.

may = can possibly.

52. **complete**[◡ ×] **steel** = dressed entirely in steel, i.e. in panoply(= full armour).

steel = 「갑옷」. 갑옷을 입은 유령이 엄숙하게 보이는 효과도 있지만 실제로 덴마크에서는 왕을 갑옷을 입힌 채 매장하는 것이 관례이기도 했다.

53. **Revisit'st thus the glimpses of the moon** = revisit the earth at this hour of night when the moon is struggling to appear from behind the clouds.

glimpse = momentary shining, flash.

54-6.　**and we fools…our souls** = and causing us weak humans to agitate our minds with thoughts that go beyond what even our souls can reach to.

54.　**we fools of nature** = victims of our weak mortal natures 「자연의 노리갯감」.

we = we는 문법적으로 Making의 목적어이므로 정확히 말해 us로 해야 옳다. 아니면 we 뒤에 are made가 생략됐다고 볼 수 있다. 여하튼 이와 같은 혼란이 화자(Hamlet)의 동요를 나내는 데 일조한다.

55.　**horridly** = horribly.

disposition = mood, nature, temperament.

56.　**reaches** = capacities.

57.　**should** = ought.

59-60.　**As if…alone** = as if it had something which it wished to communicate to you in privacy.

59.　**impartment** = communication 「전할 말, 할말」.

60.　**action** = gesture.

61.　**waves you** = invites you by waving its hand.

removed [-id] = distant, remote, secluded.

63.　**then** = as it evidently will not speak to me here 「그렇다면」.

64.　**what should be the fear?** = what is there to fear?

should be = can possibly be.

65.　**I do not set my life at a pin's fee** = I would not stake my life as an equivalent to a pin; I do not value my life at the worth of a pin.

pin's fee = the cost of a pin.

set = regard, esteem, estimate.

fee = value.

66. **for** = as regards.

can it do to that = can the ghost do to my soul.

67. **itself** = ghost.

69. **What if it tempt you toward the flood** = suppose it should tempt you to the ocean.

flood = frequently used of large bodies of water, sea.

71. **That beetles o'er his base into the sea** = that hangs frowningly over its base and dips down into the sea.

beetles o'ver = projects over like beetle brows, overhangs threateningly.

his = its.

assume = 69행의 if에 연결된다.

73. **Which might deprive your sovereignty of reason** = the sight of which might take away the controlling principle of your reason.

deprive sovereignty of reason = depose reason as ruler of your mind. 여기 사용된 of는 deprive~of의 of가 아님을 주의할 것.

deprive = take away.

75. **toys of desperation** = desperate fancies (especially suicide).

76. **Without more motive** = though it has no other inducement.

77. **fathoms** = 바다의 깊이를 재는 단위. 6피트, 약 2미터.

80. **hands** = 복수형은 84행의 gentlemen과 일치한다.

81. **Be rul'd** = suffer yourself to be controlled, over-persuaded by us in this matter.

My fate cries out = my destiny calls upon me to act.

82. **each petty** = even the most insignificant.

artery = 「동맥」.

83. **hardy** = bold, stout.

Nemean [ní:miən] **lion** = a lion said to have been killed by Hercules at Nemea, a wooded district near Argos in Greece.

nerve = sinew, tendon, muscle 「근육, 힘줄」.

84.   **call'd** = summoned.

     Unhand me = Take your hands off me, Let me go.

85.   **I'll make a ghost of him that lets me** = I'll send him who hinders me to join the ghost in the regions below, I'll kill anyone who hinders me.

     ghost = corpse.

     lets me = holds me back.

87.   **He waxes desperate with imagination** = His excited imagination is driving him into madness.

     waxes = becomes, grows.

89.   **Have after** = let us follow him.

     issue = conclusion, result, outcome.

90.   **Something is rotten in the state of Denmark** = things are unsatisfactory 정도의 뜻.

     rotten = utterly unsound, in a morbid state.

     state = kingdom, polity.

91.   **direct it** = guide the issue.

     Nay = let us not leave it to heaven to set things right, but act ourselves.

Scene V

2.   **Mark me** = pay attention to me.

     My hour = the time at which I must return to the lower regions, i.e. it is nearly dawn.

3.   **sulphurous and tormenting flames** = the flames of the Catholic

purgatory, a place of spiritual purging preparatory to entry into heaven 「연옥의 유황불」.

4. **render up oneself** = submit myself to, must return.

5. **lend thy serious hearing** = listen intently.

6. **unfold** = reveal, narrate.

bound = ready, prepared. 그러나 다음 줄에서 유령은 bound를 동사 bind의 과거분사(= compelled)로 이해하고 있다.

9. **What?** = am I to revenge! revenge라는 뜻밖의 말에 놀라고 있다.

10. **walk the night** = walk throughout the night.

11. **And for** = and during.

to fast in fires = 「지옥의 불 속에서 굶는 고통을 겪다」. purgatory(연옥)에서의 전통적인 형벌. 이와 같은 형벌은 죄인에게만 주어지는 것이므로 3막3장80행 이하가 말해주듯 이 대목은 선왕이 생전에 죄를 지었다는 것을 암시하고 있다.

12. **in my days of nature** = in the days of my natural life 「생전에」.

13. **But that I am forbid** = except that I am forbidden, if it were not that I am forbidden 「금지되지 않았다면」.

But that = Unless.

14. **my prison-house** = the place where I am confined, purgatory 「연옥」.

15. **I could a tale unfold** = If I could unfold a tale.

lightest word = 「조금만 이야기해도」.

16. **harrow up** = lacerate (the feeling), distress, confound, paralyze. 써레(harrow)의 이미지에서 온 말.

17. **spheres** = orbits of the eye, eye sockets, eyepit Ptolemy의 천문학에 의하면 천체는 몇 개의 투명한 구(球)에 둘러싸여 지구의 주위를 회전하고 있다고 생각되었다. 따라서 여기서는 눈알이 마치 천체가 구에 싸여 있듯 안와에 싸여 있는 것으로 간주되고 있다.

18. **knotted and combined** [-id] **locks** = neatly arranged hair.
lock = hair.

19. **particular** = separate, individual.
stand an end = stand on end 「거꾸로 서다」.
an = on.

20. **quills** = the spines of a porcupine 「고슴도치의 가시」.
fretful = fear-inducing, terrifying, peevish, ill-tempered, impatient.
porpentine = porcupine.

21-2. **But this … blood** = but this proclamation of the world beyond must not be made to those still in the flesh.
eternal blazon = revelation of eternity, disclosure of the mysteries of eternity.
eternal = relating to the realm of the supernatural. 많은 경우에 extreme abhorrence(극도의 혐오)를 나타내기 위해 사용되었다.
blazon = public announcement, proclaiming, publishing.
must not be = must not be delivered.

22. **To ears of flesh and blood** = 「살아 있는 사람 귀에」.
List = listen!

27-8. **Murder … unnatural** = all murders are bad but mine was especially bad.

27. **as in the best it is** = 「살인은 제아무리 그럴만한 이유가 있더라도 몹쓸 짓이다」.
in the best = at best, in the best circumstances.

28. **this** = this is.
strange = out of the common, remarkable, rare.

29. **Haste me to know 't** = let me quickly know it, quickly put me in the position of learning it.

30. **meditation** = thought. as swift as thought는 「빠르다」는 뜻으로

많이 사용된다.

31.   **sweep** = move swiftly, swoop.

       apt = easily impressed, ready to learn, responsive.

32-4.   **And duller⋯this** = and more sluggish would you necessarily prove yourself than that heavy weed whose torpid growth clings to the banks of Lethe.

32.   **duller shouldst thou be** = you would surely be duller.

       fat = dull, slow-witted.

33.   **roots itself** = rots itself로 된 판본도 있다.

       in ease = lazily and comfortably.

       Lethe wharf = the banks of the infernal river Lethe. 희랍 신화에 나오는 「망각의 강」. 황천(Hades)에 있는 강으로서, 그 물을 마시면 과거사를 전부 잊어버린다고 한다.

       wharf = bank of a river.

34.   **Wouldst thou not** = if you did not.

35.   **given out** = reported, announced publicly.

       sleeping in mine orchard = while I was sleeping in my orchard.

       orchard = palace garden.

36-8.   **so the whole⋯abus'd** = the consequences of which is that every one in Denmark is grossly deceived by a forged story of the manner in which I met my death.

       the whole ear of Denmark = the ear of all Denmark.

37.   **forged** [-id] **process** = false story, fabricated account.

38.   **Rankly** = grossly, offensively.

       abus'd = deceived.

39.   **did sting thy father's life** = stung your father to death.

40.   **prophetic** = foreknowing.

       soul = person, being 정도의 가벼운 뜻.

42.   **incestuous** = 「근친상간의」.

adulterate = adulterous.

43. **traitorous gifts** = treacherous faculties.

45. **won to** = won over to, persuaded her to yield to.

46. **will** = sexual desire.

seeming-virtuous = having a virtuous appearance. 왕비는 선왕의 생전부터 시동생인 현재의 왕과 불륜의 관계에 있었을 가능성이 높다. 그렇다면 왕비는 불륜과 근친상간이라는 2중의 죄를 짓게 된다. Hamlet은 삼촌의 아버지 살해뿐만 아니라 어머니의 이 같은 불의도 예감하고 있었는지 모른다. 그와 같은 어머니에게서 육신을 물려받았다는 생각을 할 때 1막 2장 129-30행의 Hamlet의 독백 첫 부분도 이해가 된다.

O, that this too too solid flesh would melt,

Thaw, and resolve itself into a dew!

seeming = seemingly.

47. **what a falling-off** = what a decline in standards. 'The Fall'이라고 하면 인류의 타락, 즉 아담과 이브의 원죄를 가리킨다. 여기서는 '뱀'으로 변신한 악마 사탄의 꼬임에 빠진 여인의 원형인 이브의 이미지와 겹쳐져있다.

48-50. **whose love⋯marriage** = whose love was so worthy of the name that it never for a moment swerved from the vow made to her at the altar.

48. **that** = such.

dignity = worth.

49. **even with the vow** = with the very vow.

even = just, exactly, precisely.

50-2. **and to decline⋯mine!** = and to think that she should forsake me for a miserable creature whose natural gifts could not for a moment compare with mine!

50. **decline** = fall to a lower level.

52. **To** = compared to.

53-4. **But virtue … heaven** = but just as virtue(= a virtuous person) will never be led astray even tough it be solicited by lewdness(= a lewd person) in the garb of an angel. virtue는 강조를 위해 앞에 놓였고, 바로 뒤에서 it로 다시 받고 있다.

moved = affected, stirred.

54. **shape of heaven** = an angelic form, beautiful celestial form.

55-7. **So lust … garbage** = so lust(= a lustful person), though linked in marriage with one as white of soul as a radiant angel, will ravenously glut itself with garbage even in a bed of heavenly purity.

56. **sate itself in a celestial bed** = satiate itself with the pleasure of a lawful marriage.

sate = gratify (desire, a desirous person) to the full. satiate의 줄임 꼴.

57. **prey on** = seek.

garbage = offal, refuse 「쓰레기」. 현대의 rubbish보다 더 강한 뜻으로 사용되었다.

58. **soft!** = wait (see, listen).

60. **My custom** = which, or as, is my custom.

of the afternoon = during the afternoon.

61. **Upon my secure hour thy uncle stole** = your uncle crept softly upon me in my unguarded hour, at a time when I fancied myself safe.

61. **secure** = free from care, relaxed, unsuspicious 「안심하고 있는, 방심하고 있는」.

62. **juice of hebenon** [hébnən] = poison.

hebenon = ebony(흑단) 아니면 henbane(사리풀). 정확히는 모른다.

vial = small container for liquid.

63.   **porches** = entrances.

64.   **leperous distilment** = distillation causing leprosy.

       leperous = producing upon the skin blotches like those in a leper.

       whose effect = which in its effect.

65.   **Holds such an enmity with blood of man** = is so hostile to the blood of man.

66.   **quicksilver** = mercury.

       courses = rushes.

67.   **natural gates and alleys** = veins and arteries.

       gates = gateways.

68-70. **And with…blood** = and with a sudden energy thickens and curdles with the same effect as that of acids upon milk, when dropped into it, the blood which, while in healthy state, is thin and fluid 「우유에 떨어뜨린 산처럼 묽고 건강하던 피를 응결시켜버린다」.

68.   **sudden** = speedy in action.

       vigour = efficacy (of a poison).

       posset, *v.* = curdle (like a posset), clot.

       posset, *n.* = drink composed of hot milk curdled with ale, wine, etc., formerly used as a delicacy and as a remedy 「밀크 주」.

69.   **eager** = sour, acid.

70.   **wholesome** = sound, healthy.

71-3. **And a most…body** = and a most instantaneous eruption spread over my skin, covering it with a loathsome crust such as is seen upon lepers.

71.   **instant tetter** = instantaneous skin eruption.

       tetter = a skin disease marked by sores and scabs 「피진」.

       bark'd about = covered (as with bark). 73행의 All my smooth body가 목적어.

72. **lazar-like** = like a leper.

lazar = a person afflicted with sores such as those of Lazarus in the parable. cf. *Luke* 16:20.

vile = disgusting.

loathsome = offensive, repulsive.

75. **at once** = at the same time.

dispatch'd = suddenly deprived of.

76. **in the blossoms of my sin** = when my sins were in full blossom.

77. **Unhousel'd ⋯ unanel'd** = without having received final rites.

Unhousel'd [ʌnháuzld] = without receiving the Eucharist(성찬식); without receiving the holy sacrament administered to dying persons. cf. housel = the reception of Holy Communion.

disappointed = unprepared (for death); not furnished, or appointed, with the religious consolations given to a dying man.

unanel'd [ʌnəní:ld] = unanointed, without receiving the ceremony in the Catholic Church of anointing a dying person with holy oil.

78. **No reckoning made** = no chance to ask forgiveness for my sins.

reckoning = settling of spiritual accounts (by confession of sins).

sent to my account = sent to answer for my sins before the judgement seat of God. cf. **go to one's account** = die. 죽으면 하느님 앞에서 생전에 지은 모든 죄에 대한 값을 치러야하기 때문에 생긴 표현.

my account = God's judgment of me.

79. **imperfections** = shortcomings.

81. **nature** = natural feeling. 여기서는 natural filial affection 「효심」.

bear = put up with.

83. **luxury** = lust, lechery.

84.   **howsoever thou pursuest this act** = whatever measures you may take to punish the murderer.

pursuest = proceed with.

85.   **Taint not thy mind** = do not let your mind become contaminated 「마음을 더럽혀서는 안 된다」.

85-6.   **let not⋯aught** = do not allow your mind to be in any way poisoned, or your soul to plot any injury, against your mother.

aught = anything. 앞줄 contrive의 목적어.

86.   **aught** = anything.

leave her to heaven = let God judge and punish her.

87.   **thorns** = pricks of conscience 「양심의 가책」.

89.   **glow-worm** = 「반딧불이」.

matin = morning. matin이 이런 뜻으로 사용된 유일한 예.

90.   **'gins to pale his uneffectual fire** = begins to dim its fire so that it loses its effect in the morning light. 엄격히 말해 his는 her여야 한다. 왜냐하면 개똥벌레 가운데 빛을 발하는 것은 암놈들뿐이기 때문.

91.   **Adieu** = farewell.

92-112. **O all⋯sworn 't** = Hamlet의 제2 독백.

92.   **host of heaven** = angels and ministers of grace. Hamlet은 유령의 출처를 여러 가지로 의심해 본다.

host = army.

What else? = What else shall I invoke?

93.   **shall I couple hell?** = shall I invoke the powers of hell also?

couple = join, link.

fie = an expression of disgust or reproach 「쳇, 젠장」.

Hold = Hold together. Don't break.

94.   **sinews** = tendons, muscles.

grow not instant old = don't become feeble as if with sudden ageing.

instant = instantly, suddenly.

95. **stiffly** = strongly, firmly.

96-104. **Yea, from…matter** = 지금까지 내 기억 속에 적어놓은 모든 것을 다 지워버리고 아버지의 명령만을 적어두겠다.

96-7. **while memory…globe** = so long as my brain remembers anything.

97. **this distracted globe** = this confused head.

 distracted = perplexed, confused, bewildered.

 globe = head. 본래의 뜻은 「지구」이지만 Globe Theatre의 청중에게는 말의 울림이 단순하지 않았을 것이다.

98. **table** = writing-tablet. 당시 젊은이들이 메모를 위해 가지고 다녔다.

99. **fond** = trifling, trivial, foolish.

 records [× ⌣].

100. **saws** = wise sayings, maxims, proverbs.

 forms = images, sketches.

 pressures = impressions, impressed characters.

101. **That youth and observation copied there** = that my youthful observation has set down there, i.e. in the tablets of his memory.

 youth and observation = youthful observation.

102. **live** = have lasting record.

103. **book and volume** = 강조를 위해 같은 뜻의 단어를 중복해 사용했다.

104. **Unmix'ed with baser matter** = unalloyed by anything of meaner importance.

 by heaven! = 「맹세코」.

105. **pernicious** = wicked, villainous.

106. **damned** [dǽmnid].

107. **My tables** = let me get out my tablets. 수첩을 꺼내면서 하는 말.

　　meet it is = it is appropriate that.

　　meet = suitable, fitting, proper, appropriate.

　　set it down = make a memorandum of it「적어두다」. 엘리자베스 조 시대의 멋쟁이나 법학부 학생들은 항상 수첩을 가지고 다니면서 책을 보거나 설교를 듣거나 사람들과의 대화에서 인상에 남는 말을 적어두는 것이 관습이었다.

110. **So, uncle, there you are** = so, uncle, now I have got my memorandum about you set down.

　　Now to my word = now for the injunction given me by my father; I must keep my promise to the Ghost.

113. **secure** = guard, protect from injury.

114. **So be it!** = amen! 판본에 따라서는 이 부분이 Marcellus의 몫이 되어 있다. 다시 말해 Heaven secure him!이라는 Horatio의 말에 amen(그렇게 되기를!)이라고 동의한 것이 된다. 그러나 이 대사가 Hamlet의 것이라면 그가 뭔가를 적고나서, 또는 결심을 위해 기도를 하고 난 다음에 덧붙인 amen의 뜻이 될 것이다.

115. **Illo** = hillo. 멀리 있는 사람을 부르는 소리.

116. **Hillo** = Hamlet이 Marcellus가 Illo라고 외친 것과는 달리 그를 조롱하기 위해 매사냥꾼(falconer)이 매를 부를 때 외치는 소리를 흉내 내 Hillo라고 부르고 있다.

　　Come, bird, come = 역시 매사냥꾼이 매를 부를 때 쓰는 말.

117. **How is 't** = How is it (with you), i.e. are you all right?

118. **wonderful** = miraculous.

121. **How say you** = What do you think?

　　once = ever.

122. **secret** = not revealing secrets.

123-4. **There's ne'er…knave** =「덴마크에는 대악당 아닌 악당은 없다; 덴마크의 악당이란 악당은 모두 대악당이다」.

124.	**But he's** = without his being; who is not.
	arrant = complete, thoroughgoing, out-and-out.
	knave = rogue, scoundrel.
127.	**without more circumstance** = without further ceremony, to cut the matter short.
	circumstance = ado, ceremony, formality.
128.	**I hold it fit that we shake hands and part** = it seems better that we should shake hands and part.
	shake hands = 여기서는 작별의 악수.
129.	**You, as your business and desires shall point you** = you to occupy yourselves in such a way as, etc.
	point = direct.
131.	**Such as it is** = whatever it may be.
	poor = 겸손을 위한 표현이기는 하나 현재의 Hamlet의 무력한 입장을 나타내기도 한다. 이 점은 142행과 185행의 경우도 같다.
133.	**whirling** = excited, impetuous, extravagant, inconsequent.
134.	**offend** = hurt, wound the feelings of.
	faith = in faith.
135.	**offence** = wounding of the feelings.
136.	**Saint Patrick** = 아일랜드의 patron saint. Purgatory(연옥) 지킴이 이며, 아일랜드에서 뱀을 없앴다고 알려져 있다. 흔히 어떤 맹세를 할 때 성인의 이름을 곁들이는 것이 상례이다. 그러나 이 성자의 이름이 유령이 연옥에서 왔다는 사실과 Hamlet의 아버지가 뱀에게 물려 죽었다고 알려진 사실(36, 39행) 등과의 연상에서 나왔다고도 볼 수 있다.
137.	**much offence** = crime. 135행에서 친구 Horatio가 기분 상할 일이 아니었다고 말하는 것에 대해 Hamlet은 offence의 뜻을 일부러 달리 알아들은 척하고 Claudius의 큰 범죄 사실이 있었다는 것을 암시한다.

Touching = Concerning, As for.

138. **honest** = genuine, truthful. 다시 말해 아버지의 모습을 빌린 악마가 아니었다.

   that let me tell you = let me tell you that; so much it is well you should know 「그것만은 알아두게」.

139. **what is between us** = what has passed between myself and the Ghost.

140. **O'ermaster 't as you may** = subdue your desire as best as you can; I must recommend you to curb it as best you may.

141. **As you are friends, scholars, and soldiers** = on your faith as, etc.

142. **Give** = grant.

145. **In faith** = 「맹세코」.

146. **not I** = I will not divulge it.

147. **Upon my sword** = 칼의 도신과 날밑이 십자 모양을 이루기 때문에 맹서를 위해 「검을 걸고」라는 말이 흔히 사용된다.

149. **Indeed, upon my sword, indeed** = Hamlet이 맹세를 강요하고 있다. 판본에 따라서는 indeed가 in deed가 되기도 한다. 다시 말해 말로서만 맹세할 것이 아니라 행동과 형식을 갖춰 맹세하라는 뜻.

150. **truepenny** = honest fellow. 「진짜 동전」이라는 뜻에서.

151. **cellarage** = underground. 정확히 cellar의 뜻은 아니고 cellar로 사용할 수 있는 지하 공간을 뜻한다.

152. **Propose the oath** = 「(따라 할 테니) 선창하십시오」.

153. **Never to speak of this that you have seen** = Swear never to speak of, etc.

156. **Hic et ubique** [hik et jubáikwi] = (Thou art) here and everywhere (Latin). Hamlet의 독백이라기보다 유령에게 하는 말일 듯. 이 말은 본래 신의 편재(omnipresence)를 나타내기 위해 상투적으

로 사용되는 말인데, Hamlet은 신출귀몰하는 유령에 대해 이 말을 패러디해 쓰고 있다. 당시 라틴어는 유령에게 가장 친숙한 언어로 여겨졌었다. cf. I. i. 42.

162. **Canst work i' the earth so fast?** = Can you burrow in the earth like a mole so fast that you have already reached the point directly under the spot to which we have moved?

163. **A worthy pioner!** = well done! you are an excellent pioner.

pioner [páionə] = digger, miner.

remove = move to another place.

164. **O day and night, but this is wondrous strange!** = I call day and night to witness if this be not wondrous strange; assuredly this is wondrous strange.

day and night = 맹세할 때 흔히 같이 사용되는 말.

165. **as a stranger give it welcome** = welcome it as one should welcome a stranger.

stranger = guest.

give it welcome = do not refuse to entertain it.

166-7. **There are ⋯ philosophy** = to you this may seem very strange, but that is only because there are many more things in heaven and earth than the philosophy to which you are so addicted ever conceived.

167. **your philosophy** = your는 our 정도의 뜻.

philosophy = 「학문」.

169. **Here, as before⋯** = (swear) here as you did over there before.

so help you mercy = as you hope to receive God's mercy. 맹세할 때 흔히 같이 쓰는 말.

170. **How strange or odd soe'er I bear myself** = however strange and odd I may be in my manner.

soe'er = so ever.

bear myself = behave.

171-2.   **think meet To** = think it proper to.

172.   **put an antic disposition on** = assume fantastic behaviour.

    antic = grotesque, ludicrous, quaint, fantastic.

174.   **With arms encumber'd thus, or this headshake** = with your arms folded or shaking your head in a knowing way.

    encumber'd = folded, locked one with the other, like a man in deep thought.

    this headshake = this grave shake of the head assuming intense wisdom.

175.   **doubtful** = enigmatical, ambiguous.

176.   **As** = as, for instance.

    We could, an if we would = we could tell if we wanted to.

    an if = if.

    would = wished to.

177.   **if we list** = if we should so please.

    list = should choose.

    There be, an if they might = there are those (namely ourselves) who could explain this, if they were allowed to do so.

    be = are.

178.   **giving out** = expression, pronouncement.

    note = show, indicate. 173행의 shall에 연결되며, 전체는 you…never shall…to note(아는 척해서는 안 된다)가 된다. shall과 to 사이는 삽입절. 이 때 to는 필요 없다.

179-80.   **this not to do…Swear** = swear, according as you hope that heaven's grace and mercy may help you in your time of need, not to do this.

179.   **this** = 위(169-79)에서 언급한 내용. 즉, 내가 이상한 행동을 해도 모른 척하는 것.

180.   **So grace and mercy** = 169행의 so help you mercy를 부연한 것.
most = greatest.
Swear = 다음과 같이 맹세하라는 것, 즉, I swear, so help me grace and mercy at my most need, not to do so. 이번이 세 번째 맹세이다. 첫 번째는 「본 것」에 대해, 두 번째는 「들은 것」에 대해, 그리고 마지막으로 「이상한 행동을 하는 것」에 대해 아무 말 하지 않기로 맹세하라는 것이다.

184.   **With all my love I do commend me to you** = with my best love I recommend myself to you.
commend me to you = 「잘 부탁합니다」. 정중한 작별 인사.
me = myself.

186.   **friending** = friendship shown in action.

187.   **God willing** = if it so please god.
shall not lack = shall not be wanting.

188.   **And still your fingers on your lips** = always keep the secret.
still = always.

189.   **The time is out of joint** = The world is in utter disorder. out of joint의 본래의 뜻은 「탈골」.
cursed = [kɔ́:sid].
spite = malicious fate or fortune.

190.   **set it right** = 「본래대로 바로 잡다」. 여기서는 탈골한 뼈를 다시 맞추는 일, 즉 제대로 아버지 복수를 하는 것을 뜻한다.
it = the time.

191.   **Nay, come, let's go together** = Hamlet이 「아니, 같이 가지」라고 한 것은 Horatio와 Marcellus가 Hamlet를 남겨두고 저희끼리만 가려는 것에 대해 한 말이거나, 아니면 그들이 예절을 갖춰 Hamlet을 앞세우려고 한 것에 대해 같이 가자고 한 말일 수 있다.

Act II

Scene I

1. **notes** = message, letters.

   him = Polonius의 아들 Laertes.

3. **You shall do** = you will certainly do, you should be sure to do.

   marvellous = marvelously, wonderfully, very.

4-5. **make inquire ··· behaviour** = make inquiries as to how he has borne himself since he arrived in Paris.

4. **inquire** = inquiry. 이처럼 접미사 -y의 첨가 없이 동사 그대로 를 명사로 사용하는 것은 당시에는 흔히 볼 수 있던 현상이다.

6. **Marry** = indeed, to be sure. 가벼운 뜻의 감탄사.

   well said = you are quite right.

   Look you, sir = take care you do this.

7. **Inquire me** = inquire on my account.

   me = for me. 이른바 ethical dative의 경우.

   Danskers = Danes.

8. **And how** [they live], **and who** [they are], **what means** [they live on], **and where they keep** = and what their manner of life is, who they are, what their resources, income, and in what part

of the city they live.

means = income.

keep = dwell, live.

9.   **What company, at what expense** = what company they keep, whom they entertain, and how much they spend in such hospitality.

10.   **encompassment and drift of question** = roundabout way in which your questioning drives at its purpose.

    encompassment = talking round a subject.

    drift = what one is driving at, aim 「노리는 것」.

11.   **know** = are acquainted with.

11-2.   **come you···demands** = approach the topic more closely than these particular questions 「이런 자질구레한 염탐보다 더 본격적인 문제로 접근하라」.

11.   **more nearer** = 강조를 위한 2중 비교.

12.   **demands** = questions.

13.   **Take you, as 'twere, some distant knowledge of him** = pretend that you have some distant acquaintance with him.

    Take = pretend, assume.

    knowledge = acquaintance.

14.   **As thus** = saying for instance.

17.   **but,' you may say, 'not well** = adding 'but only slightly' 「그러나 썩 잘 알지는 못한다고 덧붙여라」.

18.   **if 't be he I mean** = 「만약 그가 내가 말하는 사람이라면」.

19.   **Addicted so and so** = devoted to such and such pursuits or pastimes.

    so and so = to this and that.

19-20.   **and there···please** = and at this point, when you have got so far in your conversation, you may put upon him any imputations you think fit.

19. **put on him** = accuse him of, lay to his charge, charge him.

20. **forgeries** = invented faults.

rank = gross, offensive.

22-4. **But…liberty** = but imputations of such wildness and extravagances as are commonly found to be the accompaniments of youth when not kept in too strait-laced control.

22. **wanton** = unrestrained.

slips = an accidental or slight error, faults.

23. **companions noted and most known** = well-known accompaniments 「잘 알려진 부수물」.

noted = well known, notorious.

24. **youth and liberty** = the unrestrained behaviour of young men. hendiadys의 예.

liberty = licence.

As = For instance.

gaming = gambling.

25. **fencing** = 「칼싸움」. 검술을 잘못 가운데 하나로 간주하는 것이 이상하게 여겨질 수 있다. 당시 젊은이들 사이엔 종래의 무거운 sword 대신 이탈리아나 프랑스에서 전래된 가볍고 가는 찌르기 전용의 rapier가 유행했으며, fencing 도장은 young wild bloods가 모이는 곳이기도 했다. 칼싸움은 의례히 여자나 도박 등 좋지 않은 원인에서 출발하는 경우가 많았다. 전 시대 사람인 Polonius가 그것을 경멸하고 있음이 분명하다.

26. **Drabbing** = associating with bad women.

cf. **drab** = prostitute.

you may go so far = you may venture to bring these charges against him. 남자에게 drabbing 정도는 괜찮다는 Polonius의 태도는 그와 Laertes가 1막3장에서 Ophelia에게 강권하는 여성의

정조에 대한 태도와는 대조를 이른다. 2중 잣대(double standard)의 본보기이다.

28. **'Faith** = in faith, indeed.

   as you may season it in the charge = if you qualify the accusation, that depends on how you can modify (make light of) the accusation.

   season = qualify, temper 「누그러뜨리다」.

29. **another** = a different kind of.

   scandal = disgraceful imputation.

30. **open to incontinency** = liable to immoderate indulgence 「여자에게 헤프다」. 이것은 돈을 주고 직업적인 여자를 사는 행위와는 다르다.

   incontinency = vicious sexual excess.

   incontinent = lacking self-restraint (esp. in regard to sexual desire).

31. **breathe** = speak.

   quaintly = cunningly, artfully.

32. **taints of liberty** = slight faults that accompany independence, faults resulting from freedom.

   taints = stains.

33. **fiery** = high-spirited, impetuous.

34. **A savageness in unreclaimed blood** = a wildness typical of immature spirits, a wildness such as is found in hot-blooded young men not yet tamed by the stern discipline of life.

   unreclaimed [Λnrikleimid] = untamed, wild.

35. **Of general assault** = such as most young men are liable to, which assails or affects most men.

36. **Wherefore should you do this?** = you would ask me why I make these suggestions to you.

Wherefore = why.

37. **would** = should like to.

my drift = what I am driving at; my secret object.

38. **fetch of wit** = clever trick, witty stratagem.

fetch = trick.

39. **You laying these slight sullies on my son** = you having imputed these trivial blemishes to my son.

sullies = stains, blemishes. sally(= attacks, criticisms)로 된 판본도 있다. 어느 쪽이든 뜻은 통한다.

40. **As 'twere** = as if it were.

soil'd i' the working = by being used has lost somewhat of its first gloss 「쓰다 보니 때가 묻은」.

41. **Mark you** = 가벼운 뜻의 감탄사.

42. **Your party in converse** = the person with whom you are conversing.

converse = conversation.

him you would sound = whom you wish to probe.

him = he whom.

sound = test the depth of the bottom of the sea or the river 「물의 깊이를 측량하다」. inquire into the opinions or feelings of a person 「다른 사람의 생각을 떠보다」.

43. **Having ever** = if he has ever.

prenominate = aforenamed, before-mentioned 「앞서 거명한」.

crimes = faults 정도의 가벼운 뜻.

44. **breathe of** = speak of.

45. **He** = 42행의 Your party in converse를 반복하고 있다.

closes with you in this consequence = confides in you as follows.

closes with = agrees with.

in this consequence = to this effect, as follows.

consequence = that which follows.

46. **or so** = or something of the sort, or whatever.

47-8. **According⋯country** = according to the mode of address customary in the country or the title of the man addressed 「타고 난 고장과 신분에 따라」.

47. **phrase** = phraseology, expression, form of words. 다음 줄의 country에 걸린다.

addition = something added to a man's name to denote his rank, title. 다음 줄의 man에 걸린다.

50-1. **What⋯leave** = 「내가 무슨 말을 하려고 했지?」 정도의 뜻인데, 배우들 가운데는 대사를 잊어버린 듯한 흉내를 내서 관중을 재미있게 하기도 한다.

50. **By the mass** = indeed. 가벼운 뜻의 감탄사.

51. **leave** = break off.

55. **He closes thus** = he agrees with you in these words.

57. **Or then, or then** = or at some time or other.

with such, or such = accompanied by such and such persons.

58. **'a** = he. ha(= he)의 생략형.

gaming = gambling.

o'ertook in 's rouse = overcome by drink.

o'ertook = overpowered by drink.

's = his.

rouse = a drinking-bout.

59. **falling out** = quarreling, wrangling 「말다툼, 싸움」.

tennis = 테니스는 당시 프랑스 사람들이 특히 좋아했던 운동으로서, fencing만큼 평이 좋지 않은 운동이었다. 지금과는 달리 실내에서 행해졌으며, 영국에 소개된 것도 프랑스로부터였다.

60. **house of sale** = i.e. house of creatures of sale (= prostitutes).

61. **Videlicet** [vaidíliset] = namely, that is to say. 보통 viz.로 줄여

쓴다.

brothel = a house where prostitution takes place.

63.   **Your bait of falsehood** = this falsehood which I suggested to you to use as a bait.

    bait of = bait made of.

    takes this carp of truth = catches this fish, viz. the truth of the matter.

    carp = 「잉어」. typical of something foolish and easy to catch.

64.   **we of wisdom and of reach** = we who are wise and capable.

    reach = capacity, ability.

65.   **windlasses** = circuitous routes (used to surprise game in hunting).

    assays of biases = indirect attempts. 본래 bias는 bowl 경기에서 공이 곡선을 그려 다른 공을 피해가도록 공 안에 넣어두는 납덩이를 의미했다.

66.   **indirections** = oblique courses, indirect methods.

    directions = the things we are aiming at.

67.   **So by my former lecture and advice** = so by following out the lesson of advice I just now gave you.

    former = aforesaid.

    lecture and advice = instructions. 같은 말을 되풀이하는 hendiadys 의 예.

68.   **Shall you my son** = you shall find out my son.

    You have me = you understand me.

69.   **God be wi' you** = wi'는 with의 생략형으로서 이 구가 줄어서 오늘날의 Good-bye가 되었다.

70.   **Good my lord!** = 작별 인사.

71.   **inclination** = natural disposition.

    in yourself = for yourself, personally, not being content with what you hear of his conduct.

73. **And let him ply his music** = let him go on to what tune he pleases 「하고 싶은 대로 하게 내버려둬라」.

ply = work steadily at one's business or trade. 고대 그리스에서와 마찬가지로 구라파에서 음악은 양가집 자식의 필수 교양이었다. 따라서 또 다른 해석은 문자 그대로 Polonius가 아들이 이 교양에 전념해주기를 바라고 있다는 것이다.

Well = very good.

77. **sewing in my closet** = occupied with needle-work in my own room.

closet = private room.

78. **doublet** = a close-fitting body-garment, with or without sleeves. 14세기에서 18세기까지 남자들이 착용.

unbrac'd = unbottoned, unfastened.

79. **No hat upon his head** = 엘리자베스 시대에는 실내에서는 물론 교회에서도 모자를 썼다. 모자를 벗는 것은 예의에 반하는 것으로 여겨졌다.

foul'd = stained with dirt, muddy.

80. **Ungarter'd** = with no garters to his hose, or with his garters not fastened. garter = 「각반」. 양말이 흘러내리지 않도록 무릎 위나 아래를 둘러싸는 헝겊으로서, 족쇄처럼 흘러내린 것은 양말이다.

down-gyved [-id] = fallen to his feet like chains(gyves) or fetters.

82. **so piteous in purport** = so expressive of misery.

purport [× ´] = meaning, expression.

83. **loosed** [-id] = released.

84. **To speak of horrors** = only in order that he might tell of its horrors.

85. **Mad for thy love?** = distracted by his intense love for you?

87. **held me hard** = grasped my wrist tightly.

88. **Then goes he to the length of all his arm** = then stepped back from me at the full length of his arm.

goes = 현재형으로 사용된 것은 과거에 일어난 일을 바로 눈앞에서 보듯 생생하게 묘사하려는 historic present의 경우이다.

89. **thus o'er his brow** = 「손을 이마 위에 이처럼 가리고」.

90. **falls to** = begins.

perusal = detailed examination, scrutiny, earnest study.

91. **As he would draw it** = as if he wished to paint it.

92. **a little shaking of mine arm** = slightly shaking my arm.

93. **his head** = 같은 줄의 waving의 목적어.

95. **As it did seem to shatter all his bulk** = that it seemed to shatter his whole trunk.

As = that.

bulk = body (of a person).

96. **end his being** = 「생을 마치다」.

That done = after that.

97. **with his…turn'd** = looking all the while over his shoulder.

99. **helps** = help. Shakespeare는 앞의 대명사(their)가 복수인 경우 추상명사를 복수형으로 사용했다. cf. I. i. 173.

100. **And, to the last, bended their light on me** = and till he disappeared in the doorway, kept them fixed upon me.

bended = turned (one's eyes) in a new direction.

101. **go seek** = go to seek.

102. **ecstasy** = madness.

103. **Whose violent property fordoes itself** = whose violent nature destroys itself.

property = peculiar or particular quality, peculiarity.

fordoes = destroys.

104. **desperate** = despairing 「(자살 따위의) 절망적인」.

105.	**passion** = 「희비애락의 모든 격한 감정」.
107.	**hard words** = harsh answers to his entreaties.
108.	**as you did command** = in obedience to your commands.
109.	**repel** = reject, decline to receive.
109-10.	**denied His access to me** = refused him permission to visit me.
112.	**quoted** = noticed, observed, marked.
	trifle = play (with your affection).
113.	**wreck** = ruin.
	beshrew my jealousy = curse my suspicion, shame upon my suspicions.
	beshrew = 가벼운 형태의 저주.
	jealousy = suspicion, apprehension of evil, mistrust.
114.	**proper to** = appropriate to, characteristic of.
115	**cast beyond ourselves** = overreach ourselves, go too far, i.e. read too much into things.
	cast = (1) reach (a metaphor from casting or 'throwing' a net), (2) design, plan.
116.	**sort** = class of people.
117.	**discretion** = good judgment, discernment.
	Come = 그러나 실제로 다음 장면에 Ophelia는 등장하지 않는다.
118.	**known** = made known (to the King).
118.	**close** = secret.
	move = cause.
119.	**More grief to hide than hate to utter love** = more grief if hidden than hatred if spoken (of Hamlet's love and strange behavior). 비록 Polonius가 국무대신이라고는 하지만 왕자가 평민의 딸을 좋아한다는 사실은 국왕을 화나게 할 수 있다.

Scene II

2. **Moreover** = besides.

3. **provoke** = incite, urge, call forth, stimulate to action.

4. **Our hasty sending** = our sending for you in such haste.

5. **transformation** = complete metamorphosis 「사람이 변한 것」.

    so I call it = so we may call it. 49행에서 Polonius는 이것을 lunacy라고 부른다.

6. **Sith** = since, because.

    nor… nor = neither… nor.

    inward man = mind.

7. **that it was** = that which it was 「이전의 모습」.

    What it should be = what it is probable that it should be.

8. **that thus…** = 앞줄의 it를 받는다.

8-9. **put him… from** = deprived him… of.

10. **I cannot dream of** = I cannot conceive in the faintest degree.

11. **being of so young days brought up with him** = since you were brought up with him from your earliest days.

    of = from.

12. **neighbour'd to** = acquainted with.

    youth and haviour = youthful behaviour.

    haviour = behaviour.

13. **That** = 11행의 that와 중복.

    vouchsafe your rest = agree to stay.

    vouchsafe = allow (a person to do something).

14. **your companies** = the company of both of you 「같이 동무해주는 것」. 앞 대명사(your)가 복수형이므로 복수형의 추상명사가 사용되었다.

15. **draw him on to** = encourage him to participate in.

pleasures = indulgence in the way of amusements.

16. **So much as from occasions you may glean** = so far as opportunity will enable you to pick up stray indications.

occasions = course of events, opportunity.

17. **whether** = [hwɜə]. 운율적으로 한 음절이어야 한다.

aught = anything.

18. **That open'd, lies within our remedy** = which, if made known to us, it would be in our power to cure 「까닭을 알면 손 쓸 방도도 있을 것이다」.

open'd = if it is revealed.

20. **there is** = 판본에 따라서는 there are로 된 곳도 있다. 그러나 이처럼 복수 주어를 단수 동사로 받는 경우는 Shakespeare에게는 드물지 않았다. 현대 미국의 흑인영어에서 볼 수 있는 they is와 같은 표현은 이 같은 용법의 잔재이다.

21. **more adheres** = is more closely bound (by friendship).

22. **gentry** = generosity, courtesy.

24. **supply and profit of our hope** = support and benefit of what we hope for.

25. **visitation** = visit.

26. **As fits a king's remembrance** = as it is fitting for a king to show when bearing in mind a service rendered to him.

27. **of us** = over us.

28. **your dread pleasures** = the desires of you who can cause dread or fear.

dread = awesome, revered.

29. **But** = though you might have commanded rather than entreated.

both = both는 문법적으로는 신하 두 사람(we both obey you)을 가리킬 수도, 혹은 왕과 왕비(we obey you both)를 가리킬 수도

있다. 그러나 문맥상으로는 전자가 맞다.

30. **in the full bent** = completely, to the full extent, to the best of our power. 활시위를 끝까지 당겼을 때의 활의 모양에서 가져온 말.

bent = extent to which a bow may be bent 「활을 힘껏 당겨 구부린 모양」, (hence) degree of capacity.

32. **To be commanded** = to be put to such purposes as you may direct.

34. **Thanks, Guildenstern and gentle Rosencrantz** = 왕비는 두 신하에 대한 감사의 마음을 공편하게 나타내기 위해 감사의 순서를 왕과 반대로 하고 있다.

36. **changed** [-id]
    some of you = one of you.

37. **bring** = conduct.

38-9. **Heavens…him!** = God grant that he may find pleasure in our society and help in our actions on his behalf. presence는 다음 줄의 pleasant에 걸리고, practices는 다음 줄의 helpful(= full of medical remedy)에 걸린다.

practices = activities (with the suggestion of plots or deceit).

41. **Are joyfully return'd** = have come back full of joy at the success of their mission.

42. **Thou still hast been the father of good news** = you have ever been the parent of good news.
    still = ever, always.

43. **Assure you** = Assure yourself, be assured.
    liege = sovereign lord 「군주」.

44. **hold** = keep, observe 「지키다」.

46-8. **or else…to do** = unless the brain of mine follows up the trail of policy less keenly than it has been accustomed to do.

47. **Hunts not the trail of policy** = does not follow so successfully the trail of statecraft.

    trail = track, scent. 짐승이 지나간 발자국이나 냄새.

    sure = surely.

48. **that** = 46행의 think에 연결된다.

52. **fruit** = dessert.

53. **do grace to them** = do honour to them (by bringing them in), give them a courtly welcome.

55. **head** = source, origin. cf. well-head.

    distemper = illness, disease. 여기서는 mental derangement.

56. **I doubt** = I fear, I suspect.

    no other but = no other than.

    main = chief concern, principal point.

58. **shall sift him** = shall discover by sifting him.

    him = Polonius.

    sift = examine closely (as if through a sieve) 「채로 치듯이 철저히 조사하다」.

59. **our brother** = my fellow ruler.

60. **Most fair returns of greetings and desires** = most courteous reciprocation of your greetings and good wishes.

    returns = reciprocation.

    desires = good wishes.

61. **Upon our first** = at our first meeting, immediately after our first audience.

    sent out = issued orders.

62. **levies** = acts of levying troops 「징집」.

63. **preparation** = force equipped for fight.

    against the Polack = against the Poles.

64. **But, better looked into** = but, having looked into the matter more

closely 「보다 자세히 살펴보니」.

truly = 동사 found가 아니라 다음 줄의 was와 엮인다.

65.   **Whereat** = whereupon, because of this.

66-7.   **That so … hand** = that he, in the powerlessness to which he had been reduced by sickness and old age, had been so imposed upon.

66.   **impotence** = helplessness.

67.   **Was** = 앞줄의 sickness, age, impotence를 묶어 하나의 현상으로 보아 단수형의 was로 받고 있다.

    borne in hand = deluded, deceived, cheated.

    sends out = 명시된 주어는 없으나 물론 Norway 왕이 주어이다.

    arrests = orders, decrees (to cease activities).

69.   **Receive rebuke** = is rebuked by.

    in fine = finally, in conclusion.

71.   **give the assay of arms** = make trial of armed combat, attack, assault.

    assay = attempt, trial.

73.   **fee** = payment, income.

74.   **commission** = authority.

75.   **So levied as before** = levied in the manner already mentioned 「앞서 말씀드린 방식으로 모병한」. **as before**는 as previously levied라고 해석할 수도 있다. 그 때는 「전에 모병한」의 뜻이 된다.

76.   **entreaty** = an earnest request, supplication 「간청」.

    herein = 서류를 내놓으면서 하는 말. 80행의 therein도 마찬가지.

    shown = set forth in writing.

77.   **quiet pass** = peaceful passage.

78.   **this enterprise** = the troop to be engaged in this enterprise.

79. **regards of safety and allowance** = terms securing the safety of Denmark, and regulating the passage of Fortinbras's troops through the country.

   regards = conditions.

80. **likes** = pleases.

81. **our more consider'd time** = a time more suitable for consideration.

82. **Answer, and think upon this business** = And think upon and answer to this business.

   business [bízinès]. 세 음절.

83. **well-took labour** = well-taken pains.

84. **at night** = tonight.

86. **liege** = sovereign lord, superior to whom allegiance is due「군주」.

   expostulate = argue about, set forth one's views, discuss at length.

87. **majesty** = royalty.

   should be = ought to be, what its essentials are.

90. **brevity is the soul of wit** =「간결은 지혜의 정수」.

   soul = quintessence.

   wit = wisdom.

91. **tediousness** = prolixity, long-windedness「장황함」.

   outward flourishes = mere ostentatious embellishments.

93-4. **to define … mad?** = it would be mad to try to define madness, (rather than simply label it).

95. **let that go** = let that pass, never mind about further discussion of that point「그건 그렇다 치고」.

   More matter, with less art = get to the point more quickly by cutting out the rhetorical ornamentations.

matter = substance 「내용」, 「요점」.

art = artfulness 「꾸밈」. 왕비는 art를 figure of speech의 뜻으로 쓰고 있는 반면 Polonius는 96행에서 art를 artifice(= 계략)의 뜻으로 받고 있다.

98.　　**figure** = figure of speech, rhetorical forms of expression.

102.　　**defect** = disability.

103.　　**For this effect defective comes by cause** = for this result which is one of deficiency, is not without its own cause.

104.　　**Thus it remains, and the remainder thus** = Polonius가 약간 당황해서 100행에서 한 말을 되풀이하고 있다.

105.　　**Perpend** = consider carefully, weigh carefully what I am about to say.

106.　　**while she is mine** = until she marries.

107.　　**mark** = note, notice this.

108.　　**gather, and surmise** = understand what I am about to say and draw your own conclusion.

　　　　gather = listen (literally, collect by observation, infer).

　　　　surmise = form an idea. 둘 다 infer, deduce의 뜻.

109-10.　**To the … Ophelia** = 113행과 마찬가지로 편지 겉봉에 써진 수취인 이름(superscription).

109.　　**the celestial and my soul's idol** = the heavenly Ophelia, the object of my soul's worship.

110.　　**beautified** = endowed with beauty, beautiful.

111-2.　**'beautified' is a vile phrase** = 비평가들은 beautified라는 단어 자체는 이상스러울 것이 없어 이 부분을 이상하게들 여겼다. 그런데 전에 Greene이라는 작가가 Shakespeare를 평하면서 그를 an upstart Crow, beautified with our feathers(우리들 깃털로 예쁘게 꾸민 갑자기 출세한 까마귀)라고 혹평한 적이 있는데, Shakespeare는 당시에는 아무 대꾸도 하지 않고 있다고 여기서

조롱하고 있는 것이 분명하다.

111. **ill phrase** = bad phrase.

113. 수취인 주소(superscription)의 일부.

   bosom = fold or pocket in the front part of a bodice, used for letters, &c.

   these = these letters = this letter. cf. 라틴어에서 littera(글자)의 복수형인 litterae는 편지의 뜻을 갖는다.

   &c. =「운운」.

115. **stay** = wait.

   be faithful = fulfill my duty, read the letter accurately.

116. **Doubt** = suspect.

117. **the sun doth move** = 이 문장이 문제가 되기도 한다. 물론 이 부분은 Ptolemy의 천동설에서 오는 말이지만, Hamlet은 여하튼 Shakespeare는 천동설을 믿지 않았기 때문이다.

120. **ill at these numbers** = a poor hand at writing verses 「시가 서툴다」. 그러나 또한 sick while I write this verse 「시 쓰는 일이 역겹다」라는 뜻도 가능하다.

   numbers = verses.

121. **art** = skill, artistic ability.

   reckon my groans = 「사랑의 신음을 음절로 계산해서 (시로) 말하다」.

   reckon = count up, express in verse 「운을 세면서 시로 나타내다」.

122. **most best** = very best, absolutely best. 이 표현은 앞줄의 best를 수식한다고 볼 수 있으나 Ophelia에 대한 호칭으로도 볼 수도 있다. 판본에 따라서는 Best로 표기하기도 한다.

   Adieu = farewell.

123-4. **whilst this machine is to him** = so long as he lives.

   machine = body. 약간 비하해서 사용하고 있다.

is to him = belongs to him i.e. while he is alive.

126. **more above** = moreover, furthermore, in addition.

solicitings = 「접근해오는 것」. 128행의 given의 목적어.

127. **As they fell out by time, by means, and place** = when, how and where they were made.

fell out = happened, took place.

by = with respect to.

129. **What do you think of me?** = do you suppose me so wanting in wisdom as to allow her to receive proffers of love from one so much above her in rank as a prince?

130. **a man faithful and honourable** = Polonius는 faithful할지는 모르나 honourable하지는 않다. 그는 그의 아들이나 왕자에 대해 뒷조사를 하고 있다.

131. **fain** = willing, gladly.

132. **hot** = impetuous, urgent.

on the wing = developing very quickly.

133. **As I perceiv'd it, I must tell you that** = for, I must tell you, I certainly did perceive it.

As = because.

136. **If I had play'd the desk or table-book** = remained silent, keeping this knowledge hidden as if I had put it in a desk or a diary. 당시의 desk는 지금과 달리 경사진 뚜껑을 가진 하나의 상자로서, 글을 쓸 때는 table 위에 올려놓고 사용했다.

137. **Or given my heart a winking, mute and dumb** = given my heart a wink as a hint to keep silent.

winking = closing of the eyes 「마음의 눈을 감는 것」.

138. **with idle sight** = seeing it but doing nothing about it.

idle = indifferent, careless.

139. **I went round to work** = instead of behaving in such a supine

way, I proceeded to act with promptitude and firmness.

round = straightforwardly.

140.   **my young mistress** = my는 특별히 소유를 나타내는 말이 아니라 my lady = [miléidi](마나님, 아씨)라고 부를 수 있는 귀부인에게 쓰는 말. 그러나 이처럼 자기 딸을 객관화해서 부름으로써 엄격함을 드러내고 있다. 마찬가지로 bespeak도 speak와는 달리 꾸짖음이 함의되고 있다.

bespeak = speak to, address with words of caution.

141.   **out of thy star** = outside your destiny, beyond your (social) sphere and position, i.e. out of the question as a marriage partner. **star** = fortune. 사람을 태어날 때의 별자리의 모양에 의해 운명이 결정되는 것으로 생각되었었다.

142.   **prescripts** = orders, instructions to govern conduct.

143.   **lock herself from his resort** = shut herself up where he could not gain access to her.

resort = visitation.

144.   **tokens** = tokens of love, presents.

145.   **she took the fruits of my advice** = she followed, and profited by, my advice.

fruit = benefits.

146.   **repulsed** = refused.

147-50.   **sadness, then…raves** = 전형적인 love-melancholy(상사병)의 증세들이다. Polonius는 그것을 단계별로 나열하고 있다. 슬픔(sadness) – 결식(fast) – 불면(watch) – 쇠약(weakness) – 현기증(lightness) – 광기(madness).

148.   **watch** = sleeplessness, insomnia.

149.   **lightness** = lightheadedness 「현기증」.

declension = decline, gradual falling-off.

150.   **raves** = talks wildly or furiously in or as in delirium 「(미친 사람

처럼) 소리 지르다」.

151.   **And all we wail for** = all of us mourn for.

   Do you think 'tis this? = 이 물음은 Polonius와 왕비 두 사람
   가운데 누구에게 한 질문인지 분명치 않다. 글의 흐름으로 보아
   서는 「그 말이 정말이냐?」라고 왕이 Polonius에게 다짐해 물은
   질문 같기도 하지만 이 질문에 대해 왕비가 대답을 하고 있는
   것으로 보아서는 왕비에 대한 질문으로도 보인다.

153-4. **Hath there…otherwise?** = I would very much like to know if
   there has ever been a time when I have said positively that
   something is the case and it has turned out not be (true).

154.   **That** = 앞줄의 such a time에 걸린다.

156.   **Take this from this** = Polonius는 머리와 어깨를 가리키면서 만
   약 자기가 틀렸다면 목숨을 내놓겠다는 시늉을 한다.

157.   **If circumstances lead me** = if I have any facts to guide me, any
   clue to follow up.

   circumstances = relevant (circumstantial) evidence 「정황, 단서」.

159.   **the centre** = the center of the earth, which, in the Ptolemaic
   system, is also the center of the universe.

   try = test.

160.   **four hours together** = 「여러 시간씩」. 당시엔 막연히 긴 시간을
   나타내기 위해 four나 forty가 많이 사용되었다.

   together = at a time.

161.   **lobby** = hall, passage 「복도」.

162.   **loose** = let loose 「풀어놓다」. 교미를 목적으로 가축을 풀어놓
   는다는 뜻도 함축하고 있다.

163.   **arras** = curtain, tapestry. 프랑스 북부의 벽걸이 견직물 생산의
   중심지인 Arras에서 유래된 말.

164.   **encounter** = meeting.

165.   **from his reason fall'n** = lost his reason, descended into madness.

thereon = for that, i.e. his love.

166-7. **Let me⋯carters** = let me no longer hold the responsible post I have so long held, but be sent to the country to busy myself with such a degrading pursuit as agriculture.

166. **assistant of state** = perhaps, one who helps run a government 「정부관료」.

state = government.

167. **keep a farm and carters** = manage a farm and its workers (such as men who drive carts).

carters = cart-drivers.

SD **Enter HAMLET, reading on a book.** = 책을 옆에 끼거나 읽으면서 걷는 것은 엘리자베스 시대에는 「우울증」의 전형적인 모습으로서, 당시의 관객들은 곧 그 사실을 알아차렸을 것이다. 판본에 따라서는 Hamlet의 등장을 9행 앞으로 당긴 것도 있다. 그리하여 Hamlet이 본의 아니게 자기 딸을 풀어놓아(loose) Hamlet를 시험해보겠다는 Polonius와 왕의 모의를 엿듣게 되고, 그런 Hamlet이 다음에서 보듯 Polonius를 fishmonger(뚜쟁이)라고 부른다든가, 그가 정직한 사람이면 좋겠다는 등의 심한 말을 하는 것의 설득력이 생긴다. 다만 이때의 Hamlet의 등장은 Polonius가 161행에서 Here in the lobby라고 하면서 복도를 가리킬 때 자연스럽게 청중에게 인식되는 모양새가 될 것이다.

168. **poor wretch** = poor unhappy fellow.

169. **Away** = make haste to conceal yourselves.

170. **board** = speak to, approach.

presently = at once, instantly.

give me leave = excuse my interrupting you. 이 말을 하는 상대가 무대를 떠나는 왕과 왕비라면 작별(farewell) 인사가 될 것이지만 여기서는 책을 읽으며 걸어오는 Hamlet에게 한 말이라고 보는 것이 적절하다.

172. **God-a-mercy** = thank you, God have mercy. 손아랫사람의 인사 에 대한 공손한 대답.

174. **Excellent well** = thoroughly well.

fishmonger = 「생선장수」라는 뜻 외에 bawd(= 뚜쟁이, 포주) 의 뜻도 있다. 한편 Coleridge는 Hamlet의 비밀을 낚으려(to fish out) 온 사람이라는 뜻으로 해석한다.

176. **so honest a man** = so honest a man as a fishmonger.

177. **Honest, my lord!** = Polonius는 자기의 정직성이 의심받자 화를 내고 있다.

178. **as this world goes** = as times are now 「요즘 같은 세상에서는」.

181. **For if…** = 책을 읽으면서 하는 말.

maggots = 「구더기」.

182. **a good kissing carrion** = a good piece of decaying flesh (of the dead dog) for the sun to kiss, i.e. good for the sun to breed maggots from by his kisses. Ophelia를 두고 하는 말이다.

carrion = 「썩은 고기」. 동시에 성적 쾌락을 위해 사고파는 「육 체」의 뜻도 있다.

185. **Let her not walk i' the sun** = sun은 son과도 발음이 같다. 따라서 이 문장은 일차적으로는 「햇볕 속에 너무 많이 걷게 하지 말라」 는 뜻이지만 동시에 「Hamlet(= son) 근처에도 가지 못하게 하라」는 뜻이 되기도 한다. 햇볕을 쏘이면 구더기가 생기기도 하지만 임신(conceive)할 수도 있기 때문이다. Ophelia로 하여 금 Hamlet 근처에 가지 못하게 한 Polonius에 대한 비아냥거림 이 담겨 있다. sun과 son의 pun이다. cf. I. ii. 67. I am too much in the sun.

Conception = 「세상물정을 알게 되는 것」과 「임신」이라는 두 뜻을 pun으로 사용하고 있다.

187. **look to 't** = be cautious in the matter, take care that she does not walk i' the sun.

188. **How say you by that?** = What do you think of that? Polonius가 청중에게 앞서 한 Hamlet의 말을 어떻게 해석해야 하느냐고 묻고 있다.

by = about, concerning.

189. **Still harping on** = ever dwelling on (the subject of my daughter) 「늘 …을 생각하고 있다」. cf. to harp on the same string.

190. **far gone** = seriously affected 「정신이상 증세가 많이 진전된」.

192. **suff'red much extremity for love** = suffered the extremest pangs for love's sake.

very near this = and was almost as far gone as Hamlet.

195. **matter** = the subject matter (of the book).

196. **Between who?** = 앞줄의 matter(내용)를 일부러 the matter in dispute(사건)으로 알아들은 척 되묻고 있다.

198. **Slanders** = 「중상, 비방」.

the satirical rogue = 로마의 시인 Juvenal일 듯.

200. **purging** = discharging.

200-1. **amber, gum** = resins from trees 「(나무의) 진」.

201. **wit** = wisdom, understanding.

202. **hams** = thighs and buttocks.

203. **most powerfully and potently believe** = most thoroughly believe.

potently = mightily. powerfully과 동의어.

204-5. **I hold⋯set down** = it should not be printed, for decency's sake.

204. **not honesty** = not decent.

honesty = honest or honourable behaviour, decency.

205-6. **for you⋯backward** = 「만약 게처럼 거꾸로 나이를 먹는다면 당신도 나처럼 노인이 될 수 있다」. Hamlet은 Polonius를 자기가 늙고 Polonius가 젊은 것으로 역할을 바꾸고 이치에 닿지 않는 말로 Polonius를 어리둥절하게 만들고 있다.

206. **old** = as old.

if like a crab you could go backward = 게가 옆으로 기는 모습을 마치 거꾸로 걷는 것으로 묘사.

go backward = 「역행하다」, 「나이를 거꾸로 먹다」.

207-8. **Though this be madness, yet there is method in 't** = 「미치기는 했으나 말은 씨가 먹었다」. 이 말은 19세기 구라파 언어학자들이 예외 속에도 규칙이 있다는 사실을 발견한 뒤 There is no rule without exception이라는 속담을 There is no exception without rule (Keine Regel ohne Ausnahme)이라고 바꿔 말했던 일을 연상시킨다.

208. **method** = a certain orderliness.

209. **walk out of the air** = walk out of the air of the lobby. 「바깥 찬바람을 피하다」. 지금 말을 주고받는 장소가 lobby이므로 실제의 뜻은 찬 공기가 몸에 좋지 않으므로 「방안으로 들어가자」는 뜻이다. 그러나 Hamlet은 이 말을 「사바세계의 공기를 버리다」의 뜻으로 받고 있다.

212. **pregnant** = full of meaning. 출산과 관계된 이 말은 breed, conception, delivered of 등과 짝으로 사용되고 있다.

212-3. **a happiness** = aptness of phrasing, a felicitous turn of expression 「절묘한 표현」. cf. happy phrase.

213. **hits on** = find by chance.

214. **could not so prosperously be delivered of** = could not manage to express so pointedly and neatly.

prosperously be delivered of = give successful birth to. deliver (분만하다)는 위의 pregnant나 conception 등과 짝으로 쓴 말.

prosperously = effectively.

215. **suddenly** = immediately.

219-20. **You cannot⋯withal** = There is nothing in my possession that I could give more willingly than that (i.e. 'leave'). Polonius와 헤어지는 것이 무엇보다 기쁘다는 뜻.

withal = with의 강조형. 항상 문장 끝에 놓인다.

223. **These tedious old fools!** = How tedious these old men are!

225. **God save you** = God bless you!

228. **excellent** = extremely.

231. **As the indifferent children of the earth** = as men whose lot on earth is in neither extreme.

   indifferent = neither good nor bad, ordinary, average.

232. **Happy, in that we are not the over-happy** = happy in the fact that we are not at such a dizzy height of fortune that we need fear a sudden fall. over-happy가 ever(= always) happy가 된 판본도 있다.

233. **the very button** = knob on the top of a cap.

236-7. **about her…favour** = 「그녀의 허리 근처나 아니면 은총의 한 가운데」. 성적인 함의가 들어 있다.

237. **favour** = sexual favour.

238. **privates** = intimates 「친구」, 「졸병」. 이 단어에는 「여인의 음부」라는 뜻도 있다. Hamlet은 다음 줄에서 일부러 이것을 private or secret parts (of women)의 뜻으로 받아 되묻고 있다. pun의 예.

240. **strumpet** = a fickle, a prostitute. 운명의 여신은 변덕쟁이이므로 창녀에 비유되기도 한다.

241-2. **the world's grown honest** = What's the news?라는 물음에 이처럼 대답하는 것이 당대의 관례적인 농담이었다.

243. **doomsday** = the Day of Judgement. 「요한 묵시록」의 '최후 심판의 날(doomsday)'이 다가오면 사람들은 두려움에 정직해질 것이다.

244. **more in particular** = more closely as to the particulars of your situation.

245-6. **What have you…of Fortune** = 「무슨 잘못을 했기에 운명의 여

신으로부터 (…하게) 되었는가?」

250. **Then is the world one** = then must the whole world be a prison, if Denmark, so happy and free, is one.

251. **goodly** = large, spacious.

252. **confines** = places of confinement, prisons.

wards = cells 「독방」.

dungeons = 「토굴」.

256. **thinking makes it so** = unless it is made so by thinking it to be good or bad 「생각할 나름이다」.

258. **your ambition makes it one** = it seems to you so because you are too ambitious to be satisfied with your own subordinate position.

260. **I could be bounded in a nutshell** = I could easily be satisfied with the narrowest limits.

bounded in a nutshell = 「호도껍데기 안에 갇히다」.

263-5. **for the very…dream** = what the ambitious man succeeds in doing or acquiring is but a shadow of what he would like to, it being merely the reflection of a dream.

264. **substance** = 「실체」. 다음 줄의 shadow와 반대되는 말.

265. **shadow of a dream** = 「꿈이 그려내는 희미한 것」.

269-71. **Then are…shadows** = if ambition is but a shadow's shadow, then beggars (who are without ambition) are the only humans with substantial bodies, and kings and heroes (ruled by ambition) are only the beggars' shadow.

269. **our beggars** = 일반적인 대상을 지칭하는 'our'.

bodies = substances.

271. **outstretch'd heroes** = strutting heroes 「점잔빼는 영웅들」.

271. **Shall we to the court?** = shall we go to the court?

fay = faith.

272. **reason** = discuss, argue.

273. **wait upon you** = accompany you, serve. Hamlet은 이것을 「시중 든다」(act as your servants)는 문자 그대로의 뜻으로 받고 있다.

274. **No such matter** = I cannot allow of that (= of your waiting upon me) 「말도 안 된다」.

        sort you with = put you in the same class with 「같이 취급하다」.

276. **I am most dreadfully attended** = My attendants are a very bad lot. 지나친 감시를 받고 있다는 뜻도 된다. Hamlet을 감시하러 온 두 사람에 대한 비아냥거림도 섞여 있다.

277. **in the beaten way of friendship** = in the ordinary way of friendship 「친구로서 (묻네만)」.

        beaten way = well-trodden track.

277-8. **what make you···?** = what are you doing···? what has made you come here···? Rosencrantz는 후자의 뜻으로 받아드렸다.

279. **occasion** = business, reason, motive.

280. **Beggar that I am, I am even poor in thanks** = so utterly a beggar am I that I have hardly thanks to give you.

        even = 판본에 따라서는 ever로 된 곳도 있다. 그 때의 뜻은 「나 는 고마움을 표시하는 데 늘 인색했다」가 될 것이다.

281. **sure** = surely.

282. **too dear a halfpenny** = not worth a halfpenny [héipəni].

282-3. **Were you not sent for?** = I fancy you were sent for by the king.

283. **Is it your own inclining?** = did you come of your own accord?

        inclining = inclination.

283-4. **Is it a free visitation?** = have you come to visit me of your own free will?

        visitation = visit.

284. **deal** = act.

285. **nay, speak** = nay, do not hesitate, but speak out.

286. **should we say** = ought we to say, do you wish us to say?

287. **anything, but to the purpose** = say anything so long as it is to the point 「무엇이든 씨 먹은 말을 해주게」. 그러나 판본에 따라서는 any thing뒤에 comma가 없는 경우도 있다. 그 때의 뜻은 say anything so long as it is not to the point라는 비아냥거림이 된다. 즉, 어차피 나를 염탐하러 온 너희들이 하는 말이란 씨 먹지 않은 말일 테지, 라는 뜻이 깔려있다. 이와 같은 애매성은 작가가 의도적으로 시도했을 수도 있다.

288-90. **there is … colour** = I can see in your looks a sort of confession which your natural ingenuousness prevents you from disguising as you would do if you were more crafty.

289. **your modesties** = 대명사가 복수일 때 추상명사의 복수형을 사용하는 당시의 관례.

   modesties = modest or decent natures.

290. **colour** = disguise.

292. **To what end** = with what object.

293. **That you must teach me** = nay, that is for you to tell me, not for me to guess.

293. **conjure** = earnestly entreat, beseech.

294. **rights** = justifiable claim (of our fellowship).

   the consonancy of our youth = the harmony we enjoyed when we were younger.

   consonancy = accord, agreement, harmony.

296-7. **by what … withal** = by any stronger motive that a more skilful speaker could appeal to you by.

296. **ever-preserved love** = 「오래 지켜온 사랑」.

   by what more dear = by whatever is more valuable.

297. **proposer** = one who propounds something for consideration 「선창자」. cf. I. v. 152. propose the oath.

charge you withal = urge you with 「너희들에게 요구할 (맹서)」.
charge = exhort.

297-8. **be even and direct** = be honest and straightforward. even, direct 모두 straightforward의 뜻.

301-2. **Nay, then, I have an eye of you** = ah, if you hesitate and whisper together, I see plainly there is something you wish to hide; my eye is upon you and you cannot deceive me.
have an eye of = watch.
of = on.

302. **hold not off** = do not keep aloof from me, do not hesitate to speak out plainly.
hold off = keep at a distance, maintain a reserve.

304-5. **so shall···discovery** = my saying it first will save you from having to tell me your secret.

305. **my anticipation prevent your discovery** = my saying it first will keep you from having to reveal it 「내가 미리 말해버림으로써 너희들이 비밀을 누설하지 않도록 해준다」.
prevent = go before and so hinder, anticipate, forestall.
discovery = disclosure.

305-6. **your secrecy···feather** = your good faith to the king and queen, which binds you to secrecy in the matter, will not suffer in the smallest particular.
your secrecy to the King = 「왕의 신임」.

306. **moult no feather** = lose none of its feathers, not suffer in the slightest degree.
moult = shed feathers in the process of renewing plumage 「털갈이 때 털이 빠지다」.

307. **wherefore** = why.
mirth = fun.

308. **foregone all custom of exercises** = completely abandoned all those exercises which were customary with me. 당시의 평상적인 운동은 펜싱이나 정구, 승마.

309. **it goes so heavily with my disposition** = my spirit in general are so depressed.

309-15. **this goodly frame…vapours** = 기원 2세기 이래 유럽을 지배해 온 Ptolemy의 천동설은 Copernicus(1473-1543)의 지동설에 의해 뒤집히게 된다. 이른바 코페르니쿠스적 전환이라는 대 사건에 의해 하나님의 말씀(로고스)에 의한 세계창조의 원리도 뒤집히게 된다. 하늘과 땅의 질서가 뒤바뀐 혼돈의 세계를 묘사하고 있다.

310. **this goodly frame, the earth** = this excellent structure, the earth. 여기서 frame은 당시 Shakespeare의 연극이 공연되던『지구극장』(Globe Playhouse)를 지칭하기도 한다.
frame = structure.

310-1. **sterile promontory** = barren headland 「황량한 갑」. Hamlet 역의 배우는 무대의 맨 앞쪽에 서서 그곳이 마치 갑인 양 이 대사를 읊게 된다.

310. **promontory** = land jutting out into the sea.
most excellent canopy = supremely beautiful covering (sky). Hamlet은 지금『지구극장』의 천장(the heavens라고 불렀다)을 가리키며 이 대사를 하고 있다. 천장에는 12궁과 태양, 달, 별들이 금빛으로 그려져 있었다.

311-3. **canopy, firmament, roof** = sky, heaven.

312. **look you** = 상대방의 주의를 끌기 위해 쓰는 말.
brave = fine, glorious, splendid.

313. **fretted** = adorned (especially a ceiling).

315. **piece** = masterpiece.

316. **in reason** = in the matter of reason.

317.	**faculty** = mental power, capacity.

317. **faculty** = mental power, capacity.

form and moving = shape and motion.

express = exact, fitted to its purpose, well-framed.

319. **apprehension** = understanding.

319-20. **the beauty of the world** = the supreme excellence of creation.

319. **beauty** = ornament.

320. **the paragon of animals** = peerless among things endowed with life.

paragon = a model of excellence, supreme example.

321. **quintessence** = 「먼지의 정수」란 인간을 말한다. cf. *Genesis* 3:19. Thou art dust, and to dust thou shalt return. quintessence(= fifth essence)란 천체를 형성하는 4원소(four elements (earth, water, air, fire)) 이외에 만물 속에 잠재하는 것으로 여겨졌던 원소를 말한다.

322-3. **though…say so** = 「너희들이 웃는 것을 보니 여자라면 그렇지 않다고 말하는 것 같네만」. man이 humankind(인간)와 the male sex(남자)라는 두 뜻이 있어 이런 표현이 가능하다.

325. **there was no such stuff in my thoughts** = my mind was not filled with any such thought.

no such stuff = nothing of the kind.

328. **To think** = at the thought 「…라는 생각을 하니」.

329. **lenten entertainment** = poor, meager welcome.

lenten = meagre, scanty. 기독교의 Lent(사순절)에서 온 말. 기독교인들이 예수의 고행을 기리는 성회 수요일(Ash Wednesday)부터 부활절 일요일(Easter) 전날까지의 40일간. 이 기간 동안 당시 극장은 모두 휴관했었다.

entertainment = reception, welcome.

players = actors. 당시 덴마크에서는 영국에서와 마찬가지로 배우들이 수입을 위해 지방 공연을 다녔다.

330. **coted** = overtook and passed, outstripped「추월했다」.

333. **his majesty** =「폐하」.

    shall have tribute = shall receive from me the tribute of applause.

    tribute = payment, praise.

333-4. **adventurous knight** = the knight-errant who goes in quest of adventures.

334. **shall use his foil and target** = shall have full opportunity of displaying his valour.

    foil = light fencing sword.

    target(= targe) = light shield.

335. **the lover shall not sigh gratis** = the lover shall be rewarded for playing his pathetic part「애인의 한숨에 대해선 충분한 보상을 하겠다」. 요즘 말로 팁을 후하게 주겠다는 뜻.

    gratis = for nothing, without reward「공짜로, 무보수로」.

335-6. **the humorous…peace** = the capricious man shall have his full opportunity of venting his spleen.

335. **humorous man** = the actor playing the eccentric character.

    humorous = capricious, whimsical, moody.

336. **clown** = the actor who plays the comic roles.

337. **tickle o' the sere** = easily made to laugh.

    tickle = unstable, insecure.

    sere = part of gun-lock which keeps the hammer at full or half cock「(총의) 걸쇠」.

    lungs =「허파」는 웃음이 생기는 곳.

338-40. **the lady…for 't** = the lady shall talk as freely as she likes, or her delivery of blank verse will lose its rhythm.

338. **the lady** = the actor playing the female role.

    freely = unreservedly「기탄없이」.

339. **blank verse** =「무운시(無韻詩)」. 운을 맞추지 않는 시.

Shakespeare는 「소네트」는 운을 맞췄으나, 희곡은 무운시로 썼다.

halt for 't = 「흐름이 막힌다」.

halt = limp.

341.　　**were wont to** = used to, accustomed.

342.　　**tragedians** = actors. 배우 전반을 가리키며, 특별히 「비극배우」만을 지칭하지 않는다.

　　　the city = 연극의 배경은 Denmark이지만 Shakespeare나 관중의 머릿속의 city는 London이다.

343.　　**How chances it** = How does it come about (that).

　　　travel = on tour in the provinces 「지방 순회공연을 하다」.

344.　　**residence** = remaining in the city.

345.　　**both ways** = reputation과 profit의 중복으로 없어도 무방하다.

346.　　**inhibition** = prohibition (perhaps against playing in the city). 이것은 반드시 관에 의한 금지라기보다는 다음에서 보는 소년극단의 인기에 밀려 하는 수 없이 지방공연에 나서게 된 사정을 말하는 듯.

347.　　**the late innovation** = *Hamlet*이 쓰인 1601년에 일어난 Essex 백작의 반란을 지칭한다는 설과 바로 뒤에서 언급되는 소년배우극단의 등장을 뜻한다는 설이 있다.

　　　late = recent.

　　　innovation = alteration for the worse, political upheaval.

348.　　**estimation** = reputation.

349-50.　**so followed** = so much run after 「그때만큼 인기가 있다」.

352.　　**Do they grow rusty?** = is their acting less sprightly than before?

353-4.　**their endeavour⋯pace** = not in the least, they take just as much pains as usual 「옛날만큼 노력하고 있다」.

　　　keeps in the wonted pace = continues as usual.

　　　in = at.

354. **aery** [έəri] = nest or brood (of hawks).

aery of children = 당시 새로 생긴 *The Children of the Chapel Royal*의 boy actors.

355. **eyases** [áiəsiz] = young hawks taken form the nest for the purpose of training, or one whose training is incomplete.

cry out on the top of question = speak their lines in loud, shrill voices. 소년 배우들의 대사를 외우는 모습을 새끼들이 먹이를 받아먹겠다고 마구 짖어대는 모습에 빗대고 있다. 당시 소년 배우들은 대사가 관객 모두에게 들리도록 필요이상으로 소리를 지르도록 훈련받고 있었다.

question = talk, conversation.

356. **tyrannically clapp'd** = fiercely applauded 「열광적인 박수를 받다」.

tyrannically = vehemently, outrageously.

357. **berattle** = fill or assail with din. 여기서는 berate the public theaters 「마구 험담을 한다」는 뜻.

common stage = 이른바 public stage. *The Children of the Chapel*(『소녀극단』)의 공연이 이루어지는 *Blackfriars Theatre*는 이른바 private stage여서 입장료도 비싸고 주로 특권계급의 관객이 이용한 반면 Shakespeare의 연극이 공연되는 *Globe Theatre*는 public stage라고 불리었다.

359. **many wearing rapiers** [réipiəz] = fashionable gentlemen 「칼을 차고 극장에 오던 많은 관객들」.

360. **goose-quills** = 「소년 배우들을 위해 극본을 쓰는 극작가들」.

dare scarce come thither = i.e. lest the world think them behind the times 「시대에 뒤떨어졌다고 생각될 까봐 거의 오지 않는다」.

362. **escoted** = paid, financially supported.

363. **pursue the quality no longer than they can sing** = follow the

acting profession only until their voices change in adolescence.

363. **quality** = (actor's) profession.

no longer than = only so long as.

365. **common players** = common stage의 adult actors.

366. **if their means are no better** =「더 나은 벌이가 없다면」.

means = pecuniary means.

367-8. **exclaim against their own succession** = attack the careers they will follow. 어릴 때는 극작가가 써주는 대로 common players의 흉을 보지만 결국 자신들도 나이 들어서는 common players가 될 것이므로 자신들의 미래의 모습을 헐뜯고 있는 결과가 된다.

exclaim against = rail at「욕을 퍼붓다, 악담하다」.

succession = the future.

369. **to do** = ado, trouble.

370. **tarre** [tɑ:] = provoke, incite「도발하다」.

371-3. **There was⋯question** = no plays were salable that did not take up the quarrel between the children's poets and the adult players.

371-2. **no money bid** = no money was offered by theatrical managers「투자할 사람이 없다」.

372. **bid** = offered.

argument = plot of a play「줄거리」.

poet =「(소년 배우들을 위해 각본을 쓰는) 작가」.

373. **went to cuffs** = strike with an open hand「주먹다짐을 하다」.

question = dispute.

375-6. **much throwing about of brains** = plenty of lively wit-contest.

377. **carry it away** = carry off the prize, gain victory.

378. **that they do** = assuredly they do.

378-9. **Hercules and his load** = 그리스 신화에 나오는 장사 Hercules는 보통 어깨에 지구(globe)를 메고 있는 모습으로 그려진다. 그런데 이 그림은 Shakespeare의 연극이 상연되던 *Globe Theatre*의

간판이기도 했다. 이런 말장난으로 Shakespeare는 *Globe Theatre*도 다 함께 소년 극단에 압도되었다는 사실을 넌지시 비추고 있다.

380. **It is not strange** = there is nothing very strange in this change of fashion. 여기서 Hamlet은 극장 관객의 변덕과 덴마크 국민의 선친 국왕으로부터 숙부의 새 왕으로의 변절을 대비시키고 있다.

381. **make mows** = make derisive grimaces 「입을 이죽거리다」.
mow = (derisive) grimace.

383. **picture in little** = miniature picture. Hamlet은 초소형 초상화를 소년 배우들에게 빗대고 있다.

384. **'Sblood** [zblʌd] = God's blood로서 맹서할 때 쓰는 강한 감탄사.

384-5. **more than natural** = abnormal.

388. **Your hands** = Give your hands. Guildenstern과 Rosencrantz에게 악수를 청하면서 하는 말.
come then = do not hesitate to shake hands with me. 「어서」.
the appurtenance of welcome is fashion and ceremony = ceremonious courtesy is an essential part of welcome.
appurtenance = that which belongs to something, proper accompaniment. 「(환영에) 수반하는 것」, 즉 「악수」.

389. **fashion and ceremony** = ceremonious courtesy. 여기서는 악수를 뜻한다.

389-93. **Let me…yours** = let me show courtesy to you by the outward formality of shaking hands, lest in that welcome which I shall hold out to the players, — a courtesy that must be evidenced by formal civilities, — I should seem to be giving them a warmer reception than I do to you.
Let me comply with you in this garb = let me show you

ceremony in this manner (i.e. by shaking hands).

comply with you = exchange courtesies with you.

garb = manner (i.e. by shaking hands). Shakespeare에서는 「복장」의 뜻으로는 사용되지 않는다.

extent = extension of welcome.

391-2. **must show fairly outward** = 「보기에 친절해야 한다」.

show = appear.

fairly outward = obviously.

392-3. **more appear like entertainment than yours** = 「당신들보다 더 환영하는 것처럼 보이면 (안 되니까)」.

392. **entertainment** = reception, welcome.

393. **yours** = the welcome Hamlet has given Rosencrantz and Guildenstern.

394. **uncle-father and aunt-mother** = 국왕 Claudius는 Hamlet의 삼촌이면서 계부이며, 왕비는 어머니이지만 삼촌과 결혼함으로써 Hamlet의 삼촌어머니가 되었다.

are deceived = are deceived in my madness.

396. **I am but mad north-north-west** = I am mad only when the wind is in the north-north-west. 이 말은 분명히 매사냥과 관계가 있다. 보통 왜가리처럼 몸집이 크고 둔한 새들을 놀라게 하면 바람을 등에 지고 바람과 함께 도망간다. 따라서 바람이 북쪽에서 불어올 때 왜가리는 남쪽으로 날아가게 되고, 보는 사람은 햇빛 때문에 눈이 부셔서 그것이 매인지 왜가리인지 구분하지 못하게 된다. 반면 바람이 남쪽에서 불어올 때면 매는 북쪽으로 날아가게 되고, 사냥꾼은 해를 등지게 되므로 힘들이지 않고 매와 왜가리를 구분할 수 있게 된다. 더 정확히 말해서 바람이 북북서에서 불어오는 것은 오전 10시 반 경이어서 한참 눈이 부실 때이다. 이 밖에 바람이 사람을 미치게 한다는 옛 의술의 지식을 원용하려는 시도도 있으나 위의 설명만 못하다.

397.　　**a hawk from a handsaw** = a hawk from hernshaw(= heron(왜가리))의 잘못으로 읽는다. 만약에 handsaw를 「(한손으로 켜는) 톱」이라고 읽으면 그 때는 hawk를 「흙받기」로 읽어야 한다. 실제로 그런 번역이 있기는 하나 「톱」과 「흙받기」의 구별은 너무 자명하다. 한편 양자를 「매」와 그의 먹잇감인 「왜가리」로 놓고 볼 때, 양자의 구별이 쉽지 않을 뿐만 아니라, 국왕과 Hamlet, 그리고 Hamlet의 비밀을 찾아내려고 온 두 친구와 Hamlet의 관계를 각각 「매」와 「왜가리」의 대비로 암시하는 재미가 생긴다. 다시 말해 Hamlet은 이 두 사람이 찾아온 까닭을 훤히 알고 있다는 암시를 하고 있다.

398.　　**Well be with you** = may things be well with you, I wish you well. 약간 현학적인 당시엔 흔치 않은 인사.

399.　　**Hark you** = listen.

400.　　**at each ear a hearer** = let each of you lend me an ear.
　　　　that great baby = Polonius.

401.　　**not out of his swaddling-clouts** = 「아직 포대기를 벗어나지 못했다」.
　　　　swaddling-clouts = narrow strips of cloth wrapped around a baby to restrict its movement.

402.　　**Happily** = possibly, perhaps, by chance.
　　　　the second time = the second childhood.

403.　　**them** = swaddling-clouts.

403-4.　**an old man is twice a child** = 속담이다.

403.　　**twice** = a second time.

405.　　**prophesy** = foretell.

406.　　**mark it** = observe the outcome.

406-7.　**You say … indeed** = it is just as you say, it did happen on Monday morning. Hamlet이 Guildenstern, Rosencrantz 두 사람과 Polonius에 대한 이야기를 하고 있던 것을 감추기 위해 갑자기

딴전을 피우고 있다.

409. **My lord, I have news to tell you** = nay, my lord, first hear what I have to say.

410. **Roscius** [rɔ́ʃiəs] = 고대 로마 최고의 배우. Hamlet은 먼저 배우 이야기를 꺼냄으로써 Polonius의 기선을 제압하고 있다.

412. **Buz, Buz!** = nonsense, nonsense! 「또 그 얘기!」. 뻔한 이야기를 할 때의 야지.

414. **Then came each actor on his ass** = 옛 ballad에서 인용한 듯. Then은 410행의 When에 연결된다. 바로 앞줄에서 Polonius가 Upon mine honour라고 한 것에 (up)on his ass라고 맞장구를 쳐서 조롱하고 있다.

416-9. **for tragedy…unlimited** = 엘리자베스 조 당대의 연극 형태들을 열거하고 있다. 원래 고전극에서는 연극의 장르를 뒤섞는 법이 없이 엄격히 분리돼 있었다. 이를테면 tragi-comedy(희비극) 따위는 존재하지 않았다. *The Merchant of Venice*를 희비극의 예로 들 수 있다.

418. **scene individable** = play which observes unity of place. 아리스토텔레스는 그의 *Poetics*(『시학』)에서 연극은 하나의 이야기가 하나의 장소에서 하루에 이루어진 것이어야 한다는 「3위 통합」의 법칙을 내세웠다.

419. **poem unlimited** = poetical drama which disregards the limitations of time and place. Shakespeare 자신처럼 「3위 통합」의 법칙을 무시하는 연극.
Seneca = 고대 로마의 스토아 철학가이며 가장 뛰어난 비극작가.
Plautus = 고대 로마의 가장 뛰어난 희극작가. 이 두 사람은 Shakespeare를 위시하여 엘리자베스 조 연극에 적지 않은 영향을 미쳤다.

420-1. **For the law of writ and the liberty** = for plays that follow the classical rules of composition and those that do not.

writ = writing.

421.   **these are the only men** = these actors are the best available. 이 부분을 Seneca and Plautus are the only great dramatists로 해석 하기도 하지만 these를 actors로 보는 것이 타당할 듯.

422.   **Jephthah, judge of Israel** = 구약성서(*Judges*(사사기) 11: 30-40) 에 의하면 Jephthah는 Ammon 사람들과의 싸움에 나가기에 앞 서 싸움에 이기고 돌아올 때 제일 먼저 뛰어나오는 사람을 제물 로 바치겠다고 신에게 맹세한다. 그런데 막상 승리하고 돌아온 그를 맞이하기 위해 맨 먼저 뛰어나온 것은 그의 외동딸이었다. 맹세를 어길 수 없어 그는 딸을 제물로 바친다. Hamlet은 자기 마음을 떠보기 위해 딸을 미끼/제물로 사용하고 있는 Polonius 를 이스라엘의 사사 Jephthah에 빗대고 있다.

426-7.   **One fair…well** = 구약성서 *Judges* 11:30-40에 근거를 둔 옛날 ballad의 일부분. 원문은 다음과 같다.

I read that many yeare agoe,

When one fair Daughter and no more,

    whom he loved so passing well.

And as by lot, God wot,

It came to passe, most like it was,

Great warrs there should be,

    and who should be the chiefe, but he

427.   **The which** = which. which는 지금과는 달리 사람에게도 사용되 었다.

loved [-id]

passing = surpassingly, exceedingly.

428.   **still** = always.

432.   **Nay, that follows not** = Hamlet은 follows의 뜻을 애매하게 사용 하고 있다. Your analogy between yourself and Jephthah is false

와 That isn't the next line in the ballad의 두 뜻이 가능하며, Polonius는 첫 번째 뜻으로, Hamlet은 두 번째 뜻으로 사용하고 있다.

435. **lot** = chance.

   God wot = God knows.

438. **first row of the pious chanson** = first line of the religious song.

   pious chanson [ʃάːnsɔn] = sacred song.

439. **abridgement** = means of shortening or whiling away the time. 즉 those who cut short my remarks(내 말을 중단해서 더 이상 말하지 않게 해주는 사람들)와 pastime, entertainment의 두 뜻 이 있다. 결국 둘 다 배우들을 가리킨다.

440. **masters** = 「여러분」.

442. **valanced** = fringed with a beard. 본래는 curtained, draped의 뜻. 프랑스의 유명한 비단 산지인 Valence(Lyon 근처)에서 온 말.

443. **beard** = oppose openly, provoke.

444. **lady** = the boy actor who played female roles.

445. **my young lady and mistress** = 여성의 역할을 맡는 소년배우 (boy actor)에게 한 말. 당시 배우는 모두 남자여서 여자의 역할 은 변성기 이전의 어린 소년들이 맡았다. 참고로 처음으로 여성 배우가 등장한 것은 1660년에 공연된 *Othello*의 Desdemona이 다.

   By'r [baiə] **lady** = By our lady, i.e. the Virgin Mary 「성모마리아 의 이름을 걸고」.

   your ladyship = 「여사」.

   nearer to heaven = taller.

447. **by the altitude of a chopine** = by the height of the thick sole of a shoe called chopine 「구두 뒷굽만큼 키가 자랐다」. 실제로 는 작년보다 키가 더 자랐을 터인데 이것을 Hamlet은 농담 삼 아 뒷굽의 탓으로 돌리고 있다.

chopine [tʃopi:n] = high-soled shoe. 지금의 「하이힐」.

Pray God = I pray God.

447-8. **your voice…ring** = 금화는 종종 나쁜 사람들에 의해 모서리가 깎이는 경우가 있었는데, 금화에 새겨진 임금님의 얼굴 초상을 둘러싼 테(ring) 안쪽까지 깎인(cracked) 금화는 통용되지 못했다(uncurrent). 한편 소년배우의 황금 같은 목소리의 울림(ring)에 금이 가면(cracked), 즉 변성하면 그는 더 이상 여성인물의 역할을 맡을 수 없게 된다. 한편 ring은 여성의 가장 중요한 부분에 대한 은어이기도 하다. Shakespeare는 소년배우의 목소리에 금이 가는 것은 소녀가 처녀성을 잃는 것과 같다고 생각하고 있는지 모른다.

448. **uncurrent** = out of circulation.

crack'd within the ring = changed to an adult males's voice, hence making you unfit for women's roles.

449. **We'll e'en to 't** = We will go about it at once.

450. **French falconers** = 「프랑스인 매부리」. 조급한 프랑스인에 대한 조롱으로 들리나 실제로 당시 프랑스 매부리는 유명했다.

falconer = a person who hunts with hawks 「매사냥꾼, 매부리」.

fly at anything we see = undertake anything, no matter how difficult.

fly at = launch the birds 「사냥감을 향해 (매를) 날리다」.

451. **straight** = immediately, at once.

451-2. **give us a taste of your quality** = give us a specimen of your capabilities.

quality = professional ability. 여기서는 acting ability.

454. **me** = for me.

455. **it** = the play containing the speech.

was never acted = 「무대에 오르지는 못했다」.

457. **the million** = the multitude.

caviare to the general = too refined for the multitude 「돼지에 진주」.

caviare [kǽvià:] = 「캐비아」. 철갑상어의 알젓. 당시 일반인들은 그 맛을 잘 몰랐다.

general = 「대중」.

458. **as I received it** = in my opinion.

   receive = believe.

459. **cried in the top of mine** = spoke with more authority than mine.

   in the top of = above.

460. **well digested in the scenes** = well organized into scenes.

   digested = ordered, arranged.

   set down = written.

461. **modesty** = moderation, propriety, restraint.

   cunning = art, skill 「기교」.

462. **one said** = it was said by somebody.

462-3. **no sallets⋯savoury** = nothing piquant to give the lines a relish.

   sallets = something tasty, piquant ingredients 「양념」. 여기서는 indelicate language. salads의 변형.

463. **nor no matter⋯affectation** = nothing in the language which could charge the author with affectation.

   no matter = nothing.

464. **indict** [indáit] = accuse.

   affectation = artificiality, excess emotion.

465. **honest method** = straightforward (unpretentious) effort of composition.

465-6. **as wholesome as sweet** = equally sensible and pleasant.

466-7. **by very⋯fine** = with a very great deal more of real beauty in it than of tawdry splendour, rich not gaudy.

466. **by very much** = by far.

more handsome than fine = with more natural grace than artful workmanship.

handsome = graceful, decent. 자연스러운 아름다움을 나타내며 fine과 대비된다.

467. **fine** = highly accomplished or skilful, exquisitely fashioned, delicately beautiful, gaudy. 기교적인 아름다움을 나타낸다.

468. **Æneas' tale to Dido** = Virgil의 *Æneid*에서 주인공 Æneas는 Troy가 함락된 뒤 서쪽으로 도망가다 Carthage에 들르게 되어 여왕 Dido에게 Troy 전쟁에 대한 이야기를 하게 된다. Dido는 Æneas를 사랑하지만 Æneas는 그곳을 떠난다.

thereabout of it = around that part of it 「대강 그 근처」.

469. **Priam** [práiəm] = Troy의 왕으로서 Pyrrhus에게 살해된다.

472. **rugged** = fierce, savage.

Pyrrhus [píros] = Achilles의 아들로서 아버지의 원수를 갚기 위해 Troy 전쟁에 참가해 용맹을 떨친 전설적 영웅. 유명한 Troy 목마(476행의 ominous horse)의 뱃속에 들어가 Troy 성 안으로 쳐들어간 용사들 가운데 한 사람. Priam을 살해함으로써 아버지의 원수를 갚는다.

Hyrcanian [həkéiniən] **beast** = tiger. Hyrcania 는 Caspian Sea의 남동부에 위치한 고대 아시아의 나라 이름. 지금의 이란.

sable arms = black armour.

475. **resemble** = 주어는 앞줄의 sable arms.

476. **lay couched** = lay concealed.

the ominous horse = 「Troy의 목마」.

ominous [ɔ́mnəs] = threatening.

477. **this dred and black complexion** = this dreadful and dark appearance.

complexion = appearance. 얼굴뿐만 아니라 몸 전체.

478. **With heraldry more dismal** = with a tincture (as it is called in

heraldry) of more dismal colour. The blood Pyrrhus has smeared on his face is seen as the equivalent of the heraldic markings on his armour.

heraldry = heraldic device, blazonry 「문장(紋章)의 색」.

dismal = grim, dreadful, ill-omened.

479. **total gules** [gju:lz] = red with blood from head to foot.

gules = heraldic name for 'red'. 문장학의 용어.

tricked = smeared. 문장학의 용어.

481. **Bak'd and impasted with** = cooked (by the heat of the streets) and made into a pastry or crust.

impasted = made into a paste, encrusted 「떡지다」. Bak'd와 함께 앞줄의 blood에 걸린다.

the parching streets = 그리스 군의 침입에 의해 불타고 있는 Troy 거리.

parching = burning, scorching.

482. **tyrannous** = cruel, fierce, outrageous.

dammed = [-id]

483. **their lord's murders** = the (impending) murder of Priam, lord of Troy.

Roasted in wrath and fire = 485행의 the hellish Pyrrhus를 수식하는 말. 479행의 trick'd, 481행의 Bak'd and impasted, 그리고 484행의 o'ver-sized도 모두 Pyrrhus를 수식한다.

wrath = warlike ardour.

484. **o'er-sized** [id] = covered over as with size.

size = a sort of glue 「아교」의 일종.

coagulate [koǽgjulit] **gore** = clotted blood.

485. **carbuncles** = deep red jewels that in myth were said to glow in the dark 「석류석」.

486. **grandsire** = grandfather.

487. **So, proceed you** = go on from that point.

489. **with good accent and good discretion** = with good pronunciation and judgement.

    discretion = judgment, discernment 「신중, 분별, 사리」.

490. **Anon** = presently, soon.

    he finds him = Pyrrhus finds Priam.

491. **Striking too short** = unable to reach his opponents with his sword. 의미상의 주어는 Priam.

    antique [⌣ ×] = ancient.

492. **Rebellious to his arm** = refusing to obey his arm, i.e. his arm being too weak to wield it.

    lies where it falls = 「떨어진 칼을 주어 올릴 기운도 없다」.

493. **Repugnant** = opposing, resisting.

    unequal match'd = more than a match for the old man.

    unequal = unequally.

494. **at Priam drives** = aims at Priam.

    in rage strikes wide = in his fury misses his blow.

    strike wide = 「빗나가다」.

495. **whiff and wind** = mere disturbance of the air.

    fell = cruel, fierce.

496. **unnerved** [-id] = rendered nerveless, weak, enfeebled.

    father = old man.

    senseless = incapable of perceiving.

    Illium = tower of Troy, Priam's palace.

498. **Stoops to his base** = falls down.

    his base = its foundation.

499. **Takes prisoner…ear** = stupefies him for the moment with its din.

500. **declining** = about to fall upon.

    milky = white-haired.

501. **stick** = remain fixed, stand out in relief.

502. **as painted tyrant** = 「그림에 그려진 폭군처럼 (칼을 든 채 서있다)」.

503. **like a neutral to his will and matter** = one suspended between his intention and its fulfillment.

     neutral to = a man indifferent to, not siding with either.

505. **see** = experience.

     against = in advance of, just before.

506. **rack** = high clouds driven by the wind.

507. **orb** = the earth.

508. **hush** = hushed, silent.

509. **rend** = tear through.

     the region = the sky, heaven.

510. **sets him new a-work** = sets him working anew.

511. **Cyclops**[sáiklɔps] = 신화에 나오는 외눈박이 거인 대장장이. Vulcan위 조수로서 신들을 위한 투구와 무기를 만들었다.

512. **Mars** = 로마 신화의 전쟁의 신.

     for proof eterne = to be impenetrable for ever.

     eterne = eternal.

513. **remorse** = pity, mercy. 현대의 「후회, 가책」의 뜻은 없었다.

     bleeding = running with blood.

515. **Out, out** = 「혐오, 비난, 분노」를 나타내는 간투사.

     strumpet = prostitute. 운명의 여신을 변덕쟁이이므로 창녀에 비유되기도 한다.

516. **In general synod** = in full council 「전원회의」.

     synod = assembly of the gods.

517. **spokes** = 「(바퀴의) 살」.

     fellies = felloes = 「(바퀴의) 겉 테」.

     wheel = 운명의 여신은 눈을 가리고 마차를 타고 있는 것으로 묘사된다. 까닭도 모르고 이 마차에 깔려 죽는 것이 우리의 운명이기도 하다.

518. **nave** = 「(바퀴의) 통(hub)」.

hill of heaven = 아마도 신들의 집이 있는 Mount Olympus.

519. **fiends** = Devils.

521. **It shall to the barber's** = 긴 이야기를 수염에 비유해 이발소에 가서 자르라고 한 것은 당시의 상투적 농담이었다.

your beard = your는 Polonius를 가리킨다. 또 다른 해석은 your가 앞서 언급한 수염이 나기 시작한 소년배우를 가리킨다는 것으로서, Hamlet이 Polonius의 짜증에 동조하고 있다는 것을 나타낸다는 것이다.

522. **Prithee** = please, pray.

he's for a jig = he (= Polonius) would prefer a jig.

jig = comic entertainment including dancing, often performed as an after-piece to a tragedy.

a tale of bawdry = an obscene tale.

523. **Hecuba** [hékjubə] = Priam의 아내.

524. **who had seen** = whoever might have seen.

who = he who. 이 who는 533행에서 다시 반복된다.

525. **mobled** [-id] = muffled, veiled 「머리나 얼굴을 감싼」.

528. **Run** = 의미상의 주어는 mobled queen. 문법적으로는 525행의 who에 잇대어 who(= he who) had seen the mobed queen run barefoot이 된다.

528-9. **threatening the flames** = threatening to put out the flames.

529. **bisson** = blinding.

rheum = tears.

clout = a piece of cloth.

530. **diadem** = crown.

for = in place of.

531. **lank and all ov'er-teemed** [-id] **loins** = loins quite exhausted by excessive childbearing. Hecuba는 Priam의 애를 19명 낳은 것으로 알려져 있다.

532. **A blanket, in the alarm of fear caught up** = 「공포에 질려 급하게 집어 든 모포 한 장」.

533. **Who this had seen** = whoever had seen this.

 with tongue in venom steep'd = with a tongue steeped in poison.

534. **state** = power.

 would treason have pronounc'd = would have spoken treason against the rule of Fortune 「운명의 여신을 저주할 것이다」.

535. **did see** = had seen.

 then = 다음 줄의 When을 받는다.

536. **make malicious sport** = amuse himself maliciously.

537. **mincing** = cutting into small pieces.

538. **instant** = immediate.

 clamour = loud wailing.

539. **Unless things mortal move them not at all** = unless they(= gods) are utterly indifferent to the concerns of men 「신들이 인간사에 아주 무심치 않다면」.

540. **Would have made milch the burning eyes of heaven** = would have drawn tears from the burning eyes of heaven (as milk is drawn from the udder of a cow) 「하늘의 별들도 눈물짓게 했을 것이다」.

 milch = milk, i.e. wet with tears.

 eyes of heaven = stars.

541. **passion** = strong emotion.

542. **whe'er** = whether.

 he = 1. Player를 가리킨다.

 turn'd = changed.

543. **Pray you** = please. 배우에게 하는 말.

545. **speak out the rest** = complete the speech.

547. **well bestowed** = comfortably lodged.

548. **us'd** = treated.

they = players, actors.

abstracts = epitome, summary. 다른 판본에서는 abstract로 표시되어 후속하는 chronicles를 수식하는 형용사로 취급되고 있다. 그러나 Shakespeare는 abstract를 형용사로 사용한 경우가 없다.

549. **chronicles** = 「연대기」.

549-50. **you were better have** = it would be better for you to have.

550. **ill report** = 「험담」.

551. **I will use them according to their desert** = I will treat them as men in their station of life deserve to be treated 「신분 상응한 대접을 하겠다」.

use = treat.

554. **God's bodykins** = by God's dear body. 간투사. bodykin은 body 의 축소사. God'd body는 성찬식에서 사용하는 영성체(holy bread)가 예수의 살을 상징하는 것에서 나온 말.

555. **after** = according to.

desert = the facts of being worthy of reward or punishment.

556. **who should 'escape whipping** = nobody would escape whipping. 1572년의 법령에 의해 무허가 유랑 배우들(unlicensed players) 은 부랑자로 취급되어 태형(whipping)을 받았다.

556-7. **after your own honour and dignity** = with such courtesy and condescension as befits a man in your high position.

558. **bounty** = generosity.

561. **Dost thou⋯me** = please listen = can I have a word with you before you go?

563. **The Murder of Gonzago** [gɔnzágou] = III. ii. 274에서 Hamlet은

이것이 이탈리아 극이라고 말한다.

565. **ha't** = have it.

566. **for a need** = if it was necessary.

study = learn by heart. 연극 술어.

571. **mock him not** = 「그를 조롱하면 안 된다」. Hamlet이 Polonius를 대하는 태도를 보고 Polonius의 실력을 몰라 본 배우들이 말썽을 일으키지 않도록 주의 하는 말.

573. **Good my lord** = farewell.

576-634. Hamlet의 제3 독백.

576. **peasant slave** = base wretch, wretched bondman.

577. **monstrous** = unnatural, shocking.

578. **But in a fiction, in a dream of passion** = under the influence of nothing more real than a poet's creation, a mere imaginary passion.

But = merely.

579. **Could force his soul so to his own conceit** = could so constrain his soul so as to be in harmony with his imagination.

conceit = conception.

580. **from her working** = in response to the soul's activity.

her = the soul's.

wann'd = turned pale.

581. **distraction in's aspect** = frenzy, intensity of feeling, in his general appearance.

in's aspect [× ⌣́] = in his look.

582-3. **his whole…conceit** = everything about him completely matching in expression to what he is imagining.

585-6. **What's Hecuba…her?** = what relation is there between Hecuba and him that he should so sympathize with her woes? i.e. there is no such relation.

587. **motive** = incentive.

cue = motive for prompting 「계기」.

589. **cleave the general ear with horrid speech** = and split the ears of his audience with the horror of his words.

the general ear = ear of the public.

horrid = causing horror. 현대보다는 더 강한 뜻.

590. **Make mad the guilty and appal the free** = madden guilty spectators and terrify those who are innocent.

free = free from guilt, innocent.

591. **Confound the ignorant** = dumbfound the ignorant.

ignorant = uninformed. groundling 「무대 바로 앞의 입석(pit) 관객」을 가리킨다.

amaze = stupefy, paralyse, stun. 현대의 bewilder, astound보다는 더 강한 뜻.

592. **very faculties** = proper functions.

594. **muddy-mettled** = low-spirited.

muddy = inert and of lacking clarity. mettle을 metal과 pun으로 엮어 tarnished metal이라는 뜻도 갖게 한다.

peak = mope about 「침울하게 서성거리다」.

595. **John-a-dreams** = John of dreams = an absent-minded dreamer, a sluggish, dreamy fellow.

unpregnant of my cause = with a mind that as yet has conceived no method of action.

unpregnant = unfilled by, and therefore never to give birth (to action).

596. **say nothing** = can't speak out.

597. **property** = everything that was properly his, i.e. the kingdom of Denmark, his crown, his queen, etc.

598. **damn'd defeat was made** = ruin was brought down by most

accursed means.

defeat = destruction, ruin.

599. **breaks my pate across** = breaks my head from one side to the other.

pate = head. (고어)

601. **Tweaks** = pulls.

gives me the lie = calls me a liar.

601-2. **gives me⋯lungs** = 「나를 말 못할 거짓말쟁이라고 비난하다」. 거짓말에는 여러 등급이 있다. 입술 끝에서 나오는 거짓말부터 목(throat)에서 나오는 거짓말, 그리고 가장 깊은 폐(lungs) 속에서 나오는 거짓말 등등.

604. **'Swounds** [zwu:nds] **I should take it** = by God's wounds (i.e. those inflicted upon Christ in His crucifixion), I should accept the insult without retaliating. 'Zounds는 현재는 [zaunds]로 발음된다.

604-6. **it cannot⋯bitter** = for clearly I must have the liver of a pigeon, and be utterly wanting in that spirit which feels and resents an injury. 간(liver)은 용기, 감정, 사랑이 존재하는 곳으로 여겨졌었다.

604-5. **it cannot be But** = it cannot be otherwise than, must surely be 「틀림없이」.

605. **pigeon-liver'd** = meek, gentle, cowardly. 비둘기가 온순한 것은 쓸개(gallbladder)가 없어서 담즙(gall)을 분비하지 못하기 때문으로 여겨졌었다.

gall = spirit to resent injury or insult 「오기, 담」.

606. **make oppression bitter** = fill my distress with adequate affliction of spirit or intense grief. 여기서 bitter는 담즙이 없어 「쓰지」 않다는 2중의 뜻을 갖는다.

ere = before.

607. **fatted** = fattened.

　　the region kites = kites of the air.

　　the region = the sky, heaven.

　　kites = birds of prey. 특히 「솔개」과의 맹금류.

608. **this slave's offal** = Claudius's carcass.

　　offal = 「(특히 내장 따위의) 썩은 고기」.

　　bawdy = lewd, immoral.

610. **Remorseless** = pitiless.

　　kindless = unnatural, lacking natural feeling. kind는 본래 nature 의 뜻이 있었다.

611. **brave** = admirable. 반어적으로 쓰였음.

612. **dear** = 청중들은 deer라는 음으로도 들을 것이다. deer는 innocent slaughter라는 이미지를 가지고 있다.

613. **Prompted** = incited, moved.

　　by heaven and hell = I. iv. 40-1 참조.

614. **Must…unpack my heart with words** = cannot help exhibiting my fury in mere words.

　　unpack = unload.

615. **a-cursing** = i.e. on cursing.

　　very = true.

　　drab = whore, prostitute.

616. **scullion** = menial kitchen-servant. 모욕적인 표현. stallion(종마) 으로 된 판본도 있다.

617. **Fie** = a strong expression of disgust.

　　Foh = faugh의 변형. 혐오를 나타내는 감탄사.

　　About = get to work. bestir yourself, be active.

618. **creatures** = people.

619. **the very cunning of the scene** = sheer ingenuity of the performance.

cunning = art, skill.

scene = dramatic performance.

620.   **presently** = at once, immediately.

621.   **proclaim'd** = made a public announcement.

         malefactions = crimes.

622-3.   **will speak…organ** = will make itself known by most miraculous means.

         organ = i.e. voice.

626.   **tent him to the quick** = probe him to his most sensitive point.

         tent = apply a tent to (a wound). 여기서부터 probe. 명사로서의 tent는 a piece of lint inserted into a wound to keep it open 「거즈 심」.

         the quick = the living, sensitive part 「아픈 부분, 생살」.

         blench = flinch, start, shrink. blanch(= grow pale from shock, fear)의 변형이라는 주장도 있다. 나름대로 뜻이 통한다.

627.   **I know my course** = I shall at once know how to proceed.

630.   **Out of** = in consequence of, by exploiting.

631.   **potent with such spirits** = influential with people who are melancholy.

         such spirits = such persons as are weak and melancholy.

632.   **Abuses** = deceive, misleads.

         to damn me = i.e. by leading me to commit murder.

         grounds = motive, reason.

633.   **relative** = pertinent, relevant.

         this = i.e. the word of the Ghost (and my own suspicions).

634.   **catch** = snare.

Act III

Scene I

1. **drift of circumstance** = beating about the bush, roundabout method 「이리저리 에둘러 물어보는 것」.

    drift = what one is driving at, aim, steering.

    circumstance = detailed and (hence) circuitous narration or discourse.

2. **Get from him why he puts on this confusion** = find out from him what has led him to behave in this excited manner.

    puts on this confusion = acts in this distracted way.

    puts on = assumes.

    confusion = distraction, mental perturbation.

3-4. **Grating…lunacy** = thus disturbing his peaceful life with outbursts of dangerous madness.

    Grating = irritating, afflicting, disturbing, vexing. 여기서는 grating의 본래의 뜻, 즉 두 물체가 심하게 서로 마찰한다는 뜻을 비유적으로 사용하고 있다.

5. **distracted** = perturbed, unsettled, seriously disturbed.

7. **forward to be sounded** = eager to be questioned.

    forward = readily disposed.

sound = probe, inquire cautiously. 본래는 「바다의 깊이를 재다」의 뜻.

8. **crafty madness** = feigned madness.

   keeps aloof = keeps himself at a distance.

11. **Most like a gentleman** = with the greatest courtesy 「아주 신사답게 정중하게」.

12. **But with much forcing of his disposition** = though he was evidently very ill inclined to have much to do with us.

   forcing of his disposition = 「내키지 않는 것을 억지로」.

   disposition = mood.

13-4. **Niggard of … reply** = reluctant to talk, but willing to answer fully our questions. 만약 question을 보통 사용하는 「질문」의 뜻으로 받아들여 「질문을 많이 하지 않았다」라고 하면 사실에 어긋난다. 왜냐하면 Hamlet은 Guildenstern과 Rosencrantz 두 사람이 찾아온 진의를 알아내기 위해 여러 가지로 묻고 있기 때문이다. 그리하여 어떤 이는 niggard와 Most free의 위치가 서로 바뀌었다고 말한다. 그러면 「질문은 많이 하셨으나 대답은 별로 하지 않으셨다」라는 뜻이 된다. 또 다른 해석은 question을 또 다른 뜻인 conversation이나 discourse로 번역하는 것이다. 그리하여 전체의 뜻은 「말씀은 많이 하지 않으셨지만 질문에 대한 대답은 아끼지 않았다」가 된다. 그러나 이것도 사실에 어긋난다. 왜냐하면 Hamlet은 이들 두 사람과 많은 말을 하고 있기 때문이다. 한편 이 해석은 바로 앞 6행에서 Rosencrantz가 한 he will by no means speak라는 말과도 모순된다. 그럼에도 불구하고 이 해석을 지지하는 사람들은 이 해석이 두 사람이 Hamlet과의 면담 목적이 실패로 끝났다는 것을 호도하려고 허둥대고 있는 모습을 그려냈다고 보기 때문이다.

13. **niggard of** = reluctant.

   of our demands = 「우리의 질문에 대해서는」.

14-5. **Did you assay him To any pastime?** = did you test him as regards his inclination to take part in any amusement?

assay him to = encourage him to try.

assay = try to entice, tempt.

pastime = recreation, (pleasant) way of passing the time.

16. **fell out** = happened.

17. **o'er-raught** = overtook.

raught = reach의 옛 과거형.

18. **seem** = appear.

20. **as I think** = I believe.

they have already order = they have already received orders.

order = instruction.

22. **beseech'd** = entreated.

24. **doth much content me** = is a great satisfaction to me.

26. **give him a further edge** = incite him more forcefully, stimulate him further.

edge = incitement.

27. **drive his purpose on to these delights** = encourage his intention to undertake these pleasures.

drive his purpose on to = direct his attention to.

28. **leave us too** = 판본에 따라서는 leave us two로 된 곳도 있다. 이때 two는 Ophelia를 제외한 왕과 Polonius만을 가리키게 된다.

29. **closely** = secretly, privately.

31. **Affront** = meet face to face, confront, encounter.

32. **lawful espials** = who may justifiably act as spies in such a matter.

espials = spies.

33. **bestow** = place, position station.

34. **encounter** = meeting, interview.

frankly = freely, unrestrictedly.

35. **And gather by him, as he is behaved** = and infer from his behaviour.

36. **affliction of his love** = the passionate love he feels.

37. **That thus he suffers for** = which causes him to suffer in this way.

38. **for your part** = as regards you.

39. **your good beauties** = the fascinations of your great beauty. good 은 어감을 부드럽게 하는 것 외에 큰 뜻은 없다.

    be the happy cause = may happily prove to be the cause.

    happy = fortuitous. 왕비는 Hamlet의 실성이 자기가 시동생인 현재의 왕과 그처럼 빨리 결혼한 탓이 아니기를 바라고 있다.

40. **wildness** = madness.

41. **wonted way** = normal behaviour 「정상적인 본래의 상태」.

42. **To both your honours** = to the honour of you both.

    I wish it may = i.e. I hope you are right.

43. **Gracious** = 뒤에 lord를 첨가할 것.

    so please you = provided it is agreeable to you 「괜찮으시다면」.

44. **bestow ourselves** = place ourselves where we shall be unseen.

    this book = 47행의 devotion이나 89행의 orisons에 비추어 볼 때 prayer-book 「기도서」일 것.

45-6. **That show···loneliness** = the apparent reading of a prayer book would give a pretext for your being here all alone. 당시 양가집 젊은 여인이 나이 든 여인을 동반하지 않고 외출하는 것은 허용되지 않았다.

    exercise = religious devotion or act of worship, holy exercise.

    colour = give a specious appearance to, provide an excuse for, camouflage, disguise.

46. **loneliness** = solitariness.

    to blame = guilty, blameworthy. 판본에 따라서는 이 부분이 too

blame으로 되어 있는 곳도 있다. 이 때는 blame이 blameworthy, culpable이라는 뜻의 형용사이다.

47. **'Tis too much prov'd** = it is too often demonstrated, it is a matter of too frequent experience.

   devotion's visage = pretence (face) of religion.

   visage = appearance.

48. **action** = gesture.

49. **sugar o'er** = cover with sugar, i.e. render superficially attractive.

50. **smart** = sharp, stinging.

51. **beautied** = made beautiful.

   plast'ring art = cosmetics 「화장술」. 당시 여성의 화장은 좋은 눈으로 보지 않았다. Shakespeare 역시 여성의 화장에 대해서는 부정적인 태도를 보여 왔다.

52. **Is not more ugly to the thing that helps it** = is not more ugly in comparison with the thing to which it owes its beauty.

   to the thing that helps it = in comparison with the makeup which enhances it.

   to = compared to.

   thing = makeup.

   helps = cure, remedy, beautify.

53. **Than is my deed to my most painted word** = than are my actions in comparison with the specious language in which I dress them up.

   most painted = thickly plastered over with specious words.

56. **To be, or not to be: that is the question** = whether to continue to live or not, that is the doubt I have to solve. Hamlet의 독백 가운데서 가장 유명한 이 구에 대해서는 전통적으로 두 가지 해석이 있어 왔다. 하나는 「복수」설이고 다른 하나는 「자살」설이다. 어느 경우도 be는 exist라는 뜻의 본동사이다. 현재의

Hamlet은 아버지 망령의 분부대로 광인을 가장하고 왕에게 복수를 해야 하는 입장이다. 따라서 자살은 다소 생뚱맞다는 입장이다. 「복수」설은 18세기 최고의 비평가 Samuel Johnson 이래 주창돼 온 것으로서 Hamlet이 주검을 동반하게 될지 모르는 자기에 과해진 복수를 고민하고 있다는 해석이다. 즉 복수를 위해 왕을 죽이고 난 뒤에 스스로는 「살아남게 될 것인가, 아니면 죽게 될 것인가」라는 해석이고, 후자는 단순히 자살을 고민하고 있다는 해석으로서 「살아야 하는가, 아니면 죽어야 하는가」의 뜻이 된다. 대부분은 후자의 해석을 따르고 있다. 그래야 앞뒤 문맥과의 관계가 자연스러워진다. 대부분의 국내 번역은 「사느냐, 죽느냐」로 되어 있다. 「자살」과 「복수」 어느 쪽으로도 해석이 가능한 다소 모호한 번역이다. 그러나 이 같은 애매함이 정답일 수도 있다.

57. **Whether 'tis nobler in the mind** = whether it shows a nobler mind. 즉 자살하는 것과 고통을 감내하고 살아가는 것 가운데 어느 것이 더 고매한 행동인가. Hamlet은 우선 주검의 매력에 대해 늘어놓고 다음에 문제점을 열거한다. 결국 인간은 주검의 여러 매력에도 불구하고 이 문제점에 대한 두려움 때문에 자살을 결행하지 못한다는 결론에 이른다.

58. **slings** = properly that which casts a stone, here the missile itself, sling-shooter. 「돌을 던질 때 쓰는 끈 달린 도구」. David가 Goliath 와 싸울 때 사용한 것과 같은 것. sling은 돌을 날리는 도구이므로 slings and arrows 대신 slings and bows라고 했어야 한다는 주장도 있다. 그래서 slings를 missiles thrown by slings라고 해석하거나 심지어는 slings가 stings의 오식이라는 주장도 있다.
   outrageous = violent, cruel.

59. **a sea of troubles** = 「바다처럼 많은 고난」.

60. **by opposing end them** = bring them to an end by actively taking them on.

61. **No more** = death is nothing more than a sleep.

by a sleep = 「잠 한번 잠으로써」.

to say we end = to assure ourselves that we thus put an end to.

62-3. **natural···heir to** = natural shocks that we inherit as mortals 「육체를 가진 인간이 겪어야 할 (갖가지) 고통」.

63. **consummation** = a desired end or goal, a completion of one's life, i.e. death.

63-4. **'Tis···wish'd** = that is a conclusion for which we may well pray. J. Donne(1573-1631)의 *Death, Be Not Proud*라는 소네트의 다음과 같은 대목을 연상시킨다.

From rest and sleep, which but thy picture be,

Much pleasure; then from thee much more must flow;

(네 그림자에 불과한 편안한 잠에서 큰 즐거움이

흘러나온다면 (죽음) 너에게서는 더 큰 즐거움이 흘러나올 수밖에)

65. **there 's the rub** = there is the difficulty.

rub = obstacle, impediment. 본래 볼링에서 온 말로서 뜻은 an obstacle which hinders the bowl from keeping on its proper course.

66. **what dreams** = i.e. the thought of what dreams may come.

67. **When we have shuffl'd off this mortal coil** = when we are untangled ourselves from the flesh, i.e. when we have detached ourselves from the turmoil of human affairs 「이 번뇌의 실타래를 떨쳐버렸을 때」.

shuffl'd = cast.

this mortal coil = confused trouble of mortal life. 자주 인용되는 유명한 구.

coil = turmoil.

68. **give us pause** = cause us to hesitate.

68-9. **There's ··· life** = in that lies the consideration which makes misfortune so long-lived; if it were not for that consideration, we should quickly put an end to calamity by ending our lives.

68. **respect** = consideration.

69. **makes calamity of so long life** = makes long life such a misfortune, makes misfortune last so long.

   of so long life = so long-lived.

70. **the whips and scorns of time** = the blows and flouts to which one is exposed in this life. 구체적으로 whips에 속하는 것은 다음 4행 속의 'the oppressor's wrong,' 'the law's delay', 'the indolence of office'이며, scorns에는 'the proud man's contumely', 'the pangs of despis'd love', 'the spurns that patient merit of the unworthy takes'가 여기에 속한다. 그런데 이들은 왕자님 Hamlet과 무관한 것이다. 진짜 speaker는 Shakespeare 자신이다.

   time = the age in which we live, hence the world.

71. **contumely** [kɔ́ntjumili] = insolence, insulting behaviour or treatment.

72. **despis'd** [⌣ ×] = unrequited.

73. **the insolence of office** = the insolent behaviour with which men in office treat those who have to sue to them.

   office = those in office 「관리들」.

73-4. **the spurns ··· takes** = the insults which men of worth calmly accept from unworthy people.

   spurns = contemptuous stroke or thrust.

74. **That patient merit of the unworthy takes** = that men of merit have patiently to endure at the hands of those who have no claim to respect.

75. **might his quietus make** = pay his complete account, could get

release from life.

quietus [kwaiíːtəs] = discharge or release from life, death. 본래의 뜻은 release from debt 「채무결산」.

76. **with a bare bodkin** = with a mere dagger.

bare = unsheathed.

bodkin = small dagger.

fardels = burdens, loads.

77. **grunt** = groan.

79. **undiscovered** = unexplored.

bourn [bɔːn] = boundary, frontier.

80. **No traveller returns** = 이것은 사실과 맞지 않는다. 선왕의 유령이 다시 돌아왔으니까.

puzzles = bewilders, paralyzes.

will = resolutions.

81. **ills** = misfortunes.

83. **conscience** = consciousness, introspection, knowledge. 「양심」이라는 통상적인 뜻은 여기에 어울리지 않는다.

84-5. **And thus … thought** = and thus over the natural colour of determination there is thrown the pale and sickly tinge of anxious reflection.

native hue = natural colour.

85. **sicklied o'er with the pale cast of thought** = covered over with a sickly hue by the pale colour of melancholy.

sicklied o'er = covered over with a sickly hue.

cast = shade.

thought = anxiety.

86. **pitch and moment** = height and importance. pitch는 매사냥에서 사용되는 술어로서 매가 가장 높이 솟아오른 정점을 가리킨다.

moment = significance, importance.

87. **With this regard** = influenced by this consideration, on this account.

their currents turn awry [ərái] = divert their course.

currents = courses (as of rivers).

88. **lose the name of action** = no longer can be said to be active.

Soft you now! = you는 스스로에게 한 말.

Soft you = be quiet, wait a moment.

89. **Nymph** = young and beautiful woman.

orisons = prayers.

90. **Be all my sins remember'd** = may you remember to ask pardon for all my sins.

remember'd = mentioned.

91. **How does your honour for this many a day?** = how have you fared for these many days (during which I have not seen you)?

92. **well, well, well** = 이처럼 같은 말을 되풀이하고 있는 것은 Hamlet의 「짜증」, 「무관심」, 「광기」를 나타내려는 것이라는 여러 해석이 있다.

93. **remembrances** = gifts, love-tokens.

94. **longed** [-id] **long** = long been most desirous.

96. **I never gave you aught** = 이처럼 Hamlet이 거짓말을 하는 것은 Ophelia가 만나주지 않고 선물을 돌려주려고 하는 데 대해 자존심이 상한 때문일 것.

aught = anything.

97. **right well** = very well, well enough.

98. **words of so sweet breath composed** = words composed of so sweet breath = words so eloquent and charming.

breath = speech.

99. **their perfume lost** = now that the perfume is lost = now that their attraction has gone (because of your unkindness).

their = things를 가리킨다.

100.   **Take these again** = take these back.

100-1. **for to…unkind** = for, to a mind of any nobility, gifts, however costly, lose all their vale when their givers change from what they were. cf. A gift is valued by the mind of the giver.

101.   **wax poor** = become poor.

102.   **There, my lord** = 「자, 받으세요」. 선물을 돌려주면서 하는 말.

103-57. 지금까지의 운문에서 산문으로 바뀐다. 그 결과 Hamlet과 Ophelia 사이의 빠른 대화가 가능해진다.

103.   **honest** = 통상적인 「정직한」이란 뜻 외에 「정숙한」(chaste, virtuous)이라는 뜻도 있다. 당시 honest가 여자에 대해 쓰이면 대개 후자의 뜻이었다. 그러나 이 경우에는 전자의 뜻도 포함돼 있다. 다시 말해 Ophelia가 지금 한 말이 누군가의 사주를 받아 한 말이 아니고 네 진심이겠지 하는 다짐이기도 하며, 이것은 Hamlet이 왕과 Polonius, 심지어는 왕비까지 자기 말을 엿듣고 있다고 확신하고 있음을 나타낸다.

105.   **fair** = beautiful. fair는 「공정한」이란 뜻도 있다. 후자의 뜻이라면 「지금 날더러 배반했다고 하나 오히려 그 반대가 아닌가」라는 힐난이 된다.

107-8. **if you…beauty** = if you be virtuous and fair, your virtue should not allow itself any intercourse with your beauty. 「beauty(아름 다움)가 honesty(정숙함)를 농락하려고 다가오는 것을 허용해서는 안 된다」라는 뜻. 이를테면 Ophelia에게 Hamlet이 다가가지 못하게 하는 것도 그중 하나이다. 「아름다움」과 「정숙함」은 여인이 지니는 가장 중요한 덕목이긴 하나 이 둘은 양립하기 힘든 것으로 여겨져 왔다. Beauty and honesty seldom meet라는 속담도 있다. 왜냐하면 「아름다움」은 「정숙함」에 대한 잠재적 위협이기 때문이다.

108.   **honesty** = chastity.

discourse = familiar intercourse 「허물없이 대하는 것」.

109-10. **Could beauty … honesty?** = Ophelia는 화제를 자기로부터 일반적인 현상으로 돌리려고 한다.

110. **commerce** = intercourse. 위의 discourse와 같은 뜻.

111. **Ay, truly** = yes, assuredly it could.

111-4. **the power of … likeness** = the beauty will sooner corrupt chastity than chastity keep beauty virtuous.

112. **bawd** = pander, pimp 「뚜쟁이」.

113. **translate** = transform, change.

114. **his** = its. honesty를 가리킨다.

114-5. **This was … proof** = this was at one time considered a strange idea, but the present times have shown that it is a mere truism. 물론 어머니 Gertrude가 그 증거이다.

114. **sometime** = formerly, once. 즉 어머니가 재혼하기 이전.

115. **paradox** = a statement contrary to received opinion.
     the time gives it proof = 암암리에 왕비의 불의를 지적한다.
     the time = the present age.

118. **You should not have believ'd me** = I. iii. 127에서 Polonius가 Do not believe his vows라고 한 말을 비꼬아 되풀이하고 있다.

119-20. **virtue … of it** = virtue cannot so graft herself upon human nature but it shall smack of its original depravity 「타고난 인간 본래의 악한 원 기둥에 제아무리 훌륭한 접목을 해도 원 기둥의 악한 냄새가 난다」. 여기서 원 기둥은 어머니 Gertrude이고 접목은 Hamlet이다. 즉 그 어미에 그 자식이므로 너는 나를 믿지 말았어야 했다는 것.

119. **inoculate** = engraft.

120. **relish of it** = have a taste of it 「원 기둥의 기운을 그대로 지니다」.
     it = the stock.

121. **I was the more deceived** = then my mistake was all the more

greater.

122-3.   **why wouldst thou** = why should you desire.

122.   **Get thee to** = Go to. 여기서 상대방에 대한 호칭이 지금까지의 you(120행 참조. I loved you not.)에서 thou로 바뀐다. 존댓말이 반말로 바뀌는 것과 같다. Hamlet의 흥분 상태를 나타낸다. **nunnery** = convent(수녀원)이란 뜻 외에 brothel(매춘굴)의 뜻도 있었다. 두 곳 모두 애를 낳아서는 안 되는 곳이라는 공통점 때문일는지.

122-3.   **why wouldst ‥‥ sinners?** = 「왜 죄인들을 낳으려고 하는가」.

123.   **indifferent** = tolerably, fairly 「어지간히」. 부사로 사용되었다.

124.   **accuse me** = accuse myself.
       it were better = it would be better.

126-7.   **proud, revengeful, ambitious** = 이 세 가지 특성만큼 Hamlet과 무관한 것은 없다. 이것은 당시 복수극의 주인공들이 전통적으로 지니는 특성이다. 따라서 이 말을 엿듣고 있는 Claudius는 심히 놀랬을 것이다.

127.   **at my beck** = ready to come at my summons, whenever I choose to beckon to them 「내 마음대로 할 수 있는」.

128-9.   **thoughts ‥‥ shape** = thoughts in which to clothe them 「미처 모양을 다듬을 수조차 없을 만큼의 생각」.

129-30.   **What should ‥‥ heaven?** = What business have such wretched fellows as myself to be crawling, like noxious reptiles, on earth and heaven?

131.   **We** = humanity, or perhaps more specifically men, in general.
       arrant = thorough, utter, downright.

132.   **go thy ways** = go along. ways는 부사로 사용된 속격(genitive adverb)의 예이다.

133.   **Where's your father?** = 이 질문에 엿듣고 있던 Polonius는 찔끔했을 터.

135. **shut upon him** = shut against his going out.

136. **in 's** = in his.

137. **Farewell** = Hamlet은 나가려다 되돌아온다. 142행과 146행의 경우도 마찬가지이다.

138. **him** = Hamlet.

sweet heavens! = gracious heavens!

139-40. **this plague⋯dowry** = this curse in place of a dowry (usually provided by the woman's father).

140. **plague** = curse.

141. **calumny** = slander.

143. **needs** = of necessity. 부사적 속격의 예.

144. **monsters** = horned monsters = cuckolds. 당시 오쟁이 진 남편 (cuckold)은 이마에 뿔이 난다는 속설이 있었다.

you = you women.

148. **your paintings** = face painting (with makeup) 「여인들의 화장」. 여기서 your는 thy와 대립되는 존대의 you가 아니라 일반적인 사람을 나타내는 you. 다시 말해 지금까지 Ophelia를 thou라고 호칭하던 Hamlet의 흥분이 아직은 가라앉지 않았다는 뜻. 여성의 화장을 비난하는 것은 당시 여성혐오주의자들의 단골 메뉴.

150. **jig** = move with a rapid jerky motion.

amble = move at an easy pace. jig와 amble은 여인네들의 몸가 짐을 비판하는 말들.

151. **lisp** = speak affectedly and flirtatiously 「혀짤배기소리를 내다」. 애교의 일종. 가장 큰 특징은 [s]를 [θ]로 발음하는 것. (ex. sick [θik]).

151-2. **nick-name God's creatures** = 「(잘난 체하고) 신이 창조한 것들 에 별명을 부친다」. ex. *Romeo and Juliet*, II. i. 36. medlar (비 파). 여자의 성기를 나타낸다.

151. **nick-name** = call by the wrong name.

152. **creatures**는 생물, 무생물 모두를 포함한다.

make your wantonness your ignorance = call your immorality ignorance「음란이라고 불러야 할 것을 무지라고 부른다」= use ignorance as an excuse for foolish or immoral behaviour「음란한 짓을 해놓고는 (불리해지면) 몰라서 한 노릇이라고 둘러댄다」.

153. **I'll no more on 't** = I will allow no more of such goings on, I won't put up with it any longer.

on 't = of it.

it hath made me mad = it has made me angry. 만약 mad가 문자 그대로「정신이상」(antic disposition)이라는 뜻으로 받아들인다면 이것은 그의 정신이상의 정도가 별 것이 아니라는 주장이 된다.

155. **all but one** =「한 사람을 제외하고는」. 물론 왕을 가리킨다. Hamlet은 왕이 숨어 엿듣고 있는 것을 알고 있다. 이 말은 Ophelia에게는 이상하게 들리겠지만 관중들은 모두 이해한다.

one = the king.

156. **keep as they are** = remain unmarried.

159. **The courtier's, soldier's, scholar's, eye, tongue, sword** = the courtier's eye, the scholar's tongue, the soldier's sword. 즉 discrimination, eloquence, courage의 세 자질. Ophelia의 눈에 비친 Hamlet의 모습이다. 이것은 또한 당대 왕자의 이상적인 모습이기도 하다.

160. **expectancy and rose** = roselike hope. hendiadys(두 개의 단어로 하나의 개념을 나타내는)의 예.

rose = paragon, adornment. rose는 '젊음'과 '아름다움'의 상징이며 당대 우주관으로는 식물계의 왕과 왕비였다.

161. **The glass of fashion** = mirror or model of style.

mould of form = pattern of behaviour.

162. **The observ'd of all observers** = the admired object of all eyes.

of = by.

down = destroyed, ruined, overthrown.

163. **deject** = dejected, cast down, broken-spirited. 과거나 과거분사를 나타내는 어미 -ed는 동사의 끝이 -t로 끝날 때 종종 생략되었다.

164. **music** = (*adj.*) pleasing, delightful.

165. **sovereign reason** = sovereignty of reason. reason(이성)은 모든 기능을 지배하는 sovereign(군주)으로 여겨졌다.

166. **Like sweet bells jangled, out of tune and harsh** = like bells naturally of a sweet tone, rung in such a way as to be out of tune with each other, and so harsh-sounding.

jangled = sounding discordantly.

167-8. **That unmatch'd…ecstasy** = that peerless form and feature of youth in its full bloom now cruelly marred by madness.

167. **unmatch'd** = unmatchable, peerless.

feature = shape of body, general appearance. 현대와는 달리 신체의 특정 부위(이목구비)를 나타내지 않고 몸 전체를 가리킨다. 따라서 form and feature는 중복표현이다.

blown = blooming.

168. **Blasted with ecstasy** = blighted by madness.

Blasted = withered, blighted, devastated.

ecstasy = madness.

woe is me = woe is to me, it is a misery to me.

169. **To have seen what I have seen, see what I see!** = that I should have known him as he once was, and should know him as he now is.

170. **Love! his affections do not that way tend** = you say that love is the cause of his madness! nonsense! the bent of his mind is not in that direction.

affections = feelings, emotions.

171-2. **Nor…was not** = 현대적 감각으로는 not이 없어야 옳다. 그러나 이런 강조를 위한 2중부정(emphatic double negation)은 당대에는 드물지 않았다. 고대영어에서와 마찬가지로 부정어(Nor와 not)가 겹친다고 해서 긍정이 되지 않고 부정의 뜻이 강조될 따름이다.

171. **though it lack'd form a little** = though it was somewhat incoherent, unmethodical.

173. **sits on brood** = sits a-brooding.

174-5. **And I do…danger** = and I suspect that when the outcome of it is seen, we shall find it something dangerous.

174. **doubt** = fear.

hatch = outcome, emerging from the egg.

disclose = disclosure, breaking out of the egg. hatch와 동의어.

175. **some danger** = 표현은 완곡하고 모호하나 왕은 155행에서 Hamlet이 all but one, shall live(한 인간을 빼놓고는 살려두겠다)라고 하는 말의 뜻을 알아들었음을 나타낸다.

for to prevent = to forestall, anticipate 「앞질러 막기 위해」. for 는 purpose나 motive를 강조하기 위해 첨가된 오래된 용법이다.

176-7. **I have…down** = I have with prompt determination decided.

177. **set it down** = made a decision about it.

he shall = he shall be sent.

178. **For the demand of our neglected tribute** = to demand the tribute of money due to us, which they have neglected to pay.

our neglected tribute = 「바쳐야 할 것을 소홀히 한 조공」이란 11세기경 영국의 일부가 덴마크의 지배하에 있을 때 해마다 덴마크에 바치던 세금으로서 Danegeld라고 부르던 것.

179. **Haply** = perhaps.

180. **variable objects** = various sights and distractions.

181. **something-settled matter in his heart** = 「그의 마음속에 응어리진 것」.

    something-settled = somehow obsessive.

    something = somewhat, in some degree.

    settled = in his heart에 걸린다.

    matter = pus(고름)의 뜻도 있다.

182. **Whereon his brains beating still puts him thus** = puts의 주어가 brains라면 주어와 동사의 수가 일치하지 않는다. 그러나 brains가 단수 동사와 사용되는 예는 드물지 않았다. 그 때의 뜻은 Whereon his brains which is still beating puts him thus From fashion of himself가 된다. 한편 명사절(the fact that his brains are still beating) 전체를 puts의 주어로 볼 수도 있다.

    still = always.

182-3. **puts … himself** = 「평상시의 모습을 바꿔놓는다」.

183. **fashion of himself** = his usual behaviour.

184. **It shall do well** = the plan is certain to answer.

    yet = still, notwithstanding what you say.

185-6. **The origin and commencement of this love** = origin과 commencement는 중복적 표현이다.

186. **How now, Ophelia!** = what brings you here?

188. **We heard it all** = 이런 말을 하면 Polonius가 Ophelia가 Hamlet과 만나 한 이야기를 엿들었다는 뜻이 되겠지만 딸에게 괴로운 이야기를 되풀이시키지 않기 위한 아버지의 배려로 볼 수 있다.

    do as you please = you will act on your own judgement. 공손한 태도이다.

189. **If you hold it fit** = if you agree with me as to the propriety of doing so.

190. **queen mother** = his mother who is the Queen.

191. **griefs** = grievance.

round = forthright, plain-spoken, not mincing matters.

192-3.   **in the ear Of all their conference** = where I can hear all that passes between them. 아무래도 왕비가 어머니이고 보니 왕비가 정확히 보고하기가 어려울 것이고, 따라서 Polonius 자기가 직접 지켜보아야겠다는 것을 암시하고 있다.

  in the ear Of = within hearing of.

193.   **conference** = talk, conversation.

  find him not = does not discover his secret, fails to discover his problem.

  find = discover the true character of.

194.   **Your wisdom** = you in your wisdom.

Scene II

1.   **the speech** = perhaps the speech Hamlet has asked the player to insert.

2.   **pronounc'd** = recited.

  trippingly = lightly, nimbly, fluently.

3.   **mouth** [mauð] **it** = speak pompously.

4.   **your players** = 편하게 생각해서 players in general의 뜻으로 받아들이면 된다. 그러나 Shakespeare는 your를 자주 잘 알려진 사람을 지칭할 때 쓰기도 했다. 그러면 your players는 many players that you and I know well 정도의 뜻이 된다.

  I had as lief = I had rather, would be as glad if.

  lief = gladly.

  town-crier = one appointed to make public announcement by shouting them in the streets.

5. **saw the air** = move your arms up and down in emphatic gesture.

6. **thus** = 여기서 Hamlet이 실제로 동작을 해보일 것이다.

   use all gently = do everything with moderation, in everything act with a quiet dignity.

   use all = do everything.

6-9. **for in···smoothness** = for even when your passion is at its highest pitch, you must learn to employ a restraint which shall make it go smoothly off.

7. **acquire** = adopt.

8. **beget** = obtain.

   temperance = moderation, self-control. 이것이 이른바 '연기의 역설(paradox of acting)이라고 하는 것이다. 즉 배우는 연기를 하고 있다는 것을 잊어서는 안 되지만 그렇다고 자제력을 잃을 만큼 감정에 휩쓸려서도 안 된다.

9-10. **offends me to the soul** =「마음속까지 불쾌해진다」.

   to the soul = to the very depths of my nature.

10. **robustious** = noisy, boisterous, violent.

   periwig-pated fellow = man with a periwig on his head. 당시 배우들은 대개 가발(periwig)을 썼다. 17세기에 가서는 일상생활에서도 가발이 사용되었다.

11. **tear a passion to tatters** =「흥분한 목소리로 감동적인 말을 갈기갈기 찢어놓다」.

   passion = passionate speech.

12. **split the ears of the groundlings** =「3류 관객의 귀를 찢는」.

   groundlings = spectators who paid lowest price for admission to the theater and stood in the pit (theater yard) rather than sitting in gallery seats or around the stage. 즉 지붕도 의자도 없는 입석 관객. 당시 입장료가 1페니였다고 한다. 이것이 이 단어가 사용된 최초의 예이다.

13. **capable of** = able to appreciate.

inexplicable = unintelligible 「까닭을 알 수 없는」.

dumb-shows = 극의 줄거리를 알리기 위해 막이 올라가지 전에 행해지는 간단한 무언극.

14. **noise** = 칼 부딪치는 따위의 소리.

I would = if I had my way.

15. **whipped** = II, ii, 556행을 참조할 것.

o'erdoing = exceeding in violence.

Termagant = an imaginary Muslim deity, thought to be violent and blustering.

16. **out-herods Herod** = outdo Herod in violence 「난폭함이 헤롯왕을 능가하다」. Herod 왕은 예수가 태어날 때 예수를 죽이려고 당시 태어난 모든 아기를 학살한 것으로 유명한 유대의 왕.

out-herods = outdo를 본떠서 Shakespeare가 만든 유명한 표현으로서 out-Newton Newton이라고 하면 「Newton을 능가하는 과학자」란 뜻이 된다.

17. **I warrant your honour** = yes, sir, I promise you we will avoid all such extravagances.

your honour = a title of respect 「저하」.

18. **Be not too tame neither** = at the same time take care to act with sufficient spirit. 현대영어에서는 이런 경우 neither 대신 either 를 사용할 것이다.

18. **tame** = weak, understated.

19-20. **Suit the action to the word** = 「대사에 연기를 맞추다」.

19. **action** = gesture.

21. **observance** = observant care.

21-2. **the modesty of nature** = natural restraints or limits, moderation as nature dictates.

21. **modesty** = moderation, absence of excess.

22-3.   **is from the purpose** = 「목적에 위배된다」.

22.   **from** = contrary to, remote from.

23.   **playing** = acting.

          end = object, purpose.

23-4.   **at the first and now** = from the earliest times of the theatre to the present.

24-5.   **hold···the mirror up to nature** = 유명한 인용구이다.

25-7.   **virtue, ···scorn, ···the very age and body of the time** = 25행 show의 간접목적어.

25.   **feature** = appearance, shape, form. cf. III. i. 167.

26.   **scorn** = object of contempt, i.e. folly, scornful person.

26-7.   **the very···time** = essential reality of this moment in time. A person's general appearance is determined in the main by two things ─ his age and his body (Kittredge).

27.   **his** = its.

          form and pressure = likeness and impression.

          pressure = shape, impressed character (as it were in wax).

27-8.   **Now this···off** = now if you overdo this on the one hand, or fall short of it on the other.

28.   **come tardy off** = fallen short, done inadequately.

28-9.   **the unskilful** = those lacking judgment, i.e. the groundlings.

39.   **the judicious** = those who are sensible and prudent.

30-2.   **the censure···others** = the opinion of one of whom you must admit would far outweigh a whole theaterful of ignorant persons.

30.   **the censure of the which one** = the judgement of even one of these (the judicious).

          censure = opinion.

          of the which one = a single one of whom.

31.   **in your allowance** = by your admission, as you will allow, as

you must agree.

32.   **be** = are.

34.   **not to speak it profanely** = not intending to be profane in what I'm about to say 「벌 받을 소리를 하려는 건 아니지만」.

    that = players를 받는 관계대명사. 36행의 have so strutted의 주어.

34-6.   **that, neither⋯man** = who not being able to speak like Christians, and in the matter of carriage resembling neither Christian, pagan or man at all.

35.   **accent** = sound, pronunciation.

    Christians = respectable human beings.

    gait = bearing.

37.   **journeyman** = one who is not a master of his trade (used depreciatively), hirelings who work for daily wages. cf. F. journée (= a day).

39.   **abominably** = detestably 「혐오스럽게」.

41.   **indifferently** = fairly well, tolerably, pretty thoroughly.

    with us = in our company.

42-4.   **And let⋯them** = do not let them insert something of their own into the speeches they have to deliver. 이처럼 배우가 임기응변으로 끼워 넣는 대사를 gag라고 한다. 당대엔 배우에 따라 상당히 많은 부분을 끼워 넣는 경우가 있었다.

43.   **clowns** = comic roles.

44.   **there be of them that** = there are some of them who.

    of them = some of them.

45-6.   **to set on⋯too** = to incite some of the more barren-witted of their audience to join the laugh.

45.   **set on** = incite.

45.   **some quantity of barren spectators** = 「얼마간의 바보 같은 관객들」.

quantity = proportion. 경멸적으로 많지 않은 양을 나타낸다.

46. **barren** = dull, unintelligent, devoid of judgement. 29행의 unskilful과 같은 뜻.

46-8. **though … considered** = though at the time some important point in the play has to be dealt with.

47. **necessary question** = essential matter.

48. **villanous** = wicked, abominably bad.

49. **pitiful** = contemptible.

50. **uses it** = practices it.

51-2. **this piece of work** = 연극을 가리키지만 약간 비하한 표현. III. i. 23의 **matter**도 마찬가지 표현.

53. **and that presently** = not only hear it, but hear it at once.
presently = immediately.

58. **sweet lord** = 당시에는 흔하게 사용된 호칭.

59. **e'en as just a man** = as thoroughly upright a man. 냉정하고 실제적인 Horatio는 여러 가지 면에서 Hamlet과 대조된다. 사람은 자기와 반대되는 성격에 매료되기 쉽다.
e'en = even, absolutely.
just = honorable, honest.

60. **As e'er my conversation coped withal** = as ever I have associated with.
conversation = experience of social life, dealings with people.
coped with = encountered, has come into contact with.
withal = with.

61. **O, my dear lord** = Horatio indicates a modest denial of Hamlet's praise 「별말씀을요」.

62. **advancement** = preferment.

63. **revenue** [× ´ ×] = income.
good spirits = good sentiments.

64.   **Why should the poor be flatter'd?** = what good could there be in flattering the poor?

65.   **let candied tongue lick absurd pomp** = let the sweet-tongued flatterer direct his attention to ridiculous pomposity.

       candied tongue = 「감언」.

       candied = sugared, sweet, and so flattering.

       absurd [´ ×]

       pomp = those who absurdly boast themselves of their grandeur.

66.   **(let) crook the pregnant hinges of the knee** = (let) bend his ever-ready knees.

       crook = bend.

       pregnant = ready, prompt, inclined.

67.   **Where thrift may follow fawning** = where profit will result from his fawning behaviour.

       thrift = gain, profit, financial advantage.

       fawning = servile behavior 「아첨, 아양 떨기」.

       Dost thou hear? = please pay attention to this. 강조어.

68.   **dear** = highly prized.

       was mistress of her choice = was capable of making choice.

       mistress는 soul을 여성으로 취급했기 때문.

69.   **could of men distinguish** = could make discriminating choices of men 「사람을 볼 줄 알게 되다」.

       election = choice.

69-70. **her election Hath seal'd** = she(my soul) has selected or chosen (literally, put a legal seal (on something or someone) as a sign of ownership) 「찜했다, 점찍었다」.

71.   **As one, in suffering all, that suffers nothing** = like one who, though enduring every misfortune, seems unconscious that he is enduring any 「갖가지 고통을 겪으면서도 끄떡도 하지 않는

사람」. 처음 **suffer**는 bear with patience의 뜻이며, 두 번째 **suffers** (nothing)는 sustain (no) damage의 뜻이다.

that = who.

72. **buffets** = blows, repeated strikes.

73. **with equal thanks** = with the same imperturbability.

74. **Whose blood and judgement are so well commingled** = in whom passionate feeling and judgement are mingled in such due proportion.

   blood and judgement = passion and reason.

   commingled = mixed together.

75-6. **That they…please** = that fortune is not able to do what she will with them.

75. **pipe** = small wind instrument, like a flute.

76. **sound** = play.

   stop = note (literally, hole in wind instruments of music by which difference of pitch is produced).

   she = 운명의 여신(Fortune)은 늘 여자로 묘사된다.

77. **passion's slave** = the slave of uncontrolled emotion. Hamlet은 자신이 그런 인간이라고 생각하고 있다.

78. **my heart's core** = the centre of my heart, the heart of his heart.

   core = heart, centre. cf. L. cor (= heart).

79. **Something too much of this** = 앞에 I have talked를 보충해서 읽을 것.

   something = somewhat.

80. **before the king** = to be acted before the king.

81-2. **comes near…death** = closely resembles in detail the manner of my father's death, of which I have already told you.

81. **scene** = episode or sequence.

82. **Which I have told thee** = 1막 5장에서 Hamlet은 아버지 유령과

의 비밀을 밝히기를 거부했었지만 그 뒤 Horatio에게 자초지종 사실을 알려준 듯하다.

83. **that act** = that part of the drama.

act = performance.

afoot = going on.

84. **the very comment of thy soul** = thy most intense observation of your entire being.

comment = mental observation.

85. **occulted** = hidden, secret.

86. **itself unkennel** = reveal itself.

unkennel = discover, reveal (literally, drive a fox from its lair) 「여우를 굴에서 내쫓다」. unkennel이 앞줄의 uncle과 울림이 같다는 점을 지적하는 평자도 있다.

one speech = the speech Hamlet has had implicitly inserted. cf. II. ii. 617-23.

> I have heard
> That guilty creatures sitting at a play
> Have by the very cunning of the scene
> Been struck so to the soul that presently
> They have proclaim'd their malefactions;
> For murder, though it have no tongue, will speak
> With most miraculous organ.

87. **damned** [-id] = damnable, hateful.

88. **my imaginations** = i.e. my suspicions, based on the ghost's words.

foul = polluted, offensive.

89. **Vulcan's stithy** = forge or anvil of Vulcan.

Vulcan = the Roman god of fire and metalworking.

stithy [stíði] = smithy, forge.

	Give him heedful note = mark him most carefully.
	heedful = attentive.
90.	**rivet** = fix immoveably.
91-2.	**And after…seeming** = and when the play is over, we will compare our impressions as to his behaviour during it, and see what conclusions we come to.
91.	**after** = afterwards.
	both our judgements = the judgement of both of us.
92.	**censure** = judgement.
	seeming = appearance, behaviour.
93-4.	**If he steal…theft** = if during the play any guilty look or movement of his escapes my notice, you may punish me as you like for having allowed myself to be duped by him.
93.	**aught** = anything.
	the whilst = while.
94.	**'scape detecting** = 「못보고 놓치는 일이 생기면」.
	pay the theft = recompense the owner of the stolen goods 「도난 물에 대해 변상하다」.
	pay = pay for.
	theft = the thing stolen.
95.	**idle** = mad, crazy.
96.	**Get you a place** = find yourself somewhere to sit.
97.	**How fares…Hamlet?** = how are you, cousin?
	fares = is, does, gets on 「지내다」. Hamlet은 98행에서 fares를 eats, feeds의 뜻으로 받고 있다.
	cousin = nephew.
98.	**Excellent** = 부사로 사용되었다.
98-9.	**of the chameleon's dish** = I eat the same food as the chameleon. Hamlet은 fares를 does가 아닌 또 다른 뜻인 'eats'로 알아들은

척하고 있다. pun의 예이다. of는 eat나 drink 뒤에 쓰이는 partitive의 of이다. 프랑스어의 부분관사에 해당한다.

99. **I eat the air** = chameleon은 아주 작은 벌레를 잡아먹고 살기 때문에 흔히 공기를 마시고 사는 것으로 알려져 있다. 한편 air는 heir(후계자)와 발음이 같으며, 왕은 늘 Hamlet이 자신의 후계자라고 말해 왔다. cf. I. ii. 109. You are the most immediate to our throne; 왕이 Hamlet을 자신의 아들(son)이라고 했던 일을 sun과의 pun으로 비꼬던 일과 같은 경우이다. 따라서 전체의 뜻은 「공기와 진배없는 약속을 먹고 살고 있다」가 된다. **dish** = food.

99. **promise-cramm'd** = crammed with promise. cf. 354. Sir, I lack advancement.

promise = 왕위를 Hamlet에게 물려주겠다는 왕의 약속.

100. **cannot feed capons so** = 「알맹이 없는 약속뿐인 그런 모이로서는 닭도 키울 수 없다」.

capons = domestic cocks castrated and fattened for eating.

101-2. **I have⋯mine** = this answer has no connection with my question.

101. **I have nothing with this answer** = I get nothing out of your answer.

102. **are not mine** = don't answer my question.

103. **nor mine now** = 「내가 알 바도 아니다」.

now = now that I've spoken them. 영국 속담에 A man's words are his own no longer than he keeps them unspoken 「말이란 일단 뱉어버리면 자기 것이 아니다」라는 것이 있다.

104. **play'd once i' the university** = 지금도 그렇지만 당대 Oxford와 Cambridge대학에서는 학부생들이나 전문 연극인들에 의한 연극 공연이 자주 있었다. Shakespeare는 그것을 마음에 두고 있는 듯.

played = acted onstage.

107.   **enact** = play (a part).

107-8. **I was⋯Capitol** = 역사적 사실에 어긋난다. Plutarch는 Cæser가 살해된 것은 Capitol(신전)이 아니라 The Theatre of Pompey(폼페이 의사당)라고 밝히고 있다. 그러나 Shakespeare는 Capitol과 111행의 capital과의 pun을 위해 Chaucer의 *The Monk's Tale* 이후의 오래된 오류를 따르고 있다.

108.   **Julius Cæser** = 로마의 정복자로서 BC 44년에 Brutus에게 살해된다.

110.   **a brute part of him** = a brutal act on his part. 이 brute와 다음 capital은 각기 앞줄의 Brutus와 Capitol에 대한 pun이다. 그런데 *Julius Cæsar*가 초연된 것은 1599년이었다. 당시 Cæsar와 Brutus의 역은 각각 현재 Polonius와 Hamlet을 역을 맡은 동일한 배우들이 맡았었다고 한다. 그렇다면 Hamlet은 이미 앞의 극에서 Polonius를 죽인 것이 된다. 그런데 이 극에서 공교롭게도 Hamlet은 그 「잔인한 역」을 되풀이하게 된다.

110.   **brute** = brutish.

110-1. **kill so capital a calf** = cf. *Luke* 15:23의 Prodigal Son을 두고 한 말.

        capital = excellent.

        calf = 번제로 바치는 송아지. stupid fellow라는 뜻도 있다.

112.   **stay upon your patience** = are waiting till you give them permission.

        patience = permission.

116-7. **here's metal more attractive** = Ophelia being the magnet. 만약 Hamlet이 어머니의 권유를 받아들여 어머니 옆에 앉게 되면, 따라서 그와 왕 사이에 어머니가 앉게 되면 왕을 관찰할 수 없다는 문제가 생긴다.

116.   **metal** = 자석. mettle과 pun을 이룬다.

117.   **attractive** = 여기서는 magnetic(끌어당기는)의 뜻이지만 동시에

fair(아름다운)의 뜻으로도 사용되었다.

119. **lie in your lap** = 귀족들의 저택에서 연극 공연이 있을 때 남자들이 여자 무릎에 기대고 누워서 연극을 보는 습관이 있었다. Ophelia는 Hamlet의 말을 보다 노골적인 뜻으로 알아듣고 처음엔 거절한다.

120. **No, my lord** = Ophelia는 lie를 성적인 뜻으로 이해하고 거절하지만 Hamlet은 다음 줄에서 곧 그렇지 않다는 해명을 한다. 그러나 이것은 여전히 Hamlet의 성적 희롱(sexual innuendo)이다.

123. **country matters** = rustic proceedings 「시골 식의 야비한 행동」. country의 첫 음절의 발음[kʌnt-]이 비속어 cunt와 같은 점을 이용한 말장난. 이 같은 말장난은 당대의 극작가나 시인들이 즐겨 사용했다.

125. **lie between maids' legs** = 성적인 음담패설(ribaldry)에 가까운 이 표현은 Shakespeare나 당시 관중 모두에게 걸맞지 않게 지나친 것으로 비판을 받고 있다.

128. **Nothing** = 숫자로 치면 0. 이 때 배우는 손가락으로 동그라미를 만들어 여성의 치부를 그려보이게 되며 야비한 장난을 알아들은 Ophelia가 You are merry라고 말한다. Hamlet은 여전히 Ophelia를 희롱하고 모욕하고 있다.

129. **You are merry** = 「농담도 심하시네요」.
merry = facetious.

132. **your only jig-maker** = 앞에 I am을 보충해 읽을 것 = I am your best comedian, entertainer.
your = 일반적 용법.
only = 「천하제일의」. cf. II. ii. 421.
jig = lively, comic, or farcical performance given at the end or in an interval of a play.

135. **within's two hours** = within this period of two hours, less than two hours ago. 부왕이 돌아가신지 두 시간밖에 되지 않는다는

것은 물론 Hamlet의 과장이다.

within's = within this.

136. **'tis twice two months** = it is four months since he died. 만약 Ophelia의 기억이 정확하다면 Hamlet이 부왕의 유령과 만난 지 두 달이 지난 것이 된다. cf. I. ii. 138. But two months dead!

137-8. **let the devil wear black** = if my father has been dead so long the devil can have my mourning clothes. 「상복은 악마에게 돌려 주자」. 악마는 까만색이다.

138. **black** = mourning garments.

sables = 검은담비 털을 댄 사치스런 외투. 역시 까만색이다.

141. **by'r lady** = By Our Lady, i.e. the Virgin Mary 「성모마리아의 이름을 걸고」. cf. II. ii. 445.

141-2. **he must build churches, then** = if he wishes to keep his memory green, he must leave behind him some visible remembrance of himself.

142-3. **suffer not thinking on** = suffer oblivion, be forgotten 「잊히고 만다」.

143. **not thinking on** = oblivion, being-forgotten. 한 단어처럼 쓰인다.

the hobby-horse = 5월에 행해지는 morris-dance(May-Day 축제 때 추던 춤의 일종)에서 버드나무 따위로 만들어 허리에 차던 말 인형. Shakespeare 시대에는 청교도들의 반발 때문에 이미 이 풍속은 잊혀져가고 있었다.

144. **For, O, for O, the hobby horse is forgot** = 당시 유행한 민요에서 가져온 듯.

SD **Hautboys** [hóubɔi] = oboes.

dumb-show = a scene without words.

makes show of protestation unto him = goes through the action of earnestly declaring her love for him.

protestation = public assertion, solemn declaration, affirmation or promise.

takes her up, and declines his head upon her neck = raises her from her kneeling position, and lets his head fall upon her neck.

declines = bends.

his crown = the King's crown.

kisses it = to show how precious it is in his sight, how dearly he would like to wear it.

passionate action = sorrowful gesture.

Mutes = actors on the stage whose part is performed only in dumb show.

loath = reluctant, unwilling.

147.　**miching mallecho** [mítʃiŋ malétʃou] = sneaking mischief(몰래하는 못된 짓, 좀도둑질)가 사전에 나와 있는 뜻이지만 어원은 분명치 않다. mich는 lurk의 뜻이 있고 mallecho는 스페인어의 malhecho(= misdeed)와 관계가 있는 듯. 여기서 말하는 sneaking mischief는 Claudius가 왕관과 왕비를 훔친 일을 암시한다고 볼 수 있으나, dumb-show를 몰래 삽입해서 Hamlet의 모처럼의 계획을 망쳐버리게 될지도 모르는 배우들의 장난을 뜻할 수도 있다. 그래야 151-2행의 the players cannot keep counsel(배우들이란 비밀을 지키지 못한다)과 맥이 닿게 된다.

149-50.　**Belike this … play** = probably this dumb-show indicates the plot of the play.

Belike = by like, perhaps.

argument = plot, theme.

SD　**Enter Prologue** = 연극이 시작될 때에는 trumpet가 세 번 울리고 월계관(laurel-wreath)을 쓰고 긴 까만 망토(cloak)를 입은 사람이 나와서 연극의 시작을 알렸다.

151.　**We shall know by this fellow** = we shall soon find out from this fellow. 판본에 따라서는 this fellow가 these fellows로 된

것도 있다. 그때는 연극 전반에 대한 언급이 될 것이다.

152.   **counsel** = secrets.

153.   **this show** = this dumb-show.

154.   **any show that you'll show him** = Ophelia가 show를 단순한 연극의 뜻으로 사용하고 있는 것에 반에 Hamlet은 any show를 「(신체의 은밀한 부분을) 보여주기」의 뜻으로 사용하고 있다.

155.   **Be not you** = if you are not.
           shame to = be ashamed to.

157.   **naught** = naughty, indecent, offensive.

158.   **mark** = pay attention to.

160.   **Here stooping to your clemency** = bowing to your mercy, generosity.

162.   **posy** = a short motto, frequently in verse, inscribed inside a ring. Hamlet이 서막(Prologue)이 너무 짧다는 불평을 하고 있다.

164.   **As woman's love** = 여기서 woman은 어머니를 지칭할 수도 있다.

165-233. 극중극인 이 부분은 고풍스러운 문체에다 aa, bb조의 2행연구 (rhymed couplet)를 사용함으로써 어순이 복잡해져 다른 부분과 구분된다. 165행과 166행의 round와 ground, 167행과 168행의 sheen과 been, 그리고 그 이하의 운이 맞는 점에 주목하라.

165-70. 요약하면 The sun has gone round the sea and the earth thirty times and the moon with her reflected rays has been round the earth twelve times this number of journeys, since love and marriage united our hearts and hands in the most holy bonds.

165.   **Full thirty times hath Phoebus' cart gone round** = 「태양신의 마차가 이미 (지구를) 30바퀴나 돌았다」. 즉 30년이란 세월이 흘렀다.
           Phoebus = 「태양의 신」. 그리스 신화의 Apollo의 별칭.
           cart = chariot.

166.   **Neptune's salt wash** = the sea.
           Neptune = 로마 신화에 나오는 「바다의 신」. 그리스 신화의

Poseidon.

Tellus' orbed ground = goddess's globe, i.e. the earth.
Tellus = 로마 신화에 나오는 「대지의 여신」.
orbed [-id] = rounded, circular.

167. **thirty dozen moons** = i.e. thirty years.
borrowed sheen = light reflected from the sun.

168. **twelve thirties** = 「(1년에) 12바퀴씩 30년 동안」.

169. **Hymen** = the god of marriage.

170. **commutual** = mutual, reciprocal.

172. **done** = ended.

173. **you are so sick of late** = you have lately been so sick.
of late = lately.

174. **So far from cheer and from your former state** = so different from your usual cheerful self.

175. **distrust** = fear for you.

176. **Discomfort you⋯it nothing must** = it must not grieve you at all.
nothing = in no way, not at all.

177. **holds quantity** = keeps proportion with each other. holds의 주어가 fear and love의 복합명사임에도 불구하고 단수형으로 쓰인 것은 fear와 love 각각을 holds의 별도의 주어로 인식한 탓.

178. **In neither aught, or in extremity** = either there is no fear or love at all, or there is an excess of both, i.e. they(= women) either feel none of these passion (= fear and love), or feel them both in the highest degree.

179. **proof hath made you know** = you have learnt by experience.
proof = experience.

180. **as my love is siz'd, my fear is so** = and my fear is as great (the same size) as my love.

siz'd = of a particular magnitude.

181. **the littlest doubts are fear** = even the smallest doubt as to the well-being of the loved one becomes fear.

    littlest = least. Shakespeare 특유의 표현. 현재도 속어로 쓰인다.

184. **My operant powers their functions leave to do** = my vital powers cease to function.

    operant = active, vital, operative.

    leave to do = cease to perform.

185. **live…behind** = survive me.

    behind = after I have gone.

186. **haply** = perhaps.

    as kind = as kind as myself.

187. **shalt thou** = 뒤에 find를 첨가해서 읽을 것.

    confound the rest! = speak no more!

    confound = destroy, i.e. don't utter.

188. **Such love must needs be treason in my breast** = such love if entering my heart would be treason.

189. **accurst** = ill-fated 「저주받은」.

190. **but who** = except the one who.

191. **wormwood** = 「약쑥, 듣기 싫은 쓴 말」. wormwood라는 단어는 성경에 세 번 사용되고 있다. 지금 Hamlet은 구약성서의 *Proverbs*(잠언) 5:3-4의 다음 구를 떠올리고 있을는지 모른다. For the lips of a strange woman drop as an honeycomb, and her mouth is smoother than oil: But her end is bitter as wormwood, sharp as a twoedged sword.

192. **instances** = causes, motives, inducements.

    move = motivate, prompt, actuate.

193. **respect of thrift** = considerations of gain.

    base respects of thrift = mean considerations of gain.

        thrift = gain, profit. cf. III. ii. 67.

198.   **Purpose is but the slave to memory** = determination easily yields itself captive to memory, passes away when that which gave it birth is forgotten, i.e. purposes are easily forgotten.

199.   **of violent birth, but poor validity** = is robust enough when first formed, but soon loses its strength.

        poor validity = not well founded, i.e. without staying power.

        validity = strength, vigour.

201.   **fall** = 주어는 198행의 Purpose이므로 동사는 단수형을 써야 하지만 200행의 집합명사 fruit와 엮이면서 복수형이 되었다.

202-3. **Most necessary…debt** = It is only natural that we should forget to pay ourselves the debts we owe to ourselves, i.e. the resolutions (not to remarry) we make.

202.   **Most necessary 'tis** = it is quite inevitable that.

204-5. **What to ourselves…lose** = that which under the influence of strong feeling we propose to ourselves as a course of action, when that strong feeling passes away, loses its motive.

        passion = 희비애락의 모든 감정을 가리킨다.

205.   **the purpose lose** = the purpose forgets. 목적어는 204행 전체.

206-7. **The violence…destroy** = the violence of either grief or joy destroys those passions, and at the same time puts an end to the execution of their purposes.

207.   **Their own enactures…destroy** = destroy the execution of their purposes 「희비애락은 그 격렬함 때문에 자멸할 때 목표실현의 가능성도 함께 없애버린다」.

        enactures = fulfilment.

        destroy = 주어는 앞줄의 violence이지만 their own enactures에 잘못 이끌려(false attraction) 복수형을 취하고 있다.

208.   **Where joy most revels, grief doth most lament** = excessive

indulgence in joy is followed by excessive abandonment to grief.

209. **Grief joys, joy grieves, on slender accident** = a very slight incident turns grief into joy, joy into grief.

Grief joys = grief rejoices, grief turns into joy.

joys = enjoys.

on slender accident = for slight reason, on the slightest impetus.

accident = incident, event.

210. **This world···change** = nothing, not even the world itself, is everlasting, and therefore it is not strange that even our love should change with change of fortune.

aye = ever.

212-3. **For 'tis···love** = for it is a point still undetermined whether love or fortune proves itself the stronger influence when the two are opposed.

212. **prove** = resolve, answer.

213. **lead** = dominates, is stronger than.

214. **The great man down···his favourite flies** = the great man having fallen from his high estate, you see his former favourite at once quit his side.

down = disgraced, fallen in esteem.

mark = notice.

favourite = a specially favoured person. Folio 판에서는 복수형의 favourites로 돼 있다. great man과 favourite가 단수형으로 되어 있는 까닭에 이들을 특정인과 결부시키려는 노력들이 있어 왔다.

flies = flees, deserts him, abandons him.

215. **The poor advanc'd makes friends of enemies** = the man of humble rank raised to a high position finds his former enemies quickly turn into friends.

216. **And hitherto doth love on fortune tend** = and up to this time

love has been found to wait on fortune, to accommodate itself to fortune.

hitherto = up to this point, thus far.

love on fortune tend = love waits upon fortune.

tend on = wait upon, follow.

217.   **who not needs** = whoever is rich, he who is not in need, he who lacks nothing.

needs = is in want.

218.   **hollow** = insincere.

try = test (his friendship).

219.   **seasons him** = ripens him into (as though the test of the false friend brought his falseness to maturity).

220.   **orderly to end where I begun** = to return in due order to the point from which I set out.

orderly = properly, duly, according to rule.

begun = began. 다음 줄의 run과 운을 맞추기 위함.

221.   **contrary** [kəntréəri] = contrarily.

222.   **devices** = plans, intentions.

still = always.

223.   **ends** = outcome, result.

none of our own = not in the least in our power.

225.   **die thy thoughts** = your thoughts will die의 서술문이거나 let such thoughts die의 명령문일 수 있다.

226.   **Nor…nor** = Neither…nor.

Nor earth = may neither earth.

earth to me give = let earth give.

227.   **Sport and repose lock from me day and night!** = may the day shut me out of all enjoyment, the night fail to give me repose!

Sport = recreation, entertainment.

lock = keep. day and night가 주어이고, Sport and repose는 목적어.

228. **To desperation turn my trust and hope!** = may my expectations and hope turn to desperation!

turn = my trust and hope가 주어.

229. **An anchor's cheer in prison be my scope!** = may a hermit's food and drink be the utmost I can hope to enjoy.

anchor = anchorite, hermit.

cheer = fare, provisions. chair로 된 판본도 있다.

scope = end in view, aim, portion, limit.

230-1. **Each opposite···destroy!** = May every adverse thing that causes joy to grow pale meet and destroy everything that I want to prosper.

Each opposite = everything exactly opposed to joy.

opposite = opponent, antagonist, adversary. 다음 줄 Meet의 주어.

blanks = blanches, makes pale. makes blank라는 해석도 있다.

231. **Meet what I would have well and it destroy** = let it encounter everything to which I wish success and destroy it.

232. **here and hence** = in this world and the world to come.

hence = in the afterlife.

234. **If she should break it now!** = how terrible if she breaks her word after placing this curse on herself. 여기서 she는 Player Queen과 Gertrude 중 어느 한쪽을 가리킬 수 있다.

it = her oath.

235. **deeply** = solemnly.

236. **My spirits grow dull** = weariness is creeping over me.

spirits = vital energies.

fain = gladly, willingly.

beguile = while away.

237. **rock** = soothe.

238.   **mischance** = ill fortune.

     twain = two.

240.   **doth protest too much** = is too full of protestations of love and loyalty.

     protest = vow, assert publicly, proclaim.

     methinks = it seems to me.

241.   **O, but she'll keep her word** = O, but you will see that she will keep her word. 비꼬면서 하는 말.

242.   **Have you heard the argument?** = 이 같은 왕의 말로 미루어보아 그가 Polonius와 잡담을 하느라 dumb-show을 보지 않았거나 아니면 그가 극의 내용에 대해 의심을 갖기 시작했다는 것을 말해준다.

     argument = plot, theme.

242-3.   **Is there no offence in 't?** = does it not seem to you an objectionable one?

243.   **offence** = 왕은 nothing offensive의 뜻으로 사용하고 있는데245 행에서 Hamlet은 이것을 crime의 뜻으로 받고 있다.

247.   **Mouse-trap** = 「쥐덫」. 본래 Hamlet이 극단에 주문한 극은 *The Murder of Gonzago*였다. Hamlet은 이런 제목을 만들어냄으로 써 왕을 함정에 빠뜨리려는 그의 의도를 보이고 있다. cf. II. ii. 633-4. The play's the thing / Wherein I'll catch the conscience of the King.

     Marry = 가벼운 뜻의 감탄사.

247-8.   **how? Tropically.** = 「무슨 뜻이냐구요? 비유지요」.

247.   **how?** = how are we to understand this name?

248.   **Tropically** = figuratively.   cf.   trope(=   figurative   (e.g. metaphorical or ironical) use of a word.) 판본에 따라서는 trapically로 된 곳도 있는 것으로 보아 trap과의 말장난인 것을 알 수 있다.

image = exact representation.

249.   **duke's** = king, duke, 심지어는 count도 흔히 '군주'의 뜻으로 구별 없이 사용되었다.

250.   **anon** = soon.

250-1.   **a knavish piece of work** = i.e. the murder.

251.   **but what o' that?** = but that matters nothing.

252.   **free** = free from guilt, innocent of all crime.

252-3.   **Let the gall'd [-id] jade wince** = 속담. 뜻은 Let guilty persons flinch.

253.   **galled jade** = a horse irritated from painful chafing.

    galled = sore from chafing 「(안장이나 고삐로) 말의 피부가 벗겨진」.

    jade = an inferior or worn-out horse.

    wince = start or involuntarily shrink showing pain or distress 「움칫하다」.

    our withers are unwrung = we are unaffected, imputation does not touch us.

    withers = the ridge between the horse's shoulders.

    unwrung = not chafed, as by a bad saddle.

254.   **Lucianus** = [lu:siá:(éi)nəs]

    nephew = brother 대신 nephew를 사용한 것은 Hamlet의 의도를 지나치게 노골적으로 나타내지 않기 위함인지.

255.   **chorus** = a character who tells the audience what they are about to see. 예를 들면 *Rome and Juliet*의 시작 부분.

256-7.   **I could interpret···love** = I could play the role of narrator at a puppet show in which you and your lover are shown making love. Hamlet은 Ophelia와 가상의 그녀 애인을 인형에 빗대고 있다.

256-7.   **I could···dallying** = I could play the narrator at a puppet show that represented you playing with your lover.

256. **interpret** = cf. interpreter = 꼭두각시 인형극(puppet-show)의 해설자. 무대 위에 앉아 관객에게 해설했다.

257. **dallying** = trifling with 「노닥거리다」.

258. **keen** = sharp, incisive.

259-60. **take off my edge** = make me less sharp, satisfy my desire, blunt the edge of my sexual desire. Hamlet은 258행의 Ophelia의 You are keen이라는 말에 성적인 의미(You are sharp, penetrating)를 부여해 외설적인 말장난(double entendre)을 하고 있다.

259. **groaning** = orgasm.

edge = sexual desire. keen, edge, groan은 모두 성적인 암시를 내포하는 말들이다.

261. **Still better, and worse** = more witty and more offensive 「더 재치가 있으나 더 험하다」.

262. **So** = 「그렇게 해서」. 즉, Still better, and worse 따위의 말로서, 영국 국교의 결혼식에서 사용하는 선서문 I, (Bride's mame) take thee, (Bridegroom's name), to my wedded husband, to have and to hold from this day forward, *for better for worse*(어려울 때나 즐거울 때나), for richer for poorer, in sickness and in health, etc.…라는 문구가 생각나서 한 말. 여자들은 이 같은 서약을 손쉽게 어기면서 남자를 받아들인다.

mistake = take wrongly, falsely, improperly. mistake가 mis-take나 must take로 된 판본도 있다.

263. **pox** = plague on you! 「염병할!」.

leave thy damnable faces = have done with all the contortions of your face.

damnable faces = execrable grimaces 「보기 싫게 찡그린 얼굴」.

264. **the croaking raven doth bellow for revenge** = 당시 관객은 잘 알고 있는 작자 미상의 *The True Tragedy of Richard III*(c. 1591)

라는 희곡에 사용된 대사를 장난스럽게 줄이고 있다. 본래의 대사는 The screeking **raven** sits **croaking for revenge.** / Whole herds of beasts come bellowing **for revenge.**

266. **Thoughts black, hands apt, drugs fit** = Thoughts are black, hands are apt, drugs are fit.

apt = ready, prepared.

267. **Confederate season** = the time and occasion conspiring (with me).

Confederate = conspiring, i.e. to assist the murderer.

else no creature seeing = no one but myself being here to see what I do.

else = if not.

268. **mixture rank** = 「맹독성의 조제약」.

mixture = preparation of various ingredients.

rank = rancid, noisome, foul, offensive.

of midnight weeds collected = extracted from herbs gathered at midnight. 마녀들이 사용하는 독초는 한밤중에 뜯어 오는 것이 가장 효과가 있다고 한다.

of = from.

269. **With Hecate's ban thrice blasted** = blasted by a triple curse of Hecate's, and so trebly poisonous.

With Hecate's ban = by the curse of Hecate.

Hecate [hékət] = goddess of sorcery and witchcraft 「마녀의 왕」. 보통 세 개의 동상이 등을 맞댄 모양으로 만들어진다. thrice(3배)라는 표현은 여기에 유래한다.

blasted = cursed.

infected = made poisonous. 앞줄의 weeds에 걸린다.

270. **dire property** = evil power or capacity.

271. **On wholesome life usurp** = steal away health and life.

usurp = encroach or exercise unlawful influence upon, take wrongfully.

272-3.   **for 's estate** = in order to get possession of his kingly dignity.

273.   **the story is extant** = the story is still present. 그러나 실제로 발견된 작품은 없다.

274.   **writ** = written.

choice = beautiful.

anon = soon.

277.   **false fire** = discharge of a gun loaded only with powder 「공포」.

279.   **Give o'er** = give up, abandon.

282-4.   **Why, let the strucken deer go weep** = 당시 전해 내려오던 민요에서 가져온 말인 듯.

282.   **strucken** = struck, wounded by an arrow.

go weep = go and (*or* to) weep. 상처 입은 사슴은 보이지 않는 곳으로 가서 울다가 죽는 것으로 알려져 있었다.

283.   **The hart ungalled** = 앞에 let를 보충해서 읽는다.

ungalled = uninjured, unhurt.

284.   **watch** = stay awake.

285.   **So runs the world away** = such is the course of the world 「세상은 그렇게 돌아간다」.

286.   **this…and a forest of feathers** = 「여기다 깃털을 잔뜩 달면」. 당시 배우들은 화려한 의상을 입었으며 특히 모자에 깃털을 다는 것이 유행이었다.

this = i.e. my contribution to the play.

forest of feathers = many plumed hats.

286-7.   **if the rest…me** = if I fail in every other way to get my livelihood.

287.   **turn Turk** = change utterly for the worse. 터키인들은 이교도로서 혐오의 대상이었다.

288.   **Provincial roses** = rosettes imitating the damask rose 「장미 모양

으로 묶은 리본」. Provincial은 남부 프랑스의 Provence가 아니고 파리 근교의 Provins의 형용사. 빨강 장미로 유명한 곳이다.

raz'd shoes = 「무늬부분 이외의 것을 도려낸 신발」. 청중은 당시 때로 배우들이 신턴 raised(굽이 높은) shoes로 들을 수 있다.

raz'd = fashionably slashed.

289. **a fellowship in a cry of players** = a partnership in a theater company.

fellowship = partnership, membership.

cry = company (of people), pack of hounds 「패거리」. 사냥개들이 짖는 소리(cry)에서 나온 경멸적인 표현.

290. **Half a share** = 「반 몫, 반 구좌」. 당시 배우들은 월급이나 출연료 대신 수입의 배당을 주권(shares)으로 나누어 받았다. 즉 그들은 주주들이었다. 신인 배우들은 「반 몫」을 받기도 했다.

291. **A whole one** = I would expect a whole one.

292-5. **O Damon…pajock** = 출처 불명의 민요에서 가져온 듯.

292. **O Damon dear** = my dearest friend.

Damon [déimən] = Damon and Pythias는 그리스 사람들로서 친한 친구의 귀감으로 알려져 있다. Hamlet은 Horatio를 Damon 으로 부르고 있다.

293. **dismantled** = stripped, deprived, robbed.

294. **Jove** = Jupiter. 그리스 신화의 Zeus에 해당한다. 신들의 왕이다. Hamlet은 아버지를 Jove에 비유하고 있다.

295. **pajock** = peacock. 북부 Scotland의 하층 계급 사람들이 peacock 을 pajock이라고 발음한다는 보고가 있다. 공작은 날개가 화려하고 교만한(proud) 대신 발이 더럽고, 또한 호색적인(lustful) 것으로 알려져 있다. 또한 많은 새들이 모여 독수리대신 공작새를 왕으로 옹립했다는 우화도 있는 점으로 미루어 여기서는 물론 국왕 Claudius를 지칭한다.

296. **You might have rhym'd** = 「운을 맞출 수도 있었는데」. 292-5의

네 줄의 운을 보면 마지막 단어가 dear, was, here pajock으로 되어 첫째와 셋째 줄은 운이 맞는 데 둘째의 was와 넷째의 pajock 은 운이 맞지 않는다. 넷째 줄의 끝을 둘째 줄의 was와 운을 맞추려면 pajock 대신 ass(바보) 따위의 단어로 바꾸면 된다.

297-8.   **I'll take···pound** = I'll wager a thousand pounds that the ghost spoke the truth about my father's death「천만금을 내고라도 사겠다」. Shakespeare는 확정된 금액을 나타내는 경우 pounds 대신 자주 pound를 사용하였다.

300.   **Upon the talk of the poisoning** = as soon as the poisoning was mentioned.

   upon = at or just about the time.

303.   **recorders** = wind instruments, flutes. 여덟 개의 구멍을 가진 피리.

304-5.   **For if···perdy** = 이 두 줄은 복수극의 효시로 알려진 T. Kid의 걸작인 *Spanish Tragedy*, IV. I. 197-8에서 주인공 Hieronimo가 극중극(play-within-the-play)을 계획하면서 "And if the world like not this tragedy, / Hard is the hap of old Hieronimo'라고 한 말을 패러디한 것. Hieronimo는 복수를 성공시킨다. Hamlet 이 본래의 tragedy를 comedy로 바꾼 것은 아직 복수가 이루어 지지 않은 탓.

305.   **belike** = perhaps.

   perdy = by God. 프랑스어의 par Dieu(= by God)에서 온 말.

306.   **Come, some music!** = Rosencrantz와 Guildenstern이 염탐하러 들어오는 것을 보고 Hamlet은 다시 미친 척 딴전을 피운다.

307.   **vouchsafe** = grant.

309.   **Sir** = Guildenstern의 말투는 지나치게 공손하고 젠체하는 데가 있다. 그래서 Hamlet도 일부러 공손한 말투로 대꾸한다.

   a whole history = not merely a word, but a whole history, if you wish it.

   history = story, narrative.

312.   **his retirement** = his withdrawal to his private chambers.

313.   **marvellous distemper'd** = very much vexed, upset.

    marvellous = marvellously.

    distemper'd = out of temper「불쾌한」, disordered in body「몸이
    불편한」. Guildenstern이 전자의 뜻으로 말한 것을 Hamlet은
    후자의 뜻으로 받고 있다.

315.   **choler** [kɔ́lə] = anger. 또 다른 뜻은 bile(담즙). 중세 이래의 생리
    학에서는 인체 내에 흐르는 네 가지 기본 체액 중 하나로 간주.
    이것이 지나치면 사람은 화를 내게 된다. Hamlet은 짐짓 이것
    을 후자의 뜻으로 받는다.

316-7.   **Your wisdom···doctor** = you would act more wisely to report
    this to his doctor.

    more richer = much more rich. 당시에는 이와 같은 2중비교급
    이 드물지 않게 사용되었다.

317.   **signify** = inform, announce, tell.

317-9.   **for me···choler** = if I were administer his purge (purges being
    given for bilious disorders), I should only increase his choler.

318.   **purgation** = medical cleansing, spiritual purification「지설제」.
    담즙 병의 치료를 위해서는 설사 약을 사용한다. Hamlet은 자
    기가 왕에게 설사 약을 사용해서 병을 고쳐주려고 하면(죄악을
    고백하게 하면) 병이 더 도질 것이다(더 화를 낼 것이다)라고
    말하고 있다.

320-1.   **put your discourse into some frame** = be pleased to answer me
    in some coherent form, some orderly shape.

321.   **frame** = definite form, order.

    start not so wildly = do not rush so madly. 말에 빗댄 말.

    start = jump away (like a nervous or wild horse).

    from my affair = away from my business.

322.   **tame** = ready to hear anything you have to say. tame(길들이다)

은 특히 말에 대해 사용하는 말이다. 윗줄의 wildly와 짝지어
사용되고 있다.

pronounce = i.e. deliver your message.

326. **Nay⋯breed** = nay, my good lord, the courtesy shown in the
word 'welcome' is not of the kind proper to the occasion.

327. **of the right breed** = proper (to the occasion).
breed = sort, kind.

328. **wholesome** = sane, sensible, reasonable.

328-9. **I will⋯commandment** = I will give you the message sent by
your mother.

320-30. **if not⋯business** = if not, I will finish my business by asking
your permission to lease you.

329. **pardon** = leave, permission to depart 「작별의 허가」.

331. **I cannot** = 다다음 줄의 Make you a wholesome answer에 연결
된다.

333. **Make you a wholesome answer** = give you a healthy answer.
Hamlet은 Guildenstern의 wholesome을 문자 그대로 '건강한'의
뜻으로 받아 '정신이 온전치 못해' 제대로 답을 할 수 없다고
말한다.

334. **wit's** = mind is.

335. **you shall command** = shall be at your service, shall be rendered
to you.
command = demand with authority.

336. **my mother** = 뒤에 shall command를 보충해서 읽는다.
Therefore no more, but to the matter = therefore without further
preface let us come to the business.
to the matter = (let us come) to the point.

339. **amazement and admiration** = great surprise and wonder.
admiration = wonder, astonishment.

340-1. **O wonderful ··· mother!** = what a wonderful son I must be if I can cause wonder in my mother.

341-2. **But is ··· admiration?** = but is this all you have to tell me? is there nothing else to follow after this expression of her wonder?

342. **Impart** = Tell.

344. **closet** = private chamber. closet은 침실은 아니다. 그러나 현대 연출가들은 Hamlet의 Oedipus complex를 강조하기 위해 종종 왕비의 침실을 사용한다.

345-6. **We shall ··· mother** = Hamlet speaks as though obedience to a mother was about the last thing that could be expected of a son, instead of its being an ordinary duty.

345. **We** = 같은 줄의 our, 그리고 다음 줄의 us와 더불어 문법에서 말하는 이른바 royal 'we'의 용법이다. 우리말의 경우라면 반말이 경어로 바뀌는 것과 같다. Hamlet이 royal 'we'를 사용하는 것은 여기뿐이다. 반 농담조이지만 동시에 Hamlet은 Rosencrantz 와 Guildenstern에게 명확히 선을 그어 거리를 두려고 한다.
were she ten times our mother = 「열 배 내 어머니라 치더라도」. 다시 말해 「제아무리 죄 많은 어머니라도」.

346. **trade** = business.

348. **by these pickers and stealers** = by these hands. 이것은 Church Catechism(교리문답)에
Question. 'What is thy duty towards thy neighbour?
Answer. 'To keep my hands from picking and stealing, and my tongue from evil-speaking and slandering'에서 나온 말. Hamlet의 마음의 비밀을 염탐하러(훔치러) 온 Rosencrantz와 Guildenstern 두 사람에 대한 비아냥거림이 들어 있다.

350-1. **your cause of distemper** = the cause of your illness or disorder.

351-2. **You do ··· friend** = by refusing to communicate your griefs to your friend, you do but decline to avail yourself of the means of escaping from them.

352.   **deny your griefs** = refuse to disclose the cause of your suffering.

353.   **advancement** = 「출세, 승진」.

355-6.   **when you…Denmark** = i.e. when the King himself has said you are to succeed him on the throne.

356.   **voice** = recommendation.

         succession = succession to the throne.

358.   **While the grass grows** = 속담의 일부. 속담의 전문은 'While the grass grows, the steed starves'이다. 즉, 왕위를 넘겨받기 전에 자기는 죽고 말거라는 뜻. cf. 97-100.

         King. How fares our cousin Hamlet?
         Ham.   Excellent, i' faith; of the chameleon's
                dish. I eat the air, promise-cramm'd. You cannot
                feed capons so.

359.   **something musty** = somewhat stale, i.e. so familiar it need not be quoted in full.

360-1.   **To withdraw with you** = let me have a word with you in private. Guildenstern에게 하는 말.

         withdraw = be private.

361-2.   **go about recover the wind of me** = 「바람이 불어오는 곳에 자리 잡기 위해 이리저리 움직이다」. 사냥을 할 때 짐승들은 사냥꾼의 냄새를 맡을 수 있도록 바람이 부는 방향으로 도망을 가는데, 사냥꾼이 미리 그곳에 덫(toil)을 놓는 사냥의 한 기법이다. Hamlet은 Rosencrantz와 Guildenstern이 hunter이고 자기는 마치 quarry인 양 말하고 있다.

         recover = get, gain, reach.

362.   **toil** = net, snare, trap.

363-4.   **if my…unmannerly** = if, in my devotion to your interests, I am too bold in questioning you (asking about your distemper), it is my love for you that causes me to forget my manners.

my love is too unmannerly = my love is too genuine to trouble about manners, great affection causes me to intrudes in your affairs.

mannerly = well-mannered, polite.

365. **I do not well understand that** = I do not understand your enigmatical sentence라는 표면적인 뜻 외에 I am not sure that you are speaking the truth라는 비아냥거리는 뜻도 포함돼 있다.

366. **this pipe** = the recorder.

371. **I know no touch of it** = I do not have the skill to play it.

touch = fingering or playing of a musical instrument.

372. **as easy as lying** = 「거짓말 하는 것만큼 쉽다」. 속담적 표현. Guildenstern에 대한 빈정거림(innuendo)이다.

372-3. **govern these ventages** = apply your fingers and thumb to the stops to regulate the emission of sound.

ventages = wind-holes, the stops of a flute.

374. **discourse** = give forth (musical sound).

375. **stops** = ventages.

376-7. **But these⋯harmony** = but these stops I cannot so regulate as to make them give forth any harmonious sound.

377. **utterance of harmony** = harmonious (musical) sound or expression.

378. **unworthy** = contemptible, easy to manipulate.

379-80. **how unworthy⋯me!** = how mean an opinion you must have of me!

381. **you would seem to know** = you wish to appear that you know.

382. **pluck out the heart of my mystery** = find out my inmost secret.

mystery = (1) secret; (2) skill at a craft or trade (such as, here, playing an instrument).

381-4. **you would⋯compass** = you fancy you can interpret my every thought.

383.   **sound** = (1) bring forth a sound, play me like a musical instrument; (2) search out my depth, as with a fathom line; (3) test me for my secrets. 3중의 pun이다.

383-4.   **to the top of my compass** = to my limit.

384.   **compass** = (1) full range of an instrument's sound; (2) limits, scope.

385.   **organ** = musical instrument. 여기서는 pipe.

386.   **speak** = make music.

         'Sblood = by God's, or Christ's blood. 강한 욕.

388.   **though you can fret me** = (1) though you can manipulate my 'frets'; (2) you can make me angry.

         fret = (1) annoy, irritate; (2) torment; (3) provide a stringed instrument with frets.

         fret, *n.* = the raised parts on the fingerboard of stringed instrument that guide the fingers 「프렛」(현악기의 지판(指板)을 구획하는 작은 돌기).

392.   **and presently** = at once, immediately 「그것도 지금 곧」. 여기서 and는 immediately의 뜻을 강조한다.

393.   **Do you see…** = 지금 시간은 밤이다. 게다가 Hamlet은 지금 궁정 안에 있다. 따라서 하늘이 보일 리 없다. 따라서 대개는 Hamlet이 하늘을 쳐다보는 척하고 Polonius는 Hamlet이 미친 것으로 여기도록 연출하는 것이 보통이다. 그러나 야외에서 공연할 때에는 관중이 실제로 하늘을 쳐다보기도 하고, 현대적인 무대에서는 배우가 창가로 다가갈 수도 있다. 그러나 그렇지 않더라도 작품 *Hamlet*이 상연되고 있는 당대의 Globe Theatre의 천정은 하늘처럼 장식되어 있어 연출에 무리가 없었을는지도 모른다. cf. II. ii. 312-3.

                        this most excellent

canopy, the air, look you, this brave o'erhanging
firmament, this majestical roof…

395.   **By the mass** =「미사에 걸고 맹서하건데」. 가벼운 뜻의 감탄사.
        and = as you say.

397.   **back'd like a weasel** = its back is like that of a weasel. 「족제비」
        는 「낙타」와 사뭇 다른 짐승이다. 구름이 실제로 빠르게 모양
        을 바꾸고 있을 수도 있으나 Hamlet은 불성실한 Polonius를
        조롱하는 것으로 보이고, 여기에 대해 Polonius는 「미친」
        Hamlet에 거슬리지 않도록 편한 대로 응대하는 것으로 보인다.

400.   **by and by** = soon, before long, at once. 이 부분은 '당장'으로
        번역되기도 하나, 왕과 대결한다는 큰일을 치르고 난 뒤라서,
        '곧'이나 '조금 있다가' 정도의 여유 있는 번역이 좋을 듯하다.

401.   **They fool me to the top of my bent** =「인내의 한계까지 나를
        조롱한다.」.
        fool = trifle with.
        top of my bent = limit of my endurance.
        bent = extent to which a bow may be bent, degree of tension;
        (hence) degree of endurance.

405.   **'By and by' is easily said** = that's not a very difficult undertaking
        「말하긴 쉽다」.

406.   **witching time of night** = time when witches are active, midnight.
        여기서부터가 Hamlet의 여섯 번째 독백.

407.   **churchyards yawn** = graves open wide like mouths (to let out
        the dead).

407-8. **breathes out Contagion** = lets loose its pestilence or poison.

408.   **Contagion** = contagious or poisonous influence, infectious
        vapours.
        drink hot blood = Witches were supposed to do this.

409.   **such bitter business** = such deeds of bitter cruelty.

410.   **Soft!** = Be quiet, let me pause.

411.   **lose not thy nature** = do not deny or betray your natural (filial) feeling, do not forget your natural affection for your mother. **nature** = natural feeling, natural affection.

412.   **Nero** = 고대 로마의 폭군 Nero는 황제인 남편 Claudius를 독살하고 그 형제와 불륜의 결혼을 한 어머니 Agrippina의 아랫배를 칼로 찔러 죽였다.
       this firm bosom = this bosom of mine, fully determined though it is to punish the guilty.
       firm = resolved (i.e. against doing violence).

413.   **Let me be cruel, not unnatural** = Hamlet may assumes that it will be cruel to attack his mother verbally but unnatural to attack her physically.

414.   **speak daggers** = speak bitterly or fiercely, so as to stab the heart as keenly as daggers would pierce the flesh. 이 표현은 지금도 흔하게 쓰이는데, 그 기원이 바로 이 표현이다.

415.   **My tongue and soul in this be hypocrites** = in this matter let my soul be a hypocrite to my tongue, i.e. he will behave hypocritically or deceitfully in merely scolding his mother when in his soul he wants to do her physical harm.

416-7. **How in⋯consent!** = however roughly I may take her to task, let me never yield to the impulse to ratify my words by deeds, i.e. the deed of murder.

416.   **How⋯soever** = however.
       shent = shend의 과거분사. rebuked, punished, put to shame.

417.   **give them seals** = ratify the words by actions, confirm them (= words) by making words into deeds. Hamlet은 왕과 함께 어머니에 대한 복수도 생각하지만 아버지 유령이 말했던 것을 잊지 않고 있다. cf. I. v. 84-8.

But, howsoever thou pursuest this act,
Taint not thy mind, nor let thy soul contrive
Against thy mother aught; leave her to heaven
And to those thorns that in her bosom lodge,
To prick and sting her.

Scene III

1-2.　**I like … range** = I do not like the look of things as regards him,
nor is it safe for us to allow his madness to have free scope.

1.　**I like him not** = I do not like the way he is acting.

　　him = his condition or behaviour.

　　nor stands it safe = nor is it safe.

2.　**his madness** = him who is mad.

　　range = roam freely.

　　prepare you = prepare yourselves.

3.　**I your commission will forthwith dispatch** = I will at once make
out the commission which you are to take to England.

　　commission = authoritative letter.

　　forthwith dispatch = prepare at once.

　　dispatch = prepare in haste, prepare promptly.

4.　**shall along** = shall go along. shall 뒤에서 동작을 나타내는 동사
는 자주 생략된다.

5.　**The terms of our estate** = my position as a king.

　　terms = circumstances.

7.　**ourselves provide** = prepare ourselves.

8-10.　**Most holy … Majesty** = the anxiety you feel for the safety of those who are dependent upon you is a most holy feeling, their welfare being a sacred duty to one in your position.

8.   **holy and religious** = devoted and conscientious.

    fear = duty, apprehension, concern.

9.   **bodies** = persons. cf. any*body*, some*body*, etc.

10.   **feed** = depend (upon another) for their food. cf. feeder = servant.

11-3.   **The single···noyance** = even the individual man (who has no one to think of but himself) is in prudence bound to use every faculty of his mind to keep himself from injury.

11.   **single and peculiar life** = individual and private.

    bound = obliged.

13.   **noyance** = harm, injury.

14.   **That spirit** = the King. 뒤에 is bound to do so를 보충할 것.

    weal = welfare.

    depends and rests = 이들 동사의 주어는 다음 줄의 The lives of many이므로 복수형의 depend and rest로 해야 옳다. 그러나 여기서처럼 동사가 주어를 선행하는 경우, 즉 화자가 아직 주어를 확정짓지 못한 경우 단수형의 동사를 사용하기도 한다.

15-6.   **The cease···alone** = the extinction of majesty in the death of a king is much more than the single death of an ordinary man.

15.   **the cease of majesty** = the death of a king.

16-7.   **but, like···it** = involves the sweeping away of everything connected with it (= majesty), as a whirlpool engulfs everything that comes within its area.

16.   **gulf** = whirlpool.

    draw = pull in, attract.

17.   **It is a** = it is like a.

    massy = massive.

    wheel = 운명의 여신이 굴리는 운명의 수레바퀴.

20. **mortised** [mɔ́:tist] **and adjoin'd** = 「끼워 넣거나 붙이거나」.

mortised = securely fastened, firmly fixed.

motise, n. = a hole made in timber into which the tenon of another piece of timber is fixed.

mortise, v. = join securely by mortise and tenon.

20-2. **which,⋯ruin** = and when this massive wheel is precipitated down, everything however small, that is an adjunct of it, everything however trifling that accompanies it, is swept away in its violent overthrow.

21. **annexment** = appendage, addition.

petty consequence = trivial thing connected with it.

22. **Attends** = accompanies, participates in.

boisterous = tumultuous, violent, savage.

ruin = downfall.

23. **but with a general groan** = being echoed by the groan of the whole kingdom.

24. **Arm you** = Prepare yourselves.

speedy = imminent or perhaps hastily planned.

25-6. **For we⋯free-footed** = for I will put restraint upon this danger which now ranges abroad too freely.

25. **fear** = object of fear, i.e. Hamlet.

26. **free-footed** = 「마음대로 돌아다니는」.

haste us = make haste.

us = ourselves.

27. **closet** = private chamber. cf. III. ii. 344.

28. **arras** = a fold of tapestry, wall-hanging. cf. II. ii. 163.

convey myself = slip furtively. convey는 Shakespeare의 경우 대개 나쁜 뜻으로 사용된다.

29. **process** = proceedings, conversation, what happens. cf. I. v. 37.

warrant = guarantee, promise.

tax him home = reprimand him severely.

tax = censure, blame, accuse.

home = to the point aimed at 「정통으로」. 부사로 사용되었음.

30.   **as you said** = 사실 이 제안을 한 것은 Polonius 자신이다 (cf. III. i. 192-3. And I'll be plac'd, so please you, in the ear Of all their conference.). 신하의 도리에 따라 모든 공을 왕에게 돌리려는 겸양이라고 볼 수 있으나 책임을 왕에게 돌리려는 신중함이라고도 볼 수 있다.

31.   **meet** = fitting, appropriate.

32.   **nature makes them partial** = 「인정 상 어머니는 아들을 편애하게 된다」. them의 의미상의 선행사는 앞줄의 a mother이다. 어머니들 모두가 그렇다는 생각에 복수형의 them을 잘못 사용하고 있다.

33.   **of vantage** = from the vantage point of concealment.

33.   **liege** = sovereign lord.

34.   **ere** = before.

36-8.   **O, my offfence … murder** = O, my crime, the murder of a brother, is so foul that the taint of it has reached the very heavens, and on I rests the curse pronounced upon Cain.

36.   **rank** = offensive, foul-smelling.

37.   **primal eldest curse** = 구약의 *Genesis* 4:8. 11-12에서 Cain이 동생 Abel을 죽이는 인류 최초의 살인을 범하고 신에게서 받은 최초의 저주.

       eldest = oldest.

38.   **A brother's murder** = the murder of a brother.

39.   **Though inclination is sharp as will** = although my desire to pray is as strong as my determination to do so. 이것은 같은 말의 반복(tautology)이므로 차라리 although my desire to pray is as

strong as my will to sin으로 번역하자는 주장도 있다.

inclination = the natural disposition to do a thing.

will = the determination prompted by the understanding.

40.   **My stronger guilt defeats my strong intent** = strong as my purpose is, my guilt is stronger still, and overcomes it.

41.   **to double business bound** = obliged to undertake two tasks at once.

42.   **stand in pause** = am in hesitation. cf. III. i. 68.

43.   **What if** = even supposing that.

        cursed [-id]

44.   **thicker than itself** = 「피가 묻어 두꺼워지다」.

45-6.   **Is there···snow** = cf. *Psalm* 51:7. Wash me and I shall be whiter than snow; *Isiah* 1:18. Though your sins were as crimson, they shall be made white as snow.

45.   **sweet heavens** = gracious heavens. cf. III. i. 138.

46-7.   **Whereto···offence?** = what is the function of mercy if it does not confront guilt.

46.   **Whereto serves mercy** = what purpose does mercy serve.

47.   **confront** = face up to and deal with (a problem, difficulty, etc.) 「(피하지 않고) 직면하다」.

        the visage of offense = the sinful acts of the offender.

48-50. **this twofold···down** = i.e. the twofold force of prayer is that we not be led into temptation and that we be forgiven our trespasses. cf. *Matthew* 6:13. And lead us not into temptation, but deliver us from evil.

48.   **what's in prayer** = what is the use of prayer.

49.   **forestalled** [-id] = prevented by anticipation.

50.   **being down** = when we are fallen.

        Then I'll look up = i.e. with hopeful eyes, take courage.

look up = take courage.

51. **past** = already committed, i.e. it is too late for sin to be forestalled, but there is still the possibility of pardon.

52. **serve my turn** = answer my purpose.

turn = occasion.

53-4. **am still possess'd Of** = still possess.

54. **effects** = rewards, benefits, something acquired by an action.

55. **ambition** = 왕위에 오른 것. My crown과 동격어.

56. **May one be pardon'd and retain the offence?** = is it possible for one to be pardoned while still retaining that for which he sinned?

retain the offence = keep the profits of the crime.

offence = the thing acquired by sin.

57. **In the corrupted currents of this world** = in the corrupted ways in which this world goes.

currents = courses of events, ways of doing things.

58. **Offence's gilded hand may shove by justice** = the wealthy offender is able to thrust justice aside.

Offence's gilded hand = the gold-bearing (and guilty) hand of the offender.

shove by = push or thrust aside.

59-60. **the wicked … law** = a favourable verdict is secured by the very wealth which has been wrongfully acquired.

59. **wicked prize** = ill-gotten wealth.

prize = booty.

60. **buy out** = 「매수하다」.

'tis not so above = this is not the case in heaven.

61. **There is no shuffling** = before God's tribunal there is no evading justice.

shuffling = evasion, trickery.

61-4.   **the action⋯in evidence** = in God's court, the legal action must be brought in accord with the facts, we are forced even to testify against ourselves.

61-2.   **the action lies In his true nature** = the deed is clearly known for what it is.

61.   **the action lies** = the case lies bare, is seen in its bare colours. 상투적인 법정 술어이다.

  action = legal proceeding.

  his = its.

62-4.   **and we⋯evidence** = and we cannot escape being brought face to face with our own sins to give evidence against them.

62.   **we ourselves compell'd** = compell'd 앞에 are를 보충하여 다다움 줄의 To give in evidence(= give witness)에 연결한다.

63.   **to the teeth and forehead of** = face to face.

64.   **What rests?** = what remains (to be done)?

65.   **Try** = let me try.

  can = can achieve.

66.   **Yet what can it when one cannot repent?** = yet of what avail is repentance when one cannot repent?

68-9.   **O limed⋯engag'd** = O soul entangled in difficulties, and only more thoroughly entangled by your efforts to free yourself.

  limed [-id] = caught as a bird in lime (a sticky paste).

69.   **engaged** = entangled.

  Make assay = make vigorous effort to rescue me! 자신에게 하는 말.

  assay = an attempt.

70.   **stubborn** = stiff, inflexible.

  heart with strings of steel = naturally so unyielding.

73. **Now might I do it pat** = I could not find a time more fit for my purpose.

pat = appositely, opportunely, quite to the purpose. pat이 But이 된 판본도 있다. 그 쪽이 Hamlet의 즉각적인 회의를 더 잘 나타내는 장점이 있다.

74. **And so** = and the consequence will be that.

75. **would be scann'd** = requires careful scrutinizing.

scan = examine, consider, discuss.

76. **for that** = in return for that.

77. **his sole son** = on whom therefore the duty of revenge solely lies.

79. **this is hire and salary** = something Claudius should pay me for 「이것은 마치 아버지를 죽이기 위해 삼촌을 고용하고 죽인 보상으로 천국에 보내는 것과 같다」.

80. **He took my father grossly, full of bread** = he took my father by surprise when in a state of gross and luxurious living.

grossly = 문법적으로 grossly는 동사 took에 걸린다. 즉, He killed my father without any decency의 뜻이 된다. 동시에 살해된 아버지에 걸리기도 한다. 그 때는 He killed my father in a state of gross sinfulness의 뜻이 된다.

full of bread = full-fed, in a state of sensual satiety. cf. *Ezekiel* 16:49. Pride, fullness of bread, and abundance of idleness.

81. **With all his crimes broad blown, as flush as May** = with all his sins in full blossom, and with his blood flowing in his veins with the lusty vigour of the sap of trees in mid-spring. cf. I. v. 74-6.

Thus was I, sleeping, by a brother's hand
Of life, of crown, of queen, at once dispatch'd;
Cut off even in the blossoms of my sin,

broad blown = in full bloom. cf. I. v. 76.

flush = lusty, vigorous.

82.   **how his audit stands** = how his account in the next world stands. knows의 목적어.

his = Hamlet의 아버지 국왕.

audit = final reckoning, account. cf. I. v. 78.

83-4.   **But in our…him** = but so far as we can judge by looking at the matter from all points of view, things are in an evil plight with him.

83.   **in our circumstance and course of thought** = from my limited earthly perspective 「내 좁은 소견으로는」.

84.   **'Tis heavy with him** = his audit or list of sins is a weighty or large one 「심판은 가볍지 않다」.

85.   **To take him in the purging of his soul** = in seizing the opportunity of killing him(= Claudius) when he is purging his soul of guilt.

purging = cleansing.

86.   **season'd** = ripe, prepared.

passage = the passage from this world to the next.

88.   **Up** = back to your sheath. cf. put *up* a sword.

know thou a more horrid hent = may you have a more horrible seizure, i.e. wait to seize a more terrible opportunity.

hent = grasp (i.e. occasion to be grasped). hent를 hint(= opportunity, occasion seized)의 변종으로 보는 해석도 있다.

89.   **drunk asleep** = in a drunken sleep, dead drunk. drunk와 asleep 사이에 콤마가 있는 판본도 있다. 그 때는 drunk or asleep의 뜻이 된다.

rage = violent passion. sexual passion(Onions)이라는 해석도 있으나 다음 줄과 내용이 겹치는 문제가 있다.

90. **incestuous** = cf. I. ii. 157.

91. **At gaming, swearing** = when he is engaged in gaming or is swearing. gaming과 swearing 사이에 콤마가 없는 판본도 있는데, 그 때는「도박판에서 소리 지를 때」라는 하나의 동작을 나타내게 된다.

 swearing = using profane or indecent language.

 about = occupied with.

92. **That has no relish of salvation in 't** = that has nothing in it that savours of the salvation of his soul「구제의 기미가 보이지 않는」.

 relish = hint, trace, flavour.

93. **Then trip him, that his heels may kick at heaven** = then give him such a fall that he will go headlong to hell.

 trip him = cause him to stumble and fall.

95. **stays** = is waiting.

96. **This physic but prolongs thy sickly days** =「이 약은 잠시 네 목숨을 연장한 뿐이다」.

 This physic = this medicine, i.e. this postponement of the killing, or Claudius's purging of himself through prayer.

98. **Words without thoughts never to heaven go** = mere words of prayer, into which heartfelt penitence does not enter, never reach the throne of God.

Scene IV

1. **straight** = straightaway, immediately.

 Look you lay home to him = accuse or reprove him thoroughly.

	lay home to = attack, press hard, reprove thoroughly.
2.	**pranks** = malicious or mischievous deed or trick, reprehensible action. 현재의 jokes보다 더 뜻이 강하다.

have been too broad to bear with = have gone to too great a length to be endured any longer.

broad = free, gross, unrestrained, excessive.

bear with = tolerate.

3. **your Grace** = Queen.

3-4. **hath screen'd ⋯ him** = have interposed to shield him from much wrath which would otherwise have fallen upon him 「왕의 분노가 미치지 않도록 가운데 막아섰다」.

3. **screen** = interpose oneself as a screen.

4. **Much heat** = anger (of the king). 벽난로의 열을 직접 받지 않도록 하기 위해 사용한 이동식 칸막이(screen)에서 온 은유.

5. **be round with him** = use the plainest language possible to him.

round = plain, forthright, direct, blunt, severe.

7. **I'll warrant you** = I promise you that I will.

Fear me not = do not doubt my pressing him hard.

Fear = be anxious about.

9-21. 왕비가 Hamlet를 부를 때 thou와 you를 섞어 사용하고 있다. 부모와 자식 사이의 통상적인 호칭은 thou이다. 그러나 왕비는 때로 Hamlet를 you로 부르기도 한다. 정확하지는 않지만 thou는 우리말의 반말에, you는 경어에 해당한다. Shakespeare는 왕비가 Hamlet를 친근하게 생각하거나 흥분해서 자신을 잃을 때에는 thou를, 격식을 차려 거리를 두려고 할 때에는 you를 사용한다. 이것은 마치 선생님이 학생을 벌주면서 "숙제 안한 학생은 종아리를 맞아야지요"라고 경어를 쓰는 경우와 비슷하다. Shakespeare는 이런 방법으로 왕비의 미묘한 감정의 움직임을 묘사하고 있다.

9.	**thy father** = stepfather, i.e. Claudius.

10.	**my father** = Hamlet의 아버지인 선왕.

11.	**you answer with an idle tongue** = your answer is mere frivolity.
	idle = 보통은 foolish, frivolous의 뜻이나 여기서는 뜻이 좀 강
	해져서 void of meaning or sense 정도의 뜻이 되었다.

12.	**Go, go** = 앞줄의 Come, come과 거의 같은 뜻.

13.	**how now** = an expression of reproach.

14.	**forgot me** = forgotten that I am your mother. Hamlet의 무례를
	탓하고 있다.
	by the rood = a mild oath. by the (holy) cross 「결코」.
	rood = cross (of Christ).

15.	**your husband's brother's wife** = cf. II. ii. 393-4. my uncle-father
	and aunt-mother are deceiv'd.

16.	**would you were not so!** = I wish you were not my mother! 「그러
	지 않았으면 좋았겠지만」.

17.	**I will set those to you that can speak** = summon those who can
	speak more forcefully. 왕을 데려오겠다는 말로 들린다.
	set one thing to another = place one thing in opposition to
	another.

18.	**budge** = stir, move.

19.	**You go…you** = you will not be allowed to move from this spot
	till, as in a mirror, I have shown you your real nature. cf. III.
	ii. 23-5. whose end, both at the first and now, was and is, to
	hold, as 'twere, the mirror up to nature;
	glass = looking glass, mirror.

23.	**Dead, for a ducat** = I'll bet a ducat that he is dead.
	for a ducat = 맹세할 때의 말.
	ducat = 4s. 9d.의 gold coin.

SD	**a pass** = a thrust with his rapier. 펜싱 술어임.

30. **As kill a king** = as to kill a king. 유령도 왕비가 살인에 공모했다는 말을 하지 않았으며, 여기서 왕비가 놀라는 것을 보아서도 왕비는 살인과 무관하다는 것을 알 수 있다.

32. **thy better** = i.e. the king.
Take thy fortune = accept your fate.

33. **busy** = overactive, interfering, meddlesome「나서기 좋아하는」.
cf. busybody (= meddlesome person).
is some danger = is a dangerous kind of business.

34. **Leave wringing of your hands** = it is no good your making all this outward show of grief「손을 쥐어짜며 슬퍼하는 모양은 그만두세요」.
leave = leave off.

35. **And let me wring your heart; for so I shall** = it is your heart that should be wrung, and that I mean to do.

36. **If it made of penetrable stuff** = if it has still retained any sensitivity to emotion.

37-8. **If damned … sense** = if accursed familarity with crime has not so brazened it as to be proof against all feeling.
damned [-id] custom = habitual wickedness, accursed habit.
braz'd = brazened, hardened.

38. **proof and bulwark** = armoured and fortified, i.e. impenetrable. hendiadys의 예.
proof = invulnerable (like armour).
bulwark = rampart「성채」.
sense = natural or proper feeling (i.e. guilt).

39. **wag thy tongue** = use your tongue so freely.

40-1. **Such an act … modesty** = you have committed a deed of a nature that dims the grace of all modest blushes, the modesty of all your sex is robbed of much of its grace by the fact of a woman having done such a deed.

40. **Such an act** = 앞에 You have done을 보충할 것. 여기서의 act는 어머니의 재혼이나 불륜에 관한 것.

41. **blurs** = stains, defiles, disfigures.

the grace and blush of modesty = innocent (blushing) grace of a modest woman. grace and blush는 hendiadys의 예.

42. **Calls virtue hypocrite** = makes all real virtue seem mere hypocrisy.

42-4. **takes off…there** = and in place of the tenderness that graces an innocent love, sets upon its brow a shameless flush.

rose = idealized love.

44. **sets a blister there** = 「대신 불로 낙인을 찍다」. 옛날 감찰을 갖지 않은 창부의 이마를 불로 지지던 습관에 빗대고 있다. cf. harlot-brow. 그러나 Hamlet은 blister라는 단어로 어머니가 선왕의 생존 시부터 불륜을 저질렀다는 암시를 하고 있다. 유령이 "정숙해 보였던(seeming)"이라고 했던 대목이 연상되는 부분이다. cf. I. v. 46: my most seeming-virtuous queen.

45. **dicers' oaths** = the (rash) promises of gamblers.

dicer = one who gambles with dice.

46-7. **As from…soul** = as robs the outward form of the marriage tie of that which is its essential grace.

46. **body of contraction** = substance of a (marriage) contract.

47-8. **sweet religion…words** = turns sweet religion into a mere confusion or frenzy of words.

47. **sweet religion** = (marriage) contract. makes의 목적어.

48. **A rhapsody of words** = a string of words, a mere extravagant utterance of words without meaning.

rhapsody = jumble.

doth glow = 「하늘이 불길한 붉은 색을 띠다」.

49-51. **Yea,···act** = yea, even this solid earth, with gloom-struck face, as though expectant of the day of judgement, is sick at heart in beholding such a deed. 판본에 따라서는 Yea가 O'er(over)로 된 곳도 있다. 그때는 48행의 Heaven's face가 51행 Is thought-sick의 주어가 된다.

49. **solidity and compound mass** = i.e. earth. 자기 「육체」의 뜻으로도 해석이 가능하다. cf. I. ii. 129: this too too solid flesh.

50. **tristful** = sorrowful.

   as against the doom = as if it were doomsday.

51-2. **what act···index?** = what act of mine is it that has so stormy a prelude?

51. **thought-sick** = thick at the thought, filled with anxiety, smitten with grief.

52. **thunders in the index** = 「시작부터 요란한 소란」.

   index = table of contents prefixed to a book, hence figuratively, preface, prologue. 앞줄의 act도 「소행」, 「연극」 두 가지 뜻으로 사용되고 있다.

53. **this picture, and on this** = 이 그림에 대해서는 약간의 논쟁이 있다. 실제로 벽에 그림이 걸려 있었는지, 아니면 Hamlet이나 왕비의 목걸이에 걸린 그림인지 분명치 않다. 그러나 58행의 Mercury에 대한 비유를 고려한다면 초상화가 벽에 걸려있는 것이 자연스럽다.

54. **counterfeit presentment** = representation in portraits, exact resemblance. Shakespeare는 counterfeit를 자주 부정적인 뜻은 없는 단순한 「그림」의 뜻으로 사용하였다. 즉 counterfeit가 portrait의 뜻으로 사용된 경우이다.

55. **this brow** = 죽은 왕의 얼굴.

56. **Hyperion** = Greek god of the sun, Apollo. Hyperion is often said to be the most beautiful of the pagan deities. cf. I. ii. 140.

front = forehead, brow.

Jove = 로마 신화의 Jupiter.

57. **eye like Mars** = The war-god would have a dominating glare.

to threaten = threatening, awe-striking 「질타하는」.

58. **station** = posture, manner of standing, pose of figure.

herald = Mercury being the messenger of the gods.

station like the herald Mercury = 전령의 신 Mercury는 몸이 강건하고 자세가 바른 것으로 되어 있다. 그렇다면 Hamlet이 가리키고 있는 그림은 반신상이나 흉상이 아닌 전신상일 것이다.

station = manner of standing.

59. **New-lighted** = newly alighted or landed. Mercury는 날개를 가지고 있는 것으로 묘사된다.

heaven-kissing = reaching almost to heaven.

60. **combination** = i.e. of physical features, excellences.

form = good semblance.

61. **Where every god did seem to set his seal** = which bore the impression of the hand of all the gods, set there in attestation of his nobility.

set his seal = place his mark of approval.

62. **assurance** = guarantee.

a man = 「훌륭한 남자」.

64-5. **like … brother** = infecting and so destroying his brother as a mildewed ear of corn by its neighbourhood to a healthy ear infects and blights it.

64. **mildew'd ear** = 「곰팡이 난 보리 이삭」.

ear = ear of grain 「이삭」. 이것은 동시에 선왕의 '귀'에 독을 부어넣은 사실을 연상시킨다.

65. **Blasting** = blighting.

his = its.

66-7.	**mountain⋯moor** = 산이나 황무지나 풀의 질에는 차이가 없다. 여기서는 높낮이를 대비시키고 있다.
66.	**leave to feed** = stop feeding.
67.	**batten** = grow fat, feed gluttonously.
	moor = barren land. 이 단어는 당시 혐오의 대상이었던 Moor인 (= blackamoor)에 대한 pun이다. 동시에 앞줄의 fair가 「희다」는 뜻도 가지고 있다는 사실을 생각할 때 fair와 moor가 「흑백」의 대비를 이룬다는 점을 알게 된다.
68.	**You cannot call it love** = you cannot say that you were led astray by ardent love.
69.	**The hey-day in the blood is tame, it's humble** = passion no longer overleaps its bounds, but has become dulled and well under control.
	hey-day = state of excitement, frolic wildness. 중세영어의 hey는 high를 뜻한다.
	blood = passion.
70.	**waits upon** = follows, obeys, waits for the direction of.
71.	**step** = transfer itself, pass with idea of what is good to what is bad.
71-2.	**Sense⋯motion** = you must have some basic sense or apprehension or you would not be living and moving.
	sure = certainly.
71.	**Sense** = feeling, sensibility.
72.	**motion** = movement(움직임). impulse(충동)나 desire(욕망)라는 해석도 있다.
73.	**apoplex'd** = struck with apoplexy, paralyzed.
73.	**for madness would not err** = for even madness would never make such a mistake.
74-6.	**Nor sense⋯difference** = nor sense ever allow itself to become

so entirely the slave of passionate feeling as to leave no power of choice by which to help itself in deciding between two objects so different from each other. to ecstasy는 thrall'd 뒤에 연결된다.

74. **ecstasy** = madness, frenzy.

  thrall'd = captive.

75. **quantity of choice** = power of discrimination.

76. **To serve in such a difference** = to enable it to differentiate (in such a case).

77. **cozen'd** = cheated, tricked, deceived.

  hoodman-blind = the game of blindman's buff 「장님놀이, 술래 잡기」. a game among children in which one of them has his eyes 'hooded' or blinded, with a handkerchief, and is set to catch and name one of his companions, a forfeit being paid if he names the wrong one. Hamlet implies that his mother must have been blindfolded when she chose her second husband.

78-81. **Eyes⋯mope** = eyes without the help of touch to guide them, touch without the help of sight, etc., or even a small portion, and that a diseased portion, of a single healthy sense, would not show itself so dull and stupid.

79. **sans** [sænz] **all** = without the other senses.

81. **Could not so mope** = could not commit such stupidity.

82-5. **Rebellious⋯fire** = if hellish passion can burst out into such uncontrolled mutiny in a woman of her age, virtue in the case of ardent youth may well show itself as soft as wax and melt in the fire which she (in flaming youth) feels.

82. **Rebellious hell** = Hamlet sees sensuality as a kind of rebellion.

  hell = fiendish passion.

83. **canst mutine** = can incite mutiny.

  matron's bones = Hamlet stresses the Queen's maturity.

84-5. **To flaming ⋯ fire** = i.e. chastity (*virtue*) will be like wax for young people (who are naturally more sensual) and will melt in its own heat.

84. **wax** = candle.

85. **her** = 앞줄의 virtue를 가리킨다.

85-8. **proclaim⋯will** = i.e. do not call it shameful when youthful passion acts impetuously, since the frost of age is itself aflame and reason is acting as a pander for desire instead of controlling it.

86. **compulsive ardour** = compelling desire (of youth).

　　gives the charge = makes the attack, gives the signal for attack.

87. **frost** = old age.

　　actively = briskly, vigorously.

88. **reason panders will** = reason acts as a pander for desire instead of controlling it, reason forgives (or makes excuses for) passion.

　　panders = acts as pander to, prostitutes (*v.*).

　　will = lust.

89. **into my very soul** = so that I am forced to look into the very depths of my soul.

90. **grained** [-id] = ingrained, indelible, deep-dyed.

　　grain = permanent dye.

91. **As will not leave their tinct** = as will leave their stain there, that nothing can wash them out.

　　leave their tinct = give up their color 「얼룩이 가시다」.

　　leave = part with, give up, resign.

　　tinct = color.

92. **rank** = offensive, excessive.

　　enseamed [-id] = greasy. 이 부분을 stained with semen과 연관시키려는 해석도 있다.

93. **Stew'd** = cooked, steeped. 밑에 stew(= brothel)라는 단어를 깔

고 있다.

honeying = using love-talk, calling each other *honey*.

94.   **sty** = pigsty, (*figuratively*) abode of bestial lust.

95.   **daggers** = cf. III. ii. 414. I will speak daggers to her.

97.   **that is not twentieth part of the tithe** = literally who is not the twentieth part of the tenth part, i.e. who weighs nothing as against, etc.

    twentieth part the tithe = i.e. 1/200.

    tithe = tenth.

98.   **precedent** = preceeding, former.

    a vice of kings = a clown of a king.

    vice = 중세 이후의 도덕극(morality play)에 나오는 buffoon으로서 Fool(어릿광대)과 마찬가지로 얼룩무늬 옷을 입고 있었다. 'Vice'라는 단어는 광대가 고약한 역할을 맡아했기 때문.

99.   **A cutpurse of the empire and the rule** = one who has filched the empire and its sway as a common pick-pocket filches his stolen goods. 당시에는 전대를 허리띠에 차고 다녔으므로 소매치기의 손쉬운 대상이 되었다.

    cutpurse = pickpocket, thief.

    the rule = the government, the kingdom.

100.   **diadem** = crown.

102.   **A king of shreds and patches** = a king with nothing kingly about him, made up of nothing but the cast-off remnants of kingly dignity. 어릿광대의 얼룩무늬 옷(motley dress)을 가리키기도 한다. 당시 광대가 입던 옷이 조각(patch)으로 만들어졌던 데에서 patch는 fool, clown, simpleton이라는 뜻도 가지고 있다.

    shreds and patches = motley, the traditional variegated costume of the fool 「(광대역을 맡은 배우가 입던) 얼룩무늬 옷」.

103-4.   **Save···guards** = Hamlet appeals to angels for protection.

104. **heavenly guards** = angels.

104. **What would your gracious figure?** = what would you desire appearing thus?

106. **Do you not come your tardy son to chide** = you surely must have come to chide, etc.
    tardy = procrastinating.

107. **laps'd in time and passion** = having suffered time to slip and passion to cool.

108. **important** = urgent.
    dread command = 「어명」.
    dread = held in awe, revered 「지엄한」. cf. I. ii. 50. My dread lord.

111. **whet** = sharpen.

112. **amazement on thy mother sits** = utter bewilderment has settled down upon your mother, your mother is in a state of extreme shock.
    amazement = bewilderment, distraction, perplexity. 오늘날의 amazement보다 훨씬 강한 뜻.

113. **step between her and her fighting soul** = intervene in her mental or spiritual crisis, interpose to save her from being overpowered by the emotions now struggling in her heart.

114. **Conceit in weakest bodies strongest works** = imagination works most powerfully in those who, like women, are physically weakest.
    Conceit = imagination. 동사는 works.

116-7. **Alas, how···vacancy** = what has come over you, that you look so fixedly upon mere empty space.

117. **bend** = focus, direct.
    vacancy = empty space.

118. **incorporal air** =「허공」.

incorporal = incorporeal, immaterial「실체가 없는」.

hold discourse = converse.

119. **Forth at your eyes your spirits wildly peep** = from your eyes your soul looks out in wild amazement. Forth는 peep 뒤에 연결된다.

spirits = mind, soul.

wildly =「미친 사람처럼」.

120-2. **And, as … end** = and, like soldiers awakened by the signal of the enemy being at hand, your hair, a moment ago lying still upon your head, starts up and stands erect, like inanimate matter suddenly endowed with life.

120. **in the alarm** = roused by an alarm.

alarm = call to arms.

121. **bedded hair** = smooth-lying hair. 다음 줄 Start up and stand의 주어이다. 따라서 판본에 따라서는 bedded hairs로 된 곳도 있다.

bedded = flat-lying. sleeping soldier와 짝을 이룬다.

like life in excrements = as if hair, a lifeless outgrowth (excrements), had come to life.

excrements = anything that grows out from the body, such as hair, nails.

122. **stand an end** = stand on end.

an = on.

123. **distemper** = distraction.

124. **patience** = calmness.

125. **how pale he glares** = how pale he looks as he glares upon us.

126. **His form … capable** = his appearance, coupled with the reason of that appearance, if appealing to the very stones, would stir them to feeling.

form and cause = appearance and motive.

127.   **capable** = susceptible of feeling, responsive. cf. III. ii. 13.

128-9. **you convert My stern effects** = turn my action from its proper sternness to pity.

128.   **action** = gesture. 유령의 애처로운 표정을 일컫는다.

129.   **effects** = purposes.

129-30. **then what ⋯ colour** = then the vengeance which I have to take will lack that justification which it would otherwise have.

130.   **want true colour** = will not present its proper appearance. 여기서는 tears와 blood의 문자 그대로의 색의 대비도 밑에 깔고 있다.
        want = lack.
        colour = appearance.
        tears perchance for blood = I shall perhaps shed tear instead of shedding the blood of the king.

132.   **is** = exist.

134.   **steals away** = gradually vanishes. 유령이 사라지듯 퇴장하는 것은 Gertrude가 자기를 보지도 듣지도 못한다는 사실에 대한 놀라움과 멋쩍음 때문일는지 모른다.

135.   **in his habit as he lived** = in the very dress he wore when alive.
        habit = clothing.

136.   **Look, where** = look나 see 뒤의 where는 there 정도의 뜻을 가진다.
        portal = door.

137.   **very** = mere.
        coinage = invention. 여기서는 forgery의 뜻.

138-9. **This bodiless ⋯ in** = ecstasy is very cunning in this bodiless creation = madness is very skilful in giving birth to such illusions of the sight.

138.   **bodiless creation** = manufacture of fantasies or hallucinations.
        ecstasy = madness. 주어.

139.   **cunning** = skilful, clever (in making).

140.   **doth ··· music** = beats with as regular and healthy a rhythm as yours, its pulsations are as indicative of a sound frame of mind as yours.

143.   **re-word** = repeat word for word.

143-4.   **which madness ··· from** = whereas a madness would wander in fantastic fashion from the subject.

144.   **gambol from** = shy away from, i.e. be incapable of performing. 「(···에서 (턱없이) 빗나가다」.

        gambol = leap or spring, in dancing or sporting.

        for love of grace = for God's sake.

        grace = the grace of God.

145.   **Lay not that flattering unction to your soul** = do not try to soothe your soul by imagining to yourself that it is not your sin but my madness which calls aloud in this way.

145.   **that flattering unction** = the salve of that deceptive notion.

        unction = soothing or healing ointment, salve.

146.   **trespass** = a sin or offence.

147-9.   **It will ··· unseen** = to do so will, instead of healing the sore, only cover it as with a film, while rank corruption, eating into the core of or soul, poisons it unnoticed.

147.   **skin and film** = cover thinly like a skin or film 「엷은 피부와 막으로 싸다」.

148.   **rank** = foul, festering.

        mining = burrowing, undermining.

150.   **avoid what is to come** = avoid sin in the future. Hamlet은 159-70 행에서 그 내용을 설명하고 있다.

151-2.   **And do not ··· ranker** = and do not make what is already so foul still fouler by self-deception and hypocrisy.

151. **compost** = manure.

152. **this my virtue** = my admonition and virtuous talk 「잘난 체 화내는 것」.

153. **For in the fatness of these pursy times** = for in these times of gross and pampered indulgence.

fatness = grossness.

these pursy times = 「타락한 시대」.

pursy = short-winded 「숨이 짧은」. 비유적으로 fat, flabby, corpulent. 대개 몸이 비대한 사람들이 호흡이 짧다.

155. **curb** = bend, bow, cringe.

woo = try to win, seek.

leave = permission.

do him good = him은 앞줄의 vice.

156. **thou hast cleft my heart in twain** = 「뉘우침」과 Claudius에 대한 「사랑」의 두 쪽.

cleft = cleave(= split)의 과거분사.

twain = two.

157. **worser** = 이와 같은 이중비교(double comparative)는 강조를 나타낸다.

158. **the purer** = all the purer, by so much the purer 「나쁜 것을 버린 만큼 더 깨끗하게」.

160. **Assume a virtue, if you have it not** = act as though you were virtuous, even if you have not the feeling.

161-2. **That monster⋯this** = 「습관이라는 괴물은 악습에 대한 감각을 모두 먹어치우기도 하지만 착한 행동을 하는 습관에도 마찬가지로 입기 편한 옷을 입혀준다는 점에서는 천사이다」. 많은 편자들이 devil을 evil의 잘못으로 여기지만 angel과의 대조(antithesis)를 위해 devil을 주장하는 편자도 있다.

161. **That monster, custom** = Custom who is a monster.

162. **habit** = 통상적인 「습관」이라는 뜻 외에 164행의 frock and livery의 뜻도 있다.

163-5. **That to…on** = Just as a new dress or uniform becomes familiar to us by habit, so custom enables us readily to execute the outward and practical part of the good and fair actions which we inwardly desire to do.

163. **use** = custom, habit.

164. **He** = Custom.

likewise = if the Queen puts on the clothing or appearance of virtue, custom will make it habitual, just as custom has made her insensitive to sin.

frock or livery = coat or uniform.

165. **aptly** = easily.

166. **easiness** = facility.

168. **use can almost can change the stamp of nature** = 「습관은 타고난 성품을 바꿀 정도의 힘을 갖는다」.

use = habit, custom.

stamp of nature = inborn disposition, what nature has stamped on the character, natural inclinations.

stamp = character, disposition.

169-70. **And either…potency** = and either completely overcome the devil, or at least expel him from our nature with irresistible force.

170. **With wondrous potency** = with remarkable power.

potency = power, strength.

171-2. **And when…you** = and when you crave for a blessing from heaven, thus showing your contrition, I will ask of you a mother's blessing.

171. **be blest** = be blessed by Heaven = repent.

172. **blessing** = i.e. mother's blessing.

For = as regards.

173-5. **but Heaven···minister** = but heaven has pleased that it should be so, viz., that I should be its instrument of vengeance in order that I might be punished by being guilty of this man's death, and this man be punished by my act.

173. **Heaven hath pleas'd it so** = such is heaven's pleasure.
it = itself.

174. **To punish me with this and this with me** = as I have punished Polonius (by killing him), so I will be punished for the killing.
and this with me = and punish this (= Polonius) through me.

175. **their scourge and minister** = heaven's lash and agent of justice (to punish others and perhaps, himself). Hamlet sees himself as the chastising agent of the gods.
scourge = a whip used for punishment
minister = a person employed for in the execution of a purpose, agent.
their = heaven (= heavenly powers).

176. **bestow him** = get rid of his dead body.
bestow = remove, dispose of.

176-7. **answer well The death** = be responsible for the death either by explaining the death or perhaps by atoning for it.

178-9. **I must···behind** = 운(kind, behind)이 맞는 이 두 줄은 Hamlet이 어머니에게 한 말이라기보다는 오히려 관중을 향한 방백(aside) 으로 보는 편이 낫다.

178. **I must be cruel, only to be kind** = I must be cruel in words only to be kind in reality 「내 말은 잔인하지만 이 모두가 어머니 를 위해서 하는 말이다」.

179. **Thus bad begins and worse remains behind** = thus my harsh words must be followed by even harsher measures, *sc.* the

punishment of the king.

bad = what is bad. Polonius를 죽인 일.

worse remains behind = worse crimes or calamities will follow. 왕을 죽이는 일.

behind = to come.

181. **Not this…that I bid you do** = do anything in the world except this that I bid you do 「지금 하라고 한 일일랑 하지 마십시오」.

182. **bloat** = bloated or fat.

183. **wanton** = wantonly.

   mouse = term of endearment로 사용된다. 「귀여운 것」.

184. **reechy** = reeky, dirty, filthy.

185. **paddling** = playing fondly with the fingers.

186-8. **Make you…craft** = make you confess that I am not mad in reality, but only pretend to be so in order to effect my objects.

186. **ravel…out** = disentangle, make plain or clear, unravel, reveal. 마치 엉킨 실타래의 실을 풀듯이 비밀을 누설하라는 뜻.

187. **essentially** = really. in craft와 대조되는 말.

188. **mad in craft** = cunningly mad, pretending to be mad.

   'Twere good you let him know = 풍자적으로 한 말.

189-91. **For who…hide?** = for would anyone who was just fair, sober and wise queen think of hiding a secret of such vital importance from a filthy creature like your husband.

189. **but** = merely.

190. **paddock** = toad.

   gib [gib] = male cat. paddock(두꺼비), bat(박쥐), gib(수고양이) 는 모두 혐오동물로서 마녀와 한 패거리로 여겨졌다.

191. **dear concernings** = affairs of vital importance, important matters.

192. **in despite of sense and secrecy** = in spite of the secrecy which common sense would bid you maintain.

193-6. **Unpeg…down** = 여기서 말하는 the famous ape의 우화는 전해 지지 않고 있다. Hamlet이 하려는 말뜻은 다음과 같다. 즉, 만약 당신이 내 비밀을 누설하면 마치 조롱을 지붕으로 가져가 새를 날려 보내고 자기도 새처럼 날아보려다 떨어져 목이 부러진 원숭이 꼴이 된다.

193. **Unpeg the basket** = open the cage.

195. **try conclusions** = make experiments, see what will happen.
in = into.

196. **break your own neck down** = break your neck by falling headlong in your effort to fly like a bird.

196. **down** = toward a lower place라는 통상적인 뜻이라기보다는 utterly라는 강조어로 보는 것이 타당.

197-9. **Be thou…me** = rest assured that, if words are made of breath, and breath is made of life, it is not in me to breathe your secret to any one.

198. **breath of life** = breath be made of life.

199. **I must to England** = Hamlet과 왕비가 언제 이 사실을 알게 되었 는지 분명치 않다. Shakespeare는 이처럼 등장인물들로 하여금 청중이 알고 있는 사실을 공유케 하는 관례를 종종 사용한다.

201. **I had forgot** = 「잊을 뻔했다」.
concluded on = determined.

202. **There's letters** = 복수형 명사 letters 앞에 단수형 동사 's(= is) 가 사용되고 있는데, 이것은 Shakespeare가 letters가 공식 문서 따위를 뜻할 때는 단수형 대신 복수형을 사용하는 관례에서 비롯한 것이다. 라틴어의 litterae(littera의 복수형)의 영향으로 보인다.

203. **as** = just as much.
adders = poisonous snakes.
fang'd = having fangs.

204. **mandate** = command. 여기서는 「공식문서」 그 자체라기보다는 단순한 「명령」 정도로 이해하는 것이 좋다. 왜냐하면 봉인된 공식문서는 외교관례(protocol)상 일행의 수장격인 Hamlet이 가지고 가야하기 때문이다.

204-5. **they must…knavery** = it is for them to make the path smooth for me, and to lead me where the villanous scheme of the king may be put into execution.

204. **sweep my way** = prepare the way for me.

205. **marshal me to knavery** = conduct me towards some kind of trick or villainy.

marshal = guide, lead, conduct. marshal이라는 군사용어는 그 뒤에 enginer, petard, mines와 같은 다른 군사용어의 사용을 유발한다.

Let it work = Allow it to follow its course 「마음대로 하라지」.

206-7. **For 'tis…petar** = for it is the finest sport in the world to see the engineer blown into the air by his own engine of destruction.

206. **'tis the sport** = 「볼 만하다」.

enginer [éndʒinə] = engineer.

207. **Hoist with his own petar** [pitɑ:] = blown into the air by his own bomb. Now a proverbial saying meaning "injured or destroyed by his own device for the ruin of others." 오늘날 거의 숙어처럼 사용된다.

Hoist = hoisted. 옛날 사용된 동사 hoise의 과거분사.

petar = small engine of war filled with explosive materials, used for blowing up obstacles such as the walls and gates of a besieged city.

207-8. **and 't shall go hard** = the difficulty must be a great one if I do not manage to overcome it.

208. **delve** = dig.

mines = tunnels dug under a fortress wall (the word later used for the explosives buried in such tunnels).

209. **blow them at the moon** = blow them up to the moon.
at = up to.

210. **When in one line two crafts directly meet** = when two skilful designs come into direct opposition. 물론 counter mine도 염두에 두고 하는 말이다.
crafts = skilful designs.
directly = exactly.

211. **This man** = Polonius의 시체.
packing = pack에는 depart와 conspire의 두 뜻이 있다. 즉, 이곳을 빨리 떠난다는 뜻과 시체를 적절히 처리한다는 두 뜻이다.

212. **lug the guts** = 「시체를 끌고 가다」.
lug = drag or tug (a heavy object) with effort or violence. cf. luggage.
guts = 「내장」. 시체를 경멸해서 부르는 말. 비유적으로 「살찐 사람」을 가리키기도 한다.
neighbour = neighbouring.

214. **secret** = not revealing secrets.
grave = grave에는 dignified, somber((죽어서 말을 못하는 까닭에) 의젓한)와 weighty((시체가 되어) 무거운) 등의 뜻이 있다. 동시에 grave(무덤)도 연상시킨다.

215. **prating** = chattering, fond of idle talk.

216. **to draw toward an end with you** = make an end of my business with you라는 뜻과 함께 drag you towards your grave라는 두 뜻의 pun이다.
to draw toward an end = finish up 「끝을 내다」. 긴 연설 끝에 상투적으로 하는 말이다.

Act IV

Scene I

여기서 새로이 4막을 설정해야 하는가에 대해서는 이론이 있어 왔다. 3막4장의 왕비가 아직 퇴장하지 않은 점이 그 근거가 된다. 여기에 대한 새로운 구분의 유일한 근거는 34-5행의 Hamlet in madness hath Polonius slain / And from his mother's closet hath he dragg'd him이라는 부분일 것이다. 즉 3막4장의 무대였던 Queen's closet이 바뀐 것이다.

1.　　**matter** = something of importance, something material.
　　　　profound [⌣ ×] **heaves** = deep sighs. cf. heave a sigh.
　　　　profound = drawn from the depths of your heart, and deep in significance.
2.　　**translate** = explain.
　　　　'tis fit = it is only right.
3.　　**your son** = 'our son'이라고 하지 않는 것에 주의.
4.　　**Bestow this place on us** = be good enough to leave us alone for a short time.
6.　　**How does Hamlet?** = what is the state of Hamlet's mind?
8.　　**Which** = as to which, on the question which.

lawless = ungovernable, out of control.

fit = 「발작」.

10. **Whips out** = he hastily draws. 시제가 현재형인 것은 과거에 일어난 일을 바로 지금 눈앞에서 일어나고 일인 듯 묘사하기 위한 이른바 historical present의 예이다.

A rat, a rat = 이 부분은 아들 Hamlet을 감싸기 위한 왕비의 거짓말이다. III. iv. 22행에서 Polonius는 휘장 뒤에서 What, ho! help, help, help!라고 소리치고 있어 Hamlet은 rat가 아니라는 것을 충분히 알고 있었기 때문이다.

11. **brainish apprehensions** = mad-brained fancy.

12. **unseen** = hidden.

heavy = grievous, dreadful.

13. **It had been so with us** = I myself should have fared as Polonius has, if I had been in his place.

with us = with me. 이른바 royal 'we'.

14. **His liberty** = the fact of his being allowed to go at large 「마음대로 하도록 내버려두는 것」.

threats = risk, danger.

16. **how shall this bloody deed be answer'd** = what excuse shall we be able to make for ourselves in regard to this deed?

answer'd = accounted for, explained (to the public), justified.

17-9. **It will… man** = the blame of the deed will be laid upon us for not having used the precaution of keeping this madman under restraint where he could not have come in contact with any one.

17. **laid to us** = charged against me, blamed on me. 이 'us'도 royal 'we'.

providence = foresight.

18. **kept short** = kept under control.

short = on a short leash 「(가죽 끈 따위를) 짧게」.

out of haunt = away from others, secluded. 앞의 restrain'd와 함께 kept에 연결된다.

haunt = company, society of men.

20. **We would not understand** = we deliberately refused to perceive 「일부러 모른 척했다」.

we would not = chose not to. 앞에 that를 보충해서 읽을 것.

22. **To keep it divulging** = rather than let it be known.

divulging = becoming known. 당시 창궐하고 있던 성병을 암시하고 있다.

let = 과거형.

24. **pith** = marrow.

24. **To draw apart** = to put out of the way so that no harm may come to it.

25-7. **O'er whom···done** = over which he shed tears of repentance, his very madness showing in this a touch of soundness, like a vein of pure ore in the midst of mines of base metal.

25-6. **like some···base** = like a vein of gold in a mine of base metals 「비천한 광맥 속에 빛나는 금처럼」.

25. **ore** = precious metal. 참고로 프랑스어로 or는 gold을 뜻한다.

26. **mineral** = metallic vein 「광맥」.

base = 「비천한.」

27. **he weeps for what is done** = 텍스트 어디에도 Hamlet이 울었다는 말은 없다. 여기서도 왕비는 아들 Hamlet을 감싸기 위해 거짓말을 하고 있다.

29. **shall the mountains touch** = gild the mountains with its first rays.

29-30. **The sun···hence** = we will make him take ship as soon as dawn breaks.

30. **But** = than. 그리하여 29행의 no sooner와 함께 no sooner···than (···하자마자)의 구문을 이루고 있다.

31-2. **We must···excuse** = we must use all our authority as king to put a good face upon, and all our skill in special pleading to excuse, the deed. countenance는 majesty와, excuse는 skill과 짝이 된다. 즉 our majesty will countenance and skill will excuse.

32. **countenance and excuse** = face out and offer justification.

   Ho = Guildenstern이 등장하기 전이라면 그를 부르는 말이 될 것이고, 등장 이후라면 인사말이 될 것이다. 여기서는 「여보게!」 정도의 인사.

33. **join you with some further aid** = get more men to help you.

   some further aid = some more assistants.

36. **speak fair** = use polite language (to placate him).

38. **call up** = summon to our assistance.

40. 문장의 후반이 소실되었다. 그리하여 편자들은 [so, haply, slander]라는 말을 첨가하게 된다.

   untimely = inopportunely.

   [so, haply, slander] = in that way if we take those measures, perhaps slander.

41-4. **Whose whisper···air** = whose poisonous whisper flies from end to end of the world as unerringly and as fatally as the cannon-ball to its mark, may pass by us and only hit the air which feels no wound.

41. **diameter** = extent.

42. **as level as the cannon to his blank** = as straight as the cannon-ball reaches its mark.

   As level = with as direct aim. 부사적 용법.

   cannon = cannon-ball.

   his = its.

   blank = white spot in the center of a target.

44. **woundless** = invulnerable.

45. **My soul** = 여기서는 royal 'we'의 our를 쓰지 않고 개인으로서
의 1인칭 단수형 my가 사용되고 있는 점에 주의.

Scene II

1. **stowed** = put away (hidden).
3. **soft** = be quiet!
6. **Compounded it with dust, whereto 'tis kin** = mixed with the earth
of which it was originally formed. 판본에 따라서는 compounded
가 compound로 된 곳도 있다. 1600년경에는 compound의 과거
형이 동일한 compound였으므로 해석에 문제는 없으나 Hamlet
이 거짓말을 한다기보다는 오히려 이 부분을 명령문으로 보아
시체를 묻으라는 명령으로 해석하는 사람도 있다. 그러나 그렇
게 되는 경우 다음 7행의 Tell us where 'tis와 맞지 않게 된다.
Compounded = mixed. Hamlet이 시체를 묻었다는 인상을 준다.
dust, whereto 'tis kin = cf. *Genesis* 3:19. "for dust thou art, and
unto dust shalt thou return. cf. II. ii. 321. what is this
quintessence of dust?"
11. **That I can keep your counsel and not mine** = 「너희들 비밀은
지켜주고 내 비밀은 지키지 못한다」는 말은 뒤집으면 「자기
비밀도 지키지 못하는 자가 남의 비밀을 지킬 순 없다」는 당대
의 속담에 해당하게 된다. 다시 말해 「내가 내 비밀을 밝히게
되는 날엔 너희들이 임금의 밀정이라는 비밀도 세상에 폭로하
겠다」는 협박이 된다.
keep your counsel = keep your secret.
12. **to be demanded of a sponge** = on being questioned by a fellow
like a sponge.

demanded = interrogated.

12-3.　**what … king?** = what sort of answer do you expect to receive from one, like me, of royal birth? do you expect that such a one would submit to be sucked dry by a fellow like you?

13.　**replication** = reply. 법정 술어.

16.　**that** = 앞줄의 sponge를 선행사로 하는 관계대명사.

17.　**countenance** = favor, patronage 「은총」.

　　authorities = attributes of power.

19.　**like an ape** = like an ape does (nuts).

20.　**mouthed** [mauðd] = taken into the mouth.

21.　**glean'd** = gathered, collected.

21-2.　**it is but squeezing you** = all he needs to do is to squeeze you like a sponge.

25-6.　**a knavish speech sleeps in foolish ear** = fools never understand the point of knavish words. 유명한 구이다.

　　knavish speech = 「험담」.

　　knavish = mischievous.

　　sleeps in = is meaningless to, is not understood by.

29-30.　**The body … body** = 해석이 분분한 구절이다. 「Polonius의 시체는 부친과 함께 있지만 부친은 Polonius와 같이 있지 않고 망령이 되어 돌아다닌다」, 아니면 두 번째 King을 현재의 왕으로 보아 「Polonius는 돌아가신 부친과 함께 있지만 살아 있는 Claudius는 아직 시체와 같이 있지 않다」, 또는 「Polonius의 시체는 여기 왕 곁에 있지만 왕은 아직 시체와 함께 있지 않다, 즉 죽어야할 사람이 아직 살아 있다」 등 여러 해석이 가능하다. Hamlet이 Rosencrantz와 Gildenstern을 골탕 먹이기 위해 일부러 장난치고 있다고 볼 수도 있다.

30.　**The King is a thing** = 여기 King은 현재의 왕으로서 Hamlet은 그가 a thing(하찮은 것)이라고 말한다. a thing of nothing은

Psalms 144:4의 Man is like to vanity: his days are as a shadow that passeth away가 말해주는 「인생무상」의 사상을 반영하고 있으며, 동시에 Claudius의 살날도 얼마 남지 않았다는 것을 암시하고 있다.

32-3.   **Hide fox, and all after**=「술래는 숨고, 모두 그를 잡아라」. 숨바꼭질 (hide-and-seek)의 「꼭꼭 숨어라」에 해당하는 말. Hamlet은 아직도 미친척하고 있다.

    fox=여기서 fox는 Polonius.

Scene III

SD   **Enter KING, attended.** = 판본에 따라서는 *Enter* KING이라고만 되어 있고 그 밖의 신하들은 Rosencrantz와 함께 등장하도록 된 곳도 있다. 그 경우 1행~11행은 왕의 독백이 된다.

1.   **him**=Hamlet.

2.   **goes loose**=is allowed his freedom.

3.   **Yet must not we**=yet we must not.

    put the strong law on him=punish him to the full extent of the law.

4.   **loved of**=loved by.

    distracted=weak-brained, irrational, mad.

5.   **like not in their judgement, but their eyes**=approve not by judgement but by appearance; does not depend on the use of their judgement, but on their eyes.

    not in their=not by their.

    their eyes=by appearances. 앞에 in(= by)을 보충할 것.

6-7.   **where 'tis…offence**=where the people judge the punishment rather than the crime.

scourge = punishment.

weigh'd = taken seriously.

7-9.   **To bear···pause** = in order that things may go smoothly, this sending him away so suddenly must be made to seem the result of deliberate calculation.

7.   **bear all smooth and even** = manage everything smoothly.

9.   **Deliberate pause** = well-considered action.

9-10.   **Diseases···relieved** = Desperate diseases require desperate remedies. 속담.

10.   **appliance** = remedy, application (of remedies).

11.   **or not at all** = or there is no hope at all to be cured.

   How now! = 왕은 Rosencrantz가 혼자 돌아온 것을 보고 놀란다.

   befall'n = happened.

12.   **bestow'd** = placed.

13.   **get from him** = learn from him. get의 목적어는 앞줄의 Where the dead body is bestow'd.

14.   **Without** = outside (the door).

   guarded = under a guard.

21-2.   **a certain···him** = a certain assemblage of discriminating worms, worms that know what they like, are even now engaged upon him.

21.   **convocation of politic worms** = 1521년 독일의 서부 라인 강에 위치한 Worms에서 개최된 국회(Diet)에서 로마 황제 칼 5세가 루터를 이단자로 선고한 역사적 사건을 연상케 한다. Hamlet이 루터가 교수로 있던 Wittenberg대학 학생이라는 점도 상기할 것. cf. I. ii. 113.

   convocation = assembly.

politic = shrewd, cunning, scheming. Polonius의 성격을 빗대고 하는 말.

22.   **e'en** = just now.

    Your worm = the worm. 24-5행의 your fat king and your lean beggar의 your도 마찬가지 용법.

22-3.   **Your worm is your only emperor for diet** = 「먹는 것에 관해 구더기는 실로 따를 자 없는 제왕이다」.

23.   **fat** = fatten.

24.   **maggots** = larva.

25-6.   **but…table** = two dishes served in a different way, but placed before the same company.

25.   **is but variable service** = are merely different courses (of dishes).
    variable = various.

26.   **end** = what it all comes to.

29.   **hath eat** = has eaten. eat는 옛날 과거분사형.

30.   **of** = on.

31.   **thou** = you 대신 thou를 사용하고 있는 것은 III. iv. 9 (Queen. Hamlet, thou hast thy father much offended.)의 경우와 마찬가지로 왕의 감정이 격해졌음을 나타낸다.

33.   **go a progress** = go on progress.
    progress = royal journey.

36-7.   **the other place** = hell. Hamlet은 왕이 종국적으로 가야 할 장소를 암시하고 있다.

38.   **nose** = smell.

39.   **lobby** = corridor or ante-room. 큰 홀에 붙어 있는 복도로서 대기실로 사용되던 것.

41.   **He will stay till ye come** = you need not be afraid of his running away. 다른 판본에서는 do not make too much haste, / I'le warrant you hee'le stay till you come으로 돼 있다.

43. **tender** = care for, feel compassion for.

dearly = keenly, intensely.

44. **must send thee hence** = will render it necessary for you to leave Denmark.

45. **therefore** = for that.

46. **bark** = vessel, ship.

at help = favourable. 앞에 is를 보충할 것.

at = *a*sleep나 *a*foot, *a*fire 따위의 *a*-와 같은 구실의 접두사.

47. **The associates tend** = the companions I have chosen for your voyage are in readiness for you.

tend = are waiting for you.

bent = ready, prepared.

48. **For England!** = 판본에 따라서는 느낌표 대신 물음표가 사용된 곳이 있다. 그러나 어느 쪽이든 중요하지 않다. 왜냐하면 Hamlet은 이미 자기를 영국으로 보내려는 왕의 의도를 알고 있기 때문이다. cf. III. iv. 199. I must to England; you know that?

49. **So is it** = good it is.

50. **I see a cherub that sees them** = Heaven's angels can see Claudius's purposes.

cherub = seraph 다음 급의 천사로서 지식이 뛰어나며, 인간사를 지켜보고 있는 것으로 알려져 있다.

52. **Thy loving father** = 「(어머니가 아니고) 사랑하는 아버지라고 해야지」. 실제로 3장에는 왕비가 등장하지 않고 있다. 만약 현장에 왕비가 있다면 왕이 67행에서 The present death of Hamlet 과 같은 말을 할 수 없을 것이다. 51행에서 Hamlet은 미친 척 Farewell, dear mother라고 말하고 있다.

54. **one flesh** = 「일심동체」. cf. *Matthew* 19:5, *Mark* 10:8. they two shall be one flesh.

56. **at foot** = at his heels, closely.

    tempt him with speed aboard = persuade him to go on board as quickly as you can.

    tempt = coax, entice, encourage, urge.

57. **I'll have him hence to-night** = I am determined that he shall sail tonight.

58-9. **everything … affairs** = for everything else that depends upon the management of this business (of sending him away) is thoroughly complete.

58. **leans on** = depends on, appertains to.

60. **England** = King of England.

    if my love thou hold'st at aught = if you in the least value my love. my love는 hold'st의 목적어.

    hold'st at aught = consider to be of any value.

61. **As my great power thereof may give thee sense** = and the greatness of my power may well teach you to value my love.

62-3. **Since yet … sword** = since the chastisement you received at our hands is still fresh in your memory.

62. **cicatrice** [síkətris] = scar, wound.

63-4. **thy free … us** = awe of Denmark's power makes England pay homage to Denmark.

    free awe = voluntary obedience, uncompelled respect.

    free = not enforced.

64-5. **thou mayst … process** = you may not treat with indifference our royal mandate.

64. **coldly set** = regard indifferently, ignore.

    set = regard, esteem, estimate. cf. I. iv. 65.

65. **Our sovereign process** = my royal order.

    process = formal command, mandate.

imports = states, demands.

at full = at length.

66.   **letters** = cf. III. iv. 202.

    congruing [´ ××] = conforming, agreeing.

67.   **present** = immediate.

68.   **the hectic** = hectic or wasting fever.

70.   **Howe'er my haps, my joys were ne'er begun** = however good fortunes may happen to me, I can never feel that the happiness I long for has begun.

    haps = good fortunes. 뒤에 might be를 보충한다.

Scene IV

1.   **from me greet** = bear my greetings to.

2.   **by his license** = if he will allow it.

    license = permission.

3-4.   **Craves···kingdom** = desires that, according to promise, he may be allowed to transport his forces across Denmark.

3.   **craves** = begs for. 판본에 따라서는 craves가 claimes로 된 곳도 있다. Fortinbras의 입장에서 볼 때 영토 통과에 대해서는 이미 양해가 있었으므로(cf. II. ii. 76-82) craves보다는 여기서는 법률적인 claimes가 더 어울린다는 주장이다. 또한 그것이 강인한 성격의 Fortinbras에게 어울리기도 한다. 그러나 다른 한편에서는 craves가 냉철한(chillingly macho) Fortinbras에 어울리는 반협박적인 외교적 완곡어법(diplomatic euphemism)으로 보자는 주장도 있다.

    conveyance = escort; granting or fulfilment (of a promise)라는

해석도 있다.

4.   **rendezvous** = the appointed place of meeting.

5.   **would aught with us** = wishes to see me for any purpose. 여기서 us는 royal 'we'.

6.   **express our duty in his eye** = pay our respects in his presence.

        duty = respect.

        in his eye = in his presence, to him personally.

7.   **let him know so** = let him know this.

8.   **softly** = quietly, carefully, slowly. Denmark에 대한 존경과 배려를 나타낸다.

9.   **powers** = military forces, armies.

11.   **How purpos'd** = with what object have they marched hither?

        purposed = have as one's purpose (used with verb of motion implied). ex. He purposed to Athena.

15-6.   **Goes it⋯frontier?** = is the expedition directed against the mainland of Poland, or only some outlying portion of that kingdom?

15.   **the main** = the main part.

16.   **for** = towards.

        frontier = frontier fortress or town.

17.   **with no addition** = without exaggeration.

18.   **to gain** = to make ourselves masters of.

        a little patch of ground = 1601년 7월부터 1602년 봄에 걸쳐 Sir Francis Vere의 지휘 하의 영국군이 Ostend의 sand-dunes를 지키기 위해 스페인 군과에 대항해 용감하게 싸운 일에 대한 언급으로 알려져 있다.

19.   **That hath in it no profit but the name** = whose only value lies in the name of possession.

        name = the mere name of conquest.

20. **To pay five ducats, five, I would not farm it** = I would not pay even five ducats to rent it for farming.

farm = rent (land).

21. **Norway** = the king of Norway.

the Pole = the King of Poland.

22. **ranker rate** = higher value.

rank = high in amount.

in fee = 「세습지로 (팔리다)」.

fee = an estate feudally held of another person, fee-simple.

23. **then** = if so, if it is worth no more than that.

the Polack = the Pole, i.e. the King of Poland.

24. **garrison'd** = occupied by a defending army.

25. **Will not debate the question of this straw** = are not enough to pay for settling this trifling quarrel.

Will = 강조 용법.

debate = decide by combat.

question of this straw = this trifling issue.

27-9. **This is⋯dies** = this morbid desire in the body politic to quarrel about nothing, a desire due to superabundance of wealth and the idleness of a long peace, is like an abscess in the physical body which bursts inwardly without showing any visible cause of the man's death; too much wealth and peace lead to war.

27. **imposthume** [impɔ́stjum] = purulent swelling, abscess[ǽbses] 「곪은 종기」.

28. **That inward breaks, and shows no cause without** = 「겉에선 보이지 않지만 속에서는 곪고 있다」. cf. III. iv. 147-8.

It will but skin and film the ulcerous place,

Whilst rank corruption, mining all within,

Infects unseen.

without = on the outside.

30. **God buy you** = God be with you. 정중한 작별 인사.

31. **straight** = immediately.

SD **[Exeunt all except HAMLET.** = Rosencrantz와 Guildenstern이 퇴장하는 것은 놀랍다. 왜냐하면 이들은 왕으로부터 Hamlet을 철저히 감시하라(Follow him at foot (IV. iii. 56))는 명령을 받았기 때문이다. 아마도 이들은 퇴장한 뒤 어딘가에 숨어서 Hamlet를 계속 감시할 것이다.

32. **How all occasions do inform against me** = how everything that happens seems to denounce my irresolution! 여기서부터가 Hamlet의 제7 독백.

   all occasions = every incident that occurs.

   inform against = accuse, denounce, bring a charge against.

33. **dull** = slow, inert, inactive.

34. **market of his time** = that for which he sells his time, the best use he makes of his time.

   market = profit.

36-7. **discourse···before and after** = power of thought that looks into the past and the future (unlike that of beasts which seems concerned with the present moment only).

36. **large discourse** = extensive powers of thought or reasoning.
   discourse = power of reasoning.

37. **before and after** = past and future. Hamlet distinguishes human beings from animals because they are capable of remembering the past and thinking about the future.

38. **That capability** = 36행의 large discourse.

39. **fust** = grow fusty, become mouldy, decay.
   whether = [hwɛə].

40. **Bestial oblivion** = the forgetfulness or heedlessness characteristic

of animals rather than people.

40-1. **craven scruple Of thinking** = cowardly hesitation that results from thinking.

craven scruple = cowardly hesitation.

41. **Of thinking** = which consists in thinking.

Of = caused by.

precisely = punctiliously, with attention to minute detail.

event = result, outcome, consequence.

42-3. **A thought···coward** = a mode of thinking which, if quartered, will be found to be made up of one part of wisdom to three parts of cowardice. 앞줄의 thinking과 동격.

44. **to do** = to be done. cf. a house to let (셋집), water to drink.

45. **Sith** = since.

46. **gross as earth** = as evident as the earth itself.

gross = large, obvious.

exhort = urge.

47. **Witness** = see.

such mass and charge = such size and expense 「이처럼 막대한 인원과 비용이 든」.

mass = massiveness.

charge = expense.

48. **delicate and tender** = brought up in ease and luxury, and so not naturally inclined to such rough work.

delicate and tender prince = Fortinbras. Fortinbras란 'strong arm' 이라는 뜻이다. delicate and tender라는 표현은 Fortinbras에게 는 어울리지 않는다. Horatio는 그를 Of unimproved mettle, hot and full(I. i. 96)이라고 표현하고 있으며, 5막에서 그는 매우 기민하게 묘사돼 있다. 그러나 그는 거친 사람은 아니다. 그는 Hamlet에게는 열정과 이성의 균형이 잘 잡힌 이상적인 인물이

다. 그리하여 Hamlet은 그를 자기 대신 덴마크의 왕으로 삼으라는 유언을 남긴다.

49. **puff'd** = inflated, inspired.

50. **Makes mouths at the invisible event** = 「예측할 수 없는 결과 따위엔 아랑곳 하지 않고」.

    Makes mouths at = laughs at, scorns.

    invisible = unforeseeable.

51. **what is mortal and unsure** = his life which is mortal and unsure.

    unsure = liable to danger, unsafe.

52. **dare** = can threaten.

53. **egg-shell** = the merest, most worthless, trifle.

53-6. **Rightly…stake** = greatness does not consist in fighting only on great provocation, but on the slightest matter (a straw) if honor is at risk. not은 stir가 아니라 Is에 연결된다.

54. **argument** = cause of quarrel.

55. **But greatly to find quarrel in a straw** = but to be prompt to find in the slightest trifle provocation for fighting.

    a straw = a trifle.

56. **When honour's at the stake** = when honour is concerned.

    at the stake = at risk.

57. **stain'd** = sullied, blemished.

58. **Excitements** = motives or incentives for.

    blood = passion.

60. **twenty thousand** = two thousand라고 해야 할 것을 흥분한 나머지 잘못 말 한 것. 25행에서는 Two thousand souls and twenty thousand ducats라고 말하고 있다. 이처럼 Shakespeare는 종종 숫자에 엄격하지 못하다는 지적을 받는다.

61. **for a fantasy and trick of fame** = illusion and imposture regarding reputation or honour.

fantasy = illusion, whim.

trick = (1) trifle, (2) deceit.

62.   **Go to their graves like beds** = To be or not to be에서처럼 Shakespeare는 '죽음'과 '잠'을 연결한다.

      like beds = as readily as they would to their beds.

      plot = small strip of land.

63.   **Whereon the numbers cannot try the cause** = which is not enough for so many men to fight on it to decide the issue.

      try the cause = decide the issue 「결판을 내다」.

64-5.   **Which is not…slain** = which is not large enough to be a tomb or receptacle for those who will be killed.

64.   **continent** = container, receptacle.

65.   **hide** = i.e. provide burial space for.

65.   **from this time and forth** = henceforward.

66.   **My thoughts be bloody, or be nothing worth!** = let my thoughts be murderous, or they shall be worth nothing.

      bloody = bloodthirsty.

Scene V

2.   **importunate** = persistently troublesome, persistent in her demand.

      distract = distraught, distracted, mad.

3.   **Her mood will needs be pitied** = it is impossible not to pity her condition.

      mood = state of mind.

      will needs be = must necessary be.

      What would she have? = i.e. what does she want?

5.   **There's tricks i' the world** = there are strange doings going on in the world.

tricks = deceits, plots, deceptions.

hem = makes the 'hem' sounds, a cough or a throat clearing.

heart = breast.

6.   **Spurns enviously a straws** = takes offense angrily at trivial things.

spurns = kicks.

enviously = maliciously, angrily.

straws = something trifling or feeble. cf. IV. iv. 55.

in doubt = with no clear meaning, obscurely, in dubious language.

7-9.   **Her speech···collection** = her speech makes no sense, but the incoherent fragments cause those who listen to find coherence in them.

7.   **nothing** = i.e. nonsense.

8.   **unshaped** [-id] = disordered, incoherent.

9.   **collection** = inference.

aim at = guess.

10.   **botch the words up fit to their own thoughts** = patch the words together clumsily to match their own guesses.

botch···up = patch, especially unskilfully.

fit = fitted.

11.   **Which** = her words.

yield = render, deliver (i.e. her gestures add meaning to her words).

them = words.

12.   **thought** = supposed, conjectured.

13.   **Though nothing sure, yet much unhappily** = nothing과 much는

앞줄 might be thought의 주어.

unhappily = 1) unskilfully, 2) maliciously.

14. **strew** = scatter, unintentionally suggest, i.e. incite.

15. **ill-breeding** = always ready to conceive evil.

17. **To my soul, as sin's true nature is** = to my soul, ill at ease with itself, as is always the case when guilt is present to it.

   as sin's true nature is = in accordance with the reality of the state of sinfulness, i.e. sin, in its true nature, is a sickness of the soul.

18. **toy** = trifling thing.

   amiss = (*n. rare*) calamity, disaster, misfortune.

19-20. **So full···spilt** = guilt is so full of suspicion that it unskilfully betrays itself in fearing to be betrayed.

19. **artless** = awkward, stupid.

   jealousy = unreasonable suspicion.

20. **It spills itself in fearing to be spilt** = (Guilt produces such paranoia that) it betrays itself by its very own fear of betrayal, it destroys itself in fearing to be destroyed. 액체를 운반할 때 쏟지 않으려는 긴장이 지나친 나머지 오히려 더 쏟게 되는 사실에 빗댄 은유.

   spills = destroys.

   spilt = divulged.

21. **beauteous majesty** = Queen.

23. **How should I···** = 여기서부터는 순례를 떠난 뒤 돌아오지 않는 연인의 안부를 묻는 아가씨의 물음에 나그네가 답하는 잘 알려진 민요(ballad)이다.

   know from = distinguish from.

25-6. **By his···shoon** = by his wearing the habit of a pilgrim.

25. **cockle** = 새조개.

cockle hat = 새조개의 조가비를 꽂은 모자는 순례자가 당시 유명한 Spain의 St. James of Compostella 사원에 다녀왔다는 표시로 쓰던 것으로서 지팡이(staff)와 샌들 신(sandal shoon)과 함께 순례자(pilgrim)들의 정해진 복장이었다.

shoon = shoes.

27. **what imports this song?** = what does this song signify?

28. **Say you?** = what is it you say?

　　　mark = pay attention.

31. **grass-green** = green with grass.

32. **stone** = gravestone.

35. **shroud** = grave-clothes 「수의」.

37. **Larded** = garnished, thickly covered. shroud에 걸린다.

38-9. **Which…showers** = 판본에 따라서는 not이 생략된 곳도 있다. 예를 들어 Pope는 운율 문제도 그렇고 뜻으로 보아서도 not의 존재는 불합리하다고 생각한다. 그러나 이 부분이 충분한 애도를 표할 여유도 없이 서둘러(In hugger-mugger, cf. 84행) 묻힌 아버지 Polonius에 대한 일이나 Hamlet이 참된 사랑의 눈물에 젖지도 못한 채 서둘러 영국이라는 무덤(grave)에 가버린 사실을 말하는 것이라면 not이 있어야 한다.

38. **bewept** = made wet with tears. 뒤의 With true-love showers (i.e. his faithful lover's tears)에 연결된다.

39. **showers** = tears.

41. **'ild** = 'God yield(= reward) you'의 변형으로서 'thank you' 정도의 뜻.

41-2. **They say…baker's daughter** = 어느 날 예수가 빵가게에 빵을 사러갔을 때 그 곳 딸이 어머니가 잘라놓은 빵이 너무 크다고 작게 잘라 준 탓에 부엉이가 됐다는 이야기에 근거한 말. Ophelia의 말뜻은 '빵가게 딸은 부엉이가 됐지만 Polonius의 딸은 무엇이 될지 모른다'는 뜻.

43-4. **God be at your table!** = May God bless your table with his presence. 연회에서 주고받는 인사.

45. **Conceit upon** = (she is) thinking about.

46. **have no words of this** = have no talk about this matter.

48-66. **To-morrow…bed** = 이 노래의 출처는 밝혀지지 않았음.

48. **Saint Valentine's day** = 2월 14일로서 이날 새들이 서로 짝을 만나는 것으로 알려져 있다. 이 날 남자가 보게 되는 첫 번째 아가씨가 참된 애인이라는 속설에 따라 젊은 남녀들이 그날을 위한 애인(Valentine)을 만들어 서로 선물을 주고받는 풍습이 있다.

49. **All in the morning betime** = at the earliest dawn of day.
   All = 부사로서 betime에 걸린다.
   betime = early.

50. **at your window** = greeting you at your window.

52. **donn'd** = put on. do on (= put on (입다))이 준 말. 그 반대말인 doff (= put off (벗다))는 do off가 준 말.

53. **dupp'd** = opened. did up(= put up)이 준 말.

54. **that (let) out…more** = 「더 이상 헤어질 수 없는 여자가 나왔다」.
   maid = 처음 것은 virgin, 두 번째 것은 a young woman.

57. **la** = indeed.

59. **By Gis** = by Jesus.
   by Saint Charity = by holy charity. 가톨릭 신자들이 보통 사용하는 맹세의 말. Charity가 대문자로 시작되는 것을 보면 고유명사로 보이나 확인된 바는 없음.

60. **fie for shame!** = 「너무하다」 정도의 감동사.

61. **do't, if they come to 't** = i.e. have sex when opportunity offers.

62. **By Cock** = by God. cock은 God의 사투리. cock(= penis)와의 bawdy pun.

63.	**tumbled me** = i.e. in bed = had sex.
65.	**So would I ha' done** = Indeed I would have married you.
66.	**An** = if.
69.	**cannot choose but weep** = cannot help weeping.
	to think = at the thought that.
71-2.	**I thank you for your good counsel** = 여기서 you는 오빠 Laertes.
72-3.	**Good night, ladies** = 무대 위에는 Ophelia말고는 왕비 한 사람만의 lady가 있을 뿐이므로 복수형의 ladies는 잘못 된 것이다. 왕과 다른 신하들이 있는데도 ladies와 good night을 반복하는 것은 그녀의 실성 때문일 것이다.
74.	**give her good watch** = watch her carefully.
78-9.	**they come ··· battalions** = they do not come like single spies, but in full force.
78.	**spies** = lone soldiers sent out in advance of the main force, scouts.
79.	**battalions** = large armies.
80-1.	**and he most ··· remove** = and he by his violence the cause of his justly earned removal (= banishment) 「(추방의) 강력한 원인 제공자인 그」. he는 바로 앞의 your son과 동격.
80.	**author** = instigator.
81.	**just remove** = deserved removal.
81-2.	**muddied, Thick and unwholesome** = 모두 본래 흙탕물을 수식하는 말들.
82.	**Thick and unwholesome in their thoughts and whispers** = their thoughts and their language are polluted with unwholesome matter, i.e. dangerous ideas.
81.	**muddied** = stirred up, confused.
83.	**For** = on account of.
	done but greenly = acted in an inexperienced manner.

greenly = foolishly, showing lack of experience.

84. **in hugger-magger** = secretly and hastily, i.e. without due ceremony. inter를 수식한다.

inter = bury.

85. **Divided from herself** = estranged from her own sane judgement, out of her senses, mad. cf. beside oneself (= mad).

86. **Without the which** = which 앞에 the를 사용하는 것은 낡은 용법 으로서 특히 그 앞에 전치사가 올 때는 흔히 볼 수 있다.

pictures, or mere beasts = pictures와 beasts는 godlike reason이 없다는 점에서 공통점이 있다. cf. IV. iv. 38.

pictures = mere resemblances (of human beings).

87. **and as much containing as all these** = and a circumstance as full of import as all these put together.

as much containing = as important.

containing = comprising, importing.

88. **in secret** = 「비밀리에」라는 것은 왕의 첩자가 이 사실을 밝혀냈 다는 것을 의미한다.

89. **Feeds on his wonder** = makes wonder his food for thought, i.e. broods over the amazement caused by his father's death.

wonder = bewilderment, perplexity.

keeps himself in clouds = holds aloof mysteriously.

clouds = clouds of suspicion or uncertainty.

90. **wants not buzzers** = does not lack gossipers.

buzzers = fellows who go buzzing about like noxious insects.

91. **pestilent** = harmful, morally destructive.

92. **necessity, of matter beggar'd** = driven by necessity because of lack of substantial evidence.

beggar'd (of) = destitute of.

93. **Will nothing stick our person to arraign** = will not hesitate to

accuse me of the crime.

Will nothing stick = will in no ways refrain.

nothing = not at all.

stick = hesitate.

person = 판본에 따라서는 복수형의 persons가 사용된 곳도 있다. 그 때는 왕 자신과 왕비도 포함한다.

arraign = put on trial, accuse.

94. **In ear and ear** = one ear after another, to everyone.

94. **this** = battalion of troubles, all of these things.

95. **murdering-piece** = small cannon loaded with case-shot (a collection of small projectiles, i.e. bullets, nails, old iron, etc. put up in cases).

96. **Gives me superfluous death** = kills me many times over. murdering-piece에서 날라 오는 파편 하나만으로도 죽을 수 있는데, 여러 개의 파편이 날라 오므로 superfluous.

97. **Switzers** = Swiss bodyguards. 스위스 군인들은 대륙 여러 나라에서 예전부터 궁정 용병으로 고용되었다. 그리하여 Switzer는 guard와 동의어로 사용되었다. 지금도 교황청(Vatican) 입구는 Swiss guards(혹은 이름뿐인?)가 지키고 있다.

99. **overpeering of his list** = overflowing its boundaries. 지금은 of가 필요 없다.

overpeer = rise or tower above.

list = limit, boundary.

100. **Eats not the flats** = does not swallow up the flat regions.

flats = flatlands.

impetuous = ruthless, unpitying.

101. **in a riotous head** = with an armed force of riotous citizens.

head = armed force, army.

102. **rabble** = disorderly crowd, mob.

call him lord = acknowledge his supremacy.

103.　**as the world were now but to begin** = as if the world were to begin right now.

　　　as = as if.

104.　**Antiquity forgot, custom not known** = with tradition and custom completely forgotten. antiquity와 custom은 사회조직의 근간이다. antiquity와 forgot 사이에, 그리고 custom과 not 사이에 being을 첨가할 것.

105.　**The ratifiers and props of every word** = confirmers and supporters of every word we use. Antiquity and custom guarantee and support every word. ratifiers, props는 앞줄의 antiquity, custom과 동격.

106.　**Choose we** = Let us choose.

107.　**Caps, hands, and tongues** = by throwing up caps, clapping hands, and shouting with tongues.

　　　applaud it to the clouds = applaud it to the skies.

108.　**Laetes shall be king, Laertes king!** = 당시 덴마크는 선거제의 군주국이었다.

109.　**How cheerfully on the false trail they cry** = with what chiding these hounds hunt the false scent which they have so eagerly take up! 「사냥개가 냄새를 잘못 맡고 엉뚱한 곳에서 짖어댄다」.

　　　cry on = (of hounds) yelp on the scent.

110.　**counter** = following the trail in a direction opposite to that which the game has taken. 사냥 술어. 정확히는 「냄새를 잘못 맡는다」는 것과 「냄새의 방향을 거꾸로 따라간다」는 두 가지 뜻이 있다. 앞줄의 trail도 마찬가지 사냥 술어.

　　　false = treacherous, faithless.

111.　**broke** = broken.

112. **without** = outside.

113. **give me leave** = leave me alone with the King.

115. **keep** = guard.

118. **That drop of blood that's calm proclaims me bastard** = Laertes is not his father's son if he does not avenge his father.

118. **cuckold** = husband of an unfaithful wife, betrayed husband. Laertes thinks calmness an unnatural response that would show him to be no true son and his mother a harlot.

brand the harlot = Laertes alludes to the threat to brand prostitutes.

119. **Even here** = 이마에 손을 대면서 하는 말.

between = in the midst of.

unsmirched [-id] **brow** = untainted forehead.

120. **true** = faithful, chaste.

121. **That thy rebellion looks so giant-like?** = that you have broken out into a rebellion which has assumed such terrible proportions?

giant-like = 단순한 large의 뜻일 수 있으나 V. I. 276행의 Pelion 산이나 V. i. 306행의 Ossa 산을 쌓아 올리고 신들에 저항했던 Titan 족에 대한 언급일 수 있다.

122. **Let him go, Gertrude** = do not try to hold him back.

fear = be afraid of, be anxious about.

123. **hedge** = protect as with a surrounding hedge.

124. **That treason can but peep to what it would** = that treason is unable to do more than look over the hedge which separates it from the object of its vengeance.

would = would like to do.

125. **Acts little of his will** = is able to perform little of its desires.

125. **his** = its.

126. **incens'd** = enraged, angry.

129. **demand his fill** = let him state his demand in full.

130. **How came he dead?** = How did he become dead? How was he killed?

    juggl'd with = manipulated and thus deceived.

131-2. Laertes는 왕에 대한 충성(allegiance)과 신의 은총(grace) 모두를 저주하고 있다.

132. **grace** = religious feeling.

    profoundest = deepest. cf. *Revelation* 20:1-3에서 지옥을 bottomless pit으로 묘사하고 있다.

    pit = pit of hell.

133. **I dare damnation** = in such a cause as this I am ready to risk eternal damnation.

    To this point I stand = here I firmly take my stand, I am firm in this resolve.

134. **both the worlds I give to negligence** = I don't care what happens to me in this world or the next.

    negligence = disregard, contempt.

136. **throughly** = thoroughly.

    stay = check, prevent, stop.

137. **My will, not all the world** = nothing in the world but my own free will.

138-9. **And for⋯little** = and as regards the means at my command, I will make such prudent use of them that, though small, they shall go far.

138. **And for my means** = and as for my means.

    husband = use sparingly, manage.

140-1. **certainty Of** = truth or fact about.

141. **is't writ in your revenge?** = is it a part of the revenge you have prescribed to yourself?

writ in = required by.

142-3.   **That, swoopstake,⋯loser?** = are you going to vent your rage on both friend and foe; like a gambler who insists on sweeping the stakes, whether the point is in his favour or not?

142.   **swoopstake** = indiscriminately. 본래의 뜻은 drawing the whole stake at once라는 도박 술어.

    draw = win (a stake) 「판돈을 싹쓸이하다」.

    draw both friend and foe = i.e. take revenge on the innocent and guilty.

144.   **ope** = open.

146.   **life-rendering pelican** = The mother pelican was thought to feed her young with her own blood. 펠리컨은 부리로 가슴을 찢어 피를 새끼에게 먹이는 것으로 알려져 있다.

147.   **Repast** = feed, nourish.

148.   **good** = duteous.

150.   **And am most sensibly in grief for it** = and am deeply pained by it.

    sensibly = feelingly, keenly, intensely.

151-2.   **It shall⋯eye** = it shall force its way as directly to your judgement as the daylight.

151.   **level** = straightforwardly, directly. cf. IV. i. 42.

152.   **As day does to your eye** = 「햇빛이 직접 눈에 비추듯」.

    tears seven times salt = 「짜디짠, 혹은 쓰디쓴 눈물이여」.

    seven times = many times. seven은 막연한 숫자를 나타낸다.

155.   **the sense and virtue of mine eye!** = that sensibility and property by which the eye is enabled to see.

    virtue = power.

    mine eye = 「시력」. 후속하는 명사가 모음으로 시작될 때엔 my 대신 mine이 사용되었다.

156-7. **thy madness⋯beam** = your madness will be revenged by putting more weight into our side of the scale until it over-balances the other.

157. **our scale turns the beam** = cause the beam of the balance to bow owing to the greater weight in our scale「한쪽이 무거워 저울대가 기울다」.

　　　 of May! = in the bloom of life's spring-time.

160. **mortal** = subject to destruction.

161-3. **Nature⋯loves** = Nature is delicate in love, and sends Ophelia's sanity after Polonius as a precious token (or sample) of itself.

161. **Nature** = human nature.

162. **instance of itself** = sample of its refined nature, i.e. Ophelia's wits.

　　　 instance = sample, token.

164. **barefac'd** = with his face uncovered. 관이 없었거나 관 뚜껑이 열려있었기 때문.

　　　 bier = stretcher or litter on which a corpse is carried.

165. **Hey non nonny** = a meaningless refrain. 민요에는 이런 뜻 없는 가락이 섞이는 경우가 많다.

167. **my dove!** = dove는 term of endearment. my dove는 돌아가신 아버지보다 잃어버린 사랑에 더 어울리는 표현이다. Ophelia는 Hamlet으로 착각한 오빠와 아버지 사이를 오가고 있다.

168. **Hadst thou⋯thus** = no words of perusasion that you could urge, if you were in your senses, could stir me to revenge as these disjointed, incoherent, utterances.

　　　 persuade = urge (something upon a person).

169. **move thus** = be this moving.

170-1. **Down a-down⋯a-down-a** = 이것도 별 뜻이 없는 후렴. *The Merry Wives of Windsor*, I. iv. 44에도 나타난다. a-down-a의

마지막 '-a'는 음절은 늘리기 위한 무의미한 모음. him a-down-a를 Polonius is fallen into his grave의 뜻으로 해석하는 사람도 있다.

171. **how the wheel becomes it!** = wheel을 spinning-wheel과 운명의 여신이 굴리는 Fortune's wheel의 두 가지 해석이 가능하다. 전자의 경우는 Ophelia가 물레를 돌리는 흉내를 내면서 O, how prettily the spinning-wheel and the song go together!라고 말하는 것으로 해석해 it이 '후렴'을 가리키는 것으로, 또 후자의 경우에는 Polonius가 여신이 함부로 굴리는 운명의 바퀴에 깔겨 죽은 것으로 해석해 it이 아버지의 주검을 나타내는 것으로 해석할 수도 있다. 처녀들이 물레를 돌리면서 소박한 민요를 부르던 습관이 예전부터 있었다.

172-3. **the false steward…daughter** = 출처불명의 고사.

174. **This nothing's more than matter** = nonsense is more moving than reasonable speech.

nothing = nonsense.

matter = sense.

175. **rosemary** = 「로즈메리」. 여기서부터는 Ophelia가 머리나 옷깃에 달았거나 아니면 상상 속에 가지고 온 꽃들을 하나씩 떼어내면서 하는 말이다. 어떤 꽃을 누구에 주는지가 밝혀져 있지 않으나 꽃말(the language of flowers, flower meaning), 즉 꽃의 상징에 따라 받는 사람을 추측할 수 있다. rosemary의 꽃말은 faithful remembrance이며, 아마도 오빠 Laertes에게 아버지를 잊지 말자고 하면서 주는 말일 것이다. 한편 remembrance는 오빠를 Hamlet으로 착각하고 자기를 잊지 말아 달라는 뜻의 remembrance를 뜻한다고 볼 수도 있다.

176. **pansies** = 프랑스어의 pensée(= thought)에서 온 말로서 꽃말은 love and courtship. pansy는 주로 사랑하는 이에 대한 thought를 의미하지만 여기서는 죽은 사람에 대한 thought도 포함한다고

보아야 한다. 역시 오빠 Laertes에게 주는 꽃.

177. **for** = appropriate to.

178. **a document in madness** = 앞에 There is를 넣어 해석할 것.

  document = lesson, instruction, teaching. cf. Lt. docere = teach.

178-9. **thoughts and remembrance fitted** = Ophelia has wisely linked thoughts and remembrance.

179. **fitted** = aptly joined.

180. **there's fennel for you** = 여기서 you는 왕.

  fennel = 「회향풀」. 꽃말은 flattery와 deceit. 다음 columbines와 함께 왕에게 주는 꽃.

  columbines [kɔ́ləmbainz] = 「매 발톱 꽃」. 꽃말은 unchastity, infidelity. 밀선(nectar)이 뿔처럼 생긴데서 온 꽃말. 아내를 간통당한 사람 머리 위에는 뿔이 돋는다는 속설에서 생긴 뜻이며, nectar의 모양이 남근을 닮은 데서 온 뜻이기도 하다. fennel과 columbines는 왕에게 건넨 꽃들.

181. **there is rue for you** = 여기서 you는 왕비.

  rue = 「루타」. 꽃말은 sorrow나 repentance. cf. to rue = to grieve for, repent). rue는 또한 herb-grace, 또는 herb of grace(은총의 풀)라고 불리기도 한다.

  here is some for me = Ophelia 자신도 루타 꽃을 달고 있다.

182. **o' Sundays** = on Sundays.

182-3. **you must** = 여기서 you는 여전히 왕비.

183. **with a difference** = 문장(紋章) 술어(heraldic term)이다. 같은 가족끼리도 나이나 속하는 파(branch)에 따라 조금씩 문장의 모양을 달리해서 사용했다. 여기서는 왕비는 repentance, Ophelia는 sorrow 때문에 뜻에 차이가 있다는 의미.

184. **daisy** = 「데이지」. 꽃말이 여럿 있기 때문에 받는 사람을 특정하기가 어렵다. 만약에 꽃말이 dissembling(가식)이라고 여긴다면 이것은 왕이나 왕비가 받게 될 것이고, 또 다른 꽃말인

unrequited love(짝사랑)라면 Ophelia 자신이 가져야 할 꽃이다.

I would give you = 여기서 you는 Hamlet으로 착각한 오빠 Laertes. 또는 Hamlet의 충직한 친구 Horatio라는 해석도 있다.

violets = 「바이올렛」. 꽃말은 faithfulness, fidelity.

185.   **he made a good end** = died as a good man should die. 그러나 이것은 사실이 아니다.

187.   **for bonny sweet Robin is all my joy** = 여러 곳에서 인용되고 있으나 지금 전해지지는 않는다. Robin은 Robin Hood의 Robin. 그렇다면 Ophelia는 자신을 Robin의 애인인 Maid Marian과 혼동하고 있다.

    bonny = pleasant to look upon, comely.

188.   **Thought** = sad thought, grief, melancholy.

    passion = suffering.

189.   **favour** = charm.

190-99.   출처불명의 민요.

196.   **All flaxen** = as white as flax. all은 강조를 나타낸다.

    poll = head.

198.   **we cast away moan** = we waste or throw our moans. 이 밖에 we who are abandoned mourn이라는 해석도 있지만 부자연스럽다.

199.   **God ha' mercy** = God have mercy.

200.   **And of all Christian souls** = 앞줄의 God ha' mercy에 걸린다. 통상적으로 비문(epitaph) 끝에 흔히 사용되는 문구.

    of = on.

    God buy ye = God be with you.

202-3.   **I must⋯right** = you do me wrong unless you allow me to commune with you in your grief.

202.   **commune** [⁀ ×] **with** = share, converse with.

203.   **Or** = if not.

you deny me right = you do wrong.

Go but apart = withdraw with me, and discuss this privately somewhere else 「어디 가서 단둘이 조용히 이야기하자」.

204. **Make choice of whom your wisest friends you will** = choose out from your friends those who are likely to give you the best advice 「말귀를 알아들을 친구를 구해 와라」. Make choice of whom you will과 Make choice of your wisest friends를 혼합한 문장.

    whom = whichever of your.

206. **by collateral hand** = indirectly.

    collateral = indirect.

207. **find us touch'd** = find me implicated.

    find = judge. 법률술어.

    us = me. royal 'we'.

    touch'd = tainted with guilt.

209. **satisfaction** = compensation.

210. **Be you content to lend your patience to us** = allow yourself patiently to listen to what I have to say.

    Be you content to = be patient to.

211-2. **And we…content** = and I will endeavour as earnestly as yourself to give peace to your mind.

211. **labour with your soul** = labour with you heart and soul.

213. **means** = manner.

    obscure [´ ×] = undistinguished.

214. **trophy** = memorial placed over a grave.

    hatchment = memorial tablet showing the coat of arms of the dead person.

215. **formal ostentation** = ceremonial pomp.

    ostentation = ceremony.

217. **That** = so that.

I must call't in question = I must demand an explanation.

218. **And where the offence is let the great axe fall** = and let the fullest vengeance fall upon him who deserves it.

axe = executioner's axe.

Scene VI

1. **What are they** = what sort of men are they.

2. **letters** = a letter. cf. III. iv. 202.

5. **I should be greeted** = I am likely to receive a greeting.

7. **Let Him** = may God.

8. **an't please him** = if it please him.

10. **ambassador** = Hamlet.

bound for = on his way for.

11. **as I am let to know** = 「내가 들은 대로.」

let to know = informed.

let = cause.

13. **overlook'd** = perused, read.

13-4. **some means to the King** = some means of access to the King 「왕에 대한 배알의 기회」.

14-5. **Ere we were two days old** = before we had spent two days 「배타고 나온 지 이틀도 되기 전에」.

15. **pirate** = pirate ship.

15-6. **of very warlike appointment** = fitted out in most warlike fashion, heavily armed.

16. **appointment** = equipment, outfit.

gave us chase = pursued us.

17. **slow of sail** =「배의 걸음이 느리다」.

a compelled valour = a valour compelled by necessity「억지 용기」.

18. **grapple** = a hold or grip in or as in wrestling. 해적들은 공격할 때 마치 레슬링 선수가 상대를 움켜잡듯이 갈퀴 달린 밧줄로 상대방의 배가 움직이지 못하도록 했다.

boarded them =「그들의 배에 옮겨 탔다」.

On the instant = just as I did so.

19. **got clear of** =「떨어졌다」.

21. **thieves of mercy** = merciful thieves「의족」.

they knew what they did = they knew what they were about「빈틈이 없었다」.

22. **turn** = 몸값(ransom) 따위의「보상」.

23. **repair** = come.

24. **as thou wouldest fly death** = as if you were trying to escape from death.

25-6. **will make thee dumb** =「말문이 막히게 할 것이다」. 앞에 which 를 보충할 것.

26-7. **too light … matter** = too trivial for the importance of the subject. light(가벼운)와 bore(포구) 모두 대포에서 온 말.「내용의 중대함에 비하면 내 말이 너무 가볍다」, 즉「내용의 중대함을 이룰 말로 표현할 수 없다」는 뜻.

26. **they** = my words.

bore = caliber (= diameter of a gun tube, through which the bullet is discharged)「구경」.

29. **hold their course** = continue their voyage.

31. **He that thou knowest thine** = He whom you know to be yours.

32. **give you way for** = give you the opportunity of delivering.

33.   **And do't the speedier, that···** = and I will do it all the more quickly, so that···. the speedier의 the는 the more···the more의 구문에서 사용되는 부사.

Scene VII

1.   **Now must your conscience my acquittance seal** = you must confirm my innocence.

my acquittance seal = ratify my acquittal, acknowledge my innocence.

conscience = consciousness, conviction.

2.   **And you must put me in your heart for friend** = nor can you help heartily recognizing me as a friend 「나를 마음의 친구로 받아들이지 않을 수 없을 것이다」.

3.   **Sith** = since.

knowing = intelligent, understanding.

5.   **Pursued my life** = tried to kill me.

It well appears = it is obvious enough.

6.   **proceeded not against these feats** = did not take legal proceedings against these deeds.

proceeded not = took no action to punish.

feats = deeds, actions.

7.   **crimeful** = full of crime, desperately criminal.

capital = punishable by death, heinous.

8-9.   **As by···up** = as by all considerations of your own safety, of what wisdom dictated, and everything else, you were so strongly prompted to do.

9. **You mainly were stirr'd up** = you were so strongly prompted to do.

   so mainly = so much, so strongly.

   stirr'd up = roused from indifference, motivated.

10. **unsinnew'd** = weak. 본래의 뜻은 「힘줄(sinew)이 빠진」.

12. **Lives almost by his looks** = 「얼굴을 보지 않고서는 못 산다」.

    by his looks = on the sight of him.

13. **be it either which** = whichever of the two it may be.

14. **She is so conjunctive to my life and soul** = my life and soul are so wrapped up in her, she is so much a part of my existence.

    conjunctive = closely united. 천문학 술어.

15. **not but in his sphere** = only in its sphere. Ptolemy의 천문학에 의하면 모든 천체(star)는 각각의 천구(sphere) 안에서만 돌게 되어 있다.

16. **could not but by her** = could not move except beside her, I could not live without her.

17. **Why to a public count I might not go** = why I could not have recourse to a public trial.

    count = legal indictment, judgement.

18. **the general gender** = the common people.

19. **dipping all his faults in their affection** = 「그의 잘못을 모두 그들의 애정이라는 물에 담가서」.

20. **like the spring that turneth wood to stone** = 영국에는 물에 석회분을 다량 함유하고 있는 이른바 화석천(petrifying well)이라는 것이 있어 나뭇조각 따위를 넣으면 순간 표면이 석회질로 쌓이는 곳이 있다. Yorkshire의 Knaresborough에 있는 Dropping Well 따위가 그 예이다.

21. **Convert his gyves to graces** = 「(붙잡아) 족쇄를 채워도 그것을 오히려 장식이라고 생각한다」.

gyves [dʒaivz] = fetters, shackles.

graces = ornaments. 여기서는 faults나 crimes의 뜻으로 사용했을 듯.

my arrows = my scheme for punishing him.

22.   **Too slightly timber'd for so loud a wind** = too light to meet so strong a wind.

23-4.   **Would have··· them** = would have been blown back in my face instead of hitting the mark at which they were aimed.

    reverted = returned.

26.   **terms** = state, condition.

27.   **if praises may go back again** = if I may praise what she used to be 「그 옛날의 그녀를 칭찬을 할 수 있다면」.

    go back again = recall what she was before.

28.   **Stood challenger··· perfections** = her worth challenged all the age to equal her excellence.

    Stood challenger = challenged.

    on mount of all the age = above all the age.

29.   **perfections** = endowments, accomplishments.

30.   **Break not your sleeps for that** = do not allow your sleep to be broken by that.

    that = the fear that you may not be able to wreak your revenge.

31.   **we** = royal 'we'.

    stuff = materials.

    flat and dull = spiritless and inert to take offence.

    flat = 「김빠진」.

32-3.   **That we can··· pastime** = that we can endure to have danger flaunts in the face and treat the matter as though it were a mere joke.

32.   **let our beard be shook** = 수염을 쥐어뜯는 것은 상대방에 대한

더없는 모욕이다. cf. II. ii. 600. Plucks off my beard and blows it in my face.

shook with danger = shaken by danger. danger를 의인화했다. **with** = by.

33. **pastime** = harmless sport.

　　　You shortly shall hear more = Hamlet의 죽음을 알리는 영국으로부터의 소식을 암시하고 있다.

34. **I lov'd your father, and we love ourself** = I는 개인으로서의 자신을, 그리고 we는 royal 'we'가 사용된 왕으로서의 자신을 가리킨다.

35. **And that, I hope, will teach you to imagine** = 「이 정도면 짐작이 가겠지만」.

37. **this to the Queen** = 이 편지에 대해서는 뒤에서도 언급이 없다.

43. **High and mighty** = 「지고지대하신」. 왕을 부르는 호칭.

44. **naked** = without any possessions, defenseless, unarmed.

45-7. **eyes…recount** = 귀가 아니고 눈에다 대고 말한다는 것은 이치에 맞지 않을지 모르나, 전통적으로 '눈'은 왕에 대한 환유(metonymy)로 사용되었다.

45. **when** = and then.

46. **first asking your pardon thereunto** = first asking your gracious permission to do so.

　　　pardon = permission.

　　　thereunto = thereto = to that.

47. **occasion** = cause, reason, circumstances.

47-8. **my sudden and more strange return** = my return, the suddenness of which is only exceeded by its strangeness 「나의 갑작스러운 귀국, 갑작스럽다기보다는 이상한 귀국」.

50. **should** = can possibly.

51. **abuse** = imposture, deception, delusion.

no such thing = 「그런 일은 없다」.

52. **hand** = handwriting.

character = handwriting.

55. **lost** = bewildered, at a loss.

56. **It warms the very sickness in my heart** = 「기운 나게 해준다」.

warms = does good to.

57. **That** = to think that.

live and tell = live to tell.

to his teeth = to his face.

58. **Thus didest thou** = 칼로 찌르는 흉내를 내면서 「이렇게 했지」라고 말하겠다는 뜻. 그러나 판본에 따라서는 Thus diest thou (너는 이렇게 죽는다)로 된 곳도 있다.

If it be so = if really Hamlet has returned.

59. **As how should it be so? how otherwise?** = and yet I know not how it can be so, or how it can be otherwise 「돌아왔을 리가 없는데 편지를 보면 그렇다」.

how otherwise? = how can it be otherwise?

60. **rul'd by me** = guided by my advice.

61. **So you will not o'errule to a peace** = if you will not compel me to keep peace with him.

So = so long as, provided that, if.

62. **to thine own peace** = 「자네 마음 편한 대로」.

63. **As checking at his voyage** = refusing to pursue his voyage.

As = as it were.

checking = abandoning, stopping short at. 매(falcon)가 노리던 사냥감(quarry)을 쫓지 않고 우연히 끼어든 다른 새를 쫓는다는 것이 본래의 뜻.

and that = and if it is the case that. that은 62행의 If 대신 사용되었다.

64-5. **I will work him To an exploit** = persuade him to take part in an exploit.

65. **ripe in my device** = which I have fully developed as a scheme.
device = devising, planning.

66. **Under the which he shall not choose but fall** = beneath the weight of which he shall have no choice but to succumb.

67. **And for his death no wind of blame shall breathe** = and not the smallest breath of blame for his death shall ever light on us.
wind of blame = word of blame.

68. **uncharge the practice** = never suspect the plot, find the plot blameless (because she won't recognize it).
uncharge = acquit of guilt.
practice = strategem, conspiracy, trickery, plot, intrigue, treachery.

70. **The rather** = (I will be rule'd) all the more readily.

71. **organ** = instrument, agent.
It falls right = it turns out right, that will fit excellently.

72. **much** = much를 been와 talk'd 사이에 넣고 읽을 것.

73. **And that** = that은 Laertes를 칭찬하는 소문.
quality = accomplishment.

74. **shine** = be brilliant in some respect, excel 「뛰어나다」.
Your sum of parts = all of your good qualities put together.
parts = gifts, accomplishments. 인간은 여러 parts의 조합이라는 생각에서.

75. **pluck** = draw.

76. **regard** = opinion.

77. **unworthiest siege** = lowest in rank, least worthy of respect. 당시 프랑스와 이탈리아에서 전래된 종래의 무거운 sword 대신 양날의 가벼운 rapier를 사용하는 검술. 왕은 그것을 하찮은 것으

로 여기고 있다.

siege = rank, importance. 본래의 뜻은 seat. 식탁의 '상석', '하석'을 따지던 관습에서.

78. **A very riband in the cap of youth** = a mere decoration to youth.
ribband = ribbon.

79. **no less becomes** = no less suits.

80. **light and careless livery** = the airy, jaunty, dress.
livery = clothing. 본래의 뜻은 uniform.

81. **his sables and his weeds** = his clothes formed of sables. 중언법 (hendiadys)의 예.
sables = fur of the sable(검은 담비) or robes with sable trim. cf. III. ii. 138.
weeds = garments, clothes.

82. **Importing** = signifying.
health = welfare, well-being, prosperity. health가 '건강'으로 해석되기도 하지만 '건강'은 '검은 담비 외투'와 어울리지 않는다. '담비 외투'가 '부와 관록'을 나타낸다는 것은 말이 되지만, '담비 외투'가 '건강과 관록'을 보여준다고 하면 어색하다.
graveness = dignity.

84. **I've seen myself, and serv'd against, the French** = 「지금까지 프랑스인들을 만나보고, 또 그들과 겨루기도 했지만」.
serv'd = taken part in military action.

85. **can well** = are well skilled. can을 'know how, be skilled'의 뜻을 가진 본동사로 해석하는 것이 보통이나, well을 'perform well'의 뜻을 갖는 동사로 보는 해석도 있다.
this gallant = daring or spirited man.

86. **witchcraft in 't** = 「마술은 신기에 가깝다」. 't(it)은 horsemanship (마술).
grew unto his seat = sat as though riveted to his saddle. 「몸이

자라 안장과 하나가 되었다」.

87.　　**doing** = feats, performance.

88.　　**As had he been** = as if he had been.

　　　incorps'd and demi-natur'd = made into a single body (with the horse) to form a double-natured creature like the centaur (half man, half horse).

　　　incorps'd = made into one body.

89.　　**brave** = fine, excellent, noble.

　　　topp'd my thought = exceeded my expectation「도저히 내 생각이 미치지 못했다」.

　　　top = surpass.

90.　　**in forgery of shapes and tricks** = in conjuring up in my fancy feats of dexterity.

　　　in forgery of = in conjuring up in my fancy, in imagining.

　　　shapes = embodiments of fancy.

　　　tricks = feats.

91.　　**Come short of what he did** = fall short of his actual performance, cannot compete with what he actually performed.

　　　't = it = he. cf. II. i. 40.

93.　　**Lamord** = 프랑스식으로 읽으면 [la mɔːr], 즉 the death가 된다.

94.　　**brooch** [broutʃ] = jeweled ornament. 당시 모자에 달던 장식 전반에 대한 이름.

96.　　**made confession of you** = admitted your excellence in various exercises.

　　　confession = testimonial. confession이라는 단어는 Lamord가 덴마크인의 재주를 내키지 않는 마음으로 인정한다는 것을 보여준다.

97.　　**a masterly report** = a report of your masterly skill.「극구 칭찬을 했다」.

98. **art and exercise in your defence** = theory and practice of self-defence라고 해석할 수도 있고, 중언법으로 보아 artful exercise of self-defence로 해석할 수도 있다.

　　exercise = acquired skill.

　　defence = art of self-defence.

99. **rapier** = light and fashionable Continental sword. 당시 젊은이들 사이에는 sword대신 rapier를 사용하는 검술이 더 유행했었다.

　　most especial = most especially.

101. **If one could match you** = if anyone could be found to compete with you 「자네 상대가 될 만 한 자가 있다면」.

　　scrimers = skilled fencers 「검객들」. 프랑스어의 escrimeur(= fencer)에서 온 말.

　　their = 문법적으로는 his라고 해야 옳다. 그러나 Lamord가 our nation이라고 말했을 가능성을 생각하면 납득할 수 있는 용법이다.

102. **motion** = (correct or practised) movement. 특히 수비에 대해 공격을 뜻하는 검술 술어.

　　guard = 「방어 자세」.

　　eye = faculty of visual perception 「안력」.

104. **Did Hamlet so envenom** = so poisoned Hamlet with envy.

　　envinom = embitter, literally, poison.

106. **coming o'er** = i.e. return from France.

　　to play with him = that you might play a match with him.

　　play = fence.

107. **Now, out of this ―** = 「그건 그렇고」. 차마 간계를 밝히지 못하는 왕의 주저함이 보인다.

109. **the painting of a sorrow** = the picture of some one in deep grief.

111-2. **Not that…But that** = I say this, not because…but because.

112. **love is begun by time** = love is created by circumstance.

113. **passages of proof** = well-established instances, incidents that proves the fact.

passage = something that passes, occurrence. pass = happen.

114. **qualifies** = diminishes, lessens.

115-6. **There lives···it** = while love is burning most brightly, even then there is in it something which will sooner or later abate its fervour, just as the wick of a candle when it burns to a snuff dims its brightness; i.e. even in its fullest vigour, love contains within it the principle of its own decay. 왕은 사랑도 '자기소진'(self-consumption)에 의해 변할 수 있음을 시사하고 있다.

116. **snuff** = the burned part of the wick of a candle.

117. **nothing is at a like goodness still** = nothing remains always at the same level of goodness, nothing is immune to deterioration 「아무 것도 늘 좋은 상태로만 있을 수 없다」.

at a like goodness = at the same level of goodness.

still = continually.

118-9. **For goodness···much** = for goodness itself, growing to a fulness, dies of its own excess.

plurisy = pleurisy, excess.

119. **his own too much** = its own excess.

119-20. **That we would···would** = that which we desire to do, we ought to do while the desire is strong upon us.

119. **That** = that which.

120. **this 'would'** = this desire.

121. **abatements and delays** = 둘 다 법률술어.

abatements = diminutions, reductions.

122. **there are tongues, are hands, are accidents** = 「(세상에는) 말도 많고, 방해꾼도 많고, 사건도 많기에」.

123. **this 'should'** = this feeling of duty.

spendthrift = excessive, wasteful.

124.   **hurts by easing** = gives pain at the same time as it relieves it 「마음은 편해지지만 몸은 상한다」. 옛날 의학에서 한숨은 위안은 주지만 심장의 피를 마르게 해서 수명을 단축시킨다고 생각되었다.

        to the quick o' the ulcer = to come to the core of the matter, to the main point.

        quick = the most sensitive point.

126.   **in deed** = 판본에 따라서는 indeed로 된 곳도 있다. 어느 쪽이나 해석은 가능하지만 다음 줄의 in words와 짝이 맞는다는 점에서는 in deed가 더 적절하다.

128.   **should murder sanctuarize** = 두 가지 뜻이 있다. 하나는 「교회가 Hamlet과 같은 살인자를 감싸서는 안 된다」는 것과 다른 하나는 「교회가 네가 말하는 목 따기(throat-cutting)를 방해하는 곳이어서는 안 된다」는 두 뜻이다.

        murder = murderer.

        sanctuarize = afford sanctuary. sanctuary = church or other sacred place in which, by the law of the medieval church, a fugitive from justice or a debtor, was entitled to immunity from arrest.

129.   **bound** = boundary.

130.   **Will you do this** = if you want to do this. 왕은 Laertes와 Hamlet이 결투하기 전에 만나는 것을 염려하고 있다.

        keep close = stay concealed.

        close = hidden.

132.   **those shall** = those who shall.

        put on = instigate, incite 「(개 등을) 부추겨서 덤벼들게 하다」.

133.   **set a double varnish on** = give a fresh coating of exaggerated praise to.

fame = reputation.

134. **bring you** = 132행의 We'll에 연결된다.

　　in fine = in conclusion, finally.

135. **wager on your heads** = lay wagers as to which of you will win.

　　wager = offer a wager.

　　your heads = you와 같은 뜻.

　　remiss = careless, negligent 「범연한, 대범한, 꼼꼼하지 못한」.

136. **generous** = noble-minded.

　　contriving = treachery, deception.

137. **peruse** = carefully examine, scrutinize.

　　foils = light fencing swords.

138. **shuffling** = trickery, sleight of hand, legerdemain 「속임수」.

139. **unbated** = not blunted, i.e. not protected by a button (= a round piece of leather) on the point. 진검승부가 아닌 시합에 사용되는 검의 칼끝엔 가죽 마개를 씌웠었다. bate = to blunt.

　　pass of practice = treacherous and (skilful) thrusts.

　　practice = practice에는 보통 연습 때의 thrust라는 뜻과 treacherous thrust라는 두 뜻이 있다. cf. 68. uncharge the practice.

140. **Requite him for your father** = pay him back for the murder of your father.

141. **I'll anoint my sword** = 「칼에 독약을 발라놓겠다」. 판본에 따라서는 이 부분을 왕이 제안하는 것으로 되어 있으며, 연출가들이 그렇게 바꾸기도 한다. 사실 그 쪽이 더 자연스럽다.

142. **unction** = salve, ointment 「연고, 고약」.

　　mountebank = quack doctor. 약(nostrum) 광고를 위해 벤치 위에 올라간다는 뜻에서.

143. **mortal** = deadly, fatal.

　　but dip = if one only dips.

144. **no cataplasm so rare** = no plaster, however excellent.

cataplasm = poultice「찜질약, 습포」.

so rare = however rare in its effects.

144-6. **Collected…under the moon** = 당시엔 달밤에 모은 약초 (simples)가 가장 약효(virtues)가 크다고 믿었다.

145. **Collected from** = composed of.

all simples that have virtue = all efficacious herbs.

simples = medicinal plants.

virtue = medicinal power.

147. **withal** = with it.

touch my point = anoint or smear the (unbated) point of my sword.

148. **contagion** = poison.

gall = graze, scratch.

149. **It may be death** = the result will be death.

150-1. **Weigh…us** = let us consider how we may take such advantage of time and means as will best accommodate us.

151. **May fit us to our shape** = may suit us for the role we are to play. 여기서는 몸에 맞는 옷을 골라 입는 은유를 사용하고 있다.

our shape = our scheme.

152. **And that** = and if. 여기서 that은 63행에서와 마찬가지로 앞줄의 If 대신 사용된 것이다.

our drift look through our bad performance = our intention reveal itself through our bungling.

drift = scheme, design, plot.

153. **assay'd** = put to the test, attempted.

154. **a back or second** = backup plan. 둘 다 support의 뜻.

a back = something in reserve to strengthen it.

second = something to assist.

hold = prove effective, hold good.

155. **blast in proof** = blow up in the testing 「시험해서 폭발하는 경우가 있어도」. 대포 따위의 무기는 실전 배치에 앞서 가혹한 조건에서 미리 시험해본다.

Soft! = Wait a moment.

156. **solemn** = of great dignity.

your cunnings = your and Hamlet's fencing skills.

cunnings = skills, abilities.

157. **I ha 't** = I have it, I have hit upon a good idea.

158. **motion** = bodily exertion 「몸놀림」.

dry = thirsty.

159. **As make** = and you should. as는 거의 뜻이 없다.

make your bouts more violent to that end = with which object (that you may both become hot thirsty) take care to let your bouts be as violent as possible.

bout = round or turn (in fencing).

160. **And that** = and when.

him = for him.

161. **chalice** = drinking cup or goblet.

for the nonce = especially for the occasion.

162. **venom'd** = poisonous.

stuck = thrust. 펜싱 용어.

163. **Our purpose may hold there** = our project may by this means hold good, be carried through.

hold = be steadfast.

there = 「(독살한다는) 그 점에서」.

164-5. **One woe…follow** = 불행은 겹쳐 온다는 뜻. 같은 말을 왕도 하고 있다. cf. IV. v. 78-9. When sorrows come, they come not single spies, But in battalions.

165. **follow** = follow one another.

167. **willow** = 버드나무는 '실연'(forsaken love)의 상징.

grows = 앞에 which를 보충할 것.

aslant = across, athwart, overhanging.

168. **his hoar leaves** = 버드나무 잎의 뒷면은 silvery grey이다. 따라서 강물에 비치는 버드나무 잎은 희게 보일 터.

shows = reflects.

his = its.

hoar = grey or white.

169. **fantastic** = elaborate.

170. **crow-flowers** = buttercups 「미나리아재비」.

nettles = 「쐐기풀」.

daisies = 「데이지, 들국화」.

long purples = orchids 「자색 란」.

171. **liberal** = free-speaking.

grosser name = less decent name 「보다 험한 이름」. 자색 란 (long purples)은 생김새가 긴장했을 때의 음경을 닮았다고 해서 일명 「호색 과부」(rampant(= lustful) widow)라고 불리기도 하지만 왕비는 차마 그 이름을 입에 담지 못하고 있다. 한편 「난 꽃」의 라틴어는 orchis인데 이것의 그리스어 어원은 남자의 「고환」이다. 난의 뿌리가 그것과 비슷하게 생겼기 때문이다.

172. **cold maids** = chaste maids.

173. **pendant** = overhanging.

coronet weeds = the flowers she had woven into a chaplet. 다음 줄 'hang'의 목적어.

174. **envious silver** = malicious branch 「무정한 나뭇가지」.

envious = malicious.

silver = a small branch, twig or splinter.

175.   **weedy trophies** = i.e. the garlands.

   weedy = of plants.

176.   **Fell** = fell이라는 동사는 「사고사」를 뜻하지만 5막 1장에서는 「자살」이 암시된다.

177.   **And, mermaid-like, awhile they bore her up** = and for a time they kept her afloat like a mermaid.

   mermaid = mythical creatures, half woman and half fish.

178.   **Which time** = during which time.

   snatches = bits, fragments.

179.   **As one incapable of her own distress** = as though she were insensible of the plight in which she was.

   incapable of = insensible to, without ability to understand.

180-1.   **native … element** = native to that element (i.e. water) and endowed with qualities fitting her for living in it.

   indued = naturally adapted, habituated.

   indue = furnish, supply, endow.

182.   **Till that** = till.

   heavy with their drinks = 「물이 배어서 무거워진」.

183-4.   **Pull'd … death** = put an end to her melody by dragging her down to death at the bottom of the stream.

183.   **wretch** = 「불쌍한 것」. 애정과 동정이 섞인 표현.

   lay = song.

188.   **It is our trick** = it is a habit we cannot shake off, i.e. weeping is natural.

   trick = custom, habit.

   nature her custom holds = 「참으려고 해도 눈물이 나는 것은 인지상정」.

   her = its.

189.   **Let shame say what it will** = 「제아무리 부끄럽대도」.

189-90. **When these⋯out** = when these tears are shed, my female-like weakness will be spent.

189. **these** = these tears.

190. **The woman will be out** = this feminine weakness will be finished 「사내답지 못함도 사라질 것이다」.

191. **speech of fire** = fiery speech.
that fain would blaze = that is eager to blaze out.
fain = gladly.

192. **But that this folly douts it** = if those foolish tears do not put it out.
this folly = this foolish impulse (of weeping).
dout = put out, extinguish.

193. **How much I had to do** = how much ado I had. 'ado'는 Scandinavia 어의 'at do'에서 온 말로서, 'at'는 영어의 'to'에 해당하는 전치사이다.

194. **give it start again** = will set it in motion again 「분노를 재발시키다」.

Act V

Scene I

SD.   **Clowns** = comedian이라는 통상적인 뜻이라기보다는 rustic에 가까운 뜻.

pickaxes = 「곡괭이」.

1.   **she** = Hamlet과 Horatio는 아직 모르지만 독자나 청중은 '그녀' 가 Ophelia라는 것을 안다.

1-2.   **Christian burial** = 기독교식 장례. 무덤을 파는 사람들은 Ophelia가 자살을 했다고 생각하는 것 같다. 기독교에서 자살 은 신의 계시를 거스르는 행위로서 자살자는 성지(consecrated ground), 즉 교회에 묻히지 못하고, 심한 경우에는 가슴에 말뚝 을 박아 네거리에 묻고 그 위에 돌을 싸 올리는 경우도 있었다. 이 관례는 19세기까지 계속되었다.

2.   **wilfully seeks her own salvation** = 너무 일찍 하늘나라로 가버 렸다는 뜻이거나, 아니면 damnation이라고 해야 할 것을 salvation으로 잘못 말했을 수도 있다. 무식한 사람들이 유식하 게 보이려고 하다 범하는 실수의 경우이다.

salvation = 「구원」.

3.   **she is** = she is to be buried in Christian burial.

4. **straight** = straightaway, immediately.

4-5. **crowner** = coroner 「검시관」. 사인을 규명하는 것이 직업이다.

sat on her = conducted a formal inquest into her death.

5. **finds it Christian burial** = decided that Ophelia is eligible for Christian burial.

finds = determined and declared. 법률 술어. 현재도 사용된다. 8행의 found도 마찬가지 용법.

9. **se offendendo** = se defendendo(= in defending oneself 「정당방위」)의 잘못.

11. **wittingly** = intentionally, deliberately, knowingly 「(나쁜 짓 한다는 것을) 알면서」.

wit = know의 옛말.

argues = proves, indicates.

12. **three branches** = divisions, sections. 별 차이도 없는 것을 여럿으로 나누기 좋아하는 학자들의 현학적 태도에 대한 조롱이 담겨 있다.

branches = divisions, sections.

13. **argal** = 라틴어의 ergo(= therefore)를 잘못 말한 것.

14-5. **Goodman Delver** = master digger.

14. **goodman** = 직업을 나타내는 말에 친근감을 더하기 위해 그 앞에 사용되었다. old fellow나 neighbour 정도의 뜻.

delver = (grave-) digger.

16. **Give me leave** = Excuse (for interrupting your speech).

19. **will he, nill he** = whether he is willing or not. 여기서 willy-nilly (싫든 좋든 간에)라는 단어가 나왔다.

nill = ne(= not) + will.

he goes = 앞줄의 it is에 연결된다.

mark = take note, remember.

24-5. **crowner's quest law** = 앞에 it is를 보충할 것.

24-5.	**quest law** = inquest law 「검시법」.
26.	**Will you ha' the truth on 't?** = do you wish to know the whole truth of the matter?
	on 't = of it.
27.	**should** = would certainly.
28.	**out o'** = out of, outside.
29.	**there thou say'st** = you are right in that.
	say = speak to the point.
29-30.	**the more pity that** = it is the greater pity that 「그러니 더욱 안됐다」. 지체가 높은 사람들은 투신을 하거나 목을 매 죽어도 자살로 취급되지 않고 특별 취급을 받기 때문에 자연히 그런 기회가 많아진다는 것은 안 된 일이다.
30-1.	**should have…to drown** = should be countenanced in drowning by being allowed Christian burial.
	countenance = favour, patronage, permission, legal approval.
32.	**even Christian** = fellow Christian.
32-3.	**Come, my spade** = come, let me take my spade, and get to my work.
33-4.	**There is…grave-makers** = there are no gentlemen that can claim anything like old descent except gardeners, etc. 「예부터 점잖은 직업이라면 …밖에 없었다」.
33.	**ancient** = venerable, well-established.
34.	**ditchers** = men who make and repair ditches.
34-5.	**hold up Adam's profession** = 「아담의 직업을 이어왔다」. cf. *Genesis* 3:23. Therefore the Lord God sent him forth from the garden of Eden, to till the ground from whence he was taken.
	hold up = maintain, keep up (the noble reputation of).
36.	**Was he a gentleman?** = When Adam dolve (= delved), and Eve span, Who was then the gentleman? (아담이 밭 갈고 이브가

베 짜던 시절 양반 따위가 있었겠느냐?)라는 속요를 빗대고 하는 말. 다시 말해 태초의 Eden에는 gentleman이나 사회계층 사이의 차별 따위는 없었다는 뜻.

gentleman = 귀족과 yeoman 사이의 계급.

37.   **A'** = he. 배우지 못한 사람들이 쓰는 말.

37-8.   **bore amrs** = arms는 '문장'(coat of arms)와 '팔'(limbs)의 두 뜻에 걸친 pun이다. 여기서는 '문장'의 뜻으로 사용되었으나 42행의 could he dig without arms?에서는 '팔'의 뜻으로 사용되고 있다. 또 다른 주석가들은 arms를 '무기', 여기서는 spade(가래)의 뜻으로 해석하기도 한다. gentleman은 귀족은 아니지만 문장의 사용이 허용되었었다.

40.   **art** = art thou.

42.   **arms** = '팔'과 '무기(= 가래)'의 두 뜻으로 사용되고 있다.

44.   **to the purpose** = in a rational way, pertinently.

            confess thyself⁻ = Confess thyself and be hanged(자백하고 목을 매라)라는 당대의 관용적 표현을 중간에서 가로 막은 꼴.

45.   **Go to** = pooh, shut up. 짜증을 나타내는 감탄사. 「무슨 그런 바보 같은 소리를」.

46.   **What is he** = what kind of person is he.

47.   **shipwright** = 「조선공」.

            wright = maker or builder. cf. playwright.

49.   **gallows-maker** = 교수대 만드는 사람.

            that frame = gallows.

50.   **outlives a thousand tenants** = 「목을 매다는 사람이 천명이 넘어도 고장 나지 않는다」.

            tenants = occupants.

52.   **does well** = (1) is a good answer, (2) functions aptly.

55.   **church** = 교회는 mason이 짓는다.

            may do well to thee = may serve its purpose by punishing you.

56. **To't again, come** = make another effort to answer my question.

59. **unyoke** = unyoke the oxen (from the plough), i.e. put an end to you labour. 이 수수께끼를 맞히면 일을 그만하고 쉬어도 된다는 뜻.

60. **Marry** = by (the Virgin) Mary. 놀라움, 강조, 분노를 나타내는 가벼운 뜻의 감탄사.

61. **To't** = get on with it.

62. **Mass** = by the mass. cf. III. ii. 395. 가벼운 뜻의 감탄사.

63. **Cudgel they brains** = 「머리를 쥐어짜다」.

    Cudgel = beat with a stick.

64. **your dull…beating** = a stupid donkey does not move more quickly because it is beaten.

    your dull ass = a dull ass like you. your는 일반적인 뜻의 대명사.

    mend his pace = travel faster.

68. **Yaughan** [jɔːn] = 독일어의 Johan [jɔːhɑn] (= John)을 잘못 발음한 것으로, 당시 Globe Theatre 근처에 있던 유대인 술집 (ale-house) 이름일 것으로 짐작된다.

    stoup [stuːp] = flagon, jug or cup.

69-72. Clown이 부르는 이 노래는 1557년 Richard Tottel이 편집해 출간한 영국 최초의 시집 *Miscellany* 안에 있는 Vaux 경이 쓴 시 'The Aged Lover Renounceth Love'의 몇 소절을 고쳐 부른 것. 원문은 다음과 같다.

    I lothe that I did love,

    　In youth that I thought swete(= sweet);

    As time requires for my behove

    　Methinkes they are not mete(= meet).

70. **Methought** = it seemed to me, I thought.

71. **To contract, O, the time, for-a my behove** = shorten the time for my advantage. O나 －a(= ah)는 한숨 소리거나 신음 소리.

이 둘을 제외하면 나머지는 To contract the time for my behove 가 된다.

contract = shorten.

behove = behoof, benefit.

72.   **meet** = suitable, appropriate.

73-4.   **feeling of his business** = no sense of the sadness of the task on which he is engaged.

75-6.   **Custom … easiness** = habit makes it easy for him.

        property of easiness = thing he can do easily, a matter of indifference.

        of easiness = easy to him.

76-7.   **of little employment** = that is little used, not frequently used.

78.   **the daintier sense** = more delicate feeling 「그만큼 더 예민한 감각」.

79.   이 노래는 본래의 시 두 연을 하나로 꿰맞춰 부른 것. 원문은 다음과 같다.

For age with stealing steps,
    Hath clawed me with his crutch;
And lusty life away she leaps,
    As there had been none such,

For beauty with her band
    These crooked cares hath wrought,
And shipped me into the land,
    From whence I first was brought.

80.   **clutch** = grasp.

81.   **shipped me intil the land** = transported me to the land (of death).

        intil the land = toward my grave.

        intil = into. 주로 북부 지방에서 쓰이던 오래된 형태의 전치사

로서, 무덤 파는 사람의 출신성분에 대한 암시를 위한 것이라는
해석도 있다.

82. **such** = as I am.

84. **jowls** = dashes, hurls「내동댕이치다」. 명사로서의 이 단어의
뜻은「턱」. 다음 줄의 Cain's jaw-bone의 이미지를 미리 환기한
다.

85. **Cain's jaw-bone** = Cain이 동생 Abel을 죽일 때 사용했다고 전
해지는 당나귀의 턱뼈. 성경에는 나와 있지 않으나 속설로 전해
지고 있다. 그러나 여기서는 단순히「카인의 턱뼈」라고 해도
무방하다.

     that = Cain.

86. **might be** = may have been.

     pate = head.

     politician = schemer, plotter「책사」.

87. **ass** = grave-digger.

     o'verreaches = getting hold of (with his spade)와 get the better
of, outwit(한 수 앞지르다)의 두 뜻이 있다.

     one = politician과 동격.

     would = wished to.

88. **circumvent** = get around, outwit.

92. **lord such-a-one** = some lord or other whose name is not specified
「모모 나리」.

95. **beg** = borrow.

96-7. **my Lady Worm's** =「(그러나 지금은) 벌레 마님의 소유물」.

97. **chapless** = lacking the lower jaw.

98. **mazzard** = head에 대한 익살스러운 표현. mazer(= bowl)에서
나온 단어일 듯.

     sexton = church worker who rang bells, dug graves, and
performed other duties.

revolution = revolution of Fortune's wheel, i.e. the change, esp. as wrought by time.

99.　　**trick** = art, skill, knack, ability.

99-100.　**Did these…breeding, but** = 「이 뼈들은 오로지 …만을 위해 힘들여 키워졌단 말인가」.

　　　cost no more the breeding = gave no more trouble to breed.

100-1.　**but to play at loggats with'em?** = than that they should be used for playing at loggats.

　　　loggats = game in which thick sticks are thrown to lie as near as possible to a stake fixed in the ground.

101.　　**Mine** = my bones.

102-5.　Vaux의 시를 거의 그대로 옮겨 왔다. 본문은 다음과 같다.

　　　A pickaxe and a spade,

　　　　And eke a winding sheet,

　　　A house of clay for to be made,

　　　　For such a guest most meet.

103.　　**For and** = and also, and moreover.

　　　shrouding sheet = 「수의」.

104.　　**for to** = to.

107.　　**quiddities** = hair-splitting definitions, subtleties, quibbles 「괴변」.

108.　　**quillets** = verbal nicety or subtle distinction 「미세한 말의 차이」. 동시에 small pieces of land라는 뜻도 있다.

　　　tenures = property titles, holding of real estates.

109.　　**tricks** = legal chicaneries, law tricks 「법적 속임수」.

　　　suffer = allow.

110.　　**sconce** = head에 대한 장난스러운 속어적 표현.

111.　　**action of battery** = lawsuit charging physical assault 「폭행에 대한 소송」.

112-3.	**a great buyer of land** = Shakespeare 생존 당시 토지매매가 왕성해서 변호사들은 그 전문지식을 악용해서 사리사욕을 채우는 경우가 허다했다. 극의 배경은 덴마크이지만 많은 경우 관중들은 덴마크와 영국을 혼돈하게 된다.
113-4.	**his statutes … recognizances** = 땅을 사고팔고 소유하기 위해 필요한 법률술어들임. 토지 매매와 관련된 법률술어에 대한 Shakespeare의 소상한 그 자신 상속권을 박탈당해(disinherited) 소송에 휘말렸던 경험이 있기 때문.
113.	**statutes** = securities for debts or mortgages 「차용증서」.
	recognizances = bonds relating to debts 「변제보증」.
114.	**fines** = compromise of a fictitious or collusive suit for the possession of lands 「토지 소유를 위해 미리 짜고 일으키는 사기 소송」.
	double vouchers = 「2중증인」.
	voucher = person who is called upon to warrant a tenant's title.
	recoveries = process by which entailed estate was commonly transferred from one party to another.
115.	**the fine of his fines** = the end of all his legal practice, all that comes of his long practising as a lawyer.
	the fine = the end, the conclusion. cf. v. ii. 15. in fine.
	fines = amicable agreement of a fictitious suit for the possession of lands.
115-6.	**the recovery of his recoveries** = all that he recovers, gets in return for the recoveries in which, when alive, he was engaged.
115.	**recovery** = what he gets in return 「보수」.
116.	**recoveries** = suits for obtaining possession.
116.	**fine pate full of fine dirt** = 「고운 머리통엔 고운 가루가 가득」. fine pate (handsome head)의 fine은 fine dirt (powdered earth)의 fine과의 pun이다.

117-8. **vouch⋯ones too** = give him no better title to his purchases, even though those vouchers were double ones.

118. **double ones** = double vouchers (guarantees signed by two parties).

118-9. **than the⋯indentures** = than the mere parchment on which indentures are written.

119. **a pair of indentures** = 「종이 한 장에 같은 내용의 계약서 2통을 써서 가운데를 찢어 톱니 꼴로 만든 두 장의 계약서」. 계약서 두 장을 합쳐 톱니 꼴이 일치하면 진품 계약서임이 증명된다. 한편 두개골 정수리를 보면 한 가운데에 톱니 모양의 줄이 있다. 무덤 파는 사람이 두개골을 들어 관객에게 보이면서 이 대사를 말한다면 하나의 pun이 될 수 있다.

120. **conveyances** = document by which transference of property is effected 「양도증명서」.

  lie = be valid. 법률술어.

  this box = this skull. this coffin이라는 해석도 있다. 변호사들이 서류를 넣어두는 상자에 빗댄 해석이다.

121. **inheritor** = possessor, owner.

  no more = no more than this box.

122. **jot** = a very small amount.

123. **parchment** = animal skin used for a writing surface, especially for legal documents, vellum.

125-6. **They are⋯in that** = those who trust such documents are but dolts.

  assurance = 「등기이전」(conveyance of lands or tenements by deed)이라는 법률상의 뜻과 「안심」이라는 보통의 두 뜻으로 사용.

125-6. **They are⋯in that** = those who trust parchment are but dolts.

126. **in that** = in legal documents.

127. **sirrah** [síɾə] = sir. 손아래 남자를 부르는 호칭. 무덤 파는 사람이 Hamlet에게 You라는 호칭을 사용하는 것에 대해 Hamlet이 thou라는 호칭을 사용하는 것은 사회적 신분의 차이를 들어내기 위함.

132. **I think it be thine** =「아마 그건 자네 것이겠지」. be는 가상법의 be.

    liest in't = lie는「거짓말을 하다」와「(무덤 안에) 누워있다」의 pun으로 사용되고 있다.

133. **out on 't** = outside of it.

137. **the quick** = the living「살아 있는 사람」. cf. the quick and the dead.

139. **quick lie** =「(거짓말에 대한) 재빠른 반박」.「한방 먹었다」는 뜻.

    quick = swift.

    lie =「거짓말에 대한 비난」. cf. give the lie to…「…에게 거짓말을 했다고 비난하다」.

139-40. **'twill away…to you** =「다음은 당신 차례다」.

    'twill away = it will pass away.

141. **What man** =「어떤 사람」. Hamlet이「어떤 사람(man)」이냐고 묻자 무덤 파는 사람은 man을「사람」이 아닌「남자」라는 뜻으로 받아 대답한다.

144. **For none, neither** = for no woman, either.

147. **rest her soul** = God rest her soul!「나무아미타불」과 같은 삽입구.

148. **absolute** = particular, precise, punctilious about accuracy「깐깐한」.

149. **by the card** = with great precision. card에 대해서는 여러 해석이 있다. 선원들의「해도」(chart)나「예절 범례집」(book of manners), 등.

equivocation will undo us = 「애매한 말을 쓰다가는 당한다」.
equivocation = ambiguity, double meanings. equivocate

150. **these three years** = 「지난 몇 년 동안」이라고 해석할 수도 있으나, 정확히는 1597년에 의회를 통과한 빈민구제법(Poor Law)에 대한 언급으로 보인다. *Hamlet*이 1600년이나 1601년에 써졌다면 앞뒤가 맞는다. 이 법의 시행으로 귀족들에 대한 증세가 이루어졌다.

151. **it** = 다음에 말한 내용을 가리킨다.
     picked = smart, spruce, refined, exquisite, affected, finicky. 신발에 관해 사용될 때에는 pointed라는 뜻도 있다. 여기서는 이 두 가지 뜻으로 사용된 pun.

153. **he galls his kibe** = the peasant chafes the sore on the courtier's heel 「농사꾼이 동상으로 쓰린 대감의 발뒤꿈치를 아프게 한다」. 그만큼 양자의 거리가 가까워져 차이가 없어졌다는 뜻. 빈민구제법의 결과 귀족들에 대한 증세가 이루어져(galls his kibe) 그 결과 빈부의 격차가 준 것이 사실이다.
     galls = chafes, hurts.
     kibe = chapped chilblain on the heel 「살갗이 튼 발뒤꿈치 동상」.

155. **Of all the days i' the year** = if you wish me to be precise as to the exact day.

166-7. **it's no great matter there** = it does not much matter.

169. **'Twill not be seen in him** = 「(영국에서는) 눈에 띄지 않는다」.
     seen = noticed.

175. **Upon what ground?** = owing to what cause? 다음 줄에서 무덤 파는 사람은 ground를 「땅」이라는 뜻으로 받아 대답하고 있다.

177. **thirty years** = 무덤 파는 사람이 Hamlet이 태어난 해에 일을 시작해서 30년이 지났다고 하니까 Hamlet의 나이가 30이라는 것을 알게 된다. 평론가들은 지금까지 관객이 대학생 신분인

Hamlet에 대해 짐작했던 나이보다 약간 많게 느껴진다는 견해를 보이고 있다.

181. **pocky** = rotten (especially with syphilis). pock의 형용사. small-pox(천연두)의 pox는 pocks와 같은 단어지만 여기서 pocky는 천연두가 아니고 매독(syphilis)을 뜻한다. Columbus 일행이 신세계 미국에서 가져온 이 병은 이탈리아, 프랑스를 거쳐 Shakespeare 시대에는 영국에서 맹위를 떨쳤다.

    corses = corpse의 옛날 형태.

182. **scarce hold the laying in** = barely hold together long enough to be buried 「거의 장례식 때까지 지탱하지 못한다」.

    hold = endure.

183. **you** = ethical dative.

    year = years. 옛날 복수형.

    tanner = one who converts animal hides into leather. Shakespeare 의 아버지는 흰 가죽을 만드는 무두장이(whittawer)였다.

188. **your water** = 「물이라는 것」. 일반적인 사항을 가리키는 your.

    sore decayer = 「심하게 부패시키는 것」.

    sore = grievous.

188-9. **your whoreson dead body** = 이 your도 마찬가지 용법의 your.

189. **whoreson** [hɔ́ːsən] = 문자 그대로는 son of whore or prostitute이지만 대개는 cursed, vile, damnation 따위와 같은 뜻의 intensive 로 사용되었다.

196-7. **A pestilence on him for a mad rogue!** = curses on him, as such a mad rogue deserves! 「미친 놈 염병이나 걸려라!」.

196. **for** = as.

197. **’A** = he.

    a flagon of Rhenish [réniʃ] = a bottle of Rhine wine.

    Rhenish [réniʃ] = Rhine 지방에서 나는 백포도주. cf. I. iv. 10.

203-4. **a fellow of infinite jest** = a fellow of inexhaustible wit.

204. **fancy** = imagination, invention.

206. **how abhorred in my imagination** = 「자기를 업어주던 사람이 이렇게 된 것을 보면 상상하는 것만도 역겹다」.

abhorred = filled with horror, loathsome.

it is = 여기서 it은 지금은 해골이 된 이 광대의 등에 어릴 때 업혀 놀았다는 사실.

206-7. **My gorge rises at it** = I feel like vomiting 「구역질이 난다」.

207. **gorge** = throat, stomach, but also contents of the stomach.

209. **gibes** = taunts, scoffs 「비웃음」.

gambols = playful tricks.

211. **on a roar** = roaring (with laughter). 현대 영어로선 in a roar라고 해야 맞다.

211-2. **Not one now, to mock your own grinning?** = 「지금 해골이 되어 히죽거리는 자신의 모습을 비웃을 웃음은 없는가?」.

Not one now…? = Is there not one now…?

one = 앞의 gibes나 gambols 따위를 받는다.

212. **grinning** = Because they showed teeth, skulls were thought to grin.

chap-fallen = dejected(아래턱이 빠져 늘어진), 또는 without the lower jaw(아래턱이 없는).

212-3. **get you to** = go to. you는 재귀대명사.

my lady's chamber = 특별히 가리키는 사람이 있는 것은 아니고 my lady [miléidi](= gentlewoman)라고 부를 수 있는 신분을 가진 부인을 말한다.

213-4. **let her paint and inch thick** = 「설사 한 인치 두께로 화장을 해도」.

paint = apply cosmetics.

214. **favour** = face, countenance, appearance. cf. well-favoured (= of good looks, comely).

218-9.	**Dost thou…earth?** = 죽음에 관한 이야기가 나올 때 Alexander 대왕에 대해 언급하는 것이 관례이다. Plutarch의 *Lives*(영웅전)에 의하면 생전의 대왕의 몸은 「매우 희고 아름다우며, 향기를 내뿜고 있어 그의 옷은 마치 향수를 뿌린 듯 이루 말할 수 없는 좋은 냄새를 머금고 있었다」라고 전해지고 있다.
	o' this fashion = in this manner, like this.
219.	**i' the earth** = when buried 「땅 속에서」.
223.	**To what base uses we may return…!** = 「얼마나 천하게 쓰이는가!」.
225.	**he find it** = he는 imagination, it은 dust를 가리킨다.
226.	**bung-hole** = stopper for a cask or barrel 「술통 마개」.
	bung = stopper for a cask or barrel.
227.	**'Twere to consider too curiously** = 「생각이 지나치다」.
	curiously = fastidiously, ingeniously.
229.	**not a jot** = not at all.
	jot = a very small amount.
	but = (only) to follow him. 그 앞에 't were를 보충해서 읽을 것.
230.	**thither** = to the bung-hole.
	with modesty enough = without exaggeration.
	modesty = moderation, reserve.
230-1.	**likelihood to lead it** = with probability to lead the mediation.
231.	**it** = imagination.
232.	**returneth to dust** = cf. *Genesis* 3:19.
233.	**of earth** = with earth.
	loam = a mixture of clay and sand, moistened to make plaster 「점토」.
236.	**Imperious** = imperial.
238.	**that earth** = the body of Caesar.

239.	**expel** = keep out.

flaw = sudden gust of wind.

240.	**soft** = be silent.

Aside! = let us stand aside.

242.	**maimed** [méimid] = curtailed, imperfect.

244.	**Fordo** = destroy, kill, put an end to.

it own life = its own life. cf. I. ii. 216.

some estate = considerable class, social standing.

245.	**Couch we** = Let us hide.

mark = observe.

246.	**What ceremony else?** = what further ceremonies have to be performed? i.e. surely this does not complete the usual rites.

249.	**obsequies** [ɔ́bsəkwiz] = funeral rites.

249-50.	**as far…warranties** = 「허용될 수 있는 한도까지 해드렸다」.

249.	**enlarg'd** = extended, prolonged.

250.	**warranties** = permission, authorization.

doubtful = suspicious.

251.	**but that great command o'ersways the order** = if it were not that the king's command, which we dare not disobey, over-rules us as regards the proceedings usual in such case.

great command = the command of powerful people.

the order = the rule of the church.

252-3.	**in ground…trumpet** = in unhallowed ground been buried until the Judgment Day.

252.	**in ground unsanctified** = 이른바 consecrated ground가 아닌, 자살자나 죄인들을 묻는 장소. cf. V. i. 1-2.

253.	**the last trumpet** = 「최후 심판의 나팔」. cf. *Revelation* 8-10. *I Corinthians* 15:52.

for = instead of.

254. **Shards** = fragments of pottery, potsherd.

flints = 「돌조각들」.

255. **virgin crants** = garlands appropriate to a virgin. 젊은 여인네가 죽으면 흰 종이로 꽃을 만들어 교회에 거는 관습이 있었다.

crants = (*sing.*) garland, wreath. cf. *Ger.* Krantz.

256. **strewments** = flowers strewn on a grave.

256-7. **bringing … burial** = being brought to the grave, her last home, to the sound of the bell.

256. **home** = one's long or last home.

257. **Of bell and burial** = with the ringing of the bell and other ceremonies of burial.

259. **service of the dead** = 「죽은 자의 장례」.

260. **To sing** = by singing, if we were to sing.

requiem [rékwiem] = funeral hymn or chant.

such rest = to pray for such rest.

261. **peace-parted souls** = those who have departed in peace or died a natural death. cf. *Luke* 2:29.

263. **violets** = 순결의 상징.

churlish = rude, rough.

264. **minist'ring angel shall my sister be** = my sister will certainly be an angel in heaven.

265. **howling** = i.e. in the torments of hell.

266. **Sweets to the sweet** = Lovely flowers for the lovely maiden.

268. **I thought thy bride-bed to have deck'd** = 완료부정사 to have deck'd는 실현되지 않은 기대를 나타낸다.

deck'd = adorned, arrayed.

269. **treble woe** = 「크나큰 재앙」.

treble = threefold.

270. **cursed** [-id].

271. **thy most ingenious sense** = 다음 줄의 Deprived thee of 뒤에 놓고 읽을 것.

ingenious = intelligent, quick of apprehension.

272. **Hold off the earth awhile** = hold off from filling the grave with earth for a while.

274. **the quick and dead** = cf. 137.

275. **this flat** = this level surface 「평지」.

276. **Pelion** [píːliən] = 그리스 신화에서 신들에 거역하는 거인 족(the Titans)이 신들이 사는 Olympus 산에 올라가려고 Ossa 산 위에 쌓아올렸다고 전해지는 산.

276. **skyish** = reaching to the sky, lofty.

277. **Olympus** = 신들이 사는 그리스 최고의 산.

278. **Bears such an emphasis** = carries such an intensity of feeling, is expressed in such forceful language.

emphasis = intensity.

278-9. **whose phrase⋯stand** = whose utterance of sorrow has such magic power over the planets as to arrest their motion.

279. **Conjures the wandering stars** = 「회전하는 별들도 홀린다」.

wandering stars = planets. fixed star에 반대되는 말.

stand = stand still.

280. **wonder-wounded** = struck with amazement, wonder-struck.

280-1. **This is I, Hamlet, the Dane!** = 여기서 Hamlet은 변장했던 선원의 복장을 벗을 것이다. the Dane이라는 말에서 덴마크의 왕권에 대한 Hamlet의 결의가 보인다.

281. **The devil take thy soul** = 저주하는 말.

284. **splenitive** [splíːnitiv] = hot-tempered, splenetic. spleen(비장)은 anger가 들어 있는 곳으로 생각되었다.

286. **Which let thy wiseness fear** = which it will be prudent in you to fear.

wiseness = wisdom.

287.　**Pluck them asunder** = draw them apart.

289.　**theme** = subject.

290.　**Until my eyelids will no longer wag** = until I have no life left at all.

　　　wag = move.

292.　**forty thousand brothers** = forty thousand는 다수를 나타내는 문구로 Shakespeare가 자주 사용했다. 40이라는 수는 성경에서 예수의 40일간의 금식, 이스라엘 민족의 40년간의 방랑 등에서 신비한 의미를 갖게 되었는지도 모른다.

293-4.　**Could not…sum** = could not, however great their love, vie with me in loving her.

　　　with all their quantity of love = quantity는 경멸적인 뜻으로 사용되었다. cf. III. ii. 45.

296.　**forbear him** = leave him alone.

　　　forbear = bear with, tolerate.

297.　**'Sounds** [zwu:nds] = by Christ's wounds. cf. II. ii. 604.

　　　thou 'lt = thou wilt.

298.　**Woo 't** = Wilt thou. 경멸적인 표현. 아직도 영국 북부에서 사용된다고 함.

299.　**Woo 't drink up eisel?** = 「식초는 분노의 죽음이며 우울의 탄생이다」라는 잘 알려진 표현, 즉 식초를 마시면 분노가 가라앉고 우울해진다는 뜻에서 Hamlet의 말은 「식초라도 마시고 누이동생의 죽음을 한껏 슬퍼하는 척해보겠는가」라는 비꼬임이 섞인 표현.

　　　drink up = greedily quaff.

　　　eisel [i:zəl] = vinegar의 고어. eisel이 강 이름이라는 해석도 있다.

　　　Eat a crocodile? = 악어는 먹이를 먹으면서 눈물을 흘린다는 속설에서 「악어고기라도 먹고 거짓 눈물(hypocritical tears)이라도 흘려보겠다는 건가」라는 뜻.

300. **whine** = 「(개 따위가) 애처롭게 울다」.

301. **outface** = put out of countenance, put me to shame 「면목 없게 만들다」.

302. **quick** = alive.

303. **prate** = boast, rant.

304. **acres** = large quantities of land.

　our ground = the mound of earth piled on us.

305. **Singeing [síndʒiŋ] his pate against the burning zone** = scorching its top by touching the sun's orbit.

　his = its. our ground를 가리킨다.

　pate = head.

　the burning zone = the path of the sun.

306. **Make Ossa like a wart!** = 276행의 주 참조.

　like a wart = as small as a wart.

　wart = 「사마귀」.

　an thou 'lt mouth = if you will rant.

　mouth [mauð] = orate pompously, talk big 「큰소리치다」.

307. **rant** = mouth와 같은 뜻. use bombastic language.

　mere = utter, pure, sheer.

308. **awhile the fit will work on him** = for a time his fit of madness will exercise its power over him.

309. **Anon** = soon, shortly.

310. **golden couplets** = twin birds covered with yellow down 「비둘기는 한 번에 두 개의 알만을 낳고 새로 태어난 병아리는 노란 털로 덮여 있다」.

　couplets = twin baby birds.

　disclos'd = hatched.

311. **His silence will sit drooping** = he will hang down his head in silence.

Hear you, sir = Laertes에 하는 말.

314-5. **Let…his day** = 「제아무리 Hercules가 애써도 고양이는 고양이 대로 야옹거리고, 강아지도 강아지대로 짖어댈 것이다」. 즉, 비록 지금 Hamlet이 고양이나 강아지 취급을 받고 있지만 머지 않아 때가 올 것이라는 뜻. 또 다른 해석은 Hercules를 Hamlet 으로 보고, 한편 cat, dog을 Laertes로 보는 해석이다. 그 때는 「Hercules(내)가 제아무리 애써도 고양이와 강아지는 저이들대 로 짖어댈 것이다」. 즉, 자연의 섭리는 바꿀 수 없다는 뜻.

315. **every dog will have his day** = 「누구에게나 다 때가 있다」는 속담적인 표현.

316-7. **thee…you** = Horatio와 Laertes에게 각기 다른 대명사를 사용함 으로써 친근감의 차이를 나타낸다.

316. **wait upon** = follow, accompany.

317. **Strengthen your patience in our last night's speech** = 「어젯밤에 한 말을 생각하고 더 참으라」.

317. **in** = with, by means of, by remembering.

318. **present push** = immediate action.

320. **living** = Queen에게는 everlasting의 뜻으로, Laertes에게는 Hamlet을 죽여 산 제물로 삼자는 뜻으로 사용된 말.

321. **An hour of quiet shortly shall we see** = we shall shortly see an hour of quiet 「곧 평화로운 날이 올 것이다」.

hour = time.

322. **in patience our proceeding be** = let us act with patience and control.

Scene II

1.   **So much···other** = enough of this matter, now I will show you how the other turned out.

    sir = 친구인 Horatio와의 사이에 약간의 격식을 차리려는 것인지, 아니면 그의 주의를 끌기 위한 용법일 듯.

    shall you see the other = I will let you see the other, I have something to let you know.

    the other = the rest.

2.   **circumstance** = all the details, circumstances.

3.   **Remember it, my lord!** = How could I forget it?

4.   **fighting** = 「번민」.

5.   **Methought** = it seemed to me.

6.   **Worse than the mutines in the bilboes** = in a more miserable plight than that of the mutineers in chains.

    mutines [mjúːtinz] = mutineers.

    bilboes = shackles sliding on an iron bar which is locked to the floor, used for mutinous sailors.

    Rashly = impulsively. 12행의 Up from my cabin에 연결된다. 그 사이의 내용은 rashly에 대한 설명과 비평.

7-9.   **And prais'd···pall** = 「심사숙고한 계획이 실패하더라도 때로 무분별함이 도움이 될 때가 있으니 무모함도 고마운 일이다」.

7.   **let us know** = we should acknowledge.

8.   **indiscretion** = impulsive action.

9.   **pall** = fail, falter, lose strength. 판본에 따라서는 fail로 된 곳도 있다.

10.   **our ends** = outcome of our actions.

10-1.   **There's a divinity···we will** = 「우리가 제아무리 거칠게 깎아놓

아도 우리의 의도한 바를 마무리해주시는 하느님이 계신다」.

11.   **Rough-hew them how we will** = however roughly we ourselves shape them.

       rough-hew = shape roughly.

13.   **My sea-gown scarf'd about me** = having hurriedly wrapped myself in my sea-gown.

       sea-gown = seaman's coat; coarse, high-collared, and short-sleeved gown, reaching down to the mid-leg, and used most by seamen and sailors.

       scarf'd = wrapped loosely.

14.   **find out them** = find them out.

       them = King's letters.

       had my desires = 「목적을 달성했다」.

15.   **Finger'd** = stole, pilfered.

       in fine = finally.

16.   **room** = cabin.

       making so bold = and ventured so far.

17.   **My fears forgetting manners** = I in my fear thinking nothing as to whether I was acting honourably.

       manners = good manners.

       to unseal = as to unseal.

18.   **Their grand commission** = the commission they were so proud of having entrusted to them 「그 장한 국서」.

19.   **royal knavery** = knavery of a king.

       exact = strict.

20.   **Larded** = interspersed or enriched (speech) with particular words, ornamented.

       several = different, separate.

21.   **Importing** = stating, signifying.

Denmark's health = the well-being of the King of Denmark.

22. **With…such bugs and goblins in my life** = mentioning the terrible dangers which threatened so long as I was allowed to live.

ho = 놀라움의 감탄사라기보다는 비웃음을 나타내는 감탄사.

bugs = bugbears「애 잡아먹는 귀신」.

goblins =「악귀, 도깨비」.

23. **on the supervise** = as soon as he read it.

supervise = perusal, reading.

no leisure bated = no time wasted.

bate = deduct.

24. **not to stay the grinding of the axe** = without so much as waiting till the axe could be sharpened.

stay = wait for.

26. **commission** =「칙서」.

28. **beseech** = entreat, ask earnestly for.

29. **be-netted** = surrounded as by a net, ensnared.

30. **Ere I could…play** = before I started thinking about a course of action, my brains had already started to carry out a plan. 당시에는 *Romeo and Juliet*에서처럼 무대의 막이 올라가기 전에 연극의 대충 줄거리를 관객에게 미리 말해주는 것이 상례였다.

prologue = the outline of a play.

32. **fair** = in a formal handwriting (like that of a clerk).

33-4. **hold it…A baseness** = consider it, as our statesmen do, a lower-class skill.

hold = consider.

33. **statists** [stéitists] = statesmen.

34. **A baseness to write fair** = 당대 유명한 사람들은 악필을 자랑하는 풍조가 있었다. cf. Shakespeare's autograph.

baseness = lower-class skill, plebeian accomplishment.

35. **learning** = acquirement.

36. **yeoman's service** = good and faithful service.

   yeoman's = substantial, loyal.

   yeoman = a yeoman is a servant in a royal or noble household. 당대 군대에서는 yeoman이 가장 쓸모가 있었다.

37. **effect** = purport, substance 「내용」. cf. to this effect 「이런 취지로」.

38. **conjuration** = formal request, solemn entreaty, adjuration.

39. **England** = King of England.

   tributary = vassal, nation that pays tribute.

40. **As love between them like the palm should flourish** = according as he desired that their mutual love should flourish like the palm should flourish. cf. *Psalms* 92:12. The righteous shall flourish like the palm tree.

41. **still** = always.

   wheaten garland = 「밀 이삭 화환」. 밀은 peace and prosperity의 상징.

42. **stand a comma 'tween their amities** = continue to be a connecting link between the two countries.

   stand a comma = serve as a link. period는 「끝」을 의미하지만, comma는 「연결」을 뜻한다.

   amities = friendships.

43. **as-es** = as와 ass를 겹친 표현.

   charge = importance와 burden 두 뜻으로 사용.

44. **That** = 38행의 conjuration을 받고 있으며, 46행의 He should… 에 연결된다.

   on the view and knowing of = as soon as he read and learned.

   knowing = knowledge.

45. **Without debatement further, more or less** = without any hesitation, consideration, however slight.

debatement = consideration, deliberation.

more or less = however slight.

46. **He** = the King of England.

those bearers = the men bearing the document, i.e. Rosencrantz and Guildenstern.

sudden = immediate.

47. **Not shriving time allow'd** = without even allowing them to confess their sins to the priest and obtain absolution.

shriving time = time for confession 「참회의 시간」.

seal'd = marked as authentic with a seal impressed in wax.

48. **even in that was Heaven ordinant** = even in that particular heaven had ordained matters to the same end.

ordinant = directing, controlling.

49. **signet** = small seal.

50. **model** = counterpart, copy, replica.

51. **writ** = written document, writing.

in form of the other = 「본래 것과 꼭 같이」.

form = likeness.

52. **Subscrib'd it, gave 't the impression** = signed it, sealed it with the signet on wax.

Subscrib'd = signed.

gave 't impression = sealed it.

53. **changeling** = substitution. 요정들이 인간의 애기들을 훔쳐가면서 대신 놓고 가는 애기들.

54. **what to this was sequent** = what followed this.

was sequent = followed.

56. **go to 't** = go to their deaths라는 뜻의 완곡한 표현.

57. **did make love to this employment** = 「자기들이 좋아서 이 일을 맡았다」.

make love to = court. bawdy innuendo이다.

58. **They are not near my conscience** = they do not trouble my conscience.

defeat = destruction. cf. II. ii. 598.

59. **Does by their own insinuation grow** = comes from their own meddling in the matter.

insinuation = stealthy intrusion into the business.

60-2. **when the baser···opposites** = when men of lower rank come between the thrusts and sword-points of great men engaged in fierce and mortal duel.

60. **baser** = inferior.

61. **pass** = thrust.

fell incensed points = fierce enraged swords.

fell = fierce, cruel, destructive.

incensed [-id] = incited, instigated.

points = i.e. of swords.

62. **opposites** = opponents. i.e. Hamlet and Claudius.

63. **Does it not, thinks't thee, stand me now upon** − = Don't you think I am now under an obligation?

it = 68행의 To quit 이하를 받는다.

thinks 't thee = seems it to thee, do you think. cf. methinks.

stand me now upon = become my obligation now. 68행의 To quit (= to requite)로 연결된다.

64. **whored** = fornicated with.

65. **Popp'd in between the election and my hopes** = suddenly thrust himself in between my election to the throne and the hopes I had entertained of becoming king.

election = 당시 덴마크는 선거제의 군주국이었다. 이에 대해 election은 단순히 choice or selection by the inner circle of the nobility라는 해석도 있다.

hopes = expectations.

66-7. **Thrown out…cozenage** = so cunningly fished for my death 「교활하게 내 목숨을 낚으려 했다」.

66. **angle** = fishing-hook.

my proper life = my own life.

67. **And with such cozenage** = 「이처럼 속임수를 써서」.

cozenage [kʌznidʒ] = cheating, deception. cf. III. iv. 77.

67-8. **is 't…arm?** = am I not perfectly justified in paying him out with my own hand?

67. **is 't not perfect conscience** = perfectly justifiable.

68. **quit** = requite, pay back.

68-9. **and is 't not damn'd To…** = and would it not be a sin worthy of damnation to….

69-70. **let this canker…evil** = allow this worm of humanity to go into further mischief.

canker = sore that eats and spread, cancer.

in = into.

evil = sin.

71-2. **It must…there** = the king is certain to know very soon what is the result of his commission.

73. **It will be short; the interim is mine** = the time that will elapse before he knows the result will be short; but that short interval is wholly mine, there is nothing to baulk my vengeance.

74. **And a man's life's no more than to say 'One'** = and the taking of a man's life is as easy as to count one.

76. **I forgot myself** = allowed myself to behave with want of

courtesy.

77-8. **by the image ··· his** = I see the portrait of Laertes's situation in that of my own. 「내 슬픈 모습에서 그의 슬픔을 알다」. Hamlet 과 Laertes는 아버지가 횡사했다는 점에서 공통의 cause를 가지고 있다.

image = likeness, reflection.

78. **court his favours** = endeavour to win him to forgiveness and friendship.

79. **bravery** = extravagant display, boastful showiness.

80. **a tow'ring passion** = a violent anger.

83. **I humbly thank you, sir** = 여기서부터 Hamlet은 Osric의 서툰 궁정언어를 흉내(parody)내면서 그를 조롱하고 있다.

84. **water-fly** = 「물파리」. A water-fly skips up and down upon the surface of the water without any apparent purpose. fig. vain or busily idle person. Osric이 궁정 안을 돌아다니는 품을 물파리 가 물 위를 뛰어다니는 모습에 비유하고 있다.

86. **Thy state is the more gracious** = 뒤에 for not knowing him을 첨가해서 읽을 것.

state = condition, circumstances.

gracious = pious, holy, free from sin, in a state of grace. cf. sate of grace = 신의 은총을 입은 상태.

87-8. **much land, and fertile** = much fertile land.

88-9. **let a beast ··· mess** = No matter how bestial, a man who has money may eat with the king.

let a beast be lord of beasts = 「만약 짐승 같은 인간이 많은 가축을 가지고 있으면」.

89. **crib** = foodbox for animals, manger.

mess = meal-table.

chough [tʃʌf] = the small chattering species of the crow family, esp. the jackdaw 「갈가마귀」. fig. chatterer 「수다쟁이」.

90. **spacious in the possession of dirt** = possessed of many a broad acre 「땅 소유가 광대하다」. 「땅」이라는 뜻으로 dirt를 사용함으로써 Osric이 더러운 방법으로 땅을 사 모았다는 것을 암시하고 있다.

91. **Sweet** = 당대 궁정에서 사용된 큰 뜻이 없는 호칭.

92. **impart** = tell.

a thing = something.

94. **diligence** = attentiveness, assiduity.

95. **Put your bonnet to his right use** = put your hat on your head, for which it is intended 「모자는 쓰기 위한 것이니 쓰도록 하시오」.

bonnet = hat. 현재는 주로 여인의 모자를 가리키지만 당시는 단순히 head-gear의 뜻.

his = its.

97-104. 이 부분은 III. ii. 393-399에서 Hamlet과 Polonius가 주고받던 대화를 연상시킨다.

97. **'tis very hot** = it is on account of the heat that I carry the hat in my hand.

100. **indifferent** = fairly, pretty, somewhat.

102. **complexion** = bodily constitution, temperament 「체질」. cf. I. iv. 27.

105. **signify** = inform.

106. **a great wager on your head** = cf. IV. vii. 135.

on your head = on you.

107. **remember** = remember thy courtesy의 생략형으로서 여기서는 「모자를 쓰시오」의 뜻. 당시 통상적으로 사용되던 표현. 엘리자베스 시대에는 인사할 때를 제외하고는 실내에서도 모자를 썼다.

109.	**for mine ease** = I assure you I do it because I find it more comfortable. 앞에 I take it off를 보충해서 읽을 것. **ease** = convenience.
111.	**absolute** = complete, perfect.
112.	**differences** = distinguishing qualities, distinctions. **soft society** = refined manners in company.
113.	**great showing** = distinguished or impressive appearance. **feelingly** = appropriately, accurately, with due appreciation of his merits.
114.	**the card or calendar of gentry** = the very guide-book of good-breeding. **card** = map, chart. **calendar** = guide, directory. **gentry** = good breeding, gentility.
114-6.	**you shall⋯see** = you will find him to contain in himself every accomplishment that one could wish to see.
115-6.	**the continent⋯see** = the whole continent of which a gentleman may wish to see a part.
115.	**continent** = sum and substance. 「대륙」이라는 뜻과 겹치게 해서 당대 부유한 젊은이들 사이에 유행하던 대륙여행과 뜻이 겹치게 했다. **what part** = whatever quality. continent를 「대륙」의 뜻으로 해석할 때는 「지방」이라는 뜻으로 해석.
117-8.	**his definement suffers no perdition in you** = his description suffers no loss by your words.
117.	**definement** = description, definition. **perdition** = loss.
118.	**in you** = through you.
118-9.	**divide him inventorially** = specify his excellences one by one

in the manner of an inventory.

119.   **dizzy** = make dizzy.

   the arithmetic of memory = ability of memory to calculate.

119-29. **and yet⋯sail** = and yet only manage a roundabout voyage in comparison to his rapid sailing.

120.   **yaw** = (of a ship) move unsteadily, fall off or swerve from the course.

   neither = nevertheless.

   in respect of = in comparison with.

   quick sail = 「그의 장점을 늘어놓는 속도」. 동시에 quick sale(떨이)이라는 말과 pun. 즉, 「그의 장점을 마치 물건 떨이하듯이 그렇게 마구 늘어놓는다면」의 뜻.

121.   **in the verity of extolment** = to praise him truthfully.

122.   **of great article** = of great importance.

122-5. **his infusion⋯more** = Laertes is a fine man, so special that he can be matched only by his image in a mirror; everyone else in comparison to him is only his umbrage, or shadow.

122.   **his infusion** = what is infused into him, infused temperament, character imparted by nature, natural character.

122-3. **of such dearth and rareness** = so precious and rare.

123-4. **make true diction of him** = describe him truthfully.

123.   **diction** = speech.

124.   **his semblable is his mirror** = the only person like him is his mirror image. None but himself could be his parallel 「그와 견줄 수 있는 건 거울에 비치는 자신의 모습 뿐」.

   semblable = only true likeness.

124-5. **and who else⋯more** = and anyone who should try to follow in his steps, imitate him, would be but as the shadow to the reality.

124.   **who else** = whoever else.

125.	**trace** = follow, imitate.
	his umbrage = his shadow.
126.	**infallibly** = absolutely truly.
128.	**The concernancy, sir?** = the meaning, sir? 「Laertes의 이야기를 꺼낸 뜻은?」.
	concernancy = import, meaning.
128-9.	**wrap…breath** = clothe him in words which are too crude to do him justice.
129.	**more rawer breath** = (too) rude words.
131-2.	**Is 't…really** = 많은 주석자들은 이 부분을 Hamlet에 대한 방백 (aside)으로 해석한다. 그 때는 「그렇게 말을 돌리지 말고 좀 더 쉽게 말하면 알아듣지 않을까요?」정도의 뜻이 된다. 한편 이 부분을 Osric에 대한 방백으로 보는 경우에는 「이 멋진 말도 딴 사람이 하니까 어려운가? 노력해 봐, 알아들을 수 있어」라는 뜻이 될 것이다.
132.	**You will do 't, sir, really** = you can if you try (i.e. to speak more plainly).
	really = Shakespeare가 다른 곳에서 쓴 일이 없는 단어여서 really를 rarely(= unusually well, splendidly)로 바꿔 읽기도 한 다.
133-4.	**What imports…gentleman?** = what is the object of mentioning that gentleman?
133.	**nomination** = mention, naming.
136.	**His purse is empty already** = his verbal exchequer is already bankrupt.
136-7.	**All 's…spent** = all his wealth of fine words is exhausted.
	All 's = all his.
139.	**I know you are not ignorant** − = 「알고 계시겠지만」. Hamlet은 ignorant를 장난삼아 일부러 「무식한」의 뜻으로 받고 있다.

140. **I would you did** = I wish this were truly your opinion.

would = wish.

141. **it would not much approve me** = it would not be much to my credit.

approve = recommend.

145-7. **I dare⋯himself** = I dare not pretend to know him, lest I should imply that I am his equal.

145. **confess** = acknowledge.

146. **compare with** = vie with.

146-7. **but to know⋯himself** = but only through self-knowledge can one claim to know another. cf. Sir Thomas Browne: "No man can judge another, because no man knows himself.) (*Religio Medici* II. 4).

148. **for his weapon** = as regards his skill in the use of his weapon.

for = with.

148-50. **in the⋯unfellowed** = in the opinion of people generally his merit has no fellow, equal.

149. **imputation** = reputation.

by them = by people in general.

meed = merit.

150. **unfellowed** = (has) no equal, unmatched.

151. **his weapon** = the weapon he specially affects.

152. **Rapier and dagger** = 16세기 말에 영국에 소개되었다. 당시로서는 새로운 fencing 방법. 오른손에 잡은 rapier로는 주로 공격에, 왼손에 잡은 dagger로는 주로 방어에 사용한다. 그 전엔 sword and buckler(방패)를 사용하였다.

153. **but well** = but never mind, go on.

155. **Barbary horses** = Arabian horses. 이런 말들을 barb라고 부른다.

Barbary = 아프리카 북쪽 해안에 있는 나라 이름.

he = Laertes.

156. **imponed** = staked. impawned라는 단어를 Osric이 멋 부려 발음
한 단어로 여겨진다.

157. **poniards** = daggers.

assigns = appurtenances, accessories「부속품」.

as = namely.

girdle = sword belt.

hangers = straps on a sword-belt from which the sword hung.

158. **and so** = and the like.

carriages = hangers, literally, wheeled supports on which
cannons are mounted.

159. **dear to fancy** = pleasing to taste, fancifully designed.

responsive = well-matched, corresponding,「잘 어울리는」.

hilt =「손잡이」.

160. **delicate** = skilfully wrought.

liberal conceit = tasteful design, lavish ingenuity.

161. **What call you the carriages?** = what are you calling carriages?

162-3. **I knew···done** = I knew that a commentary would be necessary
before the whole description could be understood.

162. **edify** = inform.

163. **margent** = margin of a page of a book. 책의 여백에 주석을 적거
나 인쇄하던 사실에서「주석」(commentary) 그 자체를 가리키
게 되었다. 오늘날의 marginal note.

165. **phrase** = carriage라는 말. carriage는 보통 gun-carriage(대포를
끄는 차)의 뜻으로 사용되었기 때문에 carry cannon by our sides
라고 말하고 있다.

165-6. **germane** = relevant, appropriate. Hamlet은 carriage라는 단어는
gun-carriage로 끌고 다니는 대포(cannon)와 같은 큰 무기에 더
어울린다고 암시하고 있다.

167. **I would it might be** = I should prefer the word 'hangers'.

But on = do continue.

170. **French bet** = the bet of Laertes, who studied in Paris.

172. **laid** = bet, wagered.

172-3. **in a dozen passes between you and him** = a dozen exchanges between Hamlet and Laertes.

173. **passes** = bouts or rounds.

173-4. **he shall not exceed you three hits** = Laertes will not beat you by more than three hits.

174-5. **laid on twelve for nine** = 이 부분에 대한 해석은 이설이 분분하나 12번의 시합 가운데 3번은 Hamlet이 지더라도 계산에 넣지 않고 나머지 9번의 시합에서 Hamlet이 이기면 이긴 것으로 한다는 뜻으로 해석한다. 즉 전체로 보아 7번 Hamlet이 지더라고 5번 이기면 Hamlet이 이긴 것이 된다. 요즘 개념으로 하면 Hamlet에게 3점의 핸디(handicap)를 준다는 뜻이다. 요는 이 모두가 Hamlet를 시합에 끌어들이기 위한 계책이라는 점을 이해하면 된다.

175-6. **and that would…answer** = and the matter might be settled at once if you would condescend to meet him in combat.

176. **vouchsafe the answer** = accept the challenge. 「대련 신청을 받아드린다」. 그러나 Hamlet은 이 말을 일부러 make a reply의 뜻으로 오해하고 있다.

vouchsafe = design to accept.

176-9. **answer** = 이 말을 make a reply의 뜻으로 받아 「대답하기 싫다면?」(How if I answer 'no'?)이라고 말한 데 대해 Osric은 다시 한 번 「시합에 응한다는 뜻입니다」(the opposition of your person in trial)라고 고쳐 말하고 있다.

178. **opposition** = offering for combat.

181. **breathing time of day** = time for taking exercise 「운동시간」.

182. **foils** = weapons blunted for fencing.

182-3. **the gentleman willing** = if the gentleman be willing.

183. **hold his purpose** = keep his mind. hold에 -s가 붙지 않은 것은 가정법으로 쓰였기 때문. let the king hold (= if the king holds) 의 뜻.

183-4. **I will win for him** = him은 the king.

184. **an I can** = if I can.

185. **odd hits** = extra thrusts. 대상을 Hamlet으로 보는 것이 대부분 평자들의 해석이나 경우에 따라서는 대상을 Laertes로 보아 any hits I happen to make (despite losing the match)로 해석하는 사람도 있다.

186. **re-deliver you e'en so** = report your response in exactly these words

   re-deliver you = return this as your answer, report 「복명하다」.

187-8. **To this⋯will** = so long as you give that as my answer in effect, I do not care in what affected language you give it 「내용은 이 취지로, 표현은 당신 마음대로고」.

187. **after what flourish** = in whatever elaborate style.

188. **will** = wishes, intends.

189. **I commend my duty⋯** = I humbly offer my services⋯. 통상적 인 작별 인사.

   commend = recommend to kindly remembrance, please remember.

190. **Yours, yours** = yours는 (I am) your humble servant (cf. Yours truly)의 뜻.

191-2. **no tongues else for 's turn** = no other tongues than his own that would serve his turn (in commending him).

   for 's turn = for his purposes.

193. **lapwing** = peewit 「댕기물떼새」. 댕기물떼새는 갓 태어났을 때

알껍데기를 뒤집어 쓴 채 둥지를 뛰쳐나간다고 알려져 있다. Osric이 모자를 쓰고 궁정 안을 돌아다니는 모습을 댕기물떼새에 비유하고 있다.

195-6. **He did···it** = he is such a born courtier that we may be sure that he excused himself to his mother's breast before he sucked it.

195. **comply with his dug** = 「젖꼭지에 인사하다」.

　　　comply with = be courteous to. cf. II. ii. 390.

　　　dug = teat, nipple 「젖꼭지」.

196-7. **of the same bevy** = of the same sort.

　　　bevy = company, properly, of ladies.

197. **the drossy age** = the degenerate age in contrast with the Golden Age.

　　　drossy = frivolous, worthless.

　　　dotes on = be excessively fond of.

198. **the tune of the time** = the fashionable way of talking.

　　　habit = bearing.

199. **encounter** = manner of address, behaviour.

　　　yesty collection = frothy assortment (of foolish manners and fashionable talk).

　　　yesty = foamy, frothy, trivial.

200-1. **carries···opinions** = enables them to converse with both the vulgar and refined.

200-1. **the most fond and winnowed opinions** = the most foolish and fantastic opinions.

200. **fond** = foolish, silly. 판본에 따라서는 fond를 profound로 보아 전체를 choicest and most refined judgement라고 해석하거나 fond를 fanned로 바꾸기도 한다. fanned는 sifted as by a winnowing-fan의 뜻으로부터 over-refined의 뜻이 된다. 전체

문맥으로 보아서는 fond를 profound로 바꾼 해석이 가장 자연
스럽다.

201.   **blow⋯out** = put Osric and his kind to any test, and collapse
        like bubble in froth.

202.   **to their trial** = 「시험 삼아」.

        are out = soon burst.

203-5. **commended⋯hall** = young Osric, by whom the king sent you
        his message, brings back word that you are awaiting him in
        the hall.

        commended him = commended himself = sent his commendations
        or greetings.

204.   **brings back** = brings word back.

205.   **attend** = wait for.

206.   **if your pleasure hold** = 「의향에 변화가 없으시다면」.

        hold = continue, not change.

        play with = to fence with. 펜싱 술어.

        or that = or if.

207.   **will take longer time** = wish to put off the meeting till you have
        had further time for practice.

208-9. **they follow the King's pleasure** = my inclinations attend upon
        the king's will in the matter.

        follow = agree with, obey.

208.   **they** = my purposes.

209-10. **If his⋯ready** = if the time seems to him a fitting one, I am
        ready.

209.   **his fitness speaks** = his convenience suits.

        his = king's.

211.   **so able** = in as good condition for the contest.

214.   **In happy time** = they come at the right moment. cf. F. à la bonne

heure.

215-6. **use some gentle entertainment** = meet in a friendly way, show some courtesy.

216. **gentle entertainment** = conciliatory manner and speech, courteous greeting.

entertainment = reception, treatment.

216-7. **fall to** = begin to.

218. **She well instructs me** = Her advice is good.

220-1. **since he went···practice** = II. ii. 308에서 한 말과 모순된다. cf. foregone all custom of exercises;

222. **at the odds** = with the odds allowed me in my favour. cf. 174-5.

thou wouldst not think = you can have no idea.

222-3. **how will all's here about my heart** = 「여기 가슴이 이상하다」, 「예감이 불길하다」.

225. **foolery** = a mere silly feeling.

226. **gain-giving** = misgiving, feeling of mistrust or apprehension.

228. **forestall their repair** = intercept their coming.

forestall = deprive (a person) of something by previous action.

repair = going or coming to a place. cf. III. vi. 23.

230. **not a whit** = not at all.

whit = a very small quantity.

we defy augury [ɔ́:gjəri] = I pay no heed to presentiments.

augury = omens, forebodings.

231. **special providence in the fall of sparrow** = cf. *Matthew* 10: 29. Are not two sparrows sold for a farthing? and one of them shall not fall on the ground without your Father. 참새 한 마리 떨어지는 것도 신의 섭리에 의한다는 뜻.

231. **it** = fate, death.

231-2. **if it be now, 'tis not come** = if one's death is to come now, there will be nothing to fear in the future 「지금 죽을 것이면 앞으로는 안 죽는다」. 왜냐하면 사람은 한번만 죽으므로.

232-3. **if it be not to come, it will be now** = if one's death be not awaiting one in the future, it will come now 「앞으로 죽을 일이 없다면 그 죽음은 지금이다」.

233. **if it be not now, yet it will come** = if the death does not come now, it will come sooner or later. 「그 죽음이 지금이 아니라면 앞으로 죽게 된다」. 사람은 어차피 죽게 되어 있다.

234. **the readiness is all** = preparedness is everything.

has = really possesses.

234-5. **Since no man … betimes** = since no man can carry with him to the grave anything that is his, why should we grieve at leaving it when young? cf. *I. Timothy* 6:7. For we brought nothing into this world, and it is certain we can carry nothing out.

234. **aught** = anything at all.,

235. **betimes** = early.

Let be = leave it alone, say no more 「그만 됐다」.

SD **gauntlets** = stout gloves with a long loose wrist 「결투용 장갑」.

236. **take this hand from me** = let me make friends between you by placing his hand in yours.

237-54. 왕비의 분부에 따른 이 사죄는 사실과 다르다. Johnson 박사 (1765)도 Hamlet이 취한 부정직한(disingenuous) 태도를 안타까워하며 뭔가 달리 변명했으면 좋았을 것이라고 말한다. 그러나 여기에 대해 A. C. Bradley는 다음과 같이 Hamlet의 입장을 변호한다. "햄릿이 해주기를 바라는 변명이란 도대체 어떤 것인가? 나는 짐작이 가지 않는다. 햄릿은 진실을 말할 수 없는 것이다. '자네 부친이 아니고 왕을 죽일 참이었다'라고 말할 수는 없지 않은가"라고 말하고 있다. 음미해볼 주장들이다.

238. **as you are a gentleman** = as a gentleman like you should do.

239. **This presence** = this company, persons present here. 주로 고귀한 사람들을 지칭할 때 쓰인다.

240. **needs** = necessarily.

punish'd = afflicted.

241. **sore distraction** = serious mental derangement.

What I have done = 다다음 줄 was madness의 주어.

242-3. **That might…awake** = which may have rudely irritated your natural feelings, your sense of honour and your resentment of discourtesy.

Roughly awake = harshly awaken.

242. **might** = may have.

nature = natural feelings.

exception = dislike, dissatisfaction.

244. **wrong'd** = 앞에 who를 보충해서 읽을 것.

245. **If Hamlet from himself be ta'en away** = if the real Hamlet is absent from himself.

247. **denies it** = abjures it as his own action.

249. **Hamlet is of the faction that is wrong'd** = is among those who are wronged 「나도 피해자 가운데 한 사람이다」.

faction = party 「편」.

251. **this audience** = 239행의 this presence와 같은 뜻.

252. **disclaiming from** = denial of.

purpos'd evil = deliberate evil intention.

253. **Free me** = acquit me.

254. **That I have** = as if I had.

255. **brother** = Ophelia에 대한 언급이 없었으므로 이 brother를 굳이 brother-in-law로 해석할 필요는 없다.

255. **in nature** = in terms of my natural affection for my father and for my sister.

256-7.	**Whose motive⋯revenge** = though in this case those natural feelings would strongly incite me to demand revenge.
257.	**in my terms of honour** = in respect of my honour.
258.	**stand aloof** = I hold myself at a distance from you, am not ready to accept your apology.
	will no reconcilement = refuse all reconciliation.
	will =wish for, desire. 아니면 will 뒤에 accept를 보충해서 읽는다.
259.	**some elder masters** = some experienced men who are knowledgeable about questions of honour.
260.	**a voice and precedent of peace** = an opinion and previous example of (a similar) reconciliation, an assurance that according to all precedents Laertes may accept what Hamlet has said in self-defence and be reconciled to him.
	voice = authority.
261.	**name ungor'd** = reputation unwounded.
261-2.	**But till⋯love** = but for the meantime I accept your proffer of love as being what it professes to be. 앞서 한 Hamlet의 말이 거짓이었듯이 Laertes의 말도 거짓이다. Hamlet은 과거에 대해, 그리고 Laertes는 앞으로 할 일에 대해 각각 거짓말을 하고 있다.
263.	**wrong it** = i.e. by doubting it.
	I embrace it freely = I receive your reply gladly, I readily take you at your word.
264.	**And will this brother's wager frankly play** = and will with all the openness of friendship engage with you in this brotherly combat.
	frankly = freely, willingly.
265.	**foils** = light fencing weapons.
266-6.	**I'll be⋯indeed** = I'll act as your foil, my ignorance setting off your skill, as the darkness of night sets off the brilliance of

a star.

266. **foil** = background setting against which jewels show more brightly, (hence fig.) that which sets something off to advantage 「남을 돋보이게 하는 사람」. 물론 265행의 foils(끝이 무딘 수련 검)에 대한 점잖은 pun.

in mine ignorance = because I am unskilled.

268. **Stick⋯off** = show brightly in contrast.

269. **by this hand** = 맹서할 때 쓰는 말.

272. **laid the odds** = 「뎀(핸디)을 주다」. 단순히 bet on이라고 해석하는 주석자도 있다.

274. **is better'd** = is your superior. he has improved로 해석되기도 한다.

we have therefore odds = we have been given odds.

275. **let me see another** = Laertes는 여기서 끝이 날카롭고 독이 묻어 있는 칼을 고른다.

276. **This likes me** = this pleases me, I like this.

have all a length = are all the same length.

SD. **play** = fence.

278. **me** = Ethical dative.

stoups = jugs or cups.

280. **quit in answer of the third exchange** = requite Laertes for earlier hits by scoring the third hit.

quit = make a return, repay, reward, requite 「되갚다」.

answer = the return hit. 펜싱 용어.

281. **battlement** = i.e. the soldiers on the fortified crenellations of the castle.

ordnance = cannon.

282. **drink to Hamlet's better breath** = drink to him as wishing him breath to last out the combat 「시합 끝날 때까지 숨이 지탱하도록」.

283.   **union** = large pearl. cf. Latin, unio. 「큰 진주」라는 뜻을 갖는
라틴어의 unio는 본래는 「하나, 단일, 결합, 통합」이라는 뜻이
다. unio가 「진주」를 뜻하게 된 것은, 진주는 어느 하나 꼭 같은
것이 없는 하나뿐인 존재이기 때문이다. 술에 진주를 넣고 마시
면 기운이 나는 것으로 알려져 있으나 왕은 진주 대신 독을
넣을 심산.

286.   **kettle** = kettle-drum. 이어서 나오는 trumpets과 함께 악기 그 자
체를 의미할 수도 있고, 아니면 악사를 의미할 수도 있다.

     speak = give the signal 「전하다」.

287.   **cannoneer** = man in charge of the cannon.

     without = outside.

288.   **the heaven to earth** = i.e. by re-echoing the sound to the earth.

290.   **wary** = watchful.

291.   **Judgement** = let us have judgement.

292.   **a palpable hit** = 「깨끗한 일격」.

     palpable = tangible, definite.

293.   **this pearl is thine** = 진주를 잔에 넣는 척하면서 독을 넣도록
돼 있다.

297.   **A touch** = a touch, but so slight as not to count for a hit.

298.   **shall** = is certain to.

     fat = sweaty.

     scant of breath = 「숨이 차다」.

299.   **napkin** = handkerchief. 당시에는 「손수건」의 뜻으로만 사용되
었다.

300.   **carouses** [kəráuziz] = drinks a toast.

301.   **Good madam!** = 왕비의 건배에 대한 인사.

302.   **pardon me** = 이렇게 말하면서 그 잔을 마신다.

304.   **I dare not drink** = 이 말은 왕비가 포도주를 마신 뒤 그 잔을
Hamlet에게 권했다는 것을 암시하고 있다.

by and by = presently, immediately. cf. III. ii. 400-4.

306. **I do not think 't** = I don't think you can hit him.

307. **'gainst my conscience** =「양심에 가책을 받는다」. 독을 바른 칼을 사용하고 있기 때문에.

308. **you but dally** = you are only playing, i.e. you are not competing in earnest「진지하지 않다」.

309. **pass** = thrust, attack.

   your best violence = your utmost strength.

310. **afeard** = afraid.

   make a wanton of me = play with me as if I were a child「나를 어린애 취급한다」.

   wanton = spoilt or effeminate child.

312. **Nothing, neither way** =「어느 쪽도 득점 없다」,「무승부」. 현대 영어에서는 either라고 해야 맞다.

313. **Have at you now!** =「이 칼 받아라」.

SD **in the scuffling, they change rapiers** = 격투 도중에 어떻게 칼을 바꿔 잡는가는 연출가들의 골칫거리였다.

   they are incens'd = their blood is up.

314. **come again** = return to the struggle.

   Ho! = a call to stop the combat.

317. **as a woodcock to mine own springe** =「자업자득이다」. 앞에 I am을 보충해서 읽을 것. cf. I. iii. 115. 도요새(woodcock)를 미끼로 다른 새를 잡는데, 때로 도요새가 부주의해서 스스로가 덫에 걸리는 수가 있다.

   springe [spríndʒ] = snare, trap.

318. **with** = by, as a result of.

319. **She swounds to see them bleed** = she swoons, faints, at the sight of their blood.

   swounds = swoons, collapses, faints.

325.　**medicine** = antidote.

328.　**Unbated and envenom'd** = sharp and poisoned.

　　Unbated = not blunted (with a button). cf. IV. vii. 139.

　　the foul practice = my treacherous plot.

　　practice = conspiracy, trickery.

329.　**turn'd itself on me** = rebounded.

331.　**I can no more** = I can't say any more.

333.　**to thy work** = get to thy work 「네 일을 해라」.

334.　**Treason! treason!** = 「모반이다!」. Hamlet이 왕을 찌르는 것에 대한 반응인지, 아니면 방금 Laertes가 한 말에 대한 반응인지 분명치 않다.

336.　**damned** [-id].

337.　**potion** = a dose or quantity of medicine.

351.　**I can no more** = I can do or say nothing further, my strength fails me.

336.　**Dane** = King of Denmark.

337.　**thy union** = the pearl you spoke of. union에 해당하는 라틴어 unio에는 「결합, 통합」이라는 뜻도 있다. 다시 말해 죽어 이미 죽은 왕비와 한 몸이 되라는 뜻의 pun.

338.　**He is justly serv'd** = the retribution that has fallen upon him is a just one.

339.　**temper'd** = mixed, compounded 「조제한」.

341.　**Mine and my father's death come not upon thee** = may not the guilt of my death and my father's rest upon you!

　　Mine = my death.

　　come not upon thee = may they not count (at the Last Judgement) as charges against you.

SD　**Dies.** = 논리적으로 생각하면 Hamlet이 먼저 상처를 입었으므로 Laertes는 Hamlet이 죽고 난 다음에 죽어야 하지만 여기서는 극적인 효과를 위해 먼저 죽는다.

343. **free** = acquitted.

344. **Wretched** = unhappy.

345. **chance** = these (unfortunate) events. 여기서부터는 주위에 서 있는 사람들에게 한 말.

346. **That are but mutes or audience to this act** = that are either mere auditors of this catastrophe, or at most only mute performers that fill the stage without any part in the action.

    mutes ⋯ audience ⋯ act = 모두 연극 술어.

    mutes = actors without speaking parts.

347. **as this fell sergeant** = 「이 무서운 (죽음이라는) 포수」.

    as = because.

    fell sergeant = cruel officer.

348. **strict** = precise, rigorous.

349. **let it be** = let it alone 「그만 해두자」.

350. **Report** = describe, give an account of.

351. **the unsatisfied** = uninformed people, those who will demand an explanation.

    Never believe it = never believe that I will outlive you.

352. **antique Roman** = 「옛날 로마사람」. 기독교와는 달리 고대 로마에서는 자살을 죄로 여기지 않았다. 로마인들은 불명예스러운 삶보다는 깨끗한 자살을 택하는 것을 더 명예롭다고 생각했다. Brutus, Cassius, Antony, Cato the Younger 모두 자결했다. 여기서는 Hamlet과 같은 고매한 친구보다 더 오래 산다는 불명예.

353. **As thou'rt a man** = 「자네는 진정 사내대장부가 아닌가」. asseverative expression이다.

    As = as sure as.

355. **wounded name** = damaged reputation.

356. **Things standing thus unknown, shall live behind me!** = if the

real facts remain thus unknown, my name will live behind me stained with guilt.

358. **Absent thee from felicity** = forgo the bliss of heaven 「(괴로운 이 세상을 떠나는) 축복을 단념하고」.

359. **And in this harsh world draw thy breath in pain** = 「괴로운 이 세상에서 고통스러운 숨을 쉬면서」.

361-3. **Young⋯volley** = Fortinbras, returning victoriously from Poland, has shot off a volley of gunfire to salute the ambassadors approaching from England.

   with conquest come = who is come back victorious.

362-3. **gives This warlike volley** = fires this salute.

364. **o'er-crows** = overpowers, triumphs over. 닭싸움에서 이긴 수탉처럼.

   spirit = vital force.

366. **the election lights** = the choice (of a successor to the Danish throne) will fall.

   election = 여기서는 「선거」라는 뜻이라기보다는 choice, selection, preference 정도의 뜻.

   lights = alight.

367. **he has my dying voice** = I, on the point of dying, give him my support.

   dying voice = 죽음에 임해서 하는 유언. 세습군주국가 (hereditary monarchy)에서는 dying voice는 특히 중요하다. Hamlet은 왕의 후계자로 임명되었기 때문에 자신의 후계자를 임명할 권한이 있다. 그의 선친 Hamlet이 Fortinbras의 선친을 정복한 날에 태어난 Hamlet은 Fortinbras에게 빚을 갚는 (restitution) 셈이 된다.

368-9. **with the⋯solicited** = together with the events, great and small, which have incited me to what I have done.

368. **occurrents** = events, incidents.

more and less = occurrences, great and small.

369. **Which have solicited** − = incited (me to give him my support). 미완의 문장이다.

solicited = prompted, incited.

The rest is silence = Death releases me from further speech.

370. **cracks** = breaks. 심장을 받치고 있는 힘줄은 죽음과 동시에 끊어지는 것으로 알려져 있다.

371. **flight(s)** = flying companies, flock (of angels).

angels = 연옥(purgatory)을 묘사할 때 천사가 자주 등장한다. 천사는 영혼을 천당으로 인도하는 일을 돕는다.

SD **colours** = those carrying the flags or standards of Fortinbras's army.

373. **Where is this sight?** = Where is the sight that I had heard of?

What is it ye would see? = What do you want to see?

would = wish to.

374. **if aught of woe or wonder, cease your search** = if what you want to see is anything of woe or wonder, you need not go further (than here).

375. **This quarry cries on havoc** = this heap of dead bodies proclaims that havoc(devastation, destruction) has been at work.

quarry = heap of dead men. 본래는 사냥해서 잡은 사슴들을 가리키는 사냥 술어.

cry on havoc = give an army the order 'havoc!' as the signal for massacre and pillage 「죽여라!」 정도의 뜻.

376. **toward** = in preparation, about to take place, forthcoming. cf. I. i. 77.

377. **at a shot** = with one shot.

378. **dismal** = dreadful, disastrous. cf. dies mali = evil days. 현재보다

더 강한 뜻으로서 「재앙」에 가까운 뜻이었음.

379. **our affairs** = the narration of what occurred in England in our embassy.

380. **The ears** = the ears of the King.

senseless = incapable of sensing.

381. **To tell** = in telling.

him = the king.

383. **Where should we have our thanks?** = by whom may we expect to be thanked for our trouble. 대사는 현재의 덴마크의 왕은 누군가고 넌지시 묻고 있다.

Where = from where.

should we have = are we to have.

his = the king's.

384. **Had it the ability** = Even if the mouth had the ability.

the ability of life = 「(입이) 살아 있듯이 말할 수 있는 능력」.

386. **jump upon this bloody question** = just immediately after this bloody affair.

jump upon = immediately after.

jump = (adv.) just, exactly, precisely.

bloody question = bloody occurrences.

387. **Polack** = Polish.

389. **stage** = raised platform.

placed [-id].

392. **carnal, bloody, and unnatural acts** = carnal은 Claudius와 왕비 사이의 관계를, bloody, and unnatural acts는 왕이 형을 죽이거나(fratricide) Hamlet을 죽인 사실을 말한다.

carnal = sensual, sexual.

393. **accidental judgements** = judgements or punishments brought about by accident. Polonius나 왕비, Laertes의 죽음이 그렇다.

casual slaughters = killing brought about by chance.

casual = occurring by chance.

394. **deaths put on by cunning and forced cause** = Rosencrantz와 Guildenstern이 Hamlet을 죽이려고 한 간교한(cunning) 죽음과 Hamlet이 어쩔 수 없이(forced cause) 두 사람을 죽인 죽음 등.

put on = instigated.

395. **upshot** = conclusion.

purposes mistook = 「빗나간 계책」. 뒤에 which have를 보충해서 읽는다.

396. **Fallen on the inventors' heads** = recoiling upon their inventors.

397. **deliver** = report, narrate.

398. **And call the noblest to the audience** = 「고귀한 사람들도 청중으로 부르라」, 즉 「고귀한 사람들에게도 들려주라」.

399. **For me** = as for me 「나로 말하자면」.

with sorrow = in deepest grief.

embrace my fortune = 「(왕위 상속의) 행운을 받아들이겠다.」.

my fortune = good luck, i.e. accession to the throne.

400. **rights of memory** = rights remembered. Hamlet 선왕에 의해 Fortinbras의 아버지가 죽임을 당하고 땅을 빼앗겼던 일을 가리킨다.

of memory = unforgotten.

401. **Which now to claim, my vantage doth invite me** = which my presence here at this advantageous time invites me to claim.

to claim my vantage doth invite me = to claim은 invite me 뒤에 연결된다.

vantage = favorable opportunity, advantage 「유리한 입장」.

403. **And from his mouth whose voice will draw on more** = with words from Hamlet's mouth, whose voice will be seconded by others.

from his mouth = the words I will speak come from Hamlet 「이 말은 Hamlet이 한 말로써」.

draw on more = invite more (voices for Fortinbras).

404.　**this same** = Hamlet의 시체를 단상으로 운반하는 일.

presently = at once, immediately.

405-6.　**Even…happen** = without waiting for men's minds to grow calm, lest in the interval, while they are still excited, other calamities, due to intention or mistake, be added to the present ones.

405.　**wild** = disturbed, excited.

406.　**On plots and errors, happen** = happen as a result of plots and errors.

On = on top of.

four captains = 시체 운반은 보통 네 사람이 했다.

408.　**had he been put on** = had circumstances occurred to prompt him to action 「왕이 되었더라면」.

put on = given the opportunity (to rule as king).

409.　**royally** = royal. Shakespeare는 -ly의 형태를 보어로 사용하는 경우가 많다.

royal = noble, majestic, generous.

for his passage = as for his passage.

passage = passing (from life to death), death. cf. III. iii. 86.

410-1.　**The soldiers'…Speak** = let the…speak.

410.　**rites of war** = the firing of cannon, etc.

411.　**Speak** = let…speak.

413.　**Becomes the field** = is suitable to the battlefield.

here shows much amiss = is most out of place 「여기서는 전혀 어울리지 않는다」.

shows = shows itself, appears.

SD　**peal of ordnance** = discharge of a cannon.